Immortuos

Payton A. Sproule

Immortuos
Copyright © 2019 by Payton A. Sproule

All rights reserved. No part of this publication may be reproduced, distributed, or transmitted in any form or by any means, including photocopying, recording, or other electronic or mechanical methods, without the prior written permission of the author, except in the case of brief quotations embodied in critical reviews and certain other non-commercial uses permitted by copyright law.

Tellwell Talent
www.tellwell.ca

ISBN
978-0-2288-1146-6 (Paperback)

Mrs. Marshall,

Thank you so much for your support, I really appreciate it!

I hope you enjoy the book!

Chapter I

The princess sat up as straight as she could. Her shoulders were rolled back, pressed firmly against the wall as a reminder to keep them there. If her shoulders didn't meet the wall of the carriage then she wasn't straight enough, and that was a risk she was unwilling to take. Although her back was straight, she allowed her head to rest against the green velvet padding of the carriage. A tired neck was justified after travelling for a long time, that could be her excuse if asked why she wasn't sitting the way a princess should. She brought her arms across her body, pushing them against her stomach in hopes that the pressure on her gut would ease the knots of nervousness. She held her breath until her chest ached, until her throat stung, then slowly exhaled as to keep her anxiety hidden from the king and queen. She wholeheartedly fought the urge to lean forward, to hunch over until her head fell between her legs and groan. She desperately needed to scream, to hit something with full force, anything to relieve her nervousness. Her mind raced with mixed thoughts; some telling her to calm down and that everything was all right, and some telling her to dive out the window of the carriage and run all the way back to Serilion—the kingdom her family ruled.

Luckily her parents—the king and queen—didn't seem to notice her apprehension as their daughter masterfully kept her feelings well hidden through the many years of practice she had.

As Princess Amaryllis of Serilion suffered silently, battling against her own personal fears, the King and Queen of Serilion both stared out the windows of the carriage on either side. Their gazes were fixed on the serene land of greenery that surrounded them; the rolling hills sprouting with flowers, the thick canopies of lush forests and the rushing streams which blended with the sound of the carriage wheels rolling in the dirt, sending clouds of dust climbing up the sides of the coach.

Amaryllis accidentally exhaled just a little too loudly while trying to calm her butterflies, and the queen brought her gaze back into the carriage. Fortunately, the king continued his stare as he was mesmerized with the sublime surroundings. As they advanced closer to Arlon from Serilion, the vegetation seemed to gradually possess more magical qualities, but in reality it didn't change. The exact same type of oak, willow, and birch tree sprouted in both Serilion and Arlon. But in Arlon, everything seemed bigger, better, more breathtaking because it was the most powerful kingdom out of the kingdoms that thrived during that time. The idea alone that Arlon was omnipotent caused everything within and around the kingdom to also seem superior.

"Did you say something, dear?" Queen Margaret asked with a worried look on her face. Her blue eyes wide, her eyebrows raised. Amaryllis quickly glanced at her father, and felt a wave of relief as she didn't meet his eyes. Her mother possessed a more gentle face that was easier to deal with when she was troubled with unease, but her father's stern resting expression amplified the unease in her gut.

"I didn't say a word," she replied cautiously. If she spoke too quickly, she feared her mother would detect her discomfort through her voice.

"Oh, I thought you said something!" the queen sighed in relief. Her worried expression melted away as she resumed her gaze out the window.

Amaryllis rolled her shoulders back further, pressing half of her body weight into her back to release her emotion in the exertion of her muscles. Her eyes moved to the ceiling of the carriage. She focused on each individual stitch that secured the green velvet fabric tightly in place. Focusing on something so intently calmed her racing mind and allowed her to relax. As she became aware of her blank thoughts, her stomach pain began to settle. She felt the knots begin to untie. The butterflies flew away, until she felt her father's gaze. Her anxiety came rushing back, the butterflies pummelling her stomach aggressively as they soared back in. Her stomach was filled once again with tight knots which battled her body to stay still. She pressed into the wall again.

She met his dull green eyes, and her stomach dropped. There it was; his intimidating stare. His eyebrows were furrowed, eyes narrowed as he studied her, and his lips were pressed flat into a line. Amaryllis only hoped her body didn't react to her sudden fright with the lifting of her chest, or even worse, the widening of her eyes. He would surely suspect something was wrong if he caught her projecting her bright, emerald green eyes.

He opened his mouth to speak, and as he did so, Amaryllis was already conjuring defensive excuses to distract him, to lead him away from his trail of discovering her misery.

"How are you feeling about the ceremony?" he asked, tilting his head forward, breaking from his frightening glare. His hard expression softened, making Amaryllis slightly more comfortable speaking with her father. But even as *he* became less frightening, Arlon did not, and especially not the royal subjects from the other kingdoms who were also attending. Amaryllis would have to tell the best lies yet, putting her entire soul into her answers with pretend enthusiasm.

"I am quite excited," she began, pausing to think of another lie to really throw him off, "so excited, I can hardly stand it!" she continued to speak slowly as she did with her mother, but ensured to summon the right amount of joy. If she sounded too excited, the king would catch her in her lies, and if she wasn't excited enough, he would immediately discover the anxiety which she tried to keep hidden. He would then confront her, pestering to know of her true opinion. As a master of deceiving others of her true emotion, she had her father fooled, but she continued to pour her heart into her words, feeling disgusted with herself as she hated the rotten feeling that suppressed her when she told lies. But she had to… so often. The queen brought her attention into the carriage once again, looking over at the king, then at her daughter.

Her face lit up. "Oh, the Choosing Ceremony, what a wonderful event!" she exclaimed, reaching for the king's hand, "I am so thankful for it!" she said cheerfully, gushing at her husband. The Choosing Ceremony was a traditional gathering celebrated by each and every kingdom during that time. It was relied on for keeping the ties between the allied kingdoms so strong as it promoted love and harmony. It had been established several generations ago, after a long and merciless battle, to prevent another war from ever happening. A long time ago, the kingdoms lived in disharmony with one another, competing aggressively over who had the most power, the most commoners, the most resources. Arlon was the kingdom which came up with the idea of a series of parties and annual gatherings that would lead to marital arrangements, and force the royal subjects of each kingdom to meet and to mingle and to create friendships in an enjoyable environment. After eight years of the annual gatherings, when the sons and daughters (princes and princesses) of the royal subjects had become old enough to take over their parents' positions, there was to be a Choosing Ceremony. The ceremony involved a selection under control of the princes. The princesses were to make themselves up in beautiful gowns and present themselves to the princes. Each prince would receive a turn to choose their very own princess who was destined to rule alongside them as their bride-their queen. To create fairness on both ends, the princesses were allowed to reject a prince, but only one. After the prince and princess had become engaged, they were to return to the kingdom from which the prince descended, and take over for the prince's parents. In a short month, the princes and princesses would return to Arlon to marry in one giant wedding. The ceremony caused the kingdoms to realize that love should not be forced, but introduced. Forced marriages between the kingdoms created competition and rivalry. The princesses only wanted to marry the wisest and most handsome princes, and the princes only wanted to marry the wisest and most beautiful princesses. If they all could not get their own way, conflict would arise. The traditional Choosing Ceremony is what abolished their old, disorganized, and unfair ways. It resolved all conflict between the kingdoms. It was a beautiful event looked upon with appeasement by many people. It worked effectively, keeping peace for the longest time.

 Amaryllis' parents took part in the Choosing Ceremony long ago, and knowing it was their daughter's turn to become engaged, to head off to another kingdom to rule as queen, they were filled with pride.

 "You must be so thrilled! I am incredibly happy for you," the queen said sincerely, leaning forward to tap Amaryllis on the knee.

 "As am I," the king smiled. A forced smile spread across Amaryllis' face, her bright green eyes hid her misery.

 "What prince do you have your eye on?" the queen asked dreamily, looking to the ceiling of the carriage as if looking up into her imagination. She pictured her daughter looking radiant in a red gown, catching the eye of every prince.

 Amaryllis couldn't think of a lie to tell. She hadn't thought of the outcome of the Choosing Ceremony at all. In her mind, she wasn't travelling to Arlon to be selected by a prince, she was travelling to a castle haunted with merciless memories that disturbed her even when she wasn't in the kingdom, even when she was far away back at home in Serilion. She was heading to the culprit of her misery.

"No one, I am open to everyone," Amaryllis said honestly, telling the partial truth for the first time in eight years.

"And I am sure everyone is open to *you*! I bet all of the princes will fawn over you when they see you all dressed up," the queen crooned. Amaryllis looked down at her feet which rested on the floor of the carriage, wearing pink glass slippers. She sighed quietly, wishing what her mother said was true. Amaryllis was perpetually disgusted with herself. She believed she was hideous to gaze at, because the princesses from the other kingdoms put negativity into her soul with ruthless torment. Amaryllis was naive, and blinded of her own beauty by envious princesses. Each year, when the princesses were brought together, Amaryllis was excluded and treated poorly, convinced she was ugly in all aspects. She was nothing but kind and compassionate towards them, but they saw her love as a weakness and used it against her.

The king could suddenly sense something was wrong. Amaryllis had looked at the floor for too long, too consumed by horrific, and vivid memories of the annual parties to realize how long she had looked away from her parents for. Before he could ask her what the matter was, she made up a lie which saved her from confrontation.

"Hopefully they do," she laughed a fake laugh. "I'm just worried that I'll... get so nervous and scare them away somehow."

"They're princes, not birds!" the king snapped. The queen bursted into a fit of laughter, filling the carriage with loud giggles, loud enough for both the footman and the coachman to hear from the outside. But the king wasn't trying to be funny, he was angered. How could someone as beautiful as his daughter feel worried about attracting a potential husband? Something was wrong.

"Father, it's a huge event...weren't you nervous when you attended?"

The queen looked up at the king with love in her eyes, expecting him to gush over how beautiful she looked, and how happy he was to have selected her back in the day. He felt her expectant stare, but was in no mood for affection. He had to discover why his daughter was worried.

"Somewhat, but I had a reason to be. You do not. Every princess attending must be so worried that they have to stand in the ballroom with *you*. Every prince must be riding in their carriage picturing taking *you* home to their kingdom."

"Laurence, leave her be! She's humble is all!" the queen snapped. The king rolled his eyes in exasperation. His daughter was utterly exquisite. Not even the humblest person who was lucky enough to possess her qualities would ever resist from complimenting themselves when given the chance.

Amaryllis looked away from her father and out the window of the carriage. The glorious nature outside soothed her frustration. The leaves of the trees waved at her in the breeze, reminding her that the world was indeed a kind place.

From the corner of her eye, her parents too moved their gaze outside to look at the serene surroundings once again. The blossoming nature eased the tension between the family as an awkward silence presented itself. A light breeze entered the carriage. It swirled about, blowing Amaryllis' long auburn hair into her face. She gathered her wild hair, tucking it behind her shoulders. She moved in a graceful manner with delicate hands and a beautiful, solemn expression. She was exquisite, absolutely wonderful in every way. And her naturally compassionate personality intensified her appearance even more.

Amaryllis' stomach suddenly seized, forcing her eyes shut as she winced, succumbing to the pain her anxiety caused. Her surroundings forced a fearful feeling upon her as they became painfully familiar. She knew where they were; just miles away from the kingdom of Arlon.

"Will it be similar to the annual parties?" Amaryllis suddenly asked out of true curiosity, hoping it wouldn't.

"Yes, for the most part. You will have your routine horse ride and tea party with your friends—"

Amaryllis shuddered at the word, *friends*.

"The only real difference is that instead of leaving after the intermingling in the ballroom, you will be led into a dressing room designated for the princesses and prepare to be chosen."

The queen looked as if she were to explode with excitement as the king spoke, especially when he said the word, *chosen*. Amaryllis sank in her green velvet, padded seat. The Choosing Ceremony was similar to the annual gatherings, too similar for her poor anxiety-consumed heart to stand it. She quickly sat back up before her parents could notice her slumping. They had urged the importance of posture as a royal subject as it conveyed power and pride, but no matter how erect Amaryllis' body was, she could never attain the power that her parents told her she could have. Her fear was too strong.

Chapter 2

The wheels of the carriage bumped over small stones and twigs as the coachman impulsively led the four horses over to the path on the left with a hard tug of his reins. If he had continued on straight, he would have taken them straight to the village of Arlon. He wiped his brow with the back of his sleeve in relief. If he had taken Serilion in the wrong direction, he would have been punished by the King of Arlon.

Amaryllis felt bile rise in her throat with an additional feeling of lightheadedness as the carriage swayed slightly. Its wheels rumbled against the uneven ground, causing the carriage to vibrate sickeningly. She brought her hand to her mouth in case of any vomit slipping between her lips, and hoped the ground would even out soon. Her stomach ached to its limits, radiating unbearable pain right from her core. She couldn't hold in her anxieties anymore and the jerky wobbling of the carriage only made it worse. She finally surrendered to her fear, lying down on her seat, bringing her feet up to lay in the fetal position. The nauseating feeling settled slightly. She gasped as the feeling vacated her chest.

The king and queen jolted in surprise, full of anger and confusion. Her behaviour wasn't at all ladylike. They told her countless times how to sit correctly.

"What are you doing? Sit up!" the king snapped, flaring his nostrils. His face grew as red as a tomato, embarrassed and angry to see his daughter behaving like a child.

"Yes, Amaryllis, sit up!" the queen joined in.

Amaryllis could taste tears in her throat as her eyes began to water. She blinked her tears away, then sat up slowly. As she soon as she was settled *properly* in her seat, the wobbling of the carriage halted abruptly.

"I'm terribly sorry, I felt so sick, I couldn't contain it," she uttered weakly, her voice barely audible over the sound of the wheels rolling on the smooth dirt trail.

"Couldn't contain what?" her father's voice boomed, his loud voice echoing through the open windows and into the air. Birds resting on a nearby branch flew away as his voice filled the evening sky, and both the coachman and the footman tensed up, bringing their shoulders to their ears.

"I felt as if I was going to throw up," she muttered, looking at the king's hands which were clenched into fists on the padded seat.

"Are you that nervous?" the queen asked softly, studying her daughter's solemn, beautiful face.

"No, I am not nervous. It was from the swaying carriage," she said defensively. Amaryllis told half of a lie. The feeling of sickness came from the inevitable approaching of Arlon. The swaying of the carriage is what intensified that feeling, forcing her inner trauma out in the form of a hurl. Luckily, she didn't puke, but her body truly needed it. She needed to release her anxiety, it was with her for far too long— for the entire two hour long carriage ride. The king looked away, turning his body away from Amaryllis and towards the door of the carriage. He didn't want to face her, to look at her at all.

"Well, we're almost there," the queen assured her, gesturing to the castle out the window. Even at its great distance away, while it looked small, the royal subjects dared not call it so. It was the largest castle in the world, stretching into the clouds, spanning wide across the land. It truly was massive. Fear consumed Amaryllis completely as she stared at the gigantic structure. She shuddered as a shiver ran down her spine, covering her flesh in goosebumps. The longer she looked at the castle, the harder her heart pounded, surrendering to the ominous presence of the castle.

Amaryllis scratched at the seating of the carriage, digging her fingernails into the crisp velvet. Her nails buzzed against the fabric as she dragged them back and forth. She found herself clenching her teeth as hard as she could, but couldn't relax the muscles in her jaw. Her eyes were frozen still, locked on the colossal castle which creeped closer by the second. The pulse in her temple and the raging heart beat in her chest was all she could feel. The velvet beneath her fingers faded into air. She sat on nothing, just floating emptily in the carriage. Her parents, who she could vaguely see in the corner of her eye, disappeared completely, blending into the surroundings. The castle of Arlon taunted her with its potent presence, and there was nothing she could do to escape her arrival.

"Amaryllis?" her mother asked gently. When her daughter looked in her direction, she said, "We have arrived!"

Amaryllis blinked hard with the shake of her head. The castle which seemed so far, was now only a short walk away, guarded by a gargantuan iron gate. Time was an enigma, messing with Amaryllis' head. It was as if she had zoned out briefly at her great distance, her safe distance away, then zoned back in for the castle to jump out at her with its great, intimidating presence. She clenched her teeth harder, and her stomach seized upon seeing the structure. She eyed the castle from its base, following from the gigantic wooden door, passing humungous windows, all the way to the tips of the towers which pierced the clouds.

A crisp breeze tauntingly tickled Amaryllis' skin, seeping through the fabric of her light pink gown as the carriage door swung open. A visceral pain inhabited the princess. Her entire body trembled with fear as she knew it was time to enter the castle. She watched the queen take the footman's hand, then step down onto the stone path with a light click of her heeled shoes. The king hopped down himself with a heavy clack of his boots. Her world suddenly became unclear in a blur of disoriented waving lines and fading objects. Her heart jumped into her throat, making it too difficult to breathe. Her chest ached as she hyperventilated, taking huge gasps that didn't seem to fill her lungs no matter how hard she tried. The footman's open hand reached into the carriage. He peered inside and looked at Amaryllis patiently, oblivious to her terror. Her body reacted, reaching for his hand and taking it while her head spun rapidly in circles. She wobbled as soon as her feet touched the ground, and her knees nearly gave out when she looked once again at the castle through the iron bars of the gate.

"Thank you," she squeaked with a twitching mouth, barley able to hear herself speak through her fear-clogged ears. As she spoke, she realized how far she had distanced herself from the world. She was trapped within her mind which rushed with madness. Her fear caused her to be completely alert, and the urge to cry was prominent.

The footman nodded with a grin then jumped back onto his little seat on the outside of the carriage. The coachman took off as soon as he felt the carriage drop with the weight of the footman bringing it down. He snapped the reins fiercely with his wrist, and the horses trotted, pulling the carriage away.

"Are you ready to go inside?" the king asked impatiently with a hard toned voice. Amaryllis jolted, her muscles tensing in her lower back. His raised voice echoed inside of her troubled head, and she heard it as a thunderous holler from the effect of her fearful disorientation. She turned around slowly to face her father.

Pretend...you must pretend, she warned herself, solely focusing on hiding her fright.

"Yes, let us go," she answered with the most energy she could possibly manage to conjure. She payed close attention to her facial features, relaxing her lips and eyebrows. But she allowed her eyes to remain in their true form since her wide, frightened eyes could be perceived as excited. She stood as tall as she could, but not too straight to look stiff and uncomfortable. It was enough to fool both of her parents quite easily, but it was incredibly difficult for her to undertake.

"Let us go, then!" the queen crooned, her lips stretching into a wide, toothy smile. Her father turned around, satisfied with his daughter's energetic answer, and her mother followed. They faced the castle gate, awaiting its opening. Amaryllis forced her stiff legs to move as she walked. They shook spastically with each step. She feared she would collapse.

The twelve foot tall, iron gate with sharpened points stood before her majestically and uninvitingly, its presence warning her to turn around and run away before meeting what was inside. She looked beyond the pointed tips of the gate, spotting bright fluffy clouds that inched their way across the sky, pushed ever so gently by the breeze. She kept her gaze on the blue sky scattered with soft clouds, ignoring her pounding heart caused by the kingdom of Arlon, ignoring the gigantic gate. The sky's enchanting appearance calmed her slightly, easing her soul for only a minute.

A loud and sharp squeak penetrated her ears as the gate began to open. Her body jumped in surprise, her fear rushing back in like it had always been with her. Her terror had been momentarily hidden away by her blank thoughts as she focused on something other than how petrified she was. The gate opened fully, clearly revealing the castle of Arlon. Its flags waved at her ominously in the breeze like the castle had a mind of its own, tauntingly welcoming her inside. It was a monster of a building.

The castle's humungous size impressed the king and queen, like it did for any passing individual. Other kingdoms were envious, absolutely in love with its wholehearted structure, which caused it to emit power of intimidation to its visitors. It was a ruler's dream. The king and queen discussed its magnificence, but all their daughter heard were indistinct mumbles as she eyed the castle. Amaryllis payed no mind to its external wonderment, the internal horrors were imprinted in her mind, bringing her anxiety like a punch to the stomach.

"Thank you!" the queen said to the guards of the gate, waving excitedly to them. The four men nodded their heads, wearing stern expressions on their faces. They stared at Amaryllis, and she felt their eyes. She looked up to meet their gaze, and gasped. Under the bright, glaring sun, their faces were shadowed by darkness, making their faces too horrifying to look at. Their eyes followed Amaryllis as she quickly looked away with a racing heart. They followed her all the way down the stone brick path, until she reached the door.

Amaryllis narrowed her eyes as she focused on hiding the shakiness in her body while she walked. Each step was light, feeling like she wasn't touching the ground at all. She stumbled on herself, nearly tripping and falling hard to the ground. Her father looked over with a frown after hearing her shoes scrape against stone, his eyebrows arched angrily. His stare pummelled her heart, so she ignored him until he looked away.

"Are you feeling rather excited?" the queen cheered, leaning past the king to meet her daughter's eyes. Amaryllis groaned silently, her head growing lighter as she exhaled. Her mother's pure happiness conflicted with the inner demons she was so desperately trying to face. To continue hiding her terror, she withdrew pretend happiness from an unknown place in her body.

"I am! Very much so! I cannot wait a moment longer to go inside!" she exclaimed, each word squeezing her heart vigorously in a heated, fiery sensation. Her words were painfully untrue, she felt awful as each word slithered through her gritted teeth, weighing her soul down.

"Oh, how sweet! Have you given your future husband any more thought?"

Amaryllis groaned as the weight of guilt hung in her chest. Of course she hadn't, she had been dreading her arrival to the horrid kingdom of Arlon during the entire carriage ride. The only thing she thought of, were the people who visited the castle — the culprit of her despair. She hadn't the time to be able to clearly picture any sort of future without the painful reminders of where she was heading in the form of unbearable stomach aches.

"I am still open to everyone!" she lied, distributing her unknown energy to both her voice and the fake smile on her face. The light in the queen's face burned out, her gentle smile vanished, and her eyes widened. The king looked away from the mesmerizing castle to reveal his fearsome glare. Amaryllis sagged, full of despondency and worry. Had she used too much energy in her voice? Was her smile too wide, or not wide enough? She had been discovered, her misery must have seeped through—

"You can't be open to *any* prince."

Oh, thank goodness, she thought, relieved beyond her own comprehension.

"You must think in terms of who is best to rule, who possesses strong, kinglike qualities," the king scolded, looking to his wife hoping she would continue his lecture. After all, it was for the sake of their daughter's future. She needed to consider her options, but set herself on one. One prince whom she would spend the entire night trying to impress, trying to earn his heart. If she had wandered in aimlessly, with no prince in mind, she would end up with a random prince for an eternity, his qualities a mystery.

"Your father is right, Amaryllis. You must study them all; find whom you like, whom you do not. Remember, you may only reject one prince. It is vital that you pay close attention to the princes tonight. I know you aren't to see them until eight o'clock, but try your best to look for them…still following the rules of course," the queen said nervously, scanning her surroundings, speaking each word cautiously in case there were listening ears.

"Do you understand your mother?" the king asked hastily, also looking for listening ears while trying to get his daughter to look him in the eye. She was preoccupied, staring at her feet as she walked, attempting to fight her painful stomach aches with pure concentration.

"Amaryllis?"

"Yes," she snapped, forgetting to alter the attitude in her voice. "Yes, I understand," She said softly, trying to make up for her outburst. It was only one word, but that one word could easily expose the darkness that surrounded her pure heart.

"Good," the king said gruffly. "Then you will begin your searching as of now, right?"

A groan climbed out of her throat and settled in her mouth. She fought to keep it down. She was already trying to focus on surviving the night, and her parents were adding to her list which brought more stress to her already troubled heart. All she could manage to truly pay attention to, was trying to uplift the darkness that possessed her. She couldn't care less about the princes, although she knew how important it was to observe them. She didn't want to find herself stuck in a marriage with an imprudent man.

"Yes, father," she sighed. The queen relaxed after hearing her daughter agree to begin her search. It relieved her to know she would focus on her future, and not to end up with a monster of a man. She leaned back with a grin, hiding herself behind the king as she walked directly beside him. The king too felt waves of relief. He sighed, fixing his gaze upon the castle once again — which was only about one hundred paces away — satisfied enough with Amaryllis' answer to turn away.

"Just out of mere curiosity," Amaryllis began, earning her parents' attention, "if you were in my position, which prince would you desire?"

"The prince of Arlon!" They said simultaneously, with a tone that made it seem as if her question was painfully rhetorical. Amaryllis' stomach ache worsened at the mention of the word, *Arlon*. She inhaled deeply, hoping that the fresh air would ease her pains, but it did not. It seemed to make them even worse. She exhaled quickly, breathing the air hard out of her lungs. She was breathing in *Arlon's* poisonous air.

"As the prince of Arlon, he has great wealth, and by marrying him he will bring great worth to your name. He is potentially the best option for you, especially since Serilion is so small compared to Arlon. Just imagine: Amaryllis…The Queen of Arlon—"

Amaryllis nearly fainted. She reached for her father's arm and held it for balance. Her knees grew even weaker, shaking spastically as she stood still, pausing her father's walk. *The Queen of Arlon*, she thought, her world darkened by shadows of unconsciousness for a brief second. Her sight returned, and in her view (the only thing in her view as it was so ginormous) was the castle of *Arlon*.

"Are you all right?" the king asked, truly concerned. The queen stopped walking and turned around to face Amaryllis, who was gripping loosely onto her father's sleeve, trying to find balance as she seemed to be sinking to the ground.

"Amaryllis!" she cried, rushing over to pull her up. Her daughter's half-conscious body was limp and heavy, but she pulled hard until she stood up straight. Amaryllis' bright green, emerald eyes were glassy as tears formed. She couldn't hide her pain anymore, it had become too difficult. The horrendous castle broke her spirit from the outside, and she feared what it would do from within.

"I'm sorry," Amaryllis began. "I cannot go in. Please don't make me go in there," she croaked, a single tear racing down her cheek. She moved her gaze between her worried parents, struggling to fight more oncoming tears. Her eyes withheld an ocean of sorrow, ready to flood as they were stored behind a broken dam held together by rusted nails and rotten wood.

"What do you mean?" the queen asked gently, upset to see Amaryllis crying.

"I cannot go inside."

"Why not?" the king asked with a soothing voice. The voice he used on her when she was young.

"I cannot tell you," she replied frustratedly, wishing she could.

Suddenly, the giant wooden door of the castle creaked open, and standing in the centre of the moving door was the grand duke. He stood proudly in the shadows with his hands held behind his back, puffing his chest. Once the door was completely open, he waved to the royal family of Serilion, too far away for him to recognize the princess of Serilion was crying.

"We must go," the king said, taking the queen's hand, "come now, Amaryllis."

The queen looked at her husband in disbelief, but was too overwhelmed by the opening of the powerful castle to say anything to him. Amaryllis wiped her tears as she watched her parents approach the castle door. She looked up to the blue sky speckled with clouds in hope the world's beautiful qualities would take her tears away, but the clouds had taken over the sky completely with no blue in sight. The sky was overcast with grey clouds, hiding the sun, hiding the wonder. She looked down at the ground, discouraged. She moped to the entrance, not far behind her parents.

Chapter 3

"Hello Serilion, you all look so lovely!" the duke said excitedly, admiring the quality of their attire. His eyes lit up as he glanced the beautiful gowns of the queen and princess, and the elegant tunic of the king which was made with a few hints of purple dye—which was unbelievably expensive to purchase. "Please follow me!" said the duke after fully admiring the royal family of Serilion. Amaryllis slouched as soon as she stepped foot inside the castle, the weight of the castle's evil spirit crushing her. As she sagged, fighting the pressure, she looked at her pink glass slippers as they clacked against the perfectly polished, white, tiled floor. With each echoing step that reverberated through the empty hallway, Amaryllis shuddered. Her stomach pains burned in a fiery flame of terror, far more uncomfortable than her regular anxious butterflies. The tiles were so clear that she could nearly see her own reflection, which taunted her with ugliness that didn't exist. She quickly looked up at the ceiling, disgusted with herself, then cowered in fear. There was nowhere for her to look without feeling terrified. Her blurred reflection hissed at her on the floor, and the surroundings roared from above. The family of Serilion and the duke were very small within the castle. The ceilings stretched exceedingly high, leaving room for the sky itself. The castle never failed to make Amaryllis feel insignificant, puny, and weak, stripping her of the little bravery she had.

The king, queen, and the duke began conversing, but Amaryllis could hardly hear them. Their voices were muffled even though she walked just behind them. Amaryllis wrapped her arms around herself, pressing her fingers into her sides. Her hands were like fire, the heat of her sweaty palms seeping through the material of her pink gown. Her stomach seized as she looked at her surroundings. There were tall pillars serving no other purpose than intimidation. They stretched from the floor, all the way to the ceiling—two hundred feet above. There were large paintings hanging on the walls, revealing portraits of the royal family of Arlon. Some were portraits of the queen, many were of the prince, most were solely of the king, and there were few family portraits. They stretched down the hall, as far as Amaryllis could see. As Amaryllis examined the portrait of the prince of Arlon, she pictured her future with him, just like her parents had suggested. From the previous parties, she remembered him as an arrogant man who only cared for himself. His selfish nature was present in the portrait she looked at which was enclosed in a golden frame with a floral design; his piercing, metallic grey eyes withheld self pride, and his smug half grin reflected his narcissistic manners. His dirty blonde hair was slicked back at the time of his painting, and the painter had captured the fine details of each strand. Prince Eric of Arlon was handsome, but his egotistical personality was what permanently made up Amaryllis' mind. If he chose her, which she didn't believe would actually happen because of her lack of confidence, then she would surely reject him. She didn't like the way his bright grey eyes followed her as she passed by. They acted as a light source in the dark, torch-lit hallway.

Amaryllis jolted as a set of double doors opened dramatically. The hinges squeaked sharply as the duke pushed the ballroom doors open. Bright light from inside the room peered into the dim hall, lighting up an intimidating portrait of the King of Arlon. His ice blue, narrow eyes stared at Amaryllis as she entered the ballroom. She hurried inside to escape the hall of horrors.

Immediately after stepping foot into the bright room, lit by a magnificent, glass chandelier, her stomach pains and overall feeling of fear surrendered. Amaryllis gasped as overwhelming waves of relief radiated throughout her body. The evil butterflies flew from her stomach, making her gut feel rich with a pleasant, tingling warmth of emptiness. She hadn't been anxiety-free for the past few hours. Her mind was suddenly clear, free of spinning thoughts, free of the afflictions her horrors had on her. A tear rolled down her cheek. There was something about the bright, beautiful room that cleansed the evil which pummelled her soul. The chandelier hung magnificently. It seemed to float there, possessing uplifting powers which it radiated to the room. It was the heart of the ballroom. The uplifting of her pain brought her an immense sensation of happiness until it faded into nothing. The presence of Arlon entered her body again poisoning her good spirit with sadness. She sighed a despondent sigh, catching her mother's attention.

"Please try not to show your worries while we are here," the queen pleaded quietly, beneath the conversation between the duke and the king. Amaryllis looked into her mother's blue eyes, which demanded the impossible, overwhelmed with emotion.

"That will be incredibly difficult," Amaryllis whispered, more tears flowing.

"I don't know why you were crying back there, but it is completely unnecessary. The Choosing Ceremony is nothing to fear."

"But, mother I—"

"Don't make a fool of yourself," the queen snapped, leaning an inch away from Amaryllis' face. "Remember, you must impress the princes. It would be *humiliating* if something were to go wrong," she turned away, joining the king's conversation with the duke. Amaryllis' heart ached. She had always felt alone when visiting Arlon, but the way her mother reacted to her terror made her feel even more isolated, like she had absolutely no one to talk to. Not that she would have ever gone to anyone for comfort anyway, since she was so determined in keeping her fright to herself. Amaryllis sank away, letting her body guide herself around the room. The walls of the ballroom stared at her, making the hairs of her neck stand on end. Tall, purple drapes covering a large window hung devilishly still, looking as though they'd slide open by themselves to reveal the setting sky of many colours and remind her of how lovely it was outside and how horrid it was inside. They would remind her of how she was trapped. She looked to the ground, away from the fearsome objects. The floor was tiled with light blue, shiny slabs that reflected Amaryllis' appearance even more vividly than the tiles in the main hall. She looked away immediately upon noticing her reflection. There was nowhere to look. No area could provide her with any sense of comfort. Just as Amaryllis was about to come to terms with always being on edge for the remaining time in Arlon, feeling powerful sensations of sadness rising in her chest, she spotted something small. It was far away, and it was moving.

Amaryllis approached the moving object, her eyes full of curiosity. As she moved closer, she noticed a long tail, pointed ears, and bright green eyes. It was a small white cat standing perfectly still. The cat eyed her carefully as she came closer, watching her slow movements, ready to take off if she moved too quickly. The cat warmed her heart. To see something so pure and innocent in a place as daunting as Arlon was miraculous. She stood just a step away from the cat, kneeling down on one knee to appear less intimidating. She held out her hand, and the cat leaned forward to smell her hand. It closed its eyes and tickled the tips of her fingers as it sniffed with the bob of its head. A content grin spread across Amaryllis' face, and with her other hand she pet the cat's soft, white fur, stroking it gently. The cat meowed tenderly, then lay down on the blue tiled floor.

I wonder who he belongs to, she pondered, finding herself falling in love with the tame animal. His eyes were closed and he purred as she rubbed his back, petting him along his side.

Her stomach pains vanished once again as the happy little cat distracted her from where she was. She was too distracted to hear the rapid, clicking footsteps of the duke coming up behind her, but the cat was not.

"Shoo, shoo!" the duke cried, waving his hands madly at the stubborn feline. Amaryllis stood up quickly in surprise, watching the white cat hiss furiously at the duke with black, angry slits in his eyes, and an arched back. Amaryllis stepped away from the cat, fearing she would get scratched or bitten, but the duke charged, chasing him under a sofa at the far end of the room. The room filled with footsteps, shouts, and hisses as the cat's soft pink paws tapped the ground until sliding underneath the red and gold furniture. The duke halted before the sofa, contemplating whether or not he wanted to slide it out of the way to grab the cat and throw it outside. Amaryllis ran over hoping to defend the monster-turned cat and relax him back into his peaceful state.

"Why are you treating him that way? He's only a cat," Amaryllis uttered weakly, heartbroken that her source of happiness—an adorable, peaceful little animal—grew accustomed to the darkness of the palace with its sharp claws and violent hissing.

"That little *rat*, sneaks into the castle more often than you think, and the king *hates* him," the duke explained, slowly lowering down on the floor to peer underneath the couch. He was frightened to get a claw to the eye, carefully putting his face to the ground.

"Well, I wouldn't mind taking him outside," Amaryllis suggested, cringing as she watched the duke put his face awfully close to the bottom of the couch, worried he would get clawed.

"No good," the duke said between reaches for the cat, stretching his arm as far under the sofa as he could. "He'll only return again, and again," he sat up wincing, with a small line of red drawn by the cat's claw on the back of his hand. "Oh dear..." he murmured, taking a handkerchief from his pocket and dabbing the blood.

"Oh, well what are you to do with him?" she asked worriedly, her emerald green eyes illuminated in fear. She felt sympathy for the animal, believing he was just looking for a place to explore, to find food...he was a brave cat.

"I am hoping to drown him in a lake!" the duke hissed, yelling at the couch. Amaryllis' heart dropped.

"Please no!" she cried. She bent down to peer under the couch. Hidden in the shadows was the cat, his bright white fur painted grey by darkness, his green eyes luminous.

"Come on out," she whispered, holding her hand out to him. She could sense his anger as she examined him. The cat's angry eyes softened, and he inched forward to smell her. He recognized her lovely, flowery smell and crawled out cautiously. She took the cat in her arms and stood up.

"Princess, please put the rat down," the duke scoffed, glaring angrily at the spoiled feline. The cat seemed to smile evilly at the duke, wiggling his tail tauntingly in the air as he nestled deeper into the princess' comforting embrace.

"I mustn't! I don't want him to get hurt."

"Look at what he's done to me!" the duke cried, revealing his scratched hand.

"He wouldn't have hurt you if you hadn't chased him away," she stated, hugging the cat tightly and feeling his warmth defeat the fear in her body. The cat purred in her arms.

Suddenly, the King of Arlon entered the ballroom. The duke's stomach dropped as he spotted him in the doorway. He jumped in front of Amaryllis, shielding the cat.

"If he sees the rat—"

Stop calling him that,

"—He will get angry. Give it to me, please."

Amaryllis looked into the duke's brown eyes, brimful with fear. By giving the cat to the duke, she would lose her companion, her only source of happiness in the castle of darkness. She couldn't care less about the king's emotion. "Please, may I keep him?"

"I am sorry, but you may not! Trust me, you don't want to see the King of Arlon when he's…angry," the duke shivered. He spoke with a shaky voice, controlled by the remembrance of each and every outburst of the king: his thunderous voice, the madness in his eyes, his destructive nature. The king had a terrible temper.

Amaryllis handed the cat to the duke, regretting her decision as soon as he scurried away with him. She spotted her parents far off, near the corner of the ballroom. They watched dozens of young men lifting heavy, two-seated, wooden chairs into the room. They were the chairs in which the princes would sit as they admired the princesses before they chose them. They'd sit and observe until it was their turn to choose a woman for themselves. Only one prince could go up at a time, and it typically started with the prince of the smallest kingdom, working down to the prince of the largest kingdom. Once it was time to head up to the line of princesses, they would choose their bride and take them to sit down in the double seat.

Amaryllis' heart raced as the chairs were brought in, and it skipped a beat when they were dropped loudly onto the floor by the exhausted chair-lifters. Those incredibly large seats, crafted from the sweat and tears of the king's most trusted woodcarver, provided her with a frightening glimpse of the future. Power emitted from them, taking the form of pain in Amaryllis' gut. Her excitement to be chosen transformed into an intense nervousness.

She walked lightheadedly over to her parents, her thoughts rushing with worry.

"Did you see the cat?" she asked them, trying to take her mind off of her sudden fear. "He's quite lovely," Amaryllis said, faking the joy in her voice as the visualization of the Choosing Ceremony played in her mind. The king glared at his daughter, and her heart raced even faster. His brows were furrowed, his eyes cold.

"No; however, I saw you arguing with the duke," he said firmly. "Amaryllis, this is your one and only chance to make a good impression. Your poor behaviour will affect your chances of being chosen. What prince will want a disputatious bride for eternity? No one—"

The queen, raised a hand to the king, shutting him up. She opened her mouth to speak, thinking her words would ease the tension between her husband and daughter. She would paraphrase the king's word into a less aggressive manner,

"Please refrain from humiliating yourself. Be respectful of everyone, especially the duke," she warned. Amaryllis' fear boiled into an angered energy, spreading heat throughout her body. Her cheeks burned in frustration. She was *not* arguing with the duke, and how dare they tell her to *refrain from humiliating herself.* Tears welled in her eyes with a strong urge to cry. She looked up at the ceiling with glistening eyes, then closed them for a few seconds. A tear tried to wiggle through her eyelids, but instead it collected inside her eye.

"What is she doing?" the king asked the queen.

"I am not certain," she replied under her breath.

All Amaryllis could hear was mumbling of confusion between her parents as she tried to calm herself. This was the second time her true emotion had nearly been revealed to them—which at that moment was exasperation. The walls which had been holding her tears back had cracked, and if she succumbed to the pressure the fear was exerting she would cry for days. Years of bottling her petrifying experiences would explode from her body.

She had shown them a happy, loving girl for all of the eight years they had been attending the annual parties, but inside she was struggling to enjoy herself. She struggled to live outside of the barriers of fear; it consumed her completely from the brutal torment of envious princesses, scarring her from the young age of twelve.

She sighed and opened her eyes to look down at her feet. She suddenly had the strongest urge to run away, back to Serilion if she could. It was far away, but she would without a doubt, crawl back if necessary.

"Amaryllis?" the queen asked impatiently, glaring at her with wide eyes that longed for an answer. The princess looked up at her mother with watery green eyes that sent a shock through her parents' minds. Her lower lip began to quiver slightly, since she was fighting to keep it still, it was almost unnoticeable. They waited for an answer, both with raised eyebrows and wide eyes. They rarely saw their daughter in tears because of Amaryllis' belief that her misery bothered others, and her belief that if she showed her inner-horror she would face consequences. It was just too much. Pressure piled onto her shoulders, weighing her down. The unseen force of fear penetrated the wall which held her tears back. Amaryllis couldn't hide her emotion for a moment longer. Her eyes poured in an endless stream of tears. Her irises glistened like emeralds, and her cheeks flushed in a light red.

"What is this about?" her father asked, showing little concern. She never cried, but he didn't pay any mind to that fact. Her tears were justified at the nerve-wracking event she had found herself in. He understood her nervousness, but to him, the Choosing Ceremony was nothing to sob over. "Stop *now*," he uttered through a clenched jaw.

Amaryllis shook her head.

The queen looked at Amaryllis in horror, picturing a scenario in her head that involved her daughter's neglect. Luckily, no one around them noticed Amaryllis' tears, but the king and queen felt the entire world could see her humiliating sorrow. They looked around the room and met no gazes of the other royal subjects who started to flood into the room, then looked back at their daughter.

"I don't want to be here," she groaned as waterfalls fell from her eyes, startling her parents further.

That was all she said. Nothing more, because she was not allowed to say more than that. The king and queen peppered her with questions, but she tuned them out. Her misery blocked her ears, blocked her vision. All she could see was the blue tile before her, shining menacingly.

Chapter 4

Amaryllis sat motionlessly on the sofa where the cat once hid, as stiff as a board as her empty mind took over her actions. Her hands were clasped together in a sweaty grip, her legs crossed. Her body cried for a loving embrace, but she had no one to rely on for comfort, so she held herself in her own embrace. No matter how she sat, how she positioned herself, or what she thought of, emptiness consumed her. Her spirit vacated her chest. Her heart was penetrated and stripped of its happiness, causing a tingling void to take a place where her emotion once was. In all areas of her body, all she felt was the pain of emptiness.

A jumble of mumbling voices filled the air, echoing grimly in her blank mind. Although she heard the loud noises of the lively ballroom, she wasn't listening to them. She stared lifelessly at the floor, in shock. The feeling of despair radiated from the castle's aura, overwhelming her with fear that her body didn't know how to handle.

She blinked a painful, dry blink. Her eyes were scorched from her excessive crying. Crust formed in the corners of her eyes, pulling on the eyelashes that got stuck while she squeezed her eyes shut as her tears dried. She rubbed her stinging eyes, feeling the crusted tears pushing against her knuckles until she rubbed them free. It hurt to blink, and it hurt to stare. Her eyes burned.

She looked up from the ground, watching the ballroom door. The royal subjects began to leave the room, going in the direction which the duke pointed them. If she wasn't so despondent, she would have felt a surge of nervousness rush through her body, urging her to run out the door to find the princesses. But, she was beyond calm—beyond any form of emotion, so far beyond that she felt absolutely nothing at all. With the absence of motivation, she stood from the sofa groggily. Her body begged her to stay seated, but she ignored her temptation. It was time for her horse ride, time to socialize with the princesses. As much as she wanted to remain alone and away from them, she knew she had to go, because if she didn't they would hunt her down and find her anyway. She simply couldn't sit on the sofa for the rest of the night, because she wasn't allowed, and she wanted to escape the effect of the dreadful castle. Amaryllis recalled hearing the announcement of the activity switch, but it felt like hours ago. Time was a confusing concept when accompanying a sad soul.

She halfheartedly jogged across the ballroom, spotting her parents near the end of the line of people that were trying to leave, to head to the lounge area. The queen looked back at her daughter, filling Amaryllis with a slight hope that she would step away from the line to provide her with a source of comfort whether it was from a hug or even just a hello. But, she did not. She met her daughter's eyes with an irritated glance, then looked at the king who had his eyes focused on the people moving in front of him.

Amaryllis' heart sank as her mother's usual gentle stare which brought her inner peace crushed her. The unexpected glare caused her to freeze mid-stride. She watched her parents disappear into the hallway with a throbbing heart.

They do not care about my well-being, she thought, a single tear falling down her cheek, tickling her dry eye as it escaped. It was true in a way; they had no interest in how she felt, because all they saw was a whining child over an event she could easily dominate. They knew not of her trauma since she never told them. They thought she just couldn't handle her nervousness well, and they had no patience for it.

The duke caught her attention with the wave of his hand, pulling her out from her trance of sadness. "They've gone out into the meadow, behind the castle for their horse ride," the duke informed her, looking back and fourth from her to the moving line of royal subjects who walked aimlessly down the hallway. No matter how many times they visited, they never seemed to grow used to the castle and its many rooms. "To your right! I'll be there in a moment!" he called to them.

Amaryllis pushed past the duke and began her walk through the dark hallway. Meanwhile, the duke raced ahead of the group to lead them into the correct, designated room, his voice becoming quieter during his shouts as he advanced further down the hall.

Amaryllis rushed through the dark halls to escape the stares of the lively pantings, shielding her eyes as she passed them by holding her hands on either side of her head. She reached the open castle door, and walked outside of the castle. The light wind hit her like a punch to the face. Her mind was so disconnected from her body that even the lightest sensations seemed weighted with darkness provided by the castle.

She sauntered lifelessly into the meadow, the princesses mean stares becoming more distinguishable as she drew nearer. They looked at her with glares of hatred which brought pain to her chest. They spoke to her, but she was too sorrowful to hear them, and she didn't want to hear them. She looked past them, at the tips of the trees in the distance.

Suddenly, there were dozens of horses without saddles trotting before them. Amaryllis heard fierce whispers of complaint, making her feel more comfortable.

"Are we supposed to ride bareback?"

"This is absolutely ridiculous."

"My dress will be covered in horse hair!" the voices bickered on, but Amaryllis had already mounted a radiant horse that had caught her attention. He was tall with defined muscle beneath his greyish blue coat. Her heart pulsated with warmth when she looked at him. The complaining princesses all whipped their heads to follow Amaryllis on her galloping blue horse. His powerful hooves thumped the against ground in thundering strides, and he and Amaryllis looked rather magnificent riding into the setting sun with its golden rays shining upon them, gleaming onto their hair to make it shine.

They scoffed at the fact that she did not care about riding bareback. How revolting was that? That wasn't very lady like of her, but they too decided to ride bareback, and followed Amaryllis to wherever she wanted to go.

The other princesses never completely caught up to Amaryllis, as her horse did not tire easily with its great stamina. Plus, Amaryllis would discretely command her horse to gallop quicker whenever the princesses would gain closeness. Each time they came too close, her heart would scream, and shivers would rocket down her spine.

Her horse was truly lovely. He rode as gracefully and as beautifully as a bird could fly.

A horse's ears can be incredibly hypnotizing as they bounce in front of you, stretching forwards and back rhythmically with its strides. It distracts me from my pain. How my mind wanders as I explore the land. The overwhelming feeling is one of freedom—

"Hey!" yelled a princess, barely audible over the sound of galloping hooves. Amaryllis looked over her shoulder, gripping her horse's mane for balance. The princesses were all clumped together on their steeds, one hundred yards away from her.

She nearly answered, but decided against responding as a creeping feeling of unease rose in her chest. They would use anything she said against her in a manner of utter disrespect.

The princesses all took turns shouting something vulgar, but Amaryllis could not hear what they said over the sound of the thumping hooves and the strong wind caused by her great speed.

All she heard were indistinct calls of the voices that haunted her when she closed her eyes at night.

Impulsively, she squeezed her legs tight against her horse's sides, her action begging him to gallop even faster. She did not want to be able to hear them at all; neither the voices or the other horses. Her horse—already galloping inconceivably fast—now dashed across the meadow in a streak of blue.

Amaryllis' body jolted back as the horse zoomed forward. She reached for the horse's long mane and used it to pull herself upright, fighting the strong winds the horse created.

The princesses wanted her to slow her horse down, so they could pass her and leave her far behind them to make her feel alone and despondent. If Amaryllis was in the front, then the princesses behind her did not matter or affect her, and the princesses did not like that.

The entire horse riding session consisted of Amaryllis enjoying her freedom galloping around on her lovely horse and not having a single care about where she was. The princesses session consisted of trying to catch up to her to attempt to ruin her night, which they would anyway, but they were unsuccessful during that time.

Suddenly, a horn was blown, meaning the princesses had to move onto their next activity; the tea party. Amaryllis slowed her blue horse down to a complete stop, then pulled on his mane to spin him around to face the castle. The princesses were already on their way back, and they had a head start since they were closer to the castle. She watched them as they chuckled and squealed, becoming further and further away, their giggles quieting. Some of them turned their heads to laugh at Amaryllis for finally being at the back of the group where they wanted her to be.

Amaryllis groaned. Her hour of freedom had come to an end, and she was not looking forward to having to be put into a *room* with those awful, sniggering princesses.

Amaryllis came in from the meadow like a goddess on her Pegasus. The blue horse galloped as fast as he could back towards the stables where they greeted the princesses still dismounting their horses. The fast approaching, large animal startled the princesses and the stable boys assisting them. He came in with unnatural speed, and he was not slowing down. The stable boys grabbed the princesses and pulled them close against the castle wall while the blue horse flashed by. He sent a gust of wind into the stables, blowing the princesses dresses and hair. They all shut their eyes in fear, and when they opened them Amaryllis sat in front of them, still mounted on her horse, watching them.

"Why did you have to come in so quickly?" asked a frightened stable boy. He wasn't supposed to speak to the royal subjects unless spoken to first, but he could not control himself as his sudden scare took over his body.

Amaryllis brought her leg over one side of the horse to face him. "The horn was blown, and I did not want to be late for the tea party. Besides, it was the speed that he decided was appropriate, and I chose not to stop him," she explained, speaking softly as if she wasn't truly confident in what she was saying.

The stable boy, still startled, nodded his head and took the hand of the princess to his left to bring her back inside the castle. "It'll be all right," he assured her. She looked as if she had seen a ghost. She nervously patted his hand, keeping her gaze in an arbitrary place in front of her, trying to comprehend what had just happened. She could have sworn she was nearly trampled to death by a gargantuan, blue horse.

"Was that really too fast?" Amaryllis asked another stable boy who had his skeptical eyes on her.

"It was extremely fast, and you looked like a careless fool," he scoffed, crossing his arms across his chest. This man had no filter whatsoever. He had no respect for authority, and was philosophically negative. Although, he didn't dare speak that way in front of the royal subjects of Arlon. They would discipline him in a way so degrading and humiliating if they caught him offending royalty, and he would be absolutely traumatized. He never knew what the exact method of humiliation was, but his mouth had run a little too much one evening, and the king had overheard. He had spoken a sincere, sinister threat that frightened the stable boy into silence. However, seeing Amaryllis nearly trample everyone in a fierce, bluff-charge, caused him to forget the king's dark words. He immediately regretted calling the princess a *fool*, worrying the king was nearby.

"Well, I'm all right with being a fool if being a fool means I ride horses too quickly. You see, riding horses is very euphoric and hypnotic in sever—" she began, allowing her heart to take over in her speech. Her overall timidity had completely vanished as she pictured blurry surroundings rushing past her from up high on her blue horse, but, the stable boy interrupted her,

"Don't you tell me what riding horses is like," he snapped. "Unfortunately, horses are my life…my *job*. I don't want a *princess* to educate me on the *euphoric sensation* of riding a big, stupid animal," he scowled. The stable boy regretted these words as well, but he couldn't stop. The negativity flowed from his mouth uncontrollably. He looked all around, waiting for the king to pop out from somewhere with an unforgiving glare. He winced, waiting for Amaryllis to insult him, or to storm off to find someone to tell about the rude stable boy, but Amaryllis laughed at him. She had never heard a man so brutally honest before, and found it amusing. She hadn't laughed in a long while, and appreciated the good chuckle he allowed her to have.

"I am sorry to bother you—" she paused to pretend to think, "—what is your name?" she chuckled.

"Charles," he answered nervously, still on the lookout for the king. The other stable boys around him looked around as well, in fear for the loudmouth man. Everyone, except for Amaryllis, was aware of the king's threat for Charles to stay silent.

"Well, Charles… I hope you have a wonderful evening," she said with a grin, looking into his anxious eyes. She couldn't detect his fear over the jolt of happiness that surged through her body, a giddy sensation.

Amaryllis didn't have an effect on Charles like she did with most people she met. In fact, Charles was the only man she had met that was not stunned by her radiance or her kindness. His negative attitude blocked his vision of the lovely princess like a cloud that covered the sun.

She dropped down from her blue steed, falling for longer than she anticipated with crazed butterflies fluttering in her stomach until her feet thumped against the ground. Then, she turned the corner, leaving the stable boys' sight. The stable boys glared at Charles with worrisome expressions, and their stares intensified his feeling of fear.

Amaryllis could not see the princesses. They entered the castle without looking back. They did not bother to wait for her, but she didn't expect them to.

The duke appeared suddenly. "Right this way, Princess," he cheered. The princess wanted to follow him, but was too intrigued by the sound of metal swords clanging together in a simulated battle. "Are you not coming?"

"What is going on?" she asked, gazing at the ceiling in a stare of concentration as she listened to the chiming of the swords. The duke chuckled at her curiosity, brushing off her question as he was on a tight schedule.

"It is now time for your tea party, Princess. Hurry now. The others are waiting for you." He motioned for her to follow him with waving hands.

Utter fear swirled in her guts when reminded of *the others*. Knowing the duke was leading her to a huge, daunting room with no presence other than those of the other princesses worried her poor heart, but she could not tell him of her fears. She could not tell anyone as she was promised to receive such inconceivable torment if she did.

Her voice shook as she uttered her clarified question. "No, I mean—what is that noise?"

The duke stopped to listen. His smile faded, and he frowned as he focused on the sound, listening intently. "Ahh, that is the sound of fencing," he said after his stern face returned to his original cheerful expression as he identified the noise. "The princes are just fooling around. While you and your friends sip your tea, the princes engage in playful battles!" he said excitedly.

Amaryllis cringed at the implication of the duke calling those princesses her *friends*. They were the farthest thing from being even acquaintances. They were...enemies.

The faint sword fight boomed in volume as an upstairs door swung wide open. Just then, two princes in battle were fencing at the top of the stairs, laughing and grunting loudly as they fought. The dominant prince was pushing the other down, giving him no other place to go than down the stairs. They were laughing maniacally, enjoying themselves. The room was now filled with metal clanging against metal, and manly laughter.

They battled all the way down the stairs and continued to fence about two feet away from Amaryllis and the duke, not seeming to notice their presence as their focus was on their opponent.

The duke jolted with a surge of panic, putting an arm in front of Amaryllis and pushing her back, away from the two men. "This is preposterous," the duke squealed, "stop at once! You are supposed to contain yourselves in your room!"

"I will not," said the dominant prince between shallow breaths, "I am currently winning, and our duel is interrupted, then a true winner is not decided," he grunted through a clenched smile while beginning to increase his intensity. He seemed to have pulled great amounts of energy from deep within himself. It was the adrenaline's effect. "And if the battle *must* end now, then I *must*—" he took one big final swing at the prince, "—WIN!"

The tip of his sword lightly pressed against the other prince's chest. They breathed heavily, giggling like children. Both princes were filled with satisfaction. The battle had lasted for the longest time, commencing in their designated room ten minutes ago and continuing into the hall. It had ended decently.

Both princes were extremely skilled, especially the winning prince. Amaryllis watched in astonishment as she took notice of how beautifully the victorious prince smiled. His teeth were perfectly straight, and his soft, greyish blue eyes were full of pride. Amaryllis' heart fluttered happily as she admired him.

He felt her stare, glanced over, and met her eyes. Her stomach dropped, her body feeling lighter than air as their eyes locked. She couldn't move her gaze away.

The prince's smile disappeared upon seeing her. He had never seen anything so wonderful in his lifetime. Of course, he had seen her before during his previous visits to Arlon's annual gatherings, but he was not yet interested in finding his future queen then, and she never really stood out until right then. He hadn't been entirely observant until that moment, knowing he'd have to leave for the last time engaged to one of the princesses. She seemed to have been hiding for those eight years.

Neither of them knew what to say, both completely mesmerized with one another. Amaryllis feared the sight of her was horrid as his vanishing grin seemed to convey, to her, that she was hideous, but his smile only faded because his body had surrendered to the charms of her radiance, relaxing each muscle in his body until they seemed non-existent. He felt lighter than air.

"Hello," he said softly and simply, breaking through his dumbfounded trance to utter the simplest word. His voice was very masculine yet had gentleness to it. It put Amaryllis at ease. It calmed her knotted stomach and amplified her affection for him. His smile returned, but his teeth did not show this time. He wanted to hide his teeth so as not to seem too eager, but his excitement was too difficult to resist.

"Hello," she said contently, smiling back at him, revealing her radiant smile. All she could manage was a *hello*, nothing more.

She was too astonished by the wonders he emitted into her soul. Luckily, he was able to continue the conversation, because she would surely not have been able to.

"I am incredibly sorry that we carelessly carried our battle towards you…it was completely unintentional. I would have felt awful if you had gotten hurt," he apologized, looking down at his feet in embarrassment, then looking back up quickly to meet the sight of her beautiful complexion once again.

"Don't worry, it's all right," she assured him. "After all, it was an exciting match to watch," she blushed as the compliment slid from her mouth, full of lightheadedness. The prince chuckled, believing her comment was a sweet thing to tell him. He knew very well of the skills he possessed and was ecstatic to have shown her what he was capable of. He wanted to display himself to her as a kind and protective man.

"I apologize for nearly causing an accident," he admitted, ignoring his triumphant feelings.

"Well, it looked to me like you knew what you were doing," she smiled. The prince chuckled again in surprise. He was intrigued by her kindness, her innocence, her sweetness. The other prince and the duke did nothing but stare at them, watching the magical conversation between the two of them. Amaryllis and the prince talked as if no one was around. They had completely forgotten about the other people in the room, too focused on the lovely ones before them.

"Well, thank you princess," he gushed. Coming from the mouth of an unbelievably gorgeous and warmhearted princess, the compliment meant the world to him. She spoke with truth, simply wanting to express her admiration and expecting nothing in return. She pushed past her shyness to inform him of her admiration for his skill and humility.

Amaryllis had never experienced such a wonderful encounter at the annual parties before. She never experienced a feeling as pleasant as the one which consumed her in that moment. Her body flushed with euphoria. What she felt was love, but she didn't quite detect it yet as she had never been exposed to it before. She payed close attention to the detail of her surroundings, and more importantly, the prince, to really absorb the moment to ensure it would become a vivid memory.

He had luscious, dark brown hair that hung loosely in his eyes when he didn't brush it away. His eyes melted her heart. They were greenish blue, and the dark colour of his hair made them stand out. His shoulders were broad and strong. He stood tall over her, but he was not intimidating. He emitted a comforting feeling of protection. She loved how polite he was. He was truly lovely.

The prince took notice of Amaryllis' features as well. He was amazed with her perfect face. Her auburn hair complimented her emerald eyes, her cheek bones were defined, and her lips were as soft and delicate as flowers. She was tall for a woman but still quite a few inches shorter than him. She presented herself proudly, yet she seemed to behave shyly. She was incredibly sweet—

Amaryllis interrupted his thoughts of admiration. "We aren't allowed to see each other yet!" she exclaimed. She immediately wished she had not said anything, but the words slipped right out. She would have preferred to talk with the prince all night long rather than partaking in any more activities Arlon had planned. The duke stepped in when his strong observations of the conversation were concluded in his mind. He sensed chemistry, and did not bother to interrupt, even though it was not allowed for them to converse before eight o'clock—before the Choosing Ceremony.

"I was just about to say that," said the duke. The prince and the princess sagged inside, but did not show it.

"I suppose that's true," he said glumly. He tried to create a monotonous sound to his voice to hide his sudden sadness but did not hide it well enough to disguise it.

"Both of you, head back to the fencing area. You will be informed of your instructions for your hike through the forest momentarily," the duke told the princes, pointing up the stairs. They nodded in understanding.

Amaryllis was suddenly confused at the sight of the second prince since she never payed attention to his presence, especially after meeting lovely the Prince James of Werling. Like the prince, Amaryllis had never been searching for a possible spouse during the years before. Her mind raced with curiosity, wondering why Prince James had never caught her eye. Then, she remembered. The torment came rushing in, her stomach churned with butterflies as terror consumed her body. The princesses appeared in her mind, laughing and hissing rude things to her. She had been preoccupied with trying to survive her misery all those years, and she would have to face it one last time.

"Well, good bye, Princess Amaryllis," the Prince of Werling said sincerely. He did not smile this time as he was discouraged to part from her. Even though he would see her later in the night, he couldn't help but feel lonesome. Amaryllis appreciated the formal good bye, but she wished he had called her *Amaryllis* instead of attaching the *princess* portion, it would have sounded more personal.

"Goodbye, Prince James," she replied with the same sincerity in her voice, with the same lonesome glance.

As soon as he had made it up the stairs and out of sight, she already missed his presence, and he missed hers. She wanted to speak to him again, and soon.

Amaryllis and the duke continued their walk—which was so amazingly interrupted—down the vast hallway with its astonishingly high ceiling. The further she walked from the staircase, the more her heart pulsated sadly, feeling full and heavy.

"I think he was rather fond of you," crooned the duke with a smile on his little face. He could sense her discouragement and wanted to cheer her up, but her discouragement was overpowered by her fright. His senses were painfully erroneous.

"Do you really believe that?" she asked happily, her fear completely fleeing from her body.

"I really do, yes."

The princess suddenly felt lightheaded and her body became weightless. All she felt was her heart beating. It was as if her life took the form of only a heart and a set of eyes. She could not stop smiling, it felt so natural and effortless. She was filled with happiness and had to release it or else she would implode. She sighed peacefully, looking up to the tall ceiling hundreds of feet above, focusing on no particular area.

"Come along now," the duke chuckled, happy he improved her mood. He had to guide Amaryllis to the room where the other princesses were since she couldn't walk properly. She was truly under love's spell. Before entering the room, as her body lazily sank, escaping from the duke's helpful grasp, she let herself fall to the floor. She closed her eyes and smiled wider, giggling under her breath.

"He really was wonderful wasn't he?" Amaryllis asked rhetorically. The duke nodded. He let her swoon over the prince for a little while longer before taking her inside. He let her sit against the wall and dream.

Chapter 5

Amaryllis sat with her hands in her lap, her fingers laced, legs crossed, back straight, and her chin down as she sat timidly in a large oak chair with blue velvet padding. The princes were outside somewhere in the forest, and the princesses were in a small room with tea in hand. The princesses sat in a circle conversing about fashion, makeup, and the princes, but Amaryllis had no desire to speak. Prince James of Werling had faded from her mind. Reality had returned, and she was once again unhappy to be in Arlon.

Amaryllis had her chair pushed back slightly outside of the circle of chairs. She couldn't help but daydream. It was her only escape from the dreadful princesses. They may not have seemed so horrible, but for poor Amaryllis they were a nightmare.

She drifted off into the depths of her mind.

Amaryllis was walking through a colourful forest. The leaves were crimson red, the tree trunks were yellow, the dirt was a chalky blue, and the rain falling from the purple clouds was pink.

The tree is coloured bright yellow for a strange reason that I cannot explain. It is the most vibrant yellow I have ever seen. While I place my hands on the soft bark, I expect pigment to secrete from the wood and stain my hands. I rotate my wrist to see for myself, and nothing is there. I climb up and sit restfully on a thick branch, playfully swinging my legs up and down. As I sit here with my thoughts, I realize that the grass is coloured red. How strange is that? A yellow tree and red grass? What was there to come next? A purple sky? Yes, I look up and see pink birds flying gracefully through a purple sky. It is strange, yet extremely wonderful to encounter. The world that I seem to be existing in is breaking the earthly rules of nature. Where I am simply does not matter. I feel a sense of euphoria and that is what I am most conscious of. I can feel the soft rain sprinkling and dropping onto my skin. It is not warm nor cold, and it feels wonderful. I have not felt this happy since—

Amaryllis jolted. Her polychromatic world shattered and fell down into space.

"Where are you right now?" giggled the princess beside her with a giddy expression on her face. Her long blonde hair fell into her eyes as she laughed.

The torment began for one final time. They all had planned on giving her the worst night of her life, summing up all of the other times into one final horror show.

"What's the matter with you?" cried a princess, hysterically, laughing manically afterwards.

"I think she's afraid to speak. You know…ugly people aren't very smart, and I don't imagine she'd want to humiliate herself!" cried another.

It was typical for them to begin with verbal abuse, then they would escalate to physical torment; painful strikes of clenched fists and tips of their shoes pounding all areas of her body.

The urge to cry presented itself strongly. Amaryllis' throat was dry and full, making it nearly impossible to swallow. She needed to take deep breaths unless she wanted to completely lose herself and bawl her pretty green eyes out, but instead of crying, she stood up impulsively. She towered over the two princesses beside her who were hunched over in their chairs laughing, but even if they were standing, Amaryllis would still have had several inches on them. She looked up at the ceiling and blinked her tears away. Her throat opened and she could swallow again.

"I would appreciate that you left me alone," she said firmly. Her jaw was clenched tightly and her hands formed into fists. She had been brutally attacked for eight years and she had never stood up for herself until now. She harnessed all of her vulnerable emotion and converted it into a fiery rage. Her tears were no longer of sadness but of frustration. It must have been something to do with Prince James; watching him vigorously battle his opposing prince in an intense battle of strength and strategy. She had seen a fight, and it had inspired her.

The other princesses fell serious. The laughter had come to a dramatic halt. What was once a room full of childish feminine laughter was suddenly silent. The knights guarding the door to their room would have thought they had all dropped dead simultaneously if they hadn't fallen asleep.

"Let me be," she pleaded.

"Leave you alone?" asked the meanest on —Princess Laria of Galeston. "I'll leave you alone, and don't you doubt that."

She stood up and walked behind Amaryllis' chair. She dragged it back to the far side of the room and spun it around to face the wall. She gestured for Amaryllis to take a seat. Snickering and harsh whispers commenced. Amaryllis looked at the women around her, then back at Laria. Her chest burned in a raging fire, it spread throughout her body and it showed in her eyes, which were once light green, but changed into a darker hue with constricted pupils. The snickering and giddy glares halted once more. Amaryllis was already imposingly intimidating when she possessed a neutral physique, and it was almost impossible to comprehend how frightening she looked in that moment. The princesses were frozen in fear. Amaryllis' eyes narrowed into a frowning face of anger. Her mouth was slightly open to show her teeth, and her body language caused her to look as if she were about to charge at Laria. She normally stood shyly, with slouched shoulders and a narrow body, but now she was rigidly erect with a wide stance. Her chest moved up and down as she tried to calm herself with heavy breaths, but the rage kept piling on. No princess had ever seen her stand up for herself, not one. Amaryllis accepted poor treatment. She was afraid to express her own opinions, and worst of all, she believed that she was a hideous, worthless person from the influence of the princesses. Seeing her now, the princesses worst fear had come true: Amaryllis recovered from her torment, and she was using it as fuel to seek revenge on them. She would soon realize her true meaning and potential as the most beautiful girl in the world.

Amaryllis exited the circle of cowards and stormed up to Laria, an inch from her face.

"I have done nothing to you, so why are you so cruel to me? I come here to this very castle every year, and I am truly relieved that this will be my last time. Because of you, I have dreaded these parties, and you have given me *painful* anxieties that you won't believe are possible to feel. Although you are the daughter of a kingdom larger than my own, it does not mean that you can treat me this way, for my will is as strong as yours, and my kingdom is as great."

Amaryllis spoke with a passionate truth which felt wrong for her timid self to do but at the same time, it was the greatest outburst of the century which felt so right. Her outrage was far outside of her comfort zone, but it seemed like the perfect time to fight back, and she couldn't stop herself.

Laria was speechless. She looked up at the frightening, beautiful, tall, auburn-haired monster and opened her mouth to speak, but Amaryllis interrupted—

"If you are going to speak, then I am expecting an apology. That is the *only* thing I want to hear," she stated. Laria tried to look at the princesses for some sort of assistance, but Amaryllis followed her like a cobra, blocking her view. Laria paused, looked down at the ground for a split second to think of something witty and rude as a response, then looked up to speak.

"I am *sorry* you are the fool that you are, thinking you can just do what you please. Your parents must be so incredibly ashamed of you. I know that I would never wish to have a daughter like you. I am *sorry* that you are a ten-foot tall giant. You are so *masculine* for a woman and hideous to glare upon. You may feel victorious now, but that will not last very long since giants are monsters and should be treated as monsters," Laria snapped back. "You are going to wish that you had never said a *word* to me, you sorry, excruciating thing..." she whispered darkly.

Amaryllis' heart dropped. She took a slow and cautious step back. It was evident and could not be hidden that she was afraid and vulnerable once again, as her dark eyes faded back to their light green emerald irises. Laria pushed past her and began talking to the princesses in the circle. Their voices were muffled and could not be heard over Amaryllis' rushing thoughts. She turned around and watched them converse in their circle. They all watched Laria as she stood in the middle with her red dress flowing to the floor reminding Amaryllis of lava. Her mean, brown eyes met Amaryllis' for a moment.

"Now, it is time for you to go to where you belong," she snarled loudly. She sounded like a demon, planning something sinister, which she most definitely was. Amaryllis stared past the women in front of her and into her mind. It was there where she saw herself. Within her thoughts, she had a conversation with herself.

What are you still doing here? Leave now. Are they really going to do it? *Can't you hear them speaking? You know exactly what they're going to do to you!* Maybe they were bluffing all those years ago. They couldn't possibly— *Amaryllis, you must leave now for they are laughing and their vision is clouded with chaotic ideas that are causing them to forget your presence in the room. Leave NOW.*

Her inner voice thundered loudly, giving herself goosebumps.

Amaryllis' body filled with suspense. She snapped from her daydream with wide eyes and a pounding heart. Her vision was now clearer than before, she was more observant, noticing each detail of the room. The princesses were all standing with their backs turned to Amaryllis, so she took her chance and lightly jogged to the door and let herself out stealthily. She glanced around the hallway for people and spotted a few knights guarding the room in which the kings and queens were in. The knights guarding the princesses room were still asleep, leaning against the wall which Amaryllis was grateful for. She took off her pink slippers and began to sprint through the castle. She pumped her arms and ran as fast as she could with her long, frilly pink dress and auburn hair flowing behind her, and her bare feet hitting the floor echoing through the hall. She reached the front door of the castle after five minutes of mere sprinting and was greeted by two doormen standing on either side of the door.

"Princess, where are you going?" one asked, looking her up and down. Her curly hair was wild, cheeks red, and eyes awake. She was breathing shallowly, looking near to falling victim to madness.

"Please open the door!" she begged between breaths. She whipped her head over her shoulder and looked for the other princesses, who to her fortune were nowhere in sight. "I'm being chased! Please!"

"By whom? How did someone so dangerous get into the castle—?"

"Just open the *door*… Please!" she cried frantically.

"Princess, I—"

She screamed in an overwhelming terror, then ran past the two men and up the stairs to the left of the front door. The two men followed her until she reached a stained glass window in a large hallway.

She used her shoe to smash it. Her adrenaline providing her with enough strength to shatter the entire window. It broke with a shimmery crash and rainbow coloured glass rained from the top of the frame and onto the floor. Without hesitation she leaped through the window, avoiding the glass pieces still stuck in the frame, and fell twenty feet into a red rose garden.

Chapter 6

Princess Amaryllis looked up at the dark sky, just waiting to make an impact on the ground. During her descent, she pleaded aloud that she would not break any bones or even worse, die from landing on her neck. Her body fell rapidly to the ground, falling through a thornless rose bush. The soft roses cushioned her fall, preventing her from injuring her spine. Instead, she was winded and bruised.

The rose bush rustled as she fell through it, snapping the branches and landed on the ground in a pounding thump.

Amaryllis tried to gasp for air but her lungs were incapable of inhaling *and* exhaling, so she just lied there moving her mouth and looking around at her surroundings as her lungs burned and her back throbbed. She was stuck with the very last breath she took.

She gazed up at the sky through the rose petals. It was covered edge to edge in grey clouds, hiding the sun. She stared at where the sun would show on a cloudless day, hidden behind the brightest grey cloud as the sun's rays tried to penetrate the grey fluff.

She heard men's voices from above her. Four knights plus the two doormen, stuck their heads out the window and peered down at the obliterated rose bush where Amaryllis was wedged within the branches but they could not see her.

"What happened here?" asked one of the knights.

"What do you think happened?" one of the doormen asked angrily, "she jumped out of the window!"

"Why would she do that? She was clearly pushed!" the knight snapped.

"She was NOT. She *jumped* out," the other doorman said, "I saw her do it."

The doormen looked at each other in disbelief, the knight's skepticism infuriating them. After all, they were telling the truth.

"Why would she ever have this motive?" the knight hollered.

Amaryllis looked up at the window using her eyes, not moving her neck as she was afraid she had injured it. She peeked through the bush to see them arguing. To test her injuries, she flexed the muscles in each muscle group and to her relief nothing hurt too bad other than her back.

"Wait a second, she's all right. She is awake! Thank goodness," said one of the doormen.

"You're delirious. She fell twenty feet!" one of the knights yelled.

"The bush just moved!" the doorman screamed. Amaryllis' stomach dropped and she was filled with bewilderment since she hardly moved her body.

"If we have a dead princess on our hands, there will be an unforgiving world of trouble leading to our deaths," the knight shuddered, picturing the king's raging complexion and the cries of Amaryllis' family. The doormen threw their arms in the air.

"It is not our fault that she wanted to kill herself!" the doorman said.

"How would that be our fault?" screamed the other.

"Why would you let her pass you? She was supposed to be in the tea room!" the knight yelled. The doorman chuckled manically.

"How did she even get out of the tea room in the first place?" the doorman asked, "hmm?"

The knight's heart dropped, but they could not see the panic in his face as it was hidden by his helmet. He had dozed off.

Standing up for hours and hours had tired him, and he felt it was okay to sleep for a minute since the castle was guarded from the outside. He had never imagined that there would be an inner struggle.

"Did she say anything to you?" the knight asked, brushing the question off.

"She pleaded for us to open the door," he answered.

"You are supposed to obey the command of a princess, you fool. Even if she was let outside, the knights outside the castle would protect her. She clearly needed to leave for a reason. Why else would she jump out the *window?*"

Amaryllis could finally gasp, the sudden ability to breathe hit her hard in the chest. She inhaled, but not to her lungs's full capacity because her chest was tight. If she breathed in anymore than a regular breath, then that breath would turn into a horrid wheeze. She did not move yet, in hopes of leaving unnoticed during another argument.

They stood in the window talking above her for quite a while. There was a long period of silence that made her think they had left to come outside for her, to examine her body. She lifted her neck to look up at the window. She twisted her body and picked herself up. She wheezed a horrible wheeze and looked up again for a clearer view.

The knights and doormen were shocked as they spotted movement in the roses. They immediately left the window and headed for the stairs.

Amaryllis panicked, standing up quickly and squeezing out of the rose bush. Her pink slippers were broken, so she left them and ran barefoot into the meadow, behind the castle. Every breath she took was a raspy wheeze and for every stride she took, her back throbbed and ached.

Halfway into the meadow, she heard the rattling of knight armour. She did not dare to look over her shoulder to see how close they were. She picked up speed and ran as fast as her legs would let her. Her wheezes became more powerful and painful with each breath, the pain scratched at her chest like knives.

She made it to the tree line when she collapsed. Her body had given up. It was pointless to run. The knights were right on her tail, and gaining. Where could she have gone in her condition? She was too disoriented to realize where she was.

She did not bother to slow her pace, she just let herself tumble to the ground. Her back cracked when she made contact with the soft grass. She winced under her breath as she tumbled.

The knight's approached her hesitantly as she was incredibly close to the forest which inhabited evil itself with unearthly creatures of all kinds...the Dark Forest.

The knight dug his hands underneath her back and lifted her slowly. Her back cracked as her weight was concentrated in her mid-back. Her legs and head flopped over the knight's cradled arms. The knight felt and heard the cracks through his armour and he adjusted his hands to hold her like an infant.

"My deepest apology, Princess," he mumbled. Her eyes were wet with tears enhancing her green eyes again. She looked at the knights around her then up at the clouded sky. The world matched her mood, it was dark and gloomy.

"I do not intend to offend you or your choice, but why did you do this?" the knight asked, curiosity present in his voice. They had begun a quick speed-walk back to the castle. The rattling metal was irritating yet strangely satisfying to listen to. It was as if the sound of their armour was a slap to her face and a "ha ha, we caught you," but the repetitiveness and consistency was wonderfully satisfying.

"I was threatened. I was put in a situation in which I had to escape from danger, plus I desperately wanted and needed to leave."

"Who threatened you?"

"I am not allowed to say. I have been keeping it a secret for eight years and they made me promise to never tell," she whispered, "and they threatened to harm me right in that moment, so I ran." The knight had the strongest desire to learn the secret. He wanted to punish the people she called *they*.

"Was it a prince? I know at least two of them who could be ruthless. If that is the case, then please tell me and I shall have a *chat* with them."

"I can't say, don't you understand?"

"No princess, I do not. You are protected by Arlon, nothing can harm you."

"Well, Arlon is doing a terrible job at protecting me considering the condition I am in!" Amaryllis cried. The knight looked at the others walking beside him.

"I know that mistakes have been made, and we are fortunate to have someone like you in this situation as opposed to one of the others."

"What is that supposed to mean?" she asked through uncontrolled sobs.

"Well, we have been observing and protecting you princesses for eight years and have noticed the personalities you all have, and I have recognized how cruel some can be. But you, you are different. You do not complain or command. You are respectful and soft—"

"Are you telling me that you were fortunate to have me as the victim of this incident instead of someone else who, I am sorry, but someone who actually deserves the torment? You are telling me that you are lucky to have the silent and passive princess in pain because you know that she won't complain to the King of Arlon and have you in trouble?"

The knight was flabbergasted. He said nothing for a long while.

"I am correct, am I not?" she snapped.

"…Unfortunately, you are," he replied in a deep voice. Amaryllis was in her complete prime of feeling both intelligent and sorry for herself.

They reached the castle after a long and humiliating walk. The knight carried her into a bedroom on the main floor. They did not want another broken window.

They entered the room to see the King and Queen of Serilion seated at the foot of the tremendous, king sized bed with looks of horror. Word had spread quickly of her escape. The entire castle knew of her disappearance.

The knight gently set Princess Amaryllis down on the bed. Her back cracked in a wave of pops and she winced, sucking air through her clenched teeth and squeezing her eyes shut.

"Once again, I am dreadfully sorry," the knight apologized.

"Leave," she replied monotonously. The knight immediately left the room, leaving the royal family of Serilion alone.

Chapter 7

The first word her father said to her hurt her more than anything that the princesses could do to her, and that word was *shame*.

"Shame on you," he said firmly. He did not yell or even raise his voice slightly. The disappointment in his voice struck her soul. Tears filled her eyes, she could taste them in her throat. Her lower lip quivered. "That is *enough* of that," he ordered, watching her lip in disgust. Her mother gazed down at the floor. She did not want to participate in shaming her daughter.

Amaryllis wheezed as she cried frantically like a toddler. Her chest heaved rapidly as she inhaled and exhaled. The noise she made was excessively loud and sharp, and every so often she would let out a miserable cry.

"Father, let me explai—!"

"There is *nothing* you can do that will correct your behaviour. You are acting like an immature child! You are twenty years old, and I expect you to behave like a lady."

"But fa—!"

"Amaryllis, you broke and jumped out of a window, you ran away from your designated area. After being found by the knights you *still* ran from them, and your behaviour at the beginning of the party with that cat was absolutely *ridiculous*. You have never acted this way in all of your life, and I am giving you only thirty-seconds to explain yourself because that is all the patience I have left for you."

Amaryllis did not speak for a long time. She just stared at her father as her chest spasmed uncontrollably.

"Take one long deep breath, Amaryllis," the queen told her daughter after the long period of silence. Amaryllis refused. She felt stupid doing that. Instead, she tried to speak but her stutters were exceedingly disruptive.

"Father, I-I-I have been torm-muh-mented every y-y-year at these p-parties. I have n-not said a wo-wo-word to anyone until t-t-today. I have been b-b-bullied annually by the other princesses—" she immediately regretted telling her father who the culprit of her behaviour was, but she continued to speak. The entire time, her father looked at her with skepticism. "—I have been b-b-bottling my emotions for nearly a d-decade and I have been quite good at holding it all back up un-un-until n-now. I couldn't take it anymore father, I COULDN'T take it." The queen looked up from the floor with watery eyes.

"Oh, Amaryllis…" she said softly as a tear trickled down her cheek. Amaryllis looked back at her father who finally appeared concerned, and continued to reveal her inner tension.

"F-father, every y-year they have abused me either ph-physically or emotionally, usually both. I am perpetually cuh-cuh-called *hideous, uh-uh-ugly, stupid,* and several other names that are incredibly c-cruel. They quickly discovered that I was weak, and would never t-tell on them, so they all took turns s-s-slapping me as hard as they could in the face. You may remember me telling you that my face was r-red because I had embarrassed myself in the tea room, but that was a lie that I wish you didn't fall for. They ripped my beautiful blue dress into shreds. Mother, that was the dress you had given me from your mother and when I was just in my undergarments plus what was left of the dress, they brought in an arbitrary prince they found in the hallway and told him to put shame upon my body. He did not want to at first but Laria bribed him and so he did. My self esteem was poorly affected for all of those years but I lost all of my confidence that day. There are other exceedingly violent things they had done to me, but it would pain me to share—" Amaryllis stopped talking to witness her father comforting her mother, who was tearful, crying on his shoulder. He looked up from his wife in despair and looked extremely sad himself. Amaryllis was relieved to see her father like this, since he was so furious just a minute ago, and now he finally understood the pain from her perspective, along with the queen. Her chest had stopped spasming so she stopped stuttering. "—what they had done to me was traumatizing and cruel beyond comprehension. You would *never* believe what they did. There was no way to possibly defend myself. There were so many of them and only one of me. After the first party, I never wanted to return here but we had to as tradition, and it progressed worse and worse each time. I've always kept it to myself, and I never said anything to you but during the eighth time my heart, mind, and soul could not tolerate it anymore. This time by chance I chose the fastest horse to stay far away from them during our horse riding. It was absolutely wonderful and my anxiety had vanished for a full hour, but then it was tea time, and I could not find a mental escape in there. I tried to daydream but they could not help themselves. They could not spare me any mercy, so they subtly began to verbally attack me, and that was when I snapped and stood up for myself for the first time. I tried to show dominance and assertion and for the duration of my speech most princesses were terrified of me. All but one, and that was Princess Laria. She threatened me, then gathered the princesses in a circle to plan something. That was when I convinced myself to get out of there before they did something horrible to me. If that meant breaking a window to escape because the incompetent doormen would not open the door for me, then that was what I had to do."

    Amaryllis had finished speaking and had nothing more to say. Like the queen, the king was now in tears. Amaryllis sighed as far as her lungs would let her. It was a sigh of relief. Eight years of misery and suffering had finally been recognized. She felt at peace. It was as if an invisible weight resting on her shoulders for years had ultimately been removed. She was so used to the stress that she had forgotten it was there. She had been possessed by misery and revealing the truth was her exorcism.

"Amaryllis, I don't know what to say to you," the king cried. "This was not what I was expecting to hear."

"Amaryllis..." the queen began, but she could not speak.

"Why did you hold this despair within you for eight whole years without saying a single word? You have not showed your pain. Not once have you showed any abnormal signs of despair or anything of the sort. We thought that you were happy," the king sniffed.

"Well, father I have forgotten what happiness is like, but I think I caught a glimpse of it tonight," Amaryllis sighed, thinking of the Prince of Werling.

"How is that so?" his voice was high from the absurdity in her statement. How was it possible to have even a glimpse of happiness after being put under so much fear and stress to smash a window, and jump twenty feet?

"I know that it is not allowed but I met the Prince of Werling. I had seen and spoken with him before at previous parties but our discussions were always brief. I was also much younger and didn't find him intriguing. But tonight he was so lovely. I had never thought about him in a romantic way but now I think I love him. Our conversation was maybe a few minutes long but it went by too quickly."

The queen looked up from her husband's shoulder and smiled.

"Do you really love him, dear?" she asked. Amaryllis smiled down at her dress.

"I do."

The king and queen stood up and walked around the bed to lean over their daughter.

"Amaryllis, we are certain that you have recently discovered this within yourself but you need to be more assertive and blunt. Your confidence will surely return after doing so. Years of damage will be revived and your happiness will finally take a long term presence. Are you aware of your inconceivable beauty?" asked the queen. Amaryllis raised her eyebrow.

"Am I beautiful? I cannot see myself since I refuse to gaze upon my own reflection. Mirrors are my enemy. I do not see what you see."

The queen stepped away from the bed to raise her voice.

"Amaryllis, you are perhaps the most radiant woman to have ever walk this earth. You cannot see your winsomeness since the other princesses have been soiling your mind with filthy lies. You have believed their nonsense for nearly a decade and you may not see it now but you will... I've changed my mind, you shall see it *now*."

The queen stormed away to grab a mirror out of the drawer against the wall and she aggressively handed it to her daughter with a calm expression. "Take a look and tell me what you see," she demanded. Amaryllis held the antique mirror in her hands. It was relatively small but the reflective glass was held within golden flowers and she loved the look of it. She fearlessly held the mirror up to her face. She payed attention to the detail of her facial features. First, she glared into her own eyes and startled herself.

"My eyes are cruel and frightening," she exclaimed.

"Your eyes are soft and innocent—"

"I look like I am about to do something sinister."

"That is preposterous! Just... keep looking."

Amaryllis looked deep into her irises. The shiny emeralds that the world saw looked like a muddy green to her. Her pupils were minuscule little slits.

"Mother, I look like a dragon." Amaryllis grunted.

Your eyes are petrifying. Your eyebrows are arched downwards to make you appear permanently angry. Your cheekbones are defined in a way that causes you to look like an old woman. Your lips are—

"Amaryllis, stop looking at yourself that way!" ordered the queen

"What way?" Amaryllis snapped.

"You are thinking negatively about yourself. I can tell by the look on your face."

"This is my face…my regular face."

"*Amaryllis,* I want you to say something out loud to yourself that is positive and kind."

Amaryllis looked at her reflection with fear and disgust.

"I have a nice face," she lied.

"Use specifics," the queen demanded. She thought she was making progress with her daughter, but she was not.

"I have an interesting eye colour."

"Yes, yes, go on."

"My hair is… nice."

"Amaryllis, this is ridiculous," the queen gawped, rolling her eyes. "Say, *I am Amaryllis, the beautiful Princess of Serilion*. Say it."

Amaryllis shook her head. "No, that's absurd," she groaned. The king stepped in.

"Say it now," the king demanded.

"I… am Amaryllis, the—" she hesitated, but forced herself to say it, "—the beautiful Princess of Serilion." She looked at her parents hoping to have satisfied them.

"Again," they said simultaneously.

"I am Amaryllis, the beautiful Princess of Serilion."

"Once more—"

"No."

"Yes!"

"*I am Amaryllis…The unbelievably beautiful Princess of Serilion. I am so beautiful that angels envy me!*" she said sarcastically as she had grown tired of the pressure. She was exasperated with her parents forcing confidence upon her, and she hated talking about herself.

"Amaryllis," the king began.

"What?" She asked glumly.

"What you have just said, even though you were mocking yourself, was true."

"No, it was n—"

"Yes, it was," interrupted the queen. "Why do you think those princesses were bullying you? Because it just happened to be you that they decided to pick on since childhood? You were randomly selected? No Amaryllis, they pick on you because jealousy drives people mad. You mentioned that they called you cruel names. That is because they are jealous of you, and your intelligence. And you also mentioned all of the physical pain they put you through, that is because they are jealous of your body. They wanted to bruise you. They tried to break your mental and physical state to make themselves feel better. But you have never cowered before them or begged for mercy. You stayed silent and so they kept attacking you, hoping to destroy you. After finally standing up for yourself and probably even frightening them with your intimidating height and sudden confidence, they went even crazier. You showed false confidence and Princess Laria could sense it. However if you were *truly* confident in yourself, they could never win."

Amaryllis did not make eye contact with her mother. It all made sense at once. It *was* true and her mother was right.

"Amaryllis, you must always be prepared to defend yourself because envy will be everywhere for you," the queen affirmed.

"I do not know what to say. Mother, you are right about everything and I wish I had told you sooner but it was what they said that frightened me into staying silent."

"And what was that?" the king questioned.

Amaryllis began to sob uncontrollably. "Laria told me that she would hand me to Jack Grainson—" (The most ruthless serial killer in Arlon, jailed in the deepest part of the cellar for slaughtering forty-five women). Amaryllis looked up at the ceiling and shut her eyes, forcing big tears through her closed lids. "She said she was going to lock me in with him and hand him a dull, rusty knife to kill me slowly. I did not believe she would do such a thing but she and the other princesses held me in the air and walked me down. Laria slid a knife under the cellar door and said, *Jack Grainson, we have a hideous girl on the other side of this door who wants to be played with. Here is your knife.* As soon as Laria said the word, *girl,* the man began to holler and bang the bars with his bare hands. I screamed at the top of my lungs and they carried me back to the tea room. Laria then told me, *There's your warning and know that if you get any of us into trouble, that is where you'll go.* After standing up to her, she must have thought it was time to have me be the forty-sixth woman to die at the hands of Jack Grainson."

The king didn't think but he reacted. He ran to the door.

"NO, DON'T FATHER, PLEASE DON'T!" Amaryllis cried. The queen joined her daughter,

"LAURENCE, DON'T LEAVE!" yelled the queen. The king stood by the door with his hand on the handle.

"Those women deserve hell." He stated calmly, "I was going to give it to them."

"How were you going to do that?" The queen asked.

"I really do not know. I was going to think of it as I approached them."

"Laurence, all we can do is inform their parents and request for Amaryllis to be protected with a knight by her side because obviously they have not been doing a very good job at keeping order these past years."

"I do not think that we should say anything to their parents," said Amaryllis. She sat up in bed. Her back cracked again in a wave of pops but she did not wince this time. "You must tell the King and Queen of Arlon that you want a knight by my side to prevent me from sneaking out again. That way I am protected and they won't find out that I told you about my secrets."

The queen nodded and looked at the king, thinking of the mad women who walked among them. She was absolutely destroyed to learn Amaryllis was exposed to such vile people.

"I say it is a very wise decision," she stated through a shaky voice.

"Yes, of course but I want them to suffer," the king retorted.

"They will *suffer* when they see that Amaryllis is chosen by the finest prince, to live in the finest kingdom and live the finest life," the queen said, trying to think positively. Amaryllis thought of being selected by the Prince of Arlon. His traits were perceived as *dreamy* by the other princesses. She shuddered at the thought of having to live with him for eternity. Then, the Prince of Werling entered her mind. She remembered his smile and his ocean eyes.

"I love the Prince of Werling," Amaryllis stated. "I want to spend my life with him and only him. The Prince of Arlon is horrid."

The king sighed. "Ah yes, how could I have forgotten? He was the only good part of your day today."

Amaryllis nodded.

"Amaryllis," the queen began.

"Yes, Mother?"

"I want you to go back to the princesses. Go to the dressing room and put on a dress that compliments your eyes, a dress that makes you appear so angelic that people will not believe that you are a real person. I want you to be the easiest decision for every prince… understood?" she said with a gentle smile. Amaryllis smiled back.

"Yes, Mother."

"Those women won't be taking you anywhere. Jack Grainson won't be near you. There will be several knights guarding your door. Before you leave, look in the mirror once more," the queen demanded.

Amaryllis lifted the mirror to her face with curiosity. She wanted to learn whether or not her sudden, positive thinking would affect her self-interpreted appearance. It did. She conversed with herself.

Wow! My eyes are extraordinary. I know. *What do you mean you know?* I have always known you were lovely, but I could not convince you otherwise because they hurt you badly enough. *Well, I have excellent facial structure.* I also know that. *Am I really... beautiful?* I will let YOU answer that, Amaryllis thought to herself. The positivity and negativity in her body finally got along.

"Yes," Amaryllis chuckled, "I am beautiful, I suppose?"

"Without a doubt, yes!" the queen cheered. The king grinned at his daughter. Amaryllis stood up from the bed. Moving so quickly hurt her back quite badly, but her happiness pushed the pain away. She hugged her parents.

"I must thank you for all that you've done this evening. Thank you for listening and encouraging me to love myself. It is not complete but I will soon reach that point."

"We are overjoyed to have helped you through this. We wish we could have analyzed your inner trauma sooner. It was exceedingly difficult to see you so upset," the king replied. The queen called the knight back into the room. She gave direct orders to never leave her daughter's side and it was agreed.

Amaryllis left the room feeling confident with no presence of anxiety. The knight, not even an inch away from her, gave her a sense or relief and complete protection. It was the same knight who carried her back to the castle.

"Princess, I am sorry—"

"Please do not apologize again. It is over and done with. I appreciate your protection." The knight smiled in relief under his armour, and Amaryllis smiled to herself as they reached the door of the dressing room.

Chapter 8

Amaryllis did not hesitate. She twisted the knob and used all of her strength to push the door wide open, making a dramatic and loud entrance into the dressing room. Her parents had given her a great amount of confidence and she was overjoyed to finally be able to proudly walk into a room without feeling horrified or ashamed of herself.

The princesses were all in their undergarments selecting their dresses that would attract the prince they desired. Laria was closest to the door, staring at her. Amaryllis glared into her muddy brown eyes. She took notice of the dress in Laria's hands. It was a rich red, sleeveless dress that looked quite long and frilly. Amaryllis knew Laria wanted to symbolize love with the colour of red, but all Amaryllis could think of was how anger was more well suited to Laria's complexion.

She walked into the room and the knight shut the door behind them.

"Where did you go?" Laria asked with a skeptical and unimpressed look on her face. She payed attention to the patches of dirt, missing fabric, and rose petals on Amaryllis' dress.

Amaryllis crossed her arms.

"Nowhere of importance to you!" she snapped. Laria dismissed the tone in Amaryllis' voice, and proceeded to ask questions that

IMMORTUOS

she thought would irritate her. She knew very well that Amaryllis had run off, but she did not know where.

"I *know* that you ran from us," Laria chided as Amaryllis approached her. The knight stayed in his place guarding the door from the inside. Laria thought she would try to stand up for herself again but she did not. Amaryllis simply walked past her and stepped into the walk-in closet full of ballgowns. All of the snarling princesses behind her were disregarded and her focus was on her own beauty for the night. She walked deep into the maze of dresses and waited for *the* dress to pop out at her. Her mother instructed her to choose a dress that complimented her eyes, so she looked for pale blue, green, and red.

She looked from left to right until she saw—The one.

The sparkling dress shone like the night sky. A teal galaxy full of blue, green, and turquoise stars with hints of pink. She reached for it to feel the sparkles, taking the dress from the hanger and held it against her body. She ran to the back of the closet to try it on. As she ran, the princesses entered the closet.

"Amaryllis—" A princess yelled, attempting to taunt her, but Amaryllis had no patience anymore.

"Shut it," Amaryllis replied firmly.

Amaryllis pulled the silk curtain which provided her with privacy, isolating herself in a small space to change. Within the changing area was a tall mirror and a small wooden stool. She changed out of her dirty, pink dress and into the beautiful universal gown.

With the fact that Amaryllis was quite tall, she was surprised that the dress was long enough. It was large and flowed down to the floor majestically, and it was slim in the waist. The dress was frilly in the skirt with long sleeves. She looked at herself up and down, pleased with the dress she had chosen.

"Amaryllis, where did you go?" Laria asked impatiently. Amaryllis whipped the curtain aside with the swipe of her hand and stepped out of the changing area. The princesses were suddenly astounded at the sight of her and could not hide the fact that she looked absolutely stunning.

"It does not matter where I went. What matters more is what drove me to leave," she stated. "None of you shall ever cause me harm again," she said with a smirk. Laria placed her hands on her hips and frowned. But the other princesses cowered down, not making eye contact with Amaryllis, slouching their shoulders awkwardly while standing still.

"Who is this *new* princess?" Laria laughed. "She seems to think she's extremely omnipotent doesn't she—?" Laria paused to laugh along with herself. The jealousy was driving her mad. "Don't you forget about Jack—"

"You will do NO such thing," Amaryllis snarled as she walked up to her nemesis. She was not physical, nor did she want to be but if she had to beat her enemy down, then she definitely would. She stood one foot away from Laria.

"It is quite hilarious to see you this way, I must admit," Laria chuckled, trying to break her down. She figured it was all an act in attempt to earn respect, but it was nothing but a changed perspective. None of what she said was pretend, and she meant every word. Laria would try her best to cause her timid character to resurface, but there was no seeing that side of Amaryllis ever again.

"To see me so close to you without being frightened out of my mind you mean?" Amaryllis scoffed.

"Yes, actually…that is exactly it," Laria exclaimed.

Amaryllis frowned. Her face formed into a fierce expression. She could easily be a goddess of fear, with her power being placing horror onto people. Amaryllis sent a frightening feeling into the room, pushing the other princesses out of the closet and back into the open space. Her jawline seemed sharper than usual, her green eyes were lit with a flame of rage and her mouth was downturned into a snarl revealing her teeth. She allowed all of her inner rage to power her appearance. She had eight years worth of built up energy that she was ready to utilize.

    Laria tried to be brave, but was no longer unafraid of Amaryllis. She had succumbed to her sudden fearsome traits. Her heart began to race, it was all she could feel, and all she could see was the raging beauty before her eyes. Her eyes widened and her chest began to heave. She breathed from her mouth quietly.

    "You will *never* harm me again... Do you *understand?*" she hollered. She had the urge to wheeze, but she held it back to continue to imply that her threat was dangerous. Amaryllis had lost control of her mind and allowed her body to take over.

    Laria gasped and looked down at the floor. She closed her eyes briefly, then looked up with hope that Amaryllis was once again falsely confident, but the only thing she could see was a big, angry princess. Her fear was gone and Laria hated that.

    Laria raised her fist to strike her and Amaryllis grabbed her arm, then the other. She gritted her teeth as Laria resisted. She crossed Laria's arms, one over the other, then spun her around and pushed her to the ground. She landed hard on the floor with flailing arms, then looked over her shoulder.

    "*Answer* me."

    Laria's eyes were filled with terror and her breathing grew louder. She said nothing. She was staring at Amaryllis, trapped in a frozen state of fear. Amaryllis waited a few seconds, watching her bully. She looked down at her sparkly, vibrant dress. It was at that time when Amaryllis actually considered beating the living hell out of Laria, but refrained since she didn't want to risk ruining her perfect gown with the blood of her enemy.

    Amaryllis cautiously walked past Laria and jogged over to her assigned mirror where she was to apply her makeup. The other princesses did not make eye contact with her. They looked into the walk-in closet where Laria was still flabbergasted on the ground. Several princesses wanted to ask Laria if she was okay, and try to help her up, but they were too afraid to face the wrath of Amaryllis. She had finally realized she the power she had from within, and that was dangerous for the others.

Amaryllis looked at herself in the mirror, unable to recognize the woman that reflected back at her. She was happy to gaze upon this woman, as if she was meeting her for the first time. She admired the woman for her bravery. No one could abuse her. Although a new Amaryllis surfaced in the mirror, she could still feel her past self panicking with anxiety from standing up to the monstrous princesses, but she had the power to ignore the fear and focus on her new self. Her reflection emitted charisma and complete power.

Amaryllis could sense the princesses glaring at her from their own mirrors. She looked over at them and they instantly looked away. She stepped away from her mirror and approached them. "What are you looking at?" she asked hoarsely. They all shook their heads and shrugged their shoulders. Some mouthed the word, "Nothing."

"Laria isn't here, and without her you do not harass me? I am wondering why…" Amaryllis smiled to herself, "…perhaps it's because you are all cowards and lack your own sense of leadership." She glanced over at Laria, who was finally beginning to stand up. She paused in a crouched position when she looked at Amaryllis.

"Stand," Amaryllis ordered, drunk on newly gained confidence. Laria stood up slowly. "I never received your apology. I expect you to give it to me." Amaryllis kept her eyes locked on Laria as she approached her.

"You possess confidence now, but it shall fade," Laria warned. "Enjoy your power while you can."

Amaryllis did not listen to Laria since her sentences lacked the word she was looking for.

"Apologize to me, for if you don't, I shall automatically assume that you did not because of your envy towards me."

This angered Laria since it was true. She had been bullying Amaryllis to make herself feel dominant. It was Laria who was stronger than the *beautiful Amaryllis of Serilion*, and now that title was lost. Laria had finally been beaten, and she did not accept it nor did she like it. Without warning, she swung for Amaryllis' face with a closed fist. Amaryllis stepped back, avoiding the swing. The knight standing by the door rushed over with heavy clanging armour. He stepped between the princesses with extended arms.

"Stop this at once," he demanded.

Laria scoffed. "You cannot tell us what to do. You are merely a knight and we are the future rulers of the kingdoms," she snapped. The knight chuckled beneath his suit. He pictured Amaryllis successfully attacking each princess in the room all by herself without any struggle. He was on Amaryllis' side. She was the underdog, coming from the smallest kingdom, but she was also the princess with the kindest heart. He backed away from the fight and stood by the door once again. He gestured for Laria to take another swing at Amaryllis.

"Good luck," he mumbled.

"I do not wish to fight. All I want is an apology to set closure on my eight years of suffering," Amaryllis admitted.

Laria shook her head slowly. She was aware that what she had done was cruel, but she was *Laria, the Princess of Galeston*, whose kingdom was larger and wealthier than Serilion. All was nearly perfect; a powerful princess with a large kingdom, except she was not the most beautiful, and that was unacceptable. She would not lose now to the princess of dirty commoners. "What do I apologize for? Treating you how you deserve to be treated? *Amaryllis, the Princess of Stench*... the tiny kingdom in the middle of nowhere...you are a joke. You don't even behave like royalty. You are an animal."

"I am an animal for *pushing* you?" Amaryllis yelped. "You are calling *me* an animal. I'm curious to hear what your reasoning of an *animal* is, because if pushing you *once* makes me an animal, I wonder what you are... considering everything you've done to me. Imagine if I had done all of those things to you." Amaryllis' eyes began to water, not from sadness but frustration. She blinked them away with a few flutters of her lashes.

"I would never have let you do those things to me. But I wouldn't have to worry about it, considering you are weak and would never have done those things in the first place."

"Stop using my kindness against me!" Amaryllis yelled. "Love is not a weakness, it is a strength that people mistake as a blinding phenomenon. You are saying that it takes a strong woman to be able to bully others, but it really takes madness."

"The only mad person in this room is you, Amaryllis. Truly disgusting and I cannot say that enough," Laria had slight difficulty expressing this, since Amaryllis was god-like in the dress she wore.

It was at that moment that Amaryllis knew that trying to reason and negotiate with Laria would not be worth it. It was pointless. *You cannot argue with a fool. If you do, then that makes you the fool. She will never understand nor will she ever feel remorse,* Amaryllis thought.

Amaryllis inhaled loudly through her nose and exhaled quietly through her mouth as far as her lungs would let her. Her next statement was cautiously said. "None of this matters. We must prepare for the choosing. Nothing is getting done," Amaryllis refrained from directly blaming Laria, and she reminded her of why they were in the same room in the first place. The princesses had become so competitive each year, that they seemed to have forgotten the matter at hand; marriage and happiness. Laria looked at the princesses behind her. They hesitantly turned back to their mirrors and began to organize their makeup. Laria looked back at Amaryllis, who was already at her own mirror, isolated and far away from the others.

Chapter 9

Amaryllis' rush of adrenaline brought liveliness to her eyes. They seemed to have a new colour for each occasion. They were the brightest she had ever seen them, and she did not want to outline her eyes with any sort of makeup. The only feature of her complexion that she would artistically enhance, were her lips. She loved to colour them with deep reds that reminded her of roses.

She reached for the tray full of lipsticks and brought it close to the edge of the vanity. She took a seat on the padded stool and rummaged through the products. They weren't labeled, and the containers were opaque. She arbitrarily selected five lipsticks and pushed the tray back in its place below the mirror.

She opened each container and was pleased with what she saw: soft pink, bright red, maroon, magenta, and bright pink. She took a slip of paper from the right-hand corner of the vanity and drew a small line with each shade on the edge of the paper. She held the paper to her lips with the colour she wanted to visualize with her gown. The bright red and pinks did not quite suit the dress but the maroon colour did. She saved the maroon lipstick and carefully placed the remaining tubes back into the tray. The princesses were suddenly interrupted by their mothers on the opposite side of the door—

"Your majesty," the knight said to each queen as he let them into the dressing room. The queens all found their daughters and studied the dresses and makeup they had chosen for themselves. The Queen of Serilion approached her daughter.

"Amaryllis… I told you to make yourself stand out," she sighed, grabbing the lipstick from the vanity and giving it a little shake in the air.

"I don't like putting on makeup. Look at how beautiful my gown is, I don't need too much makeup."

The queen stared at the dress. It fit her daughter's body perfectly. It was snug in the arms and waist and flowed beautifully to the floor. It too reminded her of the stars.

"A wonderful decision you've made," the queen smiled, "however…more makeup."

Amaryllis shook her head. "No, I don't want it."

"Think of Prince James of Werling… you want him to be lovestruck when he sees you—"

"If he loves me like I think he does, then he will be lovestruck at the sight of *me*. I shouldn't have to cover my face with powder and black lines to impress the one I love. I want to look real. I want to look like the princess that he will see forever. After this event, I shall never put this much makeup on again."

"You don't have to apply too much, but you need more than just *lipstick*."

The queen analyzed her daughter's face.

"Thinly outline your lash line with black to make your eyes stand out. Apply some rouge to your cheeks and put on a bright shade of lipstick," she suggested. The queen looked at the maroon shade in disapproval. Amaryllis cringed at the mental image of having to remove the makeup and put on new products. Makeup enhanced her appearance, but it felt heavy on her face and she preferred to let her skin breathe. She didn't like the way she looked with it on, and she thought she appeared unnatural and mean, like Laria.

"I'd prefer not to," Amaryllis muttered.

The queen sighed loudly. "I insist... I could even apply it for y—"

"NO! It's fine, thank you... I'll put on *some*," Amaryllis groaned as she reached for the powdery pink blush, eyeliner, and the maroon lipstick she liked best. She scooped all of the products, pushed them into the centre of the vanity, then stared at them.

"Well?" the queen pestered.

"Mother, leave me be. I'll do a fine job," Amaryllis insisted. "Besides, I don't want you to watch me apply it."

"Well, why not? All of the other queens are helping their daughters," The queen exclaimed, crossing her arms.

"Yes, but I do not want your assistance," Amaryllis stated firmly but politely. The queen backed away from the vanity.

"I'll be over here," she said as she gestured to the sofa in the centre of the room. Amaryllis nodded, then looked back at the small pile of makeup in front of her.

"Thank you," she sighed over her shoulder. Amaryllis could see her mother nod in the mirror.

She grabbed a brush and dabbed the rouge, sending little puffs of pink pigment into the air. She pressed the pink coated brush onto her defined cheeks and applied it in circular motions. It was light enough on her fair skin to look subtle, but visible enough to make a notable difference and not to make her look like a circus clown.

She then applied eyeliner carefully. She made the black line as *thin* as possible to make her eyes seem as *bright* as possible. She stuck the pencil directly on her lash line, weaving through eyelashes to draw on her eyelid. Next, she applied her bold, maroon coloured lipstick, rather than a bright colour that her mother insisted upon. She felt that it wonderfully contributed to her dress, and her mother hadn't the simplest idea of how Amaryllis wanted to appear in front of the Prince of Werling.

Amaryllis looked at herself in the mirror. She had applied her makeup quite well, and was satisfied with her result until the queen wondered over to her daughter.

"That isn't enough, Amaryllis," she scolded. The queen pictured her daughter applying the makeup how *she* expected which was not subtle at all.

"I think it's just the right amount," Amaryllis stated as she began to clean up and return the products to their place. Her mother placed a gentle hand on her daughter's and she stopped.

"I don't think you are comprehending how important this is. Makeup does not fake your qualities, it enhances them."

"I do not want to enhance my face. I finally like the way it is."

"Amaryllis, I understand that you are finally learning to love yourself, which is truly amazing; however, you are required to look your very best to be able to increase your chances of having more options. You are the strongest person I know and I know you're strong enough to do something that you'd prefer not to, which at this moment is to simply apply more makeup. Trust me Amaryllis, although you don't need it… you need it," the queen spoke with sincerity, and the princess payed mind to what she said. She was beginning to consider following her mother's advice. "You are naturally beautiful. You light up every place you visit, but for this occasion, you must enhance your face because it is highly necessary. You want to strive for elegance and poise. I know from experience, Amaryllis. I too did not like makeup at your age, and so I did not apply very much either. I was lucky enough to have your father choose me because no other prince would. They all gawked at the princesses with unbelievable amounts of makeup on. As disappointing as it is, Amaryllis, princes are attracted to the external beauty of a princess rather than the internal."

Amaryllis understood her mother's reasoning, but the way Prince James looked at her convinced her otherwise. He fell in love with her bare face, so she truly did not need makeup. She only wanted to catch the attention of James, and no one else. She was convinced that she and James were to become engaged, so why would she need to attract the other princes? But, to please her mother, she offered to add more.

"All right, all right. I shall put on more, but only a small amount," Amaryllis agreed. "I am only doing it for you."

The queen smiled softly. "May I make a suggestion?"

"Yes, of course you may."

"Apply white powder to your face, then layer your cheeks with rouge. Then, remove your lipstick, and reapply it to only about two-thirds of your lips."

Amaryllis scoffed. "Mother, I shall never mimic French makeup. It is too much."

"It is what the princes want." She said as she gestured to the other princesses in the dressing room, all with pale faces, pink cheeks, and even drawn on beauty marks. "If you are the odd one out, they will declare you as strange."

"I am the odd one out anyway, and I am glad to be. I would hate to be or look like them."

"Amaryllis, I will not let you walk into the ballroom with a plain face."

"It is not plain. I have rouge, eyeliner, and maroon lipstick on." She pointed to her dark lips. "The lips and eyes are what I am emphasizing."

"Amaryllis—" the queen was beginning to bother her daughter, and so Amaryllis refused to listen anymore. She entered her mind to drown out her mother's pestering.

When she thought it was long enough, she snapped back into reality to hear her mother still nagging. "— please understand."

"I am not going to do it." Amaryllis stated. The queen sighed, realizing there was no point in arguing with her stubborn daughter.

"I wish you luck with your future," the queen said muttered as she calmly left the dressing room. Her mother's comment bothered Amaryllis, and a tight sensation, caused by anger, commenced within her chest. She groaned a long groan, then stood up and walked back over to the changing curtain to look at her gown.

It was breathtaking. Amaryllis was truly wearing a galaxy, and her makeup matched it perfectly. Her mother didn't understand what she was striving for.

She left the changing curtain and sat back at her vanity. She glared at the princesses with their chalky, pale faces being the most eye-catching feature on their bodies. In her eyes, they looked foolish.

A loud knock interrupted the makeup process.

"Hello princesses, it is the King of Arlon. I wanted to inform you that the Choosing Ceremony will commence in fifteen minutes," he said cheerfully in his deep voice. "I am sure you will all look beautiful."

The princesses smiled and began to compliment one another. Amaryllis rolled her eyes.

What could they possibly be saying? They all look identical. The only difference between them is determined by their gowns. It will be very easy for the princes to make a decision since their faces seem to be so generic with all of that makeup on. Their decision will be based on what dress they like the most. It's funny what women do for love. Tonight is the last night of being without a loving companion—

Amaryllis gasped quietly. Her life was filled with loneliness, it was all she knew. No friends, no lovers, little time spent with parents. Was she even ready for a husband?

Of course I am... I felt a true connection with the Prince of Werling. It was one conversation, that was all it took for me to fall in love with him. Imagine all of the years that I will have the chance to get to know him. The excitement shall never die. It will be wonderf—oh dear, what if he grows tired of me?

Amaryllis' head was spinning. She looked around the room, then stood up and walked to the door.

"You cannot leave yet, Princess," the knight stated. Amaryllis felt a wave of frustration, but she pushed it away and showed it as a plea for sympathy.

"Please understand. I just want to look at the night's sky one last time as an individual before I am married off to a prince."

"I do understand, but I am not allowed to let you leave unless I accompany you. They will indubitably behead me if I let you go because it is thought by many that you are suicidal. Besides, the hallway is filled with kings and queens. I can hear them."

"Get my father," she ordered. The knight sighed and opened the door to yell for the King of Serilion. He entered the room almost instantly.

"Your majesty, your daughter requested you."

Amaryllis ran into her father's arms.

"All I want is to look at the night's sky one last time," she pleaded. "I want to look up and absorb what is about to happen. I may not have been happy before but now I am, and I want to enjoy my happiness on my own for a while."

The king wrapped his arms around his daughter and squeezed her gently.

"We cannot delay the choosing Amaryllis, but I respect your desires. Perhaps we could accommodate a certain agreement with the prince and his family that you want your own space for a long period of time after being chosen. But for now, go outside and *quickly* gaze upon the stars." Amaryllis smiled at her father and thanked him before letting herself go from his embrace. The knight went to follow her but the king held up a hand to indicate he wanted his daughter left alone.

Chapter 10

Amaryllis walked anxiously through the castle, hugging herself tightly to protect herself from the staring eyes of the paintings. The unknown outcome of the Choosing Ceremony settled, taking a long-lasting place in her mind. What was to happen next was a mystery, which Amaryllis grew to hate. She needed time alone. The idea of marriage suddenly seemed like a terrible idea.

As she turned a corner, walked down another hallway and approached the doormen, she presented herself with involuntary sadness.

"Open the door," she demanded.

The doormen shook his head in disbelief. "I thought they were watching you. How did you pass them?"

Amaryllis rolled her eyes. "They let me go and so will you," she snapped.

"Where are you wanting to go exactly?

"Why can't you just open the door and stop asking so many questions?" Amaryllis did not want to mention that she was of higher power than the doorman, but he irritated her so much she could no longer refrain. "As a *princess*, I am *ordering* you to open the damn door." She held a grudge with this man. He left her no choice but to jump from a window and fall twenty feet to the ground, so of course she was angry with him.

"I am only concerned for your safety—"

"*Open* it."

The doorman grunted and began to pull on a rope on his side of the door while the other doorman did the same on his side. It slowly creaked open, allowing cold winds to enter the castle, blowing Amaryllis' hair back and giving her goosebumps. When it opened, Amaryllis walked out of the castle triumphantly. She turned right and walked a few steps to look at the crushed rose bush. She shuddered at the recent memory of nearly breaking her spine to escape possible death. She breathed in deeply to feel the moisture in her lungs and to remind herself that her back was bruised. Her wheezes were becoming slightly less aggressive as the night progressed.

She walked into the centre of the meadow and stood there staring up at the sky. She wanted to lay down, or at least sit, but she did not want to ruin her gown by staining.

She was astounded by the whimsical quality of the stars, they acted as a gateway leading directly to her imagination.

Because Amaryllis had finally come to know who she was and how much power she truly had, she wanted to spend a good portion of her life alone to learn more about herself since her childhood was disturbed. She needed time to herself and she wished the circumstances were different because she truly loved the Prince of Werling, and did *want* to spend her life with him, but not right this moment. She knew that she could not slow down time or visit the past but she desperately wished it was possible.

Maybe all of this is meant to be. I am supposed to struggle now. It's as if the world expects me to have perpetual difficulty in life. Oh, Amaryllis… you seem to have found happiness… I shall alter that for you. *I was put in a situation that I am not in control of to test my inner strength… but frankly, I have been tested for long enough and don't want to be tested now. There must be a way for me to change my circumstances. There is always a solution, a way out, to escape… or I can accept the timing, and prepare myself for the marriage to Prince James. Oh! How wonderful he is! But it must be possible to put a hold on the Choosing Ceremony. Not for everyone but only for me... Ah never mind, they would never do such thing for me. Perhaps they would for Princess Laria, but not for me. Although the world dislikes me, I will continue to fight it. I shall accept the challenge of rushing into this marriage. Go ahead and test me, world. I dare you.*

Amaryllis stared at the stars for ten minutes, then returned to the castle with a clearer mind, prepared to find herself engaged by the end of the night.

Chapter II

Amaryllis returned to the dressing room easily as the doormen opened the front doors for her quite quickly.

All of the princesses sat on furniture in the middle of the dressing room hunched over their legs, holding their stomachs.

"I can't believe this is finally happening," squeaked a princess. It was difficult to tell who was talking with their heads hidden between their legs.

"This is it."

"I am so nervous, I cannot handle this pressure."

"What are you nervous for?" Princess Amaryllis asked, immediately realizing it was a ridiculous question. The princesses paused their whining to look up. They groaned, but they dared not cry to ruin their makeup.

"Because it's *The Choosing!*" a princess winced as if saying *the choosing* caused her physical pain.

"Well, yes, I know that, but what aspect of the ceremony is the most frightening?" Amaryllis wanted to see if the others were also afraid of the idea of marriage, or if they feared their prince would grow tired of them.

"We are *overwhelmed*," snapped Laria. "You don't know *anything* about pressure."

Amaryllis scoffed, laughing slightly. "Well, I certainly do. You seem to have forgotten all the horrible things you have done to me." Amaryllis no longer let the past disrupt her well-being. She had let it slip from her mind and was strong enough to laugh about it. She was suddenly proud of herself for surviving perpetual torment.

"Not *that* type of pressure! The pressure to look presentable. We were given an hour to prepare ourselves to look our very best, and it took us that whole hour, but for you it took almost no time at all," she scowled.

"Is that your way of complimenting me?" Amaryllis asked in surprise. Laria shook her head, rolled her eyes, then payed full attention to the butterflies in her stomach.

Two knights came walking through the door of the dressing room. "Your highnesses, please line up in a single file line!" called the duke from the hallway. Amaryllis stood first in line in the doorway while the other princesses stood up from the couches and awkwardly made their way to the line. "We're just waiting for the music now!"

Suddenly, butterflies entered Amaryllis' stomach, fluttering and sending painful waves throughout her body. She focused on getting rid of them through deep, wheezy breaths which thankfully no one could hear. Her confidence had become distant with her new anxieties of the ceremony present within her. She finally understood why the other princesses were stressed beyond explanation. It was more than a selection, more than an engagement, it was a majorly important, historic event. Gasping and hyperventilating filled the hallway.

Violins and a piano could suddenly be heard from the ballroom a few doors down the hallway. "That is your cue princesses! I shall now lead you to the ballroom!" the duke cheered. "Stand up straight, smile, and look pretty!" he giggled. He sensed their nervousness, and he was attempting to lighten the mood, but he seemed to have made it worse. The princess at the back of the line, named Edith, threw up. She was lucky enough that she didn't get even a drop of puke on her dress. The duke was not aware, so he continued leading Amaryllis and the others to the ballroom, but the princesses were disgusted by Edith's sickness. They nearly found themselves having the urge to vomit as well.

The walk from the dressing room to the ballroom took a long time. It was a very short walk, but it felt like forever. Amaryllis was eager to get to the ballroom to prove to the world that she could handle absolutely anything that it threw in her path, but the weight the event had, its importance, fuelled her gut with nervousness at the same time.

Abusive princesses, eight years of bullying, envious royalty, misunderstanding parents, and marriage that I am not ready for... What else have you got? Amaryllis thought to herself, narrowing her eyes and paying no mind to her aching stomach. She sighed an exasperated sigh. She could say aloud that she wished things worked in her favour for *once,* but didn't, because if she did, then the world would win.

Double doors opened inwards for Amaryllis, letting bright light into the dim, candlelit hallway. The music played louder, and chatter between the royal subjects had quieted down to a whisper and then there was silence as she entered.

The kings and queens were seated in the balcony on the same side as the entrance, facing where the princesses were to stand, to witness the selection of their queen-to-be.

The princes each sat in their own doubled oak chair. Once they had selected their princess, they were to bring them to their double chair where they would sit together to watch the other selections.

Once each prince had chosen his bride, the couples would be granted freedom to each activity the kingdom of Arlon had to offer. The most common activity was a romantic horse ride to the falls and back.

Amaryllis had no idea she and her prince were to be granted an activity of any sort. She expected them to part until morning where she would be forced into a carriage back to Werling. It was in her head that Arlon was large, powerful, and cruel with no room for enjoyment.

The princes examined the princesses as they dawdled in. Some held their stomachs, held their breath, and some looked to the floor with a last minute, complete loss of self-confidence. None of the princes had even the slightest anxiety. It was almost like a princess buffet. The princes were spoiled. They looked mainly for beauty and grace. It was rarely the personality that they cared for. Since most princesses looked identical with their white, powdery faces, the attention was on Amaryllis. She was beneficially the odd one out.

Amaryllis followed the duke to her place, which was to the far left of the room underneath a white spotlight. The light reflected off her sparkly dress making it look like a universe of twinkling stars. It made her face look pale and the other princesses faces ghostly with their exceeded amount of powder. Amaryllis looked up into the light to determine its brightness. It did not sting her eyes but her vision was clouded with blue dots when she looked away. She leaned forward to look at Edith at the end of the line who was being comforted by the duke. She held her stomach with one hand and her mouth with the other. Even just a drop of vomit would have been notably obvious from miles away on her light pink dress. Amaryllis glanced from Edith to the prince in front of her. It was the Prince of Herras, and he looked incredibly concerned for Edith.

She deserves to be chosen by him. He would take good care of— what are you saying? She deserves nothing. She took part in hurting you. Yes, but no one deserves to feel what I felt. Everyone deserves love.

Next, she looked at Laria. Like Amaryllis, she was good at hiding her anxiety. She stood as tall as she could with her shoulders back and her arms by her sides. The prince in front of her gawked at her with big brown eyes. She noticed him looking and couldn't help but frown slightly as she thought it would make her to appear more beautiful. Amaryllis chuckled out of pity and looked at the prince in front of her. It was not Prince James of Werling like she hoped it would be, it was the prince of Arlon. He studied Amaryllis intently. He first looked at her gown, then worked his way up to her face. She looked away from him after their eyes met for a split second, but it was too late, he had taken notice of her beautiful eyes. He was no fool, and could recognize her loveliness even if she was dressed in rags and covered in dirt. He continued to stare at her until she looked back. When he caught her attention, he smiled softly. Amaryllis did not return the smile, all she did was blink once then look away again. Prince Eric of Arlon admired her even more for it. He was used to women falling for him wherever he went. Seeing Amaryllis as beautiful as she was, and not showing interest only made him want her more.

Amaryllis did not want the Prince of Arlon to be seated in front of her, but the order of the wealthiest kingdoms in princesses started from right to left, and it was the opposite for the princes. Prince James was near the centre, close to Laria. He sat in his double chair staring at the ground, not bothering to look at the princess in front of him.

She could feel the Prince of Arlon staring at her so she looked at him again. He didn't smile this time, instead he mimicked her facial expression, which was blank. He stared into her eyes, trying to intimidate her and scare her into loving him. He looked for her eyes to widen slightly, or her chest to lift with a small gasp, but they did not. She looked away again, back at Prince James. Prince Eric chuckled to himself.

She's difficult, he thought.

Prince James looked up from the floor and gradually made his way to Amaryllis. She smiled when he looked at her, and he smiled back. They couldn't have a conversation from their distance, but they spoke with their eyes, staring at each other. They smiled and sighed from overwhelming feelings of love and desire. Amaryllis had almost forgotten about the music until it had stopped playing. It was replaced with a trumpet that announced the King of Arlon.

It startled James and Amaryllis, breaking their gazes apart. Their visual conversation had ended. When the trumpet stopped sounding he began to speak.

"For generations…" the king began. He projected his voice well. It boomed loudly as he spoke. "…we have continued the ceremonial choosing tradition. As you know, the purpose of this tradition is to introduce and promote love rather than forcing it upon our children. We believe that they should have some form of a choice. We have kept peace, order, and continued strong relationships within our kingdoms because of this tradition. Your sons will approach these wonderful princesses—" he gestured to the line of women in the centre of the ballroom, "—and choose the bride he desires. However, to be fair to the princesses, we allow them to reject a prince, but she can only reject one." The kings and queens in the balcony nodded. They were aware of the rules and knew the king was restating them for the sake of their sons and daughters.

Amaryllis' anxiety grew stronger as she finally comprehended what was about to happen. Holding in all of her inner tension by standing still drove her body crazy. She needed to sit down, to breathe heavily. Her stomach swam with nervousness that spread to a fiery sensation in her chest. The pain radiated to all of her limbs. Her head felt airy and detached from her body. No one could have known she was anxious unless she said so, but if one looked closely, they could see that her eyes were full of pain and unease.

She looked at the King of Arlon whose lips were moving, but no sound seemed to come out. He said something humorous because the balcony, by the look of it, broke into a fit of laughter. He then said one final remark, and headed for the stairs to take his seat up in the balcony.

Calm down. Please, she begged her anxiety to vanish, but her pleading only made it stronger.

The first prince, the Prince of Herras, on the opposite end stood up and began his scan. He walked slowly along the line of princesses, speaking to them and asking questions. When he reached Amaryllis, he stopped for an extra minute. Her ears were still blocked by her inner-panic, so she attempted to read his lips.

"What is most important to you?" he whispered.

Amaryllis paused for a few seconds, trying to analyze his lips. "Please repeat the question," she croaked. Her voice was barely audible.

"Pardon?" he asked.

"Say it once more," her voice increased slightly in volume.

"What is most important to you?" he repeated. The question was simple, yet it would present a great amount of information. Amaryllis' hearing improved. Speaking with the prince helped to distract herself from the matter at hand, and relieve the butterflies in her stomach.

"I am sorry, but that question is somewhat vague. If you mean in *general*, then happiness is most important to me."

The prince nodded. "How could I provide that for you?"

"Don't choose me," she said bluntly. Her heart was set on the Prince of Werling and she wanted this *fool* to leave immediately. He looked hurt as he turned around to scan the line again. Normally his sadness would have caused her to feel sympathy, but all she wanted was to have her prince and be free from the castle's daunting interior.

The Prince of Herras picked princess Edith, and she immediately took his hand to sit in his double chair. The balcony politely clapped for the engaged couple, then halted when the second prince stood up from his seat.

Amaryllis stopped paying attention to the princes even when they approached her. She simply would not speak, and would glare at them angrily. However, when the Prince of Werling stood up, her stomach dropped and her heart skipped a beat. She was alert and full of hope.

He started at the end of the line and worked his way closer to Amaryllis. It was polite for the princes to consider everyone even if they were not interested. He spent around ten-seconds with each princess. It felt like an eternity before he reached her. Her world moved so slowly by the love in her heart, and everything was blurry except for Prince James. He stood out beautifully amongst her surroundings. It happened so slowly, yet so quickly. He now stood in front of her with his beautiful ocean eyes staring into hers.

"Hello, Prince James," she smiled, remembering how they had said goodbye by addressing their formal names. He smiled back and nodded. The other princes seated in their chairs crossed their arms in frustration that she was paying attention to Prince James rather than them.

"Hello, Princess Amaryllis. You look ravishing," he exclaimed, examining her dress, then for the longest amount of time, her face. His eyes widened bigger for each second he admired her and an involuntary smile spread across his face which he tried to retract. He could not. The love of his life stood before him as beautiful as he hoped she'd be, if not, even more beautiful than he could ever comprehend. Her presence was powerful and calming. Gazing into her eyes filled him with a vigorous love strong enough to warm his entire body.

"Thank you," she whispered, looking down at her gown then looking back at him. She didn't want to miss even a second of gazing into his wonderful eyes. He smiled tenderly, then walked away from her.

There he goes… he is going to pretend to consider choosing someone else, but then he'll turn calmly, look at me, and announce that he loves me. He'll take my hand and lead me to his double chair. We'll sit down and become engaged, and I will finally be free.

Amaryllis was drunk with love; her knees wobbling, heart beating, eyes fluttering. She breathed shallow breaths, overwhelmed with such a strong feeling of happiness that she did not think possible to experience. Everything finally seemed to be working in her favour. She was overjoyed.

The prince walked near the left side of the circle and…

he took…someone's hand.

Laria stepped away from the line, smiling and laughing, holding Prince James's hand.

The clapping from the balcony seemed louder than normal. She was disoriented enough to think the kings and queens were cheering and even whistling for them. The whole room rushed around her in colours of blue and red. The walls seemed to be caving in. Her heart was beating like a drum. Storm clouds thundered in her brain with flashes of lightning, her eyes darkened and shrunk into small slits trying to fight oncoming tears.

Chapter 12

Amaryllis died inside. Her body suddenly weighed one thousand pounds and her knees wanted to give out from under her. It took all of her energy just to stand. Tears poured down her face and she could not stop them. Her surroundings were falling apart; crashing, obliterating, and disappearing through thick tears. She felt several negative emotions at once as she cried an ocean of sorrow. Thankfully no one from the balcony could see her in her state of shock, and no princess in line could see her since they were looking at the princes in front of them. The princesses in their double chairs with their prince did not care to look at her, but rather at their fiancé. However, the last few princes showed deep concern when they went up to make their selection.

"Why are you crying, Princess?" asked the current Deciding Prince. Amaryllis looked at him with a stabbing pain in her heart. Her tears blocked her vision and she could not identify the prince before her. Misery filled her completely. What she felt in that moment was worse than any feeling the princesses had given her when she was weak.

"Nothing matters now," she sobbed uncontrollably, her despondent words barely understandable behind her misery-stricken face. Her escape from her unfortunate life was no longer applicable. Her release and her gateway to happiness was through leaving Arlon with the Prince of Werling. He was the one thing that allowed her to experience true happiness and he fooled her, played her. Her gateway to happiness had been destroyed.

The Deciding Prince held both of her hands and tried to smile. "Everything will be all right. You are the most beautiful princess here and you will be chosen by a fine prince that shall not be myself. I could never please someone as lovely as you, and I can tell that you do not want me to be yours. I wish you happiness and peace." The prince kissed her hand and chose the princess beside her.

The balcony clapped respectfully.

Amaryllis looked over at Prince James and Princess Laria in their double chair. Laria was giggling like a little girl, squeezing his hand and looking into his eyes. Laria smirked as she met Amaryllis' eyes, wrapping her arms around her prince and hugging him with closed eyes. When she let go of him she looked at Amaryllis with evil in her surly, brown eyes.

Finally, there were two royal subjects left: the Prince of Arlon and the Princess of Serilion. Prince Eric stood up from his seat and approached her with a wide smile on his face, excited to select the most exquisite woman he had ever laid eyes on.

Her tears had dried, but her eyes were bloodshot and would pour if she glanced at James and Laria once again. She stared into the oblivion of sadness, hardly noticing the prince before her.

The Prince of Arlon reached for her hand, but she pulled back.

"You have no choice now," he stated. "I am the only prince, and you are the only princess… we will become engaged. I am sorry if that is not what you want, but it is what I want, and this could not have worked out any better for me," he laughed in surprise. To her, he seemed evil and selfish. Amaryllis scoffed at his ignorance through a shaken exhale.

From the balcony, the King and Queen of Serilion stared, filled with worry. It was their greatest desire for their daughter to be chosen by the wealthiest prince, but remembering her face when she spoke about the Prince of Werling, seeing how in love she was, they felt sympathetic and confused as to why James chose Laria. The queen did not want her daughter to rule Arlon as she would be trapped in the place that haunted her most. The king fought every urge to stand up from his seat and yell at Prince James for picking the wrong woman, who sat in his double chair impishly. He was filled with rage.

"I will not accept your hand," she said quietly.

The prince rolled his eyes and snickered. "Like I just mentioned, you have no choice. I will never know why no one else chose you, but I am lucky for you to be here for me to have. Now, come on," he reached for her hand once more, and she pulled away. "Don't be difficult," he cautioned.

Amaryllis frowned and crossed her arms. "I *refuse*. I would rather die alone than to be trapped in this horrid kingdom with you."

The prince chuckled. "I must say princess, it is quite humorous that you think there is a way out of this. I will say it for the last time: *You have no CHOICE.*" He reached for her crossed arms and she shoved him away with all her might, almost making him trip back over his own feet. He frowned with a smile, then it faded when he realized she too was frowning. He finally understood she was not playing hard to get. She had no interest in him at all. What kind of bride would she make? Could he rule his kingdom with a beautiful grump who hated him? They would be miserable. He tried to calm his ego and be less forceful to calm her into allowing him to take her.

"Look Amaryllis, I think you are the most beautiful woman on this Earth and I feel privileged just to have laid eyes on you. I would be the luckiest man in history if you took my hand."

Amaryllis relaxed her angered face. She was intrigued by how men could formulate such passionate and strong words while they meant none of it. How could one say something so powerful knowing in their heart it's not how they truly felt? "Thank you, but I cannot take your hand. I will not."

The balcony buzzed in confusion. Muffled whispering between the King of Arlon's guests drove him to stand. He slammed his hands on the railing of the balcony.

"What is going on down there?" he hollered. The princes and princesses turned in their chairs to look at the angered King of Arlon, then looked back at the Prince of Arlon and the Princess of Serilion.

"We are fine down here, father!" Eric yelled back. He turned to Amaryllis and held out a stiff, shaking hand.

Amaryllis stared at his palm, then at his determined face. "For *the* last time, I will not marry you," she sneered. The prince's patience had vanished. He grabbed her arms and forcefully uncrossed them to access her right hand. Amaryllis winced, grunting frustratedly as she freed herself from his strong grip. She pulled away with a gasp.

The princes and princesses murmured in confusion, along with the kings and queens. The King and Queen of Arlon, and the King and Queen of Serilion stormed down from the balcony.

"Eric… do not ever touch me again," Amaryllis demanded, noticing how her wrists burned in an aching pain. He squeezed her too forcefully. The prince was breathing short breaths of anger when his father came up behind him.

"What is going on?" the king roared.

The prince kept his eyes on Amaryllis. "She refuses to take my hand, father."

The king's angered face relaxed into a calm and sincere expression when he looked at Amaryllis. He sighed. "Princess Amaryllis, why do you refuse my son's hand?" he asked softly. He slowly approached her until he was close enough to not have to raise his voice.

"I do not love your son. If I am to marry, then it will be for love. I am allowed to say no once, and there is only one prince left, meaning there is no one else for me to have. I said no, so we will *both* be without someone to become engaged to. Your son was constantly spoken highly of between the other princesses during my eight years of coming here, so he will most definitely find another princess to marry, but she will not be me."

The king shook his head in confusion. "I do not understand. My son is strong, compassionate, and diligent. He will make a wonderful husband, and a great king. He will love you until the end of time, Princess." He pulled the prince in beside him and placed his hands on his shoulders. The prince looked at Amaryllis with hope in his eyes.

No one in the ballroom ever imagined the Prince of Arlon having to beg someone to love *him*. It was a strange thing to witness. Everyone sat on the edge of their seat watching to see whether or not Amaryllis would agree to marry him… even if she did not, she would be forced into it. No one saw any reason to change the outcome of the ceremony for Amaryllis. At the end of the night, whether she wanted to or not, she would be married to Prince Eric of Arlon and she would rule the kingdom she despised.

"I understand, but please… I don't love him," she begged for the king to cancel the engagement.

"I am sorry princess, but you must take my son's hand now," the king said firmly.

Amaryllis shook her head and stepped back from the spotlight, her head spinning with terror. There was no way out.

"No."

"Amaryllis, there is no other choice. You *will* be engaged to my son. You can drag this out as long as you want, but you *will* be the Queen of Arlon, and the wife to my son."

Amaryllis took another step back, then looked over at her parents who had petrified looks on their faces. She glanced at the door to see two knights guarding it.

"Take his hand NOW!" the king boomed, causing the people around him to shudder from his unsettlingly loud voice.

"NO!" Amaryllis hollered, her shout reverberating in the room. Prince Eric marched up to her with an outstretched arm and she smacked his forearm as hard as she could. He winced as a stinging pain tingled where she contacted him. He ignored the pain and reached again. She pushed him back, twisting her face angrily. The prince then charged at her with wide arms. He grabbed her and trapped her within his grasp. A wave of panic coursed through her. Her arms were trapped under his. She kicked her legs up and tried to wiggle free, letting out yelps for help and cries of misery.

"That's *enough*!" the King of Serilion hollered at the top of his lungs.

"Stop this!" added the two queen's in screechy, panicked voices. The prince stopped trying to walk with the princess. He stood still, holding her tightly. Amaryllis kept thrashing around, kicking her legs about.

"Leave her be! She does not love your arrogant son!" Amaryllis' father yelled at Eric's father.

"She has no choice!" the King of Arlon screamed. Amaryllis twisted her body as far as the prince would let her and looked into his cold eyes. As the kings had their quarrel, Amaryllis whispered to the prince.

"Please do not make me do this," she pleaded with sadness in her voice.

This angered him. No *one* could refuse the Prince of Arlon.

He smiled at her. "You shall be mine forever," he said smugly. As he shut his eyes to laugh, Amaryllis jammed her high-heeled shoe into his ankle. The prince screamed in agony, letting her go to examine his wound. The heel broke the skin with oozing, black blood seeping through the material of his pants.

As soon as his grip loosened, Amaryllis kicked off her shoes to be able to sprint. She held onto them as she ran, cringing at the blood on the heel of her shoe. She sprinted towards the door leading from the ballroom and into the hallway. She looked at the Prince of Werling as she passed him. He stared at her in disbelief, along with other mixed emotions she was too disoriented to identify. She looked away with the shake of her head and kept sprinting, fighting back tears, breathing shallow breaths through a closed throat.

The Prince of Arlon lay on the ground holding his leg. "After her!" he screamed menacingly, pointing a bloody finger at Amaryllis. The knights guarding the door pointed swords at her, and at least twenty more knights ran from the opposite end of the ballroom charging after her, with the sound of clanging metal, and yelling echoing in the room.

She stopped to look behind her. A herd of knights came charging at her like a stampede of wild animals. She ran all around in circles stopping, pivoting, sprinting, stopping, pivoting again to just barely escape them.

The King of Serilion drew his sword and began fighting three knights all by himself, leaving seventeen for Amaryllis to run from. Feeling guilty, the King of Herras also joined the battle between the king and the knights, taking away three more. Several princes stood up from their double chairs and drew their swords as well, feeling empathy for Amaryllis. There were now three knights left; the two guarding the door, and the knight who chased her earlier in the evening.

The Prince of Werling watched in horror as Amaryllis ran frantically for her own freedom, trying to escape the mess which *he* caused for her. His hand, which was holding onto Princess Laria's, reached for his sword.

"Don't go out there," she ordered, trying to hold his hand again. The few princes who remained seated shook their heads at Prince James, and so did all of the princesses as if leaving to fight off the knights was a pointless and stupid idea.

"You all sit here watching her in pain… imbeciles." He stood up from his double chair and sprinted full speed at Amaryllis. He caught up to her quickly as she gradually lost her energy. She dodged him at first, as she was used to instinctively running from everyone who ran at her, but she let him put his hand on her back as he lead her away from the ballroom.

The two knights guarding the door charged at them with raised weapons, leaving a large gap between them and the door. Running beside the prince and having him so close to her after shattering her heart, made her cry. She said nothing to him, but he spoke to her as they ran. She drowned out what he said by staring down the knights, only focusing on what she could see. She threw her high heel at one of the knights helmets, sending vibrations through his skull. He was disoriented for a split second, which Prince James used to disarm him and push him down. As soon as he did, he spun around and fought the last knight standing. He disarmed him easily and pushed him down as well. This reminded Amaryllis of when she first started to love him, when she witnessed him duelling down the staircase. She looked at him with wet eyes then pulled the door open and ran out without looking back. The sound of swords gradually silenced as she ran further and further away from the ballroom.

"You idiots! Stop fighting! She's running away! Go and retrieve my bride!" the Prince of Arlon shouted overtop of the duelling. The fight instantly settled and every knight, king, and prince left the ballroom, sprinting down the hallway after Amaryllis. The Prince of Werling followed the crowd too, but with different intentions. He wanted to be the one to protect Amaryllis if she could not herself. As soon as all of the men left, the Queen of Serilion walked up to Prince Eric, who began to stand up slowly, and grabbed his face.

"You monster, you drove my daughter away! You don't even know what she's been through!" The queen tried to push him down, but he was too strong, so she jammed her own high heel into his wound, causing him to wail like an infant. He stood weakly, held up by the queen's trembling hands until she shoved him down. She picked up her dress and stormed away, ignoring the prince's crying as she was consumed by overwhelming emotion.

The other queens and princesses looked at her in horror. What she had done was sickening and cruel, but the Queen of Serilion dismissed that fact.

Amaryllis greeted the doormen with a wet face and a heaving chest. "OPEN THE GOD DAMN DOOR!" she screamed. She did not have time to be pestered by the nosy doormen. She desperately needed to get out of the castle and fast. Amaryllis had never been so frightened before; her thoughts were uncontrollably scattered—one hundred thoughts raced rapidly, all saying different things. The princesses repetitive attempts to destroy her soul seemed mediocre compared to what she was currently going through. The whole castle seemed to be chasing after her with sharp weapons and screaming voices. She could hear them coming, sprinting through the halls in mixed sounds of shuffling armour and heavy boots worn by the kings and princes.

She was about to run for the upstairs window to jump again until the doormen surprisingly opened the door as quickly as possible. As soon as it opened wide enough for her to run through she bolted. She ran through the crack like a shooting star in the night's sky holding onto her galaxy dress to be sure she wouldn't trip on it.

The doormen shut the door immediately after she made it through, and when the men arrived, they presented an urgency just as strong as the petrified princess' for the door's opening.

"OPEN THIS DOOR!" demanded the King of Arlon. His face contorted into a horrific expression, revealing cruel and angry eyes. The doormen nodded and opened it as slowly as they could. The determined pursuers watched in exasperation. "HURRY IT UP!" he boomed.

The doormen stopped to speak. "It is quite heavy sir," they lied, determined to help the troubled princess. They felt more sympathy for her, especially since it was their fault she nearly perished by jumping out the window. They owed Amaryllis' escape to her. The king ran over and pushed them aside, nearly causing them to trip over themselves and bash their heads against the wall.

"I WILL DO IT MYSELF!" he looked at an arbitrary prince, "HELP ME, YOU FOOL!" The prince scurried over to the other rope and began pulling. The door opened easily, and the men ran out of the castle. The king gave the doormen a threatening glance before dashing out with the other men. The doormen looked nervously at one another, then followed the crowd out the door. In the far distance they could see Amaryllis sprinting, and about fifty yards behind were the kings, princes, and knights chasing after her.

Chapter 13

Amaryllis' heart thundered in her chest. She breathed sharply as her body worked to allow her to escape. She was warm in the cold night, producing seemingly endless quantities of adrenaline and sweat. She pumped her arms and legs as her bare feet pounded the ground. All of her muscles ached. She had been running for too long without rest. Back and forth her legs moved as she sprinted away from her unfortunate future. Her arms felt non-existent and airy, but her legs were heavy and sore. A radiating pain inhabited itself within her chest, and it continued to grow stronger with each stride she took. Amaryllis groaned in frustration. She did not dare to look back, she didn't even care to listen for them. If she payed attention to anything other than trying to mobilize her exhausted body she would surely slow down.

She started to cough, which stung her throat. Frustration took over her mind completely. She was left with no choice but to run away from everyone, and to do so she had to push her body's limits in regard to stamina and mental determination. Her only fear during that time was the worry that her muscles would tire to the point of failure, leading to her collapsing in the grass. Then it would be over, and she would be caught, forced to live in the castle of darkness.

She wanted to scream at them to leave her alone but that would waste a breath. She groaned instead.

"She'll tire herself out eventually," breathed the King of Arlon. "Did you hear that sound she just made?"

The kings and princes beside him nodded, panting like dogs, and the knights at the far back of the group nodded as well. Their armour restricted their full potential of sprinting.

This meadow never ends! Amaryllis thought to herself. Her perspective changed greatly when she eyed the forest at the end of the meadow…the Dark Forest. It was forbidden to enter as it was filled with sinister creatures that would show no mercy on any human that foolishly dared to step foot within the tree line.

Amaryllis saw no other beneficial option. If she ran in circles in the meadow she would tire herself out quickly, and would be caught within an instant to be brought back to the castle where she would become engaged to Prince Eric of Arlon. She couldn't fight, the odds were unfair. It was a guaranteed loss if she decided to fight them, a suicidal idea. The only option she found best, although it was devilishly stupid, was running directly into the Dark Forest. She would rather die at the hands of a goblin or a ghost than marry that man. There was nothing the world had to offer her on the outside that would keep her from running into the forest.

Amaryllis continued to sprint forward, now driven by the idea of making her escape through the Dark Forest. She now had a new sense of purpose, which was not only to run away but to run towards something. As she advanced closer and closer, the urge to turn around grew stronger. The ominous forest made constantly produced a cacophony of monsters' cries. She heard piercing screeches, deafening roars, strange clicking sounds, thumping, and fierce whispers all combined together into one petrifying roar.

Without even a second of hesitation, as soon as she had reached the tree line, Amaryllis ran into the Dark Forest. She hopped over roots, stumps, and bushes. Her stomach dropped as she entered with the weight of terror bringing it down. There was an evident difference in spirit between the two locations. The feeling exuding from the trees attacked her soul, making her want to scream at the top of her lungs. She could not refrain, and so she did. The trees seemed to emit an overwhelmingly stressful aura, like the feeling of utter fear—a near death experience—which never went away. The feeling attacked the vulnerable ones constantly.

The men behind her halted before the forest and helplessly watched her run deeper within the trees, listening to her screaming a high pitched scream that faintly added to the many other screeching sounds in the forest.

The King of Arlon, along with every man there, could sense the darkness and dared not go in. However, the Prince of Werling considered it. He was very well aware that it was *he* who caused Princess Amaryllis her pain, and her need to run away from everyone. He felt obligated to go after her.

"I say we go in," stated Prince James between heavy panting. The crowd looked at him as if he had two heads.

"Are you mad? It is suicide!" proclaimed a prince. The crowd nodded along, mumbling cruel remarks.

"Absolutely suicidal!"

"An absurd idea that is."

"Well, standing here doing nothing is just as absurd," Prince James groaned. "The Princess of Serilion is in there and we must save her at once—"

"*Absolutely no one* will be entering the Dark Forest. It is her own fault for going inside. She is a lost cause and most likely dead already. If we go in we'll all die as well, and there will be no kings to rule. It's one woman versus forty men. What do you *think* the right decision is?" snapped the Prince of Herras.

The Prince of Werling exploded in rage. The longer they stood and waited the further into the woods Amaryllis advanced, and the more likely it was that she would perish. "If none of you cowards will help me then I shall go in alone!" he yelled. The prince withdrew his sword and impulsively ran into the forest.

"Even the bravest man does not come out of there alive!" yelled a voice James did not recognize from behind him in a panic. The prince ignored their remarks, although they were most likely true, and chased after Amaryllis, following where shrubs had been defaced and where the smallest droplets of blood could be seen.

Amaryllis involuntarily slowed down to a light jog. Her body was far too tired to continue sprinting. Her sight became clouded with blackness which ate its way from the outside-in until she could only see through a tiny pinhole. She had to stop. She looked behind her and couldn't see the way out of the forest anymore or where the night's sky shone through the skinny trees. She was completely surrounded by darkness. The pounding of her feet against the ground somewhat drowned out the horrible noises, but since she'd stopped, they became vivid and *loud*.

Amaryllis looked down at her twinkling dress, which in the sheer blackness looked surprisingly intact, and sighed inconsistently in fearful hiccoughs caused by pure fear and discomfort. The only part of the dress that looked different from the rest was the bottom. There were thick blades of grass in random places with slimy mud, and dirt sticking to it.

Nothing could distract her from the horrendous sounds the forest made but it wasn't the forest itself she was afraid of…she loved nature…it was the creatures within that she did not want to meet. The fact that she would definitely see at least one monster, frightened her and caused her to panic. She was not ready but was forced to become so.

She put her hands on top of her head and weaved her fingers down through her hair. She dug her nails into her scalp, spinning around in circles looking for a threat. The noises disoriented her. Her eyes were wide as if they would pop out of their sockets. She let out a dry, scratchy cry of agony wanting to sob her fear away, but was too frightened to cry. Her body was in shock. The noises came from everywhere and seemed to echo within her brain, haunting her.

She let herself fall to the ground, keeping her eyes shut tight and covering them for an additional feeling of safety. She laid whimpering on the ugly forest floor, trying to scream louder than the forest's sounds to drown them out, but to no avail.

She stopped screaming when she heard very faint footsteps. They nearly made her fall unconscious, frightened by what it could be. They moved quickly towards her. She suddenly pushed off of the ground within one half of a second and bolted once again.

Her knees immediately hurt and her legs ached, but she ran as fast as her body would let her, deeper into the forest.

"Stop!" She heard from behind her. It was a man's voice. She did not dare to look back to see who it was, she kept pumping her arms and legs until—

She could not run anymore.

Her legs physically could no longer move. She collapsed to the ground, then crawled slowly behind a large black tree and waited for the footsteps to pass by, or to turn around. She scratched anxiously at the tree until a big piece of bark chipped off. She attempted to use it as a weapon to scare whoever was behind her, but if she hit anything with it, it would crumble to dust, so she held it as gently in her hands as possible. The weapon was useless but she was too disoriented to care.

"Amaryllis!" the voice hollered. Amaryllis groaned, fighting every urge to run towards the person. The forest was driving her insane and she would even run to the Prince of Arlon if it were him yelling for her.

"Amaryllis, where are you?" he asked worriedly. By the tone of his voice, he wasn't afraid of the forest, he was afraid of not being able to find the princess. She peeked her head around the tree and became mixed with emotions: happiness, relief, anger, sadness, annoyance. She stood up with wobbly legs and limped around the tree to see Prince James holding a sword in front of his body, scanning around the forest with worried eyes. His shoulders sank in relief as he sighed at the sight of her. He had the urge to cry.

Her auburn hair looked black in the forest's shadows, her eyes were wild with fear, and she looked miserable. He had never seen her in such horrid conditions. She was immediately under the effect of the treacherous place, looking like a miserable spectre. He hated seeing her unhappy, it hurt him. Even though she appeared despondent and petrified, she was still beautiful.

"Amaryllis!" he cried, holding his arms out and running to her. She couldn't run to him, but limped slowly in his direction. She did not want to see him as he fractured her heart, but it was relieving to have someone to hold and someone to share fear with.

He wrapped his arms around her and sighed, filled with solace to have her in his arms. For a moment, the Dark Forest didn't seem as horrible until she pushed away from him.

"Don't take me back there," she pleaded, ignoring her emotions and focusing on her most dreadful problem; the seemingly unsolvable problem of her impossibility to live in peace. The prince's chest stung as she pushed him away, but then he remembered why she would have the right to feel that way; he chose the wrong princess. He knew it was a mistake from the beginning, but it was not his intention. He looked at her, standing a foot away from him which felt like a mile. She was wobbling and looking at the ground trying to balance herself.

"I know you don't want to hear this, but I must get you out of here immediately. I am surprised that we haven't been attacked yet."

Amaryllis took a shaky step back staring into his eyes that still managed to astound her, even though she was angry with him. She hated that a part of her still loved him. "I'd rather die," she spat. Then, her legs spasmed and she dropped, but the prince caught her and pulled her up. He held her in his arms.

"You must be exhausted," he exclaimed, picturing her running all around the ballroom.

"I *am* exhausted."

The deafening roar of the Dark Forest loudened in a booming thunder, sending shivers rocketing down their spines. Amaryllis covered her ears, and the prince groaned in agony as he couldn't cover his ears as he chose to hold Amaryllis instead. It lasted for what felt like an eternity while sending treacherous winds in their direction, blowing Amaryllis' hair all over the place.

"What do we do?" she asked frantically under the wind. The prince checked his surroundings, finding no place to go, then kicked a hole into a nearby hollow black tree where Amaryllis once hid. It was large enough in diameter for both of them to fit inside. He ran in and set Amaryllis down gently.

"I know this tree isn't strong, but as long as we're quiet nothing can find us," he insisted as he covered the open hole in the tree with the piece he had kicked in. He balanced it perfectly in its place. As he covered the hole, enclosing them in blackness, anger boiled inside of her. Amaryllis did not want to hide from death with the man that caused her the most grief she had ever felt in her lifetime, but when the deafening roar occurred again, her anger abandoned her body and she appreciated the coverage from the tree…and James.

Amaryllis sat with her knees pulled up to her chest which she rested her head on to cope with her sudden surge of emotion. The prince sat the same way, except he kept his head up to peer through the darkness at Amaryllis' silhouette. It was difficult to see because it was so dark, but just the slightest bit of light came through a crack in the tree that outlined her body.

"Amaryllis—" he began, intending on explaining the twisted turn of the Choosing Ceremony. He felt truly awful about the incident and as long as Amaryllis didn't know about the truth, the guilt ate him alive. The stress tore at his heart, squeezing the air out of him.

"Don't talk to me," she whispered fiercely, interrupting him. Silence was utterly vital. She listened to the sounds, along with a new sound that seemed to be getting louder. The creature or whatever it was, was approaching with an unexplainable screech that moved between the trees.

The prince cautiously shuffled closer to Amaryllis in an attempt to tell his story. He brought his lips to her ear to whisper nearly inaudibly. He remembered the importance of silence, but *had* to explain himself.

"I am sorry," he breathed, afraid of making too much noise. She rolled her eyes and simply ignored him. She did not want to hear a single word from the man who betrayed her, he misled her in one of the worst possible ways. "I—"

Amaryllis touched the prince's shoulder to silence him. "Stop...talking," she warned, tears beginning to well in her eyes. His presence brought a heavy weight of sadness upon her shoulders, weighing her down. Being so close to him made her feel empty inside like he was draining the life out of her. How dare he? How could he possess the audacity to fool her that way, in a romantic affliction, when she finally thought she found something wonderful?

Prince James could not tell whether or not she was angry with *him*, or if she was just frightened by the creatures. She was truly both frightened *and* angry; the two emotions battled one another within her body, taking the form of frustrated tears. Amaryllis did not want him to speak and she made herself crystal clear from all of the things she didn't say.

The prince sat in silence wanting to express himself, not caring for the situation they were in because all would make sense and hopefully she would forgive him. He desperately needed to explain why he chose Princess Laria, but after thinking about it for a short while with the sounds of death surrounding them, he decided to stay quiet.

The sounds became significantly louder and the coverage of the tree didn't seem to be blocking out the noise anymore. Amaryllis and James covered their ears, but even that did not seem to help. Amaryllis screamed in pain. The resonance of the forest was too overpowering to hear herself. Prince James yelled to Amaryllis, but she could not hear him or even read his lips because it was too dark.

They felt vibrations in the ground. The monsters were right outside the tree running around looking for something to kill. By the deafening sound and thunderous vibrations, the creatures were gigantic.

Amaryllis' world was dark, loud, terrifying, and filled with man-eating creatures. She had never felt so small and worthless until she laid whimpering and cowering within that tree.

Suddenly, the sounds halted and were replaced by ringing in both the prince's and princess' ears. Amaryllis looked over at Prince James' silhouette. She could see his widened eyes scanning the crack of light peering into the tree. He looked as if he were hesitating to check to see if the monsters were gone.

Amaryllis sighed with relief and rested her head against the wall of the tree. She shut her eyes and listened to the ringing in her ears. Now that the sounds had stopped, she could feel her heart beating, and the butterflies in her stomach seemed more present.

Grey light streamed into Amaryllis' vision underneath her closed eyes. She opened them to see Prince James moving the piece of wood that covered the hole in the tree. Her stomach dropped.

"Stop!" she whispered.

He whipped his head back, still holding the bark in the same position, letting in light. "What?"

Amaryllis crawled over to him as quickly as possible and put her hands on top of his and used them to cover the hole back up. "Are you insane?" she retorted.

The prince put his hands on her shoulders and pulled her close to him. "If the noises have stopped, we should take our chance to get out of the tree and run out of the forest. You don't want to wait for more creatures to appear do you?"

Amaryllis listened for more noises and the usual music of the Dark Forest was present. "There will always be noise... always."

She pushed his hands off of her. "I am not leaving the Dark Forest." She struggled with this sentence, because she desperately wanted to leave but chose the Dark Forest over Arlon. "I'd rather die in here."

The prince hated to hear her speak that way. He wanted her to be safe and unhappy ruling Arlon, rather than constantly petrified and unsafe in the Dark Forest where she would most likely die. "I know that things haven't worked out for you, but please listen to me when I tell you that living in Arlon with Eric is much, much better than living—" he paused as the forest's music chilled him to the bone. He shivered and shut his eyes as if doing so would grant him with more protection, "—here... Amaryllis, I feel like I need to tell you—"

"Don't say a word," she muttered. "I don't want to hear about Princess Laria."

The prince found Amaryllis' hands and held them. He brought them to his chest. "I had to choose her," he sobbed.

"*Enough!*" she snapped, yanking her hands away from his grasp. She stood up from her seated position and towered over him in his crouched position.

"You crushed me," she said firmly.

Prince James stood up and tried to hug her, not for her comfort but for his. She pushed him away again. "Amaryllis, please let me explain. Please." He reached out for her again.

"Stop touching me!" she shoved him against the tree's inner wall, and the *door* shifted slightly, letting in grey light.

Amaryllis looked at his sad, despondent face, which looked exquisite in the shadows of the hollow tree. She ignored the fact that their coverage was nearly exposed and started to cry. She could sense his love for her, but he confused her to the point of visceral frustration.

If he loves me, why didn't he chose me. It should be simple... choose the woman you love. Her heart sank as she came to her own conclusion. *He never loved you… it had to have been pretend, somehow,* she pondered.

As if reading her mind, he proclaimed through sobs of sadness, "Amaryllis… I love you…I do." He spoke with sincerity and he meant it deeply. He looked into her eyes with a plea for mercy. He needed to hear that she loved him back, that somehow she could forgive him. He truly did not want to choose Princess Laria.

This angered her. She felt tension in her chest, and groaned impatiently. "How dare you…" she began, then fell to the ground after her wobbly legs gave out from beneath her once again. She decided against ranting to him about how evil it was to fool her heart. The long pause brought discomfort to the prince. Her response, and the lack of mentioning her affection for him, squeezed his heart viciously. He did not know what to say next. He had just expressed himself in three simple words and she did not seem to comprehend in the way he wished she would. He lifted her up off the ground and repeated himself but with an uncontrollable sadness. Amaryllis opened her mouth to speak, to tell him how she hated what he did but screamed instead.

Several sets of gigantic hands wrapped their long, sharp black fingers around the loose piece of wood that hid the prince and princess within the tree. The door came off with an effortless tug and it flew one hundred feet behind the creatures as they whipped it back. They peered their heads in, and Prince James and Princess Amaryllis could not move. There were eight shadow figures surrounding them, revealing piercing blue slits as their eyes. They seemed to glow compared to their pitch black bodies. After a moment, the shadow creatures screeched a horrifying scream that sounded like boiling water mixed with a baby's cry. It was the same deafening sound from earlier. It was exceedingly loud. Amaryllis and James covered their ears, and like before it was ineffective.

When the screaming concluded, they removed their hands from their ears to feel blood trickling down the sides of their face.

Amaryllis snapped herself free from her petrified state and crawled to the back of the tree.

"James!" she screamed, but he was still frozen in fear. She pulled him by the collar to the back of the tree. She thought that the creatures could not fit inside, but whether or not they could did not matter. They disappeared briefly, then cracking sounds filled the air. The tree was lifted above their heads, exposing them to the open forest once again, making Amaryllis and James feel terrifyingly vulnerable. The roots surfaced through the crumbling soil and the tree was thrown fifty feet.

The creatures themselves stood eight feet tall. They were shockingly slim, looking like shadows of long, stretched, malnourished people. Their mouths were the most frightening feature. They were wide and extended to where a person's ears would be. When they opened their mouths, their jaws dropped unnaturally low.

The shadow creatures charged at Amaryllis and James. He withdrew his sword and Amaryllis fearfully readied herself to fight with her bare hands with nothing but panic overpowering her. She and James were separated and surrounded by four creatures each. Using their long, black blade-like fingers as daggers, James struggled to maintain dominance in his battle. He was slashed frequently, but rarely impaled, so he managed to strike them back. When he did hit them, they would scream, disorienting James long enough with their powerful screeches for them to strike back.

Amaryllis had no chance from the beginning. She was frightened out of her mind, watching the eight foot tall shadow creatures tower over her with their gaping mouths, approaching her slowly. As soon as they were close enough, Amaryllis jammed her elbow into the nearest creature's stomach. Because they had thick, scaly, skin, her attack did not hurt them. They showed no signs of pain or disorientation. This frustrated her. She punched and kicked them until she tired herself out and while she was doing so, the shadows ran around her in a circle. The creatures enjoyed watching her struggle, they toyed with her for the longest time. It wasn't until Amaryllis grabbed a sharp rock from the ground and jammed it into one of the creatures eyes, that they began to take her seriously. The injured creature shrieked a shrill cry of pain and grabbed her by the throat, pressing its sharp fingers against her neck, nearly breaking the skin. It lifted her from the ground, which added pressure to the knives against her neck. Higher and higher it lifted her. Her legs dangled motionlessly but she rested her hands on top of the creature's arms, looking into its sinister, piercing blue eyes.

From behind her, Prince James defeated his four shadow creatures and began to run over to help her.

She kept her eyes on the narrowed blue eyes before her until she moved her gaze to the mouth. It began to build up and gush red, chunky liquid which came from the back of the throat and dripped out of the front of the mouth. The creature tilted its head back slowly then spat the gunk out onto her face, making a strange, gushing sound as it left its mouth. The other monsters, behind the creature holding onto Amaryllis, charged and tried to grab her because they knew very well what that red gunk was used for consumption. Once the red liquid was formed, it was spat onto the victim's face, acting as a stimulant, disorienting them for a brief period of time as the shadow creature devoured them.

Amaryllis could immediately feel the effects of the horrible red gunk. She no longer felt pain as the shadows fought for her soon-to-be-dead body, cutting her skin and leaving gashes everywhere. They shrieked in frustration which would have caused her to wince and cover her ears, but it was unnecessary to do so within her trance. Her ears streamed with rivers of fresh blood. Her body was cut and disfigured, her pupils were large. She stared at the monsters feeling nothing but defeat. She accepted her fate. She had come to terms with her death and was just waiting for it to happen; for her vision to fade to black, for her soul to fade into non-existence.

After realizing that the one shadow creature would not share Amaryllis to devour, they all pulled at her limbs at once. Although she was delirious, she could feel the tension, like her arms were about to be ripped off. She lazily looked over at Prince James who was sprinting towards her with a scrunched face, open mouth, and a raised sword. He too was covered in fresh blood, gashes and small cuts on his face. James was nearly there, until he became drastically further away. The monsters accidentally flung Amaryllis about one hundred feet away when they were tugging at her. She felt no breeze, and couldn't hear whistling in her ears either. Her senses were strictly limited to only her vision. She did not know what was going on until she landed in murky, black swamp water.

Chapter 14

Prince James watched in horror as Amaryllis' lifeless body soared through the air at an unbelievably high speed.

"NO!" he screamed. All of his efforts, in the end, were pointless. He ran into the Dark Forest to *save* Amaryllis thinking he would be the one to die, but she would live.

The monsters sharply turned their heads to look at Prince James, who was on his knees whimpering. He looked up glumly, then stood up to run. The monsters charged, and the prince ran away, out of the Dark Forest, crying. He ran without growing tired, reaching the kings, princes, and knights on the other side of the woods and leaving the shadow creatures behind him hissing like snakes. They could not leave the Dark Forest, there was an unseen barrier that all creatures of evil instinctively knew not to cross.

The prince noticed a significant difference between areas. Being exposed to the night's fresh air relieved him of the unseen stress that the forest emitted upon its victims.

The bored expressions that the men wore drastically changed when they saw Prince James emerge covered in blood. They had been waiting for a long while, and seeing him in his condition startled them.

"What happened to you?" asked the King of Arlon.

"Where is my daughter?" cried the King of Serilion. He had just arrived after staying behind to comfort his wife. Several other questions were asked, but the King of Arlon, and the King of Serilion's wonderings concerned him more. He disregarded the other men and tried to speak, but his despair made him temporarily mute.

"Well?"

The prince hesitated, then whispered,

"I think Amaryllis is dead," he choked on that sentence, not wanting to believe it, but felt overwhelmed that it was most likely true. The whole crowd sank. They did not expect for her to be dead or alive. They wanted to keep their minds open, but learning the news destroyed them.

Amaryllis' father crumbled to the ground and sobbed quietly. He looked at Prince James with glassy eyes. "Are you certain—" the king gasped involuntarily, "—certain she's... *dead?*"

"Well, sir, she was thrown incredibly far..."

"What happened exactly?" asked the King of Arlon monotonously, showing no signs of sadness.

"I found her... but then we had to hide from these... dark, tall, skinny, *loud* monsters. They found us nearly immediately after I entered, and we were separated. There were so many of them. I fought four all alone, and so did she, but I had my sword and she had nothing. After I killed my group of monsters, I ran to find her dangling in the air, held by the throat, then scratched at and fought for her. She was flung deeper into the woods, and tossed very quickly, and quite high from the ground... I do not imagine she would have survived the impact of her fall."

The King of Serilion stood up from the ground, then fell back down as his sadness weighed him down.

"Thank you for at least *trying* to save her," he wailed. The king pushed himself up from the ground, then fell again. "My daughter is dead! What if you *all* went in after her? Imagine the outcome..." the king trailed off as he no longer had the energy to speak.

The crowd of men dropped down on one knee with guilt on their shoulders. They bowed their heads morosely, all except for the King of Arlon, who stood facing the Dark Forest listening to the internal horrors.

Chapter 15

Amaryllis' senses slowly returned. She could hear fish swimming around her with the thrashing of their fins. She tasted the repulsive pond water as her mouth hung open, and could feel the bone-chilling temperature of the liquid she was submerged in. Her muscles were too weak to move. Even her eyelids couldn't move. As she laid at the bottom of the black pond, her eyes were lazily half-open looking at strange fish that didn't seem to care too much about her being there. The worst part of it all was that Amaryllis was out of breath, and she didn't have the strength, or the energy, to swim up for air.

Her throat was the first to feel pain. It stung like hot fire, which spread to her chest and radiated throughout her whole body. She wanted to scream in pain, but her body wouldn't allow it. She was very close to the surface as the pond was shallow, but she didn't realize how close to the surface she was because the water was so translucent and dark. She could only see her torso, and the fish if they were within arms reach.

The pressure drove her insane, but she relieved her frustration by widening her eyes. She screamed, releasing black bubbles to the surface of the pond. Her limbs had not yet gained mobility, but she was nearly there. Her whole body was on fire, then suddenly she felt nothing once again. She became lightheaded, and her facial muscles relaxed. Amaryllis knew it was the end. She thought of Prince James and how much she loved him. She wished her circumstances had been more fair and generous. She wanted to see him one last time to show her affection, just one additional minute to hold him in her arms and tell him that she loved him too. She thought of when they were fighting the shadow monsters just *minutes* ago, when he told her he loved *her,* and how she pushed him away. If Amaryllis was not submerged in water, a tear would have trickled down her cheek. She groaned gently, bubbles escaping her mouth and drifting to the surface. Her lungs were empty, and so was her mind. She slowly began to drift away...

A low, gurgling sound rumbled in the water, it was all Amaryllis' drifting mind could process. As the pond floor shook rapidly, the black water bubbled and gurgled on the surface like boiling water. Beneath Amaryllis' body, her back was pummelled with surges of pressure ejected by the pond floor, pushing her around with great force. A large jet of air suddenly spewed vigorously, striking the small of Amaryllis' back and pushing her right out of the water. As soon as her face met the air, she gasped. Amaryllis was air-born, and when she reached the peak of her toss from the pond, she was alert and had full ability of her senses. She landed on her feet for just a moment then crumbled to the ground.

Amaryllis breathed rapidly, her body trembling from trauma. She stared into the night sky, hidden by dark trees, thinking of absolutely nothing.

Chapter 16

The kings, princes, and knights walked back to the castle with slouched shoulders and lowered heads. The doormen quickly opened the door for them with hope that they had brought Amaryllis back, but they too slouched their shoulders when they saw she was not present. Neither doorman dared to ask about her. Once each man had entered, they sullenly released the ropes to close the doors.

The men walked through the halls, not saying a word. Only the sound of footsteps could be heard with occasional sniffing coming from the King of Serilion, and the Prince of Werling. The two miserable royal subjects walked side by side at the back of the group silently expressing their agony.

At the back of his mind, the King of Serilion thought of punching Prince James square in the nose. *If he had chosen my daughter none of this would have happened. He loves her... so why didn't he choose her?* the king grunted, pushing his sadness away temporarily to say,

"You are an arrogant, imbecilic man and you deserve to rot in the Dark Forest where you led my daughter."

The prince groaned in response, looking at the ceiling to reveal his watery eyes. "I had no choice…" The prince's humble and confident behaviour seemed to have vanished. The death of his true love ate away at his soul, and he could not hide it.

"That is *ridiculous!*" the king scowled. "Choose the woman you *love*. Amaryllis was last to be chosen somehow, so you had SEVERAL opportunities to choose *her*... not the witch of a woman that you picked," the king's voice boomed, but the men in the front minded their own business.

"I wanted to choose Amaryllis! I assure you of that... it killed me to take Laria's hand and sit there looking at the woman I love still standing in line. I wanted *her* sitting beside me...but like I said, I did not have a choice."

The king was puzzled, but by the time he had thought of his next question they had arrived back at the ballroom. The queens had hopeful expressions on their faces, and so did the princesses, except for Laria who looked displeased to see the men.

The princesses truly felt sorry for Amaryllis and felt strong remorse for following Laria in her eight years of torment and threats. They wished they had been kinder to her. When the poor girl's life was in danger, it allowed them to realize to a full extent what they had done to an innocent, kind-hearted princess. Laria; however, felt no remorse or sense of empathy for Amaryllis.

As they entered, the queens and princesses gasped when they realized by the look on the men's faces, and the absence of Princess Amaryllis that she must be dead.

"Where is she?" sobbed the Queen of Serilion, running into her husband's arms, crying onto his shoulder. The queen was hyperventilating, and even if the king had spoken she would not have heard him over her loud crying. The king waited for her to calm down, but her tears seemed to be flowing faster and her breathing was becoming louder.

"The Dark Forest..." he began. His own crying stopped a few minutes ago in the hallway, but when confessing to his wife what had happened to their only daughter, the tears instantly flowed once again. "...she's dead."

As if the king's words had caused the queen physical pain, she dropped to the floor and groaned. Everyone in the room knelt down and bowed their heads in respect for Amaryllis. The princesses joined and even began to cry themselves…except, of course, for Laria. She knelt to blend in with the crowd but did not shed a single tear.

The ballroom echoed with cries and sent sadness into the world. People from all over the land could sense misery in their day whether it was from sudden rainfall, or just the feeling of sorrow. The people could feel it, but they did not know what it was from.

Chapter 17

The frightening noises surrounding Amaryllis did not bother her any longer. As she looked up to the starry sky with hope in her heart, she ignored the forest's music, gasping for air, and thinking about how thankful she was for her event of coincidence… or perhaps even the event of a miracle.

She did not have complete control over her muscles as the effects of the shadow creature's gunk had not worn off yet, so she laid flat on her back waiting for her muscles to regain their strength and for her brain to once again have command over them. She was out of breath, trying to calm her lungs with heavy swallows of air. She was just at the bottom of a disgusting black swamp, unaware of where she was… and she was saved by the pond itself, which literally spit her out of the water. Amaryllis was grateful. The world was cruel to her, but for once it seemed to grant her with luck.

She slowly picked herself up from the dirt and looked down at her legs. They could be seen from the absence of her sparkling dress that used to cover her completely, but is now merely a torso with ripped sleeves. The bottom portion—the skirt—was completely gone, torn and sliced off by the shadow monsters' bladed fingers. Her legs were covered in deep wounds, which gushed with fresh blood. Her entire body ached in pain from her stab and slash wounds.

Now that the red gunk's pain killing and mind numbing effects had worn off, Amaryllis could feel everything.

She walked away from the black pond, glaring at it briefly before she left, analyzing what she nearly died in. The thought of the shadow monsters crossed her mind.

Where have they gone? One minute, they surrounded me, the next, I nearly drowned. Did they get Prince James? Amaryllis unintentionally filled herself with anxieties regarding Prince James. She missed him and wanted him to be by her side in the Dark Forest, then she remembered how he had gone in to bring her *out,* and she wanted no part of that.

She continued to walk away from the pond, listening for shadow monsters. Their sounds were easily identifiable from their volume and stood out among other sounds. Her ears still rang in a consistent tingling sound that was overpowered by the Dark Forest's screeches and roars.

After dealing with beings as terrifying as the shadow monsters, Amaryllis felt she could overcome anything. What could be more frightening than eight feet tall shadow figures with gaping mouths full of red slime?

With every step Amaryllis took, her legs ached even more than the previous step. They hurt from her wounds and from her engaged muscles that she was not used to using for such a long period of time. She wanted to sit down, but then she would never be able to get up again, so she kept walking; stepping over tree stumps, rocks, streams of blood from dead animals, and even human skeletons (there were very few since no one has entered the Dark Forest in decades).

In the distance, Amaryllis could see deer and other forest animals being torn apart by large winged creatures.

Dragons.

Dragons indubitably existed during this time, but no one believed in their existence because they never appeared. Like every other creature of the Dark Forest, the dragons had limited freedom to where they could go. They could not fly higher than the tips of the trees, so they did not bother to fly at all because many parts of the forest consisted of dense areas of closely packed trees with rare open spaces. The dragons got around by weaving through the trees, and if they could not fit they would either break them with the force of their strong, massive bodies, or if they were angry they'd set trees on fire, burning them to instant dust.

Amaryllis avoided eye contact with the gargantuan beasts. She left them to be with their prey so that their attention did not shift from their half eaten animals to her. She began to walk faster still staying cautious of the nature before her. Although the dragons were far away, she could hear the disturbing sounds of them digging into their prey with additional sounds of grunts and snorts, releasing smoke from their nostrils. There were five dragons in her area, all eating different creatures.

Amaryllis' vision of herself being able to successfully survive in the forest changed drastically when in the presence of the dragons. The shadow creatures seemed so small and irrelevant compared to the gigantic fire-breathing monsters. The shadow creatures were loud and intimidating, but the dragons could easily kill in seconds.

She started to sweat nervously which was hot in the cold temperatures of the forest. Plus, being drenched in swamp water wasn't helping her body temperature either. Amaryllis shivered in fear, holding her arms crossed in front of her, making sure to avoid touching any of the gashes on her arms. The dragons weren't too bothered by the wandering princess anyway. In fact, many of the horrid creatures did not seem to pay any mind to her even though she was like a ray of light in a place of perpetual darkness.

She noticed how they did not attack her and was relieved beyond words. Some would look at her then look away, not caring for her presence, and some wouldn't even see her at all. Amaryllis was the luckiest woman to ever enter the Dark Forest as she hadn't been killed yet. Aside from luck, it was possible to survive inside if you were wise enough.

A loud sharp roar coming from every direction engaged her senses, her body rushed with adrenaline. As soon as the roar began, she picked up her pace to a light run; less than a sprint, and more than a jog. It badly hurt her legs to run, but she did so anyway as her body was already in constant pain in all areas. She couldn't tell where the danger could be. The whole forest vibrated and echoed with the alarming roar, so she kept running in the same direction.

The further she ran, the louder the roars became. She stopped abruptly to look for any signs of a threat. All that jumped out at her were the dark, oddly shaped trees that looked as if they might come to life and impale her. She could have been running straight into danger and she would have had no idea. She looked all around and saw nothing out of the ordinary, so she kept running in her original direction.

The roars were excessively loud for another few *minutes* until they finally started to quiet down. Amaryllis noticed a significant difference, so she assumed the roars came from behind her, and slowed her run down to a stiff walk. She could no longer see any creatures, but only regular forest animals like rabbits and squirrels.

She kept walking until she found herself in an area of silence. She heard no screeches, roars, or screams coming from the forest. This startled her, causing her to believe that the noises had driven her insane. She was thankful for the sound of silence, but she had started getting used to the Dark Forest's music and found the regular sound of the world to be disturbingly quiet.

Amaryllis flinched aggressively if she heard the sound of a twig snap. When a small toad crossed her path, she jumped and squealed. In her mind, the quietness was a warning that something was lurking, watching her in the open space without any trees to hide her. The moonlight from the regular world shone through the trees of the Dark Forest, lighting her journey. She could finally see where she was going and the objects around her. The grey light from the moon made her cold, gash covered flesh appear extremely white and dead.

If Amaryllis was not as beautiful as she was, she would have looked like an unearthly, horrifying corpse wandering aimlessly through the forest—looking like she was one of the lurking creatures that belonged there, but her radiant face and strong body would still have made anyone's jaw drop even in her horrible conditions.

She sauntered aimlessly through the open space, unsure of where she was going and what she was looking for. Perhaps a place to rest, to energize, or somewhere that could provide her with warmth. Her heart was finally at a pace that was not affected by fear, and all she could focus on was Prince James. The thought of him kept her in high spirits, even though he chose Princess Laria over her. Amaryllis focused on the positive encounters and shied away from the negative and saddening moments. His eyes were a clear memory in her mind and so was the look on his face when he saw her after his foolish duel down the staircase. He revealed a look of wonder and pure love at first glance.

Amaryllis smiled to herself as if reliving the memory. For a moment, she forgot about how cold she was. Her pain vanished, and she nearly forgot *where* she was until she heard a new foreign sound coming from in front of her.

Enchanting harp melodies radiated from the sky, putting the princess' soul at peace. She dared not question where they came from. She enjoyed the sound contentedly. Before her stood a bright area of beautiful, golden willow trees. Amaryllis wondered how she had not noticed the enchanting group of trees before. She walked up to them and pressed her ear to one of the trees. She discovered that the harp music seemed to be coming from inside the trees and sighed with relief. But how could the Dark Forest hold something so pure within its evil boundaries?

She wandered into the grove of golden trees, out of the Dark Forest, and immediately cried with happiness. Her heart filled with peace. Her body and mind were healed with the magical wonders of the golden forest. She looked down at her arms and legs and watched them heal in seconds. Her large gashes closed, along with her tiny cuts and bruises. All that were left were the goosebumps caused by the cold night.

Amaryllis looked out from the Forest of Enchantment to the dark, foreboding trees where she had been surviving and chuckled nervously to herself, her goosebumps growing harder. What a truly horrible place it was. She had never fully comprehended how awful it was until she left it, until she had a moment to let her racing mind relax. Amaryllis allowed the magic of the Forest of Enchantment to take over her thoughts. The magic entered her brain and removed all of the negative energy then replaced it with positive energy. The depressing memory of the Choosing Ceremony was seen from a new perspective of happiness. The princesses bullying her was transformed into a simplified memory of teasing, and Amaryllis' general placement in life, where jealousy of others affected her, was changed into a memory of pure joy. The forest's magic temporarily erased each one of her bad memories and made Amaryllis feel a sense of euphoria. She smiled and allowed herself to fall slowly to the ground without tired, aching muscles. She crawled underneath the nearest willow tree with its beautiful leaves dangling to the rich, green grass. She allowed herself to fall into a deep, dream-filled slumber with an effortless grin on her face.

Chapter 18

Amaryllis' "death" was the most dramatic and depressing event to occur in Arlon for the longest time. It did not take long for the commoners of Arlon to discover what had happened, and the news was slowly spreading throughout the country, breaking the hearts of hundreds of families from all of the kingdoms who were quite fond of her, especially breaking the hearts of the ones who knew and loved her personally.

Amaryllis was under the impression that everyone disliked her, or envied her completely, but she never knew how many people loved her. The men adored her, and young girls too. Older women thought she was lovely. The only people who really disliked her were the women around her age. She never knew of the positive side since she was always surrounded by negativity.

Her funeral was held the night of her "death." Every king, queen, prince, and princess in Arlon attended her funeral, along with the maids, knights, doormen, and stable boys. Commoners were not allowed to attend since the location of her funeral was inside the castle gates, but they all laid flowers down at the foot of the gate in her honour and shared a few words of their own. Some cried hysterically. Amaryllis had shown a surprising amount of kindness to dozens among dozens of commoners. She had impacted their lives with genuine smiles, simple hello's, and even a few pieces of gold if the people looked desperate for it.

Her funeral was held at the tree line of the Dark Forest. Because they did not have her body, the king and queen asked for Prince James to scratch her name into the tree sticking the furthest out into the regular world to represent her bravery in the Dark Forest. The group collectively chose Prince James, because he was the one thing that Amaryllis loved with all of her heart, and he was the one who had seen her last. No one had seen her so happy about anything before.

He grabbed his dagger which was belted around his waist beneath his coat, and delicately scratched Amaryllis' name into the black tree. He struggled to perform this task because his hands shook and tears lightly streamed down his cheeks. He felt her death was completely his fault. All he wanted was for her to be alive and well, standing next to him asking why he was scratching her name into the tree in the first place. He would respond with something like, *Because, Amaryllis, I love you, and I want everyone to know it now, and everyone in future generations to know it as well.*

Instead of...

Because, Amaryllis...you're gone...dead...and I want everyone to remember you for your bravery. You're the only one in decades to enter this dreaded place.

Prince James needed to take a few moments in between each letter to breathe and calm himself down.

Laria was infuriated to see her prince crying over *Amaryllis*. After he finished carving Amaryllis' name, she waltzed up to Prince James and kissed him on the shoulder since she was too short to reach his face and because he would not bend down for her. The kings and queens almost said something out of anger, trying to protect the amount of respect shown for Princess Amaryllis' funeral, but then remembered that Prince James was never Amaryllis' to begin with. Their romance was unheard of until Prince James offered to go into the Dark Forest to search for her.

James pushed his fiancé off him then glared at his father, the King of Werling, with cold, icy blue eyes. The king looked down at the grass and sighed a shaken sigh, then lifted his head with a shake and cleared his throat. "May I please have everyone's attention?" he asked politely. The whole crowd nodded along. "My son never intended on choosing Princess Laria—" he paused to apologize to her, then kept speaking. He ignored her scoffs and questioning. "—James told me about Princess Amaryllis a few hours ago, telling me about how lovely she was and how he thought he was in love with her," the king looked glumly at his son. "But I told him that he was merely in love with her appearance, and I demanded that he stopped thinking about her for the Choosing Ceremony. I told him to choose Princess Laria because she seemed like she would know how to run a kingdom. After watching the princesses grow up over these past few years, I have noticed that Princess Laria has the personality traits of a queen: tenacious, bold, and determined. But after watching Princess Amaryllis run all over the palace and then directly into the Dark Forest, she showed me the most queen-like traits I have ever witnessed. Amaryllis was strong. She was a fighter and would never agree to something that she wouldn't want to do. She was wise, outsmarting all of us, and she made my son happy beyond words. Princess Amaryllis was the *most* fit to be queen in any kingdom. She would have excelled absolutely anywhere and I feel as if her death is my fault. I should have let my son choose the woman he wanted. If he had, then she never would have run away. And I am certain that no other princess here would have run into the Dark Forest to avoid marriage with the man they did not want to marry. All I wanted was for my son to carry on our kingdom successfully, and I thought to do so, he had to choose Princess Laria. So, I threatened James. I shall not say how, but I did and for that I am sorry."

Everything finally made sense to everyone, including Laria. She did not like the truth, not one bit.

Prince James sighed, ignoring his father's apology, thinking of how he wanted Amaryllis back. He wished he hadn't fallen victim to his father's threat and chose the right princess. If he were in the right state of mind, he would have hollered at him, arguing for hours until he had grown tired of it. He was too heartbroken to be truly upset with the King of Werling. But what would arguing have done? It would have released his inner tensions but it wouldn't bring his princess back to him.

The rest of the crowd had different reactions. Many kings and queens scoffed at the King of Werling for disturbing a blossoming romance, and the rest said nothing, appreciating his honesty.

"Things will never be the same, and I take full responsibility. This guilt will affect me for the rest of my life," he said glumly, looking at his son with eyes pleading for forgiveness, but James did not meet his father's gaze. He felt his cowardly stare, it seemed to fuel his anger. The longer his father waited to meet James' eyes, the angrier James became.

"I want to find her body," James finally said. "I'd rather have her buried here, than to rot away out in the open for monsters to devour her corpse," his voice weakened. "She deserves the best treatment in death since she was not treated well in life." The princesses gushed at the prince in his moment of determination. They wished they had someone as caring as him for themselves.

"I forbid you to enter," said the King of Arlon in a deep voice. The crowd of royals looked at the king in agreement. It was far too dangerous to enter the forest for a second time. He was lucky enough to survive the first run. The odds would not work in his favour twice, it was simply impossible.

"Why?" James questioned, with a simple frown made ominous under the moonlight.

"We've had enough royal deaths in my kingdom. One too many," The king affirmed, then marched away from the funeral like what he stated was final and there were to be no exceptions. Prince James stared into the Dark Forest, already deciding to disobey the king. He fought urges to break loose, to just sprint into the trees as the other royal subjects were still standing there watching him. He wouldn't run off until they had left.

The King of Werling put his hand on his son's shoulder. James turned away from the forest and pushed him off.

"This is all *your* doing," he stated angrily. The king ignored his son's accusation which in the king's mind seemed nearly accurate. Of course, there were other occurrences that drove her away. It couldn't have been all *his* fault.

"James, I have just apologized—"

"Well, thanks, Father. I suppose all is fine now that you've apologized!" James snapped, tears falling down his cheeks. He looked back to the forest, feeling his father's gaze on the back of his head.

"You will not be going in there. I don't care if you want to find your lover's corpse, you aren't going. There are three outcomes of you returning to that wretched place: one; you will die immediately upon entering; two; you will find her mutilated corpse—which I don't imagine you'd be able to bear—then die trying to carry it all the way back out; or three; you will manage to find her, and successfully carry her back, which is *impossible*. It is a suicidal mission that I forbid you from endeavouring. You must carry on with your life. Marry Princess Laria, and take over Werling. Move on and accept that what you had with Amaryllis was wonderful but it is over now. It's over."

James glared at his father with narrowed eyes as he listened. As the words left the king's mouth, James' wounds stung harder as if the pain in his father's words battled his physical pain.

"I must go in!" James said through heavy exhales of rage. "It's only right."

"You will do no such thing!" his father hollered. "Think of what Amaryllis would want...she would want you to be happy, not to grieve—"

"Amaryllis would *not* want me to marry Princess Laria, and frankly, neither do I," he whispered as Laria stood nearby. Then he stormed away from Amaryllis' memorial tree, deciding against running into the place of death. He was too destroyed by his loss to think clearly.

Chapter 19

Everyone in Arlon had horrible dreams that night, all except for Amaryllis. Kings and queens dreamed of their children being chased into the Dark Forest to their deaths by creatures they'd never seen before. Princes and princesses dreamed of Amaryllis all dead and decayed, sprinting out of the forest, barging into their rooms and scratching their eyes out. Meanwhile, Amaryllis dreamed of beautiful landscapes full of peaceful animals at rest. She slept tranquilly in the Forest of Enchantment, surrounded by the Dark Forest. Safety consumed her. She felt protected from the people *outside* the forest and from the monsters *within* the Dark Forest. The Forest of Enchantment was relatively small. It was about one quarter of the size of the meadow around the castle of Arlon and it was just enough space for her to be satisfied.

When morning came, Amaryllis awoke with a smile on her face. She sat up and stretched out her arms, leaning back to stretch her newly healed body. She jumped up with a strong sense of energy and immediately began exploring the magical place of wonder.

There was a pond in the centre with frogs resting on lily pads, a small oak sapling beside the pond, and a group of flat boulders in the far corner. The green grass was sprinkled in dew, and the land was covered in red and blue flowers. So much beauty was enclosed in such a small space. Amaryllis could live there forever.

She spun around in circles smiling to herself.

All was well until her mind snapped awake from its drunken happiness. Her euphoria faded abruptly. The radiant trees surrounding her seemed to arch forward, about to collapse on her all at once. All she heard was a light breeze whistling through her ears.

A shiver twisted down her spine as she felt a touch on her thigh; a warm, gentle touch. Someone, or something, placed a hand on her leg. She turned around with tense shoulders and a clenched jaw. Her heart pounded. Who ever was there, was going to—

Amaryllis met the eyes of a young girl around the age of five. Her hazel eyes shone with a glistening moisture as she was near an agonizing cry. Her lower lip quivered, and her face wore sheer terror. She gripped her white dress anxiously, twisting and puling the fabric as if trying to tear it off her body. Amaryllis' shoulders relaxed with a sigh of relief. It was only a girl. She had worried that she would turn to find a prince or a king standing behind her, ready to snatch her and drag her back to the castle.

Amaryllis knelt down to meet eye-level with the frightened child. "What is the matter?"

"Please, help me," she whispered, scanning her surroundings as if watching for something.

What could possibly be causing this little girl to be so afraid? She's in the enchanting forest.

"What could I help you with?" Amaryllis asked kindly, speaking slowly to avoid revealing her fear through a shaky voice. She patted the girl's back in an attempt to help calm her down. It had no effect. The little girl stared at Amaryllis, her hazel eyes growing darker with each second that passed.

"I'm lost," she sobbed. "I was in the scary forest for a long time, and then I found this place."

"I'm so sorry. How long were you there for?"

The little girl paused and looked away for a long time, as if the question angered her. She looked back slowly. "Two days." She looked down at her bare feet.

Amaryllis was skeptical, inching away from the child hesitantly. She focused on the girl's dress which had no missing pieces, tears, or even a mark of dirt on it. She looked at her bare legs to see smooth, ageless skin. Amaryllis was in the forest for *one* day and nearly died. Her dress was ripped to pieces and walking into the Forest of Enchantment did not mend it back to its original form. Either the little girl had the best luck in the universe or the forest's magic mended her dress and not Amaryllis', which seemed odd.

"Did you see any monsters?" Amaryllis asked calmly. "I've seen quite a few myself. They're awful…utterly horrendous. I hope they didn't scare you too m—"

The little girl started to wail, looking impatient. "*Please* help me!" she yelled in a pouty voice, her cheeks beginning to flush.

"I don't know what you want me to help you with," Amaryllis said firmly, watching the child cry with pity.

"My mom and dad taught me… secret things."

"Secret things?" Amaryllis scoffed.

"Yes… um, magic, but I'm not big enough to do it… you are." Her voice was calm now, and her red face faded back to pale in an instant.

"I still do not understand how I can help you," Amaryllis said, disregarding the word, *magic*.

"I don't know how to find my way home, but I can light my path with magic… well, *I* can't… if I was big enough I could."

"You want me to light your way home with *magic*? I don't understand how I'll be able to do that."

I thought magic was a myth. No one in any kingdom I know of speaks of it anymore, and how can I believe anything she's saying? She's a child.

"It's all in your hands," the little girl replied, reaching out to grab both of Amaryllis' hands. She let her little hands hold hers. "You don't know how to get magic, so I'll give you some."

The little girl held the backs of Amaryllis' hands, making her palms face the sky. Amaryllis watched her palms fill up with different colours of bright light: gold, silver, pink, purple and blue. It felt weightless and cold. She watched in amazement as actual, sparkling magic was in her grasp. The light sunk into her hands like rainwater into dirt. The magic illuminated her hands, all the way up to her forearms. Her arms glowed brightly.

Amaryllis studied the child more closely, looking for a sign or a symbol to indicate that she was not a human being. Perhaps she was the daughter of a witch, but she really did not know what she was. All she knew was that in her palms were sparkling, weightless gems of magic.

"Wow," Amaryllis whispered to herself, completely astonished. "What do I do now?"

The little girl smiled excitedly and pointed to the border of the Forest of Enchantment. "You have to point your hands to where the dark meets the light and go all around in a circle, then you have to aim the light in the middle of the light forest and make a line from the middle to the outside. It should keep going by itself, leading me… *home*."

Amaryllis stared at her hands then looked at the girl.

"Why do you need a *big* person to do this? It seems easy enough for you to be able to do it yourself."

The little girl smiled a wide smile with tiny baby teeth showing. She scrunched her nose. "Because the magic is strong, and I am not strong enough to hold it… I'm too *little*." The little girl stared at Amaryllis with pleading eyes. Amaryllis looked past the girl, looking at where the Dark Forest's boundaries were disrupted by the magic of the Forest of Enchantment. She then met the child's eyes which seemed lifeless and blank. "Do it. Please. I want to go home," the girl pleaded.

Amaryllis thought of the end result of leading this girl home, and out of the forest. She'd be able to live alone, isolated in a wonderful place where no one could bother her anymore. If Amaryllis was going to live in the Forest of Enchantment, she'd want to be alone. Besides, she'd be helping the strange little girl get home to her parents. She would no longer be her problem.

She lifted her arms and rotated her wrists to face her palms out to the trees. The bright, psychedelic light left her hands in a straight line, hitting the trees in a surge of power. She did as the little girl said, circling the perimeter of the "light forest." The magic left her hands in a powerful beam, creating resistance between her and the magic itself. She had to lean back slightly so as to not be pulled forward by the magic. She understood why the small child would not be able to undertake it. She did it quickly, drawing a line in the centre of the forest which directed the line out to illuminate a directional path. She didn't know how the light would know where to find the girl's parents, but she did not want to question *magic*.

As she was finishing the centre line, she looked at the little girl. Her eyes were wide, and a huge smile spread across her little face. She was giggling to herself, holding her stomach and looking to the sky. Her laughter didn't sound childlike at all, which disturbed Amaryllis, sending a jolting shiver down her spine.

The magic drained from her forearms to her hands until it was all gone. "Are you excited to go home?" Amaryllis asked as kindly as she could, ignoring the strange chuckling. She looked at what she had done to the forest and waited for the next portion of the spell to take place. The path didn't seem to be forming quite yet.

"Oh yes, yes, I am," the little girl said in a deep voice between laughs. She was sitting in a crouched position, hunched over. Amaryllis looked at her hands which no longer held magic, then looked at where she drew the line.

"Why isn't the path—?"

An unearthly, white lightning bolt struck the centre of the Forest of Enchantment, causing the ground to rumble. The forked surge of electricity nearly struck Amaryllis. She fled to the opposite corner, her heart pounding in her chest. She covered her ears as strong winds circled the area, strong enough to nearly lift her from the ground. She looked up at the blue sky which was being swallowed by a swirling mouth of black: a vortex. The vortex painted the sky a dark red hue then became covered in red clouds.

Amaryllis screamed as loud as she could overtop of the strong winds. "What's happening?" She looked through the hair that danced frantically in her face, at the little girl who did not look phased by the unnatural occurrences.

The little girl's eyes glowed yellow. Her dress stretched and ripped as her limbs grew longer and longer. Her short curly hair shrivelled up and fell from her scalp. Her flesh began to bubble as if it were under fire, burning through several layers of skin. Her skin was red and black with defined, masculine muscles showing through. The adorable face she once possessed distorted and formed into a frightening, abnormal face with an odd facial structure of high cheekbones and a long chin. It was as if she was struck by an arrow carrying a growth serum that simultaneously burned her to the bone, a horrible spell or an unearthly cancer that attacked her in a matter of seconds. Her skull showed in some areas on her head, along with some bone showing through the arms and legs. The thing laughed a deep, maniacal laugh, sending chills throughout Amaryllis' body. She fell to her knees in utter shock.

The Forest of Enchantment's barriers were eaten by the darkness of the Dark Forest, bringing back Amaryllis' deep gashes, cuts, and bruises. She felt the pain all over again and screamed in agony as her forgotten wounds were recreated. The Forest of Enchantment no longer existed, it was now a part of the Dark Forest! Amaryllis' heart lurched into her throat as she watched the magic disappear into thin air.

The red and black burnt giant walked over to Amaryllis, taking big thundering steps that shook the ground. The beast stood over her in silence until it yelled easily over the wind,

"Thank you for freeing me. It's been a long *two-thousand years!*" it chuckled in its thunderous voice, then shrunk down a few feet to be able to run stealthily through the Dark Forest.

Amaryllis was speechless. It was difficult to breathe. Her throat seemed to close tighter with each second that passed. Her chest hurt and her heart raced. She looked at her surroundings that once released actual happiness into its area but now blended in with the darkness that surrounded it. The red coloured clouds casted red light upon the trees, making the Dark Forest seem even more threatening than it was. She stood in silence, looking at what she had done.

Chapter 20

Two thousand years ago when the demon roamed the Earth freely, the world was an inhospitable place with petrifying creatures taking over each and every area. It was dark and somber, and too dangerous for people to thrive there. The people hid, dashing through the shadows of trees, never daring to venture out into the open plains. Only the strongest humans could survive.

A discovery was made: magic. It could be used to counteract the demon's wrath of destruction. Three brave men—sorcerers—who had made the discovery of light magic battled the great demon in a weeklong combat until they finally contained the devilish creature in a small area of purity. They had also managed to contain all of the demon's effects of evil, the monsters and the soul crushing aura the evil emitted, into the form of a widespread forest…the Dark Forest. The Dark Forest was the living works of the ancient demon. All of the Earth's evil was stored within those woods, magically held there by the barrier created by the sorcerers.

For two whole millenniums, the demon suffered. The area of purity—The Forest of Enchantment—became the demon's prison, bringing pain both physically and spiritually.

The demon laid angrily beneath the boulders, thinking of nothing. It had been trapped in the purest place on Earth for far too long. For the first five hundred years, the demon tirelessly attempted to destroy the barriers to free itself from its imprisonment, but to no avail. It was impossible. For the next five hundred years the demon attempted to morph into innocent creatures to try and walk out of the Forest of Enchantment in hopes of fooling the unseen entities of the Forest of Enchantment.

It could only be freed by the hands of an innocent and pure being withholding great amounts of power as the sorcerers believed it would be the safest way to ensure that the demon would never walk the earth again. They believed only someone so powerful and pure would not be able to be fooled by the cunning creature. So, for the thousand years after that, the demon knew it was trapped for eternity. Since the forest of enchantment constantly emitted golden magic from the trees, the demon could not kill itself, because it would be instantly healed every time. It was left to suffer despairingly for every second of every minute of every day…seven hundred and thirty-thousand days.

The demon was overwhelmingly relieved to see the first ever human to visit the Forest of Enchantment since the capture by the sorcerers: Amaryllis. She collapsed shortly after entering and the demon waited until sunrise to morph into a little girl with a plan to fool her into freeing it.

It successfully fooled the woman into destroying the light forest's barriers. The demon supplied its dark magic in her hands but since she was so pure the magic changed colours, hiding the evil. The demon was overjoyed and struggled to successfully hide its excitement, but its plan had worked and it brought the evil back into the world.

The Forest of Enchantment's magic also affected the barriers that separated the Dark Forest from the regular world, meaning the creatures from inside could roam wherever they pleased.

Chapter 21

I must go back, Amaryllis thought to herself, visualizing Arlon being attacked by dragons and princesses being spit on and eaten by shadow creatures. *I must return... to warn them... then I will fix this... somehow.*

The incident was too new for Amaryllis to be able to react in any form of guilt. This brought on an intense fear which led her to adopt a sense of protection that she wanted to bestow among the people of Arlon. She owed it to them.

Amaryllis sprinted through the forest with limited movement from her aching legs. She arrived in the meadow without being attacked by *any* creature. The monsters had already spread out and invaded the land which was once protected by the Forest of Enchantment.

She left the tree line of the Dark Forest, discouraged. The entire world was glowing red beneath the crimson clouds. All of the good in the world was non-existent, not hidden but truly gone. The meadow that once harnessed a peaceful energy, that cured Amaryllis' stress, now possessed a foreboding sensation. The tall grass looked like a hiding place to some lurking creature about to pop out. The flowers shrivelled, coiled into dead stems, and the sky itself amplified her fears with its dark red, abnormal colour. It was an evil sunset screaming with horror.

Amaryllis stopped running to catch her breath. The longer she stood still with the sound of silence penetrating her disturbed mind, the more the reality of her situation screamed—allowing her to begin to realize what had happened.

The goliath, cobblestone castle of Arlon was unaffected by dragons like how Amaryllis envisioned and she saw no dark creatures anywhere.

Once her breathing had slowed down slightly she took off running again straight towards Arlon. She made it to the doors and banged her fists loudly against the wood.

"Open the door!" she demanded. There was silence and then sudden whispers.

"Who is that?" whispered one doorman to the other, pressing his ear to the door.

"I don't know...her voice sounds so familiar."

Nothing happened. Amaryllis heard no more voices or motion from inside. She knocked again, but harder. "Please open the door! I must hurry," she whimpered. "Did you not feel the vibrations in the ground? Can you not see the fiery sky? Can you not sense the evil that surrounds us? I was the cause of it, and I need to inform everybody of the dangers." Amaryllis had just about enough of the stubborn doormen. Instead of letting them ask her thousands of questions she told them as much as she thought was necessary.

The doormen looked at each other skeptically. "Who is out there?" they asked, truly confused.

Amaryllis groaned. She did not think she would need to identify herself. She thought by now they would be able to recognize her voice since she was constantly in and out of the castle.

"Who do you think?" she asked impatiently. The doormen both had wide eyes.

"It can't be..." one of them whispered. The other doorman nodded. "Princess Amaryllis?" he shouted unsurely.

She rolled her eyes. "Wha—yes—of co—just open the door please!"

The doormen opened the door as quickly as they could. Amaryllis ran inside, running past the doormen saying, "Thank you!" as she passed them.

Her bare feet smacked against the floor during her sprint through the halls, echoing faintly in the colossal building. Assuming the royal subjects would be in the ballroom, that was where she ran.

Although she was only gone for two days and she felt as if she were gone for an eternity, it felt normal to be running around in the castle. She thought of what she would say as soon as she saw everyone. They could have believed she was dead, or perhaps it would be easier to assume she was gone forever, living in the Dark Forest like a fool, rejecting the royal life. They could live better with themselves assuming she was crazy and it would have been less of a loss.

Amaryllis was preparing herself to be greeted by angered kings, queens, princesses and princes, especially the Prince of Arlon since she put everyone through a frenzy just to avoid him. Then, Prince James entered her mind once again. She hoped to see him standing in the ballroom with an angry face, yelling at her. She preferred him to hate, and be angry with her for an eternity, than to be dead in the Dark Forest.

She reached the doors of the ballroom and pushed them open, barging into the room at full speed. The entire room filled with gasps, cries, and screams. Amaryllis had nearly forgotten about her appearance. Her skin was dirty and her hundreds of gashes were infected by dirt and forest slime. Her auburn hair was knotted, full of black twigs and pieces of dead leaves. Her dress was gone except for the top and sleeves. Her white underpants were stained with dirt and blood and her green eyes were wild. She looked like the undead.

Her parents were frozen, along with Prince James. They were motionless, as well as their minds, which were completely in shock. No one moved a muscle. They were petrified, thinking they were visited by her ghost. Amaryllis wondered why they were still in the ballroom. Perhaps trying to arrange marriage for Prince Eric... she did not know and that did not matter.

"I must—" she began,

"Amaryllis?" asked her mother in disbelief. Amaryllis looked at her mother, down at her gashed legs then back. Her body would never be the same again. Once the gashes healed, she would be scarred in hundreds of tiny lines all over her body.

"Yes—?"

The queen ran as fast as she could over to her daughter. She wanted to hug her but refrained, fighting every urge to wrap her arms around her because she did not want to harm her daughter. She did not want to put any pressure on her fresh wounds. The queen balled her eyes out, standing awkwardly in front of her unsure of what to do.

Amaryllis wrapped her arms around her mother and gritted her teeth through the pain, tears trickling down her cheeks as her wounds stung in an excruciating fire. The queen cried into Amaryllis' blood stained shoulder.

"I don't know what to say... I am SO incredibly happy that you're alive," she cried in a high pitched, shaky voice. The King of Serilion ran over and hugged his wife who was still holding onto their daughter. He said nothing and let his tears flow. The hug lasted a painfully long time and Amaryllis was finished with it after about ten-seconds. It became a distraction from what she had to do. She gently pushed her parents off of her and tried to speak again but was interrupted.

"Why go through all of *that* just to end up here again?" sneered the Prince of Arlon. The whole room glared at him. Prince James grunted and crossed his arms, then his heart melted and his knees wobbled as he looked back at Amaryllis. He was lightheaded, overjoyed beyond his own comprehension.

"I did not plan on returning," she snapped, looking harshly into Eric's smug eyes. "I came back to—"

"What happened to you? How are you alive?" asked the Prince of Herras. "You look awful."

Amaryllis crossed her arms, winced as her wounds touched, then placed her hands on her hips instead. "I survived the Dark Forest—"

The princess was interrupted by a room full of voices. The ballroom filled with mumbling and shouting.

"Stop!" she demanded, ignoring the hundreds of questions.

Prince James was the only silent person in the room, the noise around him was unnoticed. He heard nothing as he stared at the princess, afraid to approach her, not knowing what to say. Amaryllis was alive, and he was full of emotions.

"I'm sure you've noticed the red sky, the dramatic change in the environment... and a while ago you should have felt vibrations from the ground, yes?" Amaryllis asked.

"Yes, we've noticed. We are expecting a storm—" said the King of Arlon. He showed no concern for her return. She had ruined the tradition, causing a catastrophe in his kingdom.

"A storm? That's what you think this is? I am afraid to say it, but you are wrong. The storm you are expecting is a storm I suppose, but it's a storm of evil and has nothing to do with the environment. Something has been awakened and I was the one who did it. It was unintentional... I thought I was helping someone, but I was tricked. I came to inform you that I will need an army to accompany me to defeat this thing."

Amaryllis found she had risen above her shyness through her near death experience. Speaking in front of the people who frightened her away was a simple task. She felt as thought she was in control until the room exploded in fear.

"What are you talking about, Amaryllis?" asked the King of Arlon, his voice booming over the panicking crowd. Her parents looked at her in shock, holding each other for comfort.

"On my journey I encountered a magical place of protection which separated the Dark Forest from our world. I slept there and staying there healed my mental *and* physical wounds. When I awoke, a young girl approached me and she tricked me into destroying the barrier between the Dark Forest and the magical place in which I slept. Once I did, she transformed into… a demon I can only assume. Red clouds covered the blue sky, lightning struck the ground, and the barrier was broken. All of the creatures from within the Dark Forest are now able to enter our land. The enchanting forest protected all of us, and now dragons, shadow creatures, goblins, and spectres roam our land…we are in grave danger."

"How do you think you will go about solving this?" the King of Arlon asked angrily. "Do you think that a group of men will assist you in defeating that demon? No, I will not provide you with anyone… it's impossible. Mortal men of good cannot defeat one evil, omnipotent *demon*… and *you* cannot defeat it yourself."

"I am not asking for your opinion," Amaryllis snapped, "I am asking for a group of men brave enough to join me in a quest to restore the good in this world and the magic I never knew we had."

"Magic does not exist! It is a myth!" the King of Arlon scoffed.

"That is what I thought as well, but it is without a doubt, *real*. I have seen it."

"You are beginning to sound like Akar," he mumbled.

Amaryllis paused. "Who is Akar?" she asked calmly.

The king glanced at his wife to see her shaking her head as if disapproving of him providing her with the answer. "A man I jailed twenty years ago," he said anyway, "he is in the cellar. He claims to be a sorcerer." The Queen of Arlon sighed at her husband.

"I would like to meet him. He could teach me how to use magic against the demon since I don't seem to be getting any help from *anyone*," she grunted, looking around the room at all of the princes, kings, and knights. Her heart skipped a beat when finding Prince James. He was cut up as well but he looked much better than Amaryllis, much more *alive*. She was suddenly at peace to see him. She forgot about her anger and her confusion since everything seemed to make perfect sense as she simply looked at him.

"James?" she asked softly. The whole room followed Amaryllis' gaze as she looked at him. He approached her slowly and shook his head when he was close to her.

"I-I cannot believe you are here. Please don't leave again," he pleaded, fighting tears. The rest of the crowd did not matter. They seemed to have disappeared, along with their piercing stares. Amaryllis was his world and she was all he could see.

"But it is what I must do, James," she stated nervously, looking at the King of Arlon to see if he was leaving to bring the sorcerer. He was not moving at all. He stared at James as she spoke to him.

"Look at you, Amaryllis. You need time to heal. To rest," he urged, lightly brushing a cut on her wrist. "You must be in so much pain," he exclaimed. He looked at her with the smallest, sad grin on his face, "I want to correct my future and arrange a marriage with the right princess. It is what must be done immediately," he spoke softly, moving his hand from her wrist to hold her hand. She squeezed it then wiggled her hand free.

"I want to marry you... it is what I desire, James, more than anything, but I must fix what I have done." It pained her to push him away again, but she had to do what was right. "Will you help me defeat it?" she asked, ignoring her feelings.

"Yes of c—" he began,

"Actually no," she interrupted. "I would prefer for you to stay here. Don't come at all."

"What? No, Amaryllis, please let me help you. I couldn't live with myself if something happened to you. I wanted to die when you were thrown by those dark creatures. Your body looked so lifeless and limp. It was horrifying," he whispered.

"I want you to stay here and protect my mother, father, and everyone else... even Laria." Amaryllis said, glancing over at Laria who stared back at her with a disturbingly angry look on her face.

"But I want to be there to protect *you*," he said stubbornly.

"No, James, if something happens to me, then that is the way it must be. Everything happens for a reason. Freeing this demon was... *meant* to happen, you choosing Laria was meant to happen. Hell, being tormented for nearly my entire adolescence was meant to happen. I am who I am because of it. James, I don't think that now is my time to die. My life is just beginning. I won't let anything happen to me, I shall fix my mistake and restore the barrier. If I must die doing so, then that is the way it will be... as long as I save the people of the world from evil." She backed away from Prince James, meaning every world. Of course she would fight her hardest, think as wisely as possible to make the correct decisions and push her tiredness to her very limit of exhaustion to get closer and closer each day, but death didn't frighten her. Surviving wasn't her main objective. Restoring the world was. If her death was what saved the world then that was perfectly all right with her.

He chased her and reached for her hand, but she jerked it away.

"Bring Akar to me," she ordered the King of Arlon. Prince James' world expanded and the people in the room could be seen again. Amaryllis was crushing his heart in her hand.

"If that is what you desire..." the king mumbled like her decision was foolish. "Bring me Akar!" he shouted at the knights standing against the wall. They jolted as his loud voice startled them, they nodded, then jogged out of the room with rattling armour. The king never believed in Amaryllis. He was eager for her to begin her quest so she could *die* and stop causing problems in his kingdom. He was already prepared for ruling his kingdom in a land of red surroundings. He was planning on how to defeat different creatures, and thinking about what defensive strategies he'd have to conjure up to guard his castle. He had never seen a dragon before, a ghost, a goblin or a shadow creature, but he was ready to prepare different strategies to keep them away from his castle. He was a sneaky, ruthless, and heartless king. He cared not for the commoners and that was *one* of his greatest flaws.

"If what you want is to do this alone, then I will leave you be," James said sincerely although it pained him. He hardly believed what he was saying as he spoke. "I will protect everyone... for you."

Amaryllis grabbed his hands and rested her forehead on his shoulder. She would have wrapped her arms around him in a loving embrace, but the pain from her wounds was far too excruciating. Laria stared in frustration. She knew Prince James did not love her and that everyone was in support of Amaryllis and James' relationship. She was not. She was jealous, and it was then that she could finally admit her envy to only herself

Prince James squeezed Amaryllis' hands and rested his head on top of hers. The crowd kept their "awes" to themselves and watched the young couple in amazement. The kings and queens who strongly believed in the annual tradition of introduced love felt warmth in their hearts. It had brought love to themselves, and it was bringing love to the next generation. Being in the room with Amaryllis gave her mother and father a strong sense of pride and joy, along with James' father who was one of the happiest people in the room. To know she was not dead at his hands relieved him greatly.

Prince James and Princess Amaryllis embraced their moment together for as long as possible. They stood with their hands clasped, their eyes closed and their heads resting on each other. She desperately wanted to wrap her arms around him in a comforting hug as love overcame her with feelings of euphoria. She wanted to get as close to him as possible, to simply ignore the pain, but it would hurt too much. Amaryllis wished they had their own space as she could feel everyone staring, but Prince James did not care, as long as he had Amaryllis with him he couldn't be happier or more in love.

"Promise me, you'll return," he pleaded.

Amaryllis smiled. "I cannot promise you that, but I will always be thinking of you…always."

"I know you probably don't want to come back because everyone was so cruel to you, and you probably have no pleasant memories here. Being away in the most horrible place on Earth gave you freedom, and must have allowed you to feel grateful to be out of this kingdom. But I promise, if you come back to me I will make you the happiest woman in history, and you will make me the happiest man just by being here."

Amaryllis smiled wider and sighed, overwhelmed with emotion. "All right then, I promise you, Prince James… I will return to you."

James smiled for a moment, then it faded when he pictured Amaryllis on her journey—walking through groves of twisted trees, running from unearthly beings, and screaming to release the tension caused by her terror.

Their moment of affection was interrupted by the ballroom doors slamming. Amaryllis lifted her head from James' shoulder and let go of his hands. An emaciated, short, bearded man stood at the doors with his hands tied behind his back, held by two knights.

"Who is Princess Amaryllis?" he asked in a groggy voice, looking lazily around the room. He wore nothing but a blue cape, and brown, cotton pants.

"I am Princess Amaryllis," she answered. The man smiled, revealing worn down, yellow teeth. The room was skeptical of Akar except for Amaryllis. She believed that he would be an advocate to her success in defeating the demon. She ignored his ridiculous appearance, while his appearance was what every other person in the room focused on.

"Well, I look forward to speaking with you," he grumbled, after clearing his throat full of phlegm.

"As do I."

The King of Arlon stared at Akar in disgust, then at Amaryllis in disbelief.

Amaryllis led the knights holding Akar to an arbitrary room in the castle, away from the ballroom. They entered a sitting room and settled there. Akar sat down with his hands still tied, looked at the knights who guarded the door behind him, then he looked at Amaryllis who sat with her hands folded.

"It has come to my understanding that you have some questions about magic?" he asked with a grin. "I have been practicing for fifty years and know all of its laws… which there are hardly any of. Magic tends to break the laws… in good ways; however it can be used for bad things."

"Yes, of course. I do not have a lot of time, but I must learn about magic urgently. I need to use it in ways to defend myself and to inflict harm upon dark creatures—"

"Ohhh…" he began, with a sinister tone in his voice. He looked out the window and shivered at the sight of the red clouds. "…you've released Immortuos, haven't you?" he whispered, as if saying *Immortuos* was frowned upon. Akar's nervous voice sent chills throughout Amaryllis. Her heart began to pound hard in her chest.

"Immortuos?"

"Yes, Immortuos: the demon of the dark, the most ruthless entity to exist," he said cautiously, looking directly into her eyes.

Amaryllis' heart skipped a beat. She felt a wave of guilt course through her.

"I suppose I did," she said weakly, tears welling in her eyes. She looked up at the ceiling and tried to blink her tears away, but they would not stop flowing. Her throat swelled and it was difficult to breathe, difficult to swallow. She pictured Immortuos standing before her, laughing. Laughing at her stupidity and how easy it must have been to fool her.

"He—"

"He? Oh no-no, Immortuos is not a *he*. Nor is Immortuos a *she*. Immortuos has never walked the Earth in human form, taking no particular gender, having never lived as a human being. It came to be through unknown ways, born in a malicious realm completely unheard of as to where it is. *I don't even know where it is. The only thing I know is that it is a place far worse than any place ever dreamed of in anyone's worst nightmare.*"

Amaryllis sat uncomfortably in her chair, having to slump down as the weight of the information compressed her into a tiny, trembling ball. Her stomach cramped in an excruciating pain beyond the discomfort of anxiety.

"Well, then, *it*—"

"Shape-shifted? Morphed into something to trick you? Yes, Immortuos has had *lots* of time to practice that. You found the enchanted forest then?"

This man knows exactly what he's talking about.

"Yes I did, but it no longer exists... I—"

"Destroyed it, I know," Akar interrupted. "Immortuos was placed there by three sorcerers thousands of years ago. The entire world used to be a dark and gloomy place until the evil was contained in the forest in Arlon which has been named 'the Dark Forest.' They placed Immortuos in a pure place surrounded by evil to taunt it. Well, surrounded by evil because there was no other place to put it. The evil could not be utterly banished for it is *impossible* to completely destroy it. As long as Immortuos is, I suppose, *existing*, evil will never die. It could not escape the torture, because only a pure and innocent person could free it... and that person was you."

Amaryllis slumped in her seat, still struggling to breathe.

"The world you see before you is what the world used to look like centuries ago when Immortuos was actively terrorizing people," he explained.

"I know you don't mean to upset me, but I already have enough guilt on my shoulders, and you're simply making my anxieties worse. Just teach me magic please, so I can leave and try to solve this," she sighed, struggling to hide her sadness.

"Well, there isn't enough time to make you powerful enough to restore the barrier. There is no hope there. You'll have to restore the barrier by *killing* Immortuos which will be terribly difficult since it is immortal, but every evil source or entity has a weakness. I don't know what it would be but I pray that you will discover it."

Amaryllis was overwhelmed with information. The fact that she had released the culprit of evil back into the world destroyed her. It all seemed painfully impossible.

"If you had to guess, what would the weakness be?" she asked.

"Well, obviously something to do with purity. It was tortured in the enchanted forest, but since there is no place like that to exist anymore, you'll have to attack Immortuos with an overload of handheld golden magic, or just kill it by… NO! You must coat your weapons in golden magic, and use that to kill it. That seems as if it could work!" he screamed excitedly, startling Amaryllis. "Enough talking, I must teach you!" He stood up and went to hold his arms out wide above his head, but the ropes around his wrists stopped him. He looked at the knights ferociously. "How am I supposed to help this princess potentially save the world if my hands are TIED?" he bellowed. Amaryllis stood up and held her hand up to stop the knights from grabbing the deranged man. She nodded, untying him would be all right.

"Please untie him," she ordered. The knights thought Akar was the biggest threat in the castle and did not want to free his hands but did as they were instructed. They feared him to be an unpredictable psychopath. Akar rubbed his wrists. He moaned as he did so.

"My hands—ow-ow. I have been in chains against a wall for twenty years," he groaned.

"Why were you imprisoned?" she asked. She did not fear him like others did, she found him interesting to watch. Amaryllis studied him.

Akar looked at her blankly. "I don't know any more than you. A man showed up to my door one day and brought me to the king. I was thrown in the Arlon cellar. I don't think the king liked me practicing magic instead of working," he giggled to himself. "You see, I was originally a blacksmith—enough about that! I will teach you some things and send you on your way."

Akar was indeed an interesting man. He was very skittish, yet bold. Intelligent, yet dim, and was very scatterbrained.

He stood up from his seat and grabbed Amaryllis by the arm, not paying attention to where her gashes were. She yelped in pain but he didn't hear it over his own excitement. His grip tightened to pull her along. The knights raised their swords and started marching towards Akar.

"It's fine," Amaryllis said under her breath. The knights backed away and watched Akar drag Princess Amaryllis to the back of the room where he let go of her to grab the wooden table against the wall. He slammed his palms down making a loud, hollow sound. Amaryllis looked at her arm and payed no attention to Akar quite yet. She rotated her arm to check her wounds to make sure they were not bleeding. He slammed his hands down again. Amaryllis looked up from her arm once she was done examining it.

Smack.

"What are you doing?" she snapped.

He looked at her as if she were an idiot and shook his head. "Just wait," he laughed. He slammed his hands down again, looking like a toddler throwing a fit. Suddenly, sparks flew up from the table from beneath his bony hands. Amaryllis leaned forward, astounded.

Smack. Fire ignited in his palms lighting up the curtain-closed room. His pale grey eyes looked into his creation, then at Amaryllis.

"You're going to teach me how to spark and hold onto fire?" Amaryllis questioned.

Akar smirked. "Yes, Amaryllis, all magic is in effect once you conquer your communication with the stars," he snickered.

"Communication with the stars?" she asked skeptically with a raised brow.

"Yes, the stars—the cosmos… do you really believe that the *Earth* supplies magic? NO, of course it doesn't. There are so many wonders in the universe that our ancestors were wise enough to discover and I thank them for it. My dear, magic comes from the entire universe, and once you learn how to communicate with it, you'll be a-uh-uh-an enchantress!"

"Communicating with the stars…" she repeated. "…that sounds absolutely wonderful." Amaryllis pictured herself standing in an open field during the night with no clouds in the sky to reveal the shining stars in the galaxy. She held her arms out wide, and the stars fell from the sky and into the Earth's atmosphere, rushing past her, then flying above her to drop into the ground. The stars then circled her, lifted her up, and carried her into space. They formed a path in the dark atmosphere, making the starry path appear more magical. Amaryllis weightlessly walked on it with a chill of excitement crawling down her spine, giving her goosebumps outside of her daydream. In her mind, space was frigid yet warm enough to enjoy herself—

Amaryllis' green eyes glowed a bright turquoise colour for a moment, startling Akar. He yelped, snapping Amaryllis from her daydream.

"You were doing it just now! How did you do that? I've taught you nothing yet!" he stammered.

"What was I doing?" she asked, truly clueless of what he was talking about. She was simply imagining herself—

"Your eyes... they were *glowing*! You were *communicating* and the universe's light was shining through your eyes!" he screamed. He was pacing in the room, putting his hands on his head. "Even I have not been able to do that! And I've been practicing for years. YOU BARELY EVEN STARTED YOUR LESSON!"

Amaryllis stared at him in shock.

"Are-are you *testing* me? Are you a witch? Have you practiced magic before? How *old* are you—"

Amaryllis slammed her fist down onto the table, silencing him. He looked to see if she made any sparks, but she had not. "I am not *testing* you. I don't know how I could have been communicating. I've never done it before and I don't know how to do it. I was simply daydreaming." She spoke monotonously to hide her irritation with Akar, who was acting too rambunctious for her liking.

Akar chuckled nervously. "I really doubt that. Vivid imaginations and communication with the cosmos are completely separate things. You were not daydreaming, you *were* communicating. The universe was present within you for just a moment. If I teach you all that I know, you will become so-so-SO powerful," he cheered, patting her hand. "You *will* defeat Immortuos."

Amaryllis sighed in vexation, still not understanding the concept of being able to communicate with stars, but she was relieved that someone finally believed that she could fix what she had done. Akar was the only person to show acceptance, not skepticism like the others did. The royal subjects wore faces of terror while Akar only expressed determination.

"I need to learn just a few things. I need to solve this now and don't have time to be completely educated. Maybe just teach me how to hold fi—"

"I will teach you what you will *need* to know but I expect—actually—I demand for you to return alive so you can understand your full potential. I want to teach you everything... sorcerers all over the world would be envious of your abilities… you don't even understand."

Amaryllis was amazed with this new information, and she was happy with herself for subconsciously understanding the ways of magic. She was exposed to a whole new world that existed upon her own, it was wonderful. "Yes, just please teach me *something* so I can be on my way."

"Of course, of course." He waved a hand in the air and magically opened the curtains, letting in red light.

Chapter 22

"Oh my," he said darkly, putting his hands to his face as he peered outside.

"What is it?" Amaryllis asked, walking over to look out the window. She stared at what stood outside.

"Immortuos formed a lair," Akar muttered. Several miles away beyond the Dark Forest, stood a gigantic, rocky mountain built magically by the demon's uprising. It was strangely shaped with defined jagged edges. A moat of lava surrounded the mountain. "That is where it currently resides."

The mountain was menacing, giving anyone who looked at it a feeling of utter terror. The shape was truly disturbing because of its unnatural appearance, and the red sky provided it with an additional look of hellishness.

Amaryllis finally understood what was happening. She finally felt in the moment, holding her stomach to ease her anxiety. The realization that it was she who had to destroy an omnipotent demon to save mankind made the world spin. Everything around her was unclear, all except for Immortuos' lair which seemed to taunt her from its great distance away.

She did not want to begin her quest, instead she wanted everything to return to normal. Sure, she and Prince James were closer than ever before, but she'd rather be trapped in Arlon with Prince Eric than to be living in the current time of hell on Earth.

Prince Eric revolted her, but everything in Amaryllis' life was getting worse and worse. Her solutions were becoming issues and there seemed to be no escape, but she tried.

Amaryllis looked away from the mountain. "Teach me something, now!" She had no time left for kindness. The world wanted a battle and Amaryllis was ready for war. The winner earned freedom.

Akar smiled. "I admire your enthusiasm in a time such as this," he stared at Amaryllis' legs until she felt nothing beneath her. She looked down and noticed how much higher she was from the ground. She was levitating. "Telekinesis—it should be easy for you to master since your communication is so strong." Akar looked at Amaryllis, who looked ten feet tall from where she floated in the air. He was pleased with himself for being able to use telekinesis quite well, considering his involuntary, twenty year break from magic.

"Put me down and teach me something. All you've done is shown me how *you* can perform magic… *I* need to learn…*I* am the one fighting Immortuos."

"Yes, yes, of course. I am sorry. I have never actually taught magic to anyone before. Everyone assumes you are crazy when you explain that you're practicing it, and you are the only one who believes me… ha ha… sorry. I don't know what to do." He lowered Amaryllis back to the ground in fear of her angry face.

She recognized his fright and took a deep breath. "Telekinesis… how do you do it?" she asked gently.

"Like everything, you communicate with the universe; concentrate on what or who you want to move, and in what way you want it to move. Do you want this thing to change locations? To explode, implode, crush, stretch? You must feel what this thing is touching, breathe the air it's breathing, feel the ground it stands on—" he paused to look for an object in the room, "—yes, remove the cushioned seat from the chair," he suggested.

Feel what the chair is touching... understand its surroundings... breathe the air it's breathing?

Amaryllis stared at the red and gold floral chair cushion. She imagined what the weight of each individual feather that stuffed it was like. She felt the stitching, the texture of the fabric. She felt the gravity that kept it rested on the wooden chair. Amaryllis felt everything surrounding the chair cushion, staring at it. Her body felt full of a cold energy. She stared until the cushion rose from the chair. It dropped when she snapped from her focus.

"I did it," she stated, then she smiled and repeated herself. "I *did* it!" she laughed, running her fingers through her hair.

Akar rolled his eyes, tuning out her excitement. "That was nothing. Are you going to defeat Immortuos by lifting cushions from its chairs? Next, I want you to remove the *paint* from the chair," he smirked.

"Remove the paint from the chair?" she repeated, feeling the request was absolutely ridiculous.

"Yes, the coating... *remove* it."

Amaryllis ignored her doubtful thoughts and completed the same process of concentration. It was magic she was dealing with, nothing was impossible. After a minute of staring, she removed the dark brown colouring from the pale wooden chair. It floated in a gaseous pigment. She did not lose focus but waited for the next instruction. It wasn't any more difficult than lifting the cushion.

"Paint the chair," he ordered. Amaryllis pushed the pigment onto the chair, returning it to its original form. "Now, was that difficult for you?" he asked seriously.

Amaryllis shook her head. "It was... not terribly difficult."

Akar giggled to himself having too much fun watching a *princess,* the type of which he believed are egotistical and closed-minded, perform magic that took him months to discover. He looked at her in bewilderment. No such princess should exist in this world. She was too unique. With Akar having no filter, he asked, "Why are you this way?"

Amaryllis took his question as a compliment, but he was asking out of true confusion. "Thank you?" she chuckled as if confused by his absurd wonderings. He was a crazy old man after all.

Akar shook his hands in her face. "No-no-no! Women such as yourself simply do not exist, especially a woman being a princess."

"I don't understand," her laughter had halted in an instant.

"No-one of your authority would have had the bravery to encounter the most dangerous demon in existence, come back to the castle and ask for an *army* rather than to ask for protection, and offer *yourself* to defeat it. And NO-ONE would be so open-minded to something as unheard of as magic… I don't understand, so please tell me why are you the way that you are?"

"Why am I so open-minded? Well, I have been through so much, and I believe that everything should be better eventually. Enough about me, I must leave," Amaryllis said before walking out of the room. She had forgotten to thank him. Once she left, the knights tied Akar back up, and he did not resist. He was powerful enough to kill everyone in the castle and escape; however, he did not. The knights led him back to the wall in the cellar where he was chained, and left slamming the door. The half-hour of magic was enough to keep him mentally entertained for another few years.

Amaryllis returned to the ballroom, greeted by stares of scepticism. Prince James ran up to her and held her hands.

"Did you learn magic?"

Amaryllis was filled with sudden amazement as she realized what she had done. "Yes, I certainly did!" She let go of his hands and pointed at the chandelier above them. "I could make this move if I wanted to!" She pointed at the curtains by the gigantic window. "I can remove the dye from those curtains too."

James looked at her with pity. How were any of those abilities going to help her on her deadly journey? But she looked so hopeful, so ready to tackle the problems before her, so he said nothing.

"Everyone," she began, earning everyone's attention, "I have learned many things about magic that I will utilize in defeating the demon of the dark, Immortuos." Her audience shivered at the mentioning of the demon's name: the demon of the dark... *Immortuos.* "I shall be on my way."

Prince James stared at her knowing she would not allow him to travel with her if he volunteered to join her. He focused on her lips as she spoke. Princess Amaryllis gazed around the quiet, motionless room. Feeling the silence of the room as her cue to leave, she turned to go, before being grabbed by Prince James.

Please don't go, he wanted to say, but did not. He could not think of anything to tell her, all he could do was stare. He wanted her to stay in the castle, to be safe with him and to let someone else resolve the worldly, evil issue. James believed in her abilities, she amazed him; however, her quest was unimaginably threatening. She was destined to die by heading into those woods again, and if she survived the demon would be the next thing to kill her.

Amaryllis brushed his arm off of her, looking into his pleading eyes. He did not have to say a word, she knew what he wanted to say, what he was keeping inside. She walked to the door fighting the sadness from deep inside of her, not even saying goodbye. She avoided hugging him because it would have made her want to stay. To the others in the room, she looked like a coldhearted witch.

The Queen of Serilion chased after her daughter and met her at the door.

"You're returning to the woods like that?" she whispered pointing at her mutilated legs. Amaryllis shook her head in annoyance. She just needed to leave and it seemed nearly impossible to do so. Everyone wanted to stop her. She jolted suddenly as the queen wrapped her arms around Amaryllis in a loving embrace. The hug magnified Amaryllis' appearance as a coldhearted witch because she hardly hugged her mother back.

"I'll go to the dressing room before I leave," she muttered, lightly pushing the queen off of her. Amaryllis wanted no emotions to be affecting her on her journey. She needed to keep her mind only on sheer survival and strategy. Her loved ones were making it difficult for her to push her emotions away, but she managed a stern expression and tearless eyes. She could present herself as focused, when on the inside she was fighting a battle within herself. The logical side of her wanted her to stay in the castle but her daring side forced her to leave, and her guilt contributed to her motivation to venture off.

She left the ballroom, feeling a strange sensation as dozens of eyes were fixated on the back of her head. She stormed into the hallway, leaving the royal subjects feeling rather cross. They simply did not understand why she had to leave. She had only just returned from the Dark Forest and already she was leaving again? They too were in shock, too bewildered by the new, red-coloured world to accept her decision. While they viewed the new world as dangerous, it only reminded Amaryllis that the new world crawling with devilish beings was all her fault.

Amaryllis opened the door to the dressing room, scoffing at the girly frills full of expensive gowns and makeup. She stood in the door frame for half a second before spinning around, closing the door behind her.

None of this will help me whatsoever.

Amaryllis stormed to the men's dressing room, which consisted of armour, swords, towels and water for wounds, and cotton and fleece clothing. She reached for the smallest stack of clothes and unfolded a long sleeved, beige shirt. She ripped the remaining piece of her dress off of her body with an effortless pull and threw the beige shirt on. She put on matching beige pants made from the same cotton material. The clothing fit her surprisingly well.

The armour was difficult to put on but she managed to find the smallest suit and fit inside of it decently. Her movement was limited, but it was worth it for protection. She practiced sprinting from one side of the room to the other finding the armour to be quite light in weight.

The only thing she lacked was a helmet. They were all too heavy for her neck and shoulders so she went without one. Before leaving, she grabbed a small diamond encrusted sword.

Amaryllis greeted the doormen dressed in her manly ensemble, looking perfectly eligible to wear what the men wore with her austere appearance.

"Where are you going now?" they asked curiously. This time, the many questions that followed after, did not bother her. She smiled at them, looking feminine and beautiful in armour and men's clothing.

"I am leaving to kill the demon of the dark…the culprit of the red sky, and the release of evil creatures."

"Well, wouldn't that be you then?" one of them teased. They hadn't looked outside to see the sinister landscape; therefore were oblivious to the seriousness of what had happened. Amaryllis laughed softly to herself, seeing through her serious approach to her journey for a moment, then her chuckles stopped abruptly.

"You did tell us it was your fault!" the doorman pointed out, trying to lighten the mood. The look of defeat on her face allowed him to sense her troubles.

"It *was* my fault," she mumbled, looking at the ceiling impatiently. There was an awkward silence and the doorman had no more jokes to ease the tension. He looked at the other doorman and with a simultaneous nod they opened the door as quickly as possible.

"Thank you," she barked, gripping her sword tightly.

"Good luck to you. I know you will fix things," the doorman promised. Amaryllis nodded and started walking to the meadow.

"Hey!" shouted a voice from behind her. She turned to see a stable boy. It was the sarcastic one…Charles. He walked up to her leaving the blueish grey horse he was tending to, the one she selected for her horse riding activity, in the stable. "You did this, eh?" he asked looking up at the bloody sky.

Amaryllis nodded.

"Doesn't surprise me."

Amaryllis didn't take offence to his comment but she waited for another insult. "Is that all?" she asked, studying his face, which was painted red from the sun peering through the red clouds. He always made the same facial expression which was *unimpressed*, but he looked concerned all of a sudden.

"No, Princess, I only came over to insult your clumsiness—" he began, then shook his head. It was almost impossible for his mouth to release anything other than sarcasm or rudeness. She normally found it funny, but not then. Amaryllis looked to the Dark Forest impatiently. "—I mean… no, I was going to offer you a ride," he admitted, pointing to the blueish grey horse.

Amaryllis forced a smile. "That's very kind of you, but there's a high chance he will be severely injured or killed and I don't want that. I don't want to be riding him when he gets attacked by a shadow creature or a dragon!"

Charles disregarded everything she said once she said the word *dragon*. "Dragons don't ex—"

"Yes, they do. And so does magic. I can prove it to you, but not now. Anyway, thank you, but no thanks."

"Well, how about Ronnie?"

"Ronnie?"

"He's insanely stubborn. He'll get you to the tree line, then throw you… make your trip to the Dark Forest a little shorter," Charles said with a smirk. "And if he's behaving *decently*, he may go into the woods and help you out. You'll save a lot of energy. And if something gets him, so what? He's a dimwit."

Amaryllis ignored the implication of the death of Ronnie and considered taking a horse to hurry her journey to Immortuos's lair. Walking would take weeks. "I'll take a horse, but not Ronnie or the blue one," she stated.

"I do recommend Ezro actually. He's the fastest and most obedient. If he does die, think of it as a sacrifice for our safety," Charles said shrugging his shoulders. "It's just a horse after all."

"Why are you a stable boy? You seem to hate horses."

"Well, Princess, I am merely being realistic. I am getting him for you," he declared, running to the stable. He returned in an instant with Ezro, who was equipped with brown leather horse armour and a black leather saddle with red reins.

"That's why you're a stable boy," she exclaimed, impressed at the short amount of time it took to prepare Ezro for riding.

"You'll take him then?" he asked.

Amaryllis mounted the blue horse, her armour rattling. "I shall take him. Thank you, Charles." She began leading Ezro into a gallop towards the Dark Forest. She did not want to delay her journey any longer.

Although Amaryllis did not want to take her favourite blue horse into the Dark Forest, Charles convinced her that it was a wise decision. It was truly idiotic to think she could travel efficiently on foot. Surely taking Ezro would put him at risk, but the risk was worth taking. If Ezro was killed and Amaryllis made it to the lair, it would be because of Ezro, which would make him a sacrifice for the good of the world.

Charles grinned as he watched Amaryllis get closer and closer to the place he feared most. He was glad to have provided her with Arlon's most noble steed, anything to help her restore Earth. The new world which he desperately felt he needed to escape from, petrified him immensely. However, as he completely realized where she was heading, his small grin—caused from the good deed of helping the princess—vanished. He thought he could faintly hear the forest's nightmarish melodies. As they played through his mind, his body tensed. He froze in fear, watching Amaryllis disappear as she rode into the forest.

Chapter 23

Amaryllis had already been in and out of the Dark Forest once, but it was just as frightening to enter for the second time. Although the darkness had spread and the border was non-existent, it still had a strong effect on those who crossed.

A sick feeling inhabited the pit of Amaryllis' stomach as she entered the birthplace of evil, and as obedient and brave as Ezro was, he couldn't help but stand on his hind legs and whinny. The unseen, horror-afflicting energy affected him too. Amaryllis squeezed with her legs and held the reins to keep herself from falling.

"It's all right, it's all right!" she quivered, trying to speak as calmly as possible, over and over until he calmed himself down. Once he dropped back down on all fours, Amaryllis squeezed her legs against his ribs to introduce a trot. Galloping in a forest without trails was as foolish as sailing a ship in a storm. Eventually, the horse would run full speed into a trench or run just beneath a tree to have Amaryllis knocked off by a low hanging branch, just like how the ship would have been swallowed by a wave, or knocked over by strong winds.

She kept Ezro moving slowly to be able to intently watch for danger: for herself and for Ezro. She felt safer with her armour and with Ezro elevating her from the ground. The sounds weren't as loud and didn't have as much diversity in terms of the overall noise.

The music was a consistent, low hum, as apposed to screeches, roars, screams, clicking sounds, and other unknown noises. It was still disturbing, very noticeable, but compared to the last time Amaryllis was there it was wonderful to hear.

Ezro had finally adjusted to the forest's energy. Even though the discomforting feeling spread beyond the forest, it was stronger in the Dark Forest as it was the heart of Immortuos' wrath, containing its vigorous energy. He whinnied occasionally, sounding afraid, but his loyalty kept them moving in the right direction. Any other horse wouldn't have lasted as long as Ezro, their fear would be too strong taking over their minds and naturally leading them away. They certainly wouldn't have entered in the first place, and Ronnie would have thrown Amaryllis for *sure*.

"You're riding wonderfully," Amaryllis told Ezro. His ears flipped back to listen as she spoke, then forward when she was finished. "Hopefully Charles fed you before this because we will not be stopping for quite awhile. I'll need to make sure to find a safe place to rest or else we'll be in trouble when night falls," she said softly, leaning forward. She felt that if she spoke too loud, then creatures would emerge. She feared the monsters were waiting for her to summon them with a noise just loud enough for them to find out where she was. Ezro nickered.

The Dark Forest wouldn't have seemed so unsettling if Ezro stopped looking from side to side. Amaryllis tried to calm him down by speaking to him, and even though he listened, he was still alert. It frightened her to see an animal activated by its survival instincts. "It's all right," she whispered, passing the reins to her right hand to pet the side of his face with her left. She loosely gripped the reins to allow him to choose his own path. She did not want to put too much stress on him as he was already petrified. When he started to trot the wrong way she would lightly pull the reins back in the right direction and the transition would always be smooth. "You are an extraordinary horse," she told him.

Imagine if Prince James were here. It would be wonderful, yet horrible. I could never live with myself if something happened to him. She pictured James as she thought of their long handheld embrace before she left to meet Akar. *Oh, I should have hugged him goodbye,* she sighed quietly. *What if I never see him ag—NO Amaryllis... none of that!*

Her eyes narrowed, and she looked angrily off into the distance as she relived the guilt of freeing Immortuos all over again. They had trotted into the area of what *used* to be the Forest of Enchantment but now horribly blended into the rest of the wretched woods. Although she had seen the magic it once possessed, she could not sense it anymore. Even as her mind vividly projected her memory of the Forest of Enchantment, she couldn't really believe what it once was. It looked like it had always been that way, and that haunted her the most. The way the trees seemed to follow her with unseen eyes, the way they were planted in the ground—having the appearance that they were mobile creatures that would charge at her if not imprisoned by their own roots—it all haunted her.

Amaryllis looked away from the menacing trees with a racing heart. She wanted Immortuos dead. As the fear from glaring at the haunting trees still stirred in her gut, she pictured the entire world frightening people with its new, adopted appearance, to the point of a loss of control. That demon disrupted the harmony of the world. That demon, Laria, and the ceremonial tradition were the things that stood in Amaryllis and James' way of official togetherness. She scoffed.

"He would have loved to be in here with us," she told Ezro. "He has a liking for adventure." Amaryllis caught herself within a love-induced trance. She had entered the forest wanting to focus on nothing but Immortuos, and thinking of James or anyone was a distraction.

Amaryllis and Ezro had been riding for a long time and had not run into any sort of danger. The creatures seemed to have spread out with their new freedom, but the silence worried Amaryllis. To help with her nervousness, she spoke to Ezro some more.

"We're lucky that nobody's out here," she whispered, nearly expecting a response from him which she knew was strange. A small portion of Immortuos' lair could be seen through the thick branches that touched the sky; she glared at the visible rock and shivered.

"Last time I was in here, I faced shadows and paralyzation in a black swamp all within moments of entering." Amaryllis looked at the back of Ezro's head and listened to the sound of his hooves clopping against the dirt, thinking of the suffering and pain she had experienced in the black swamp. She shuddered, shaking her head.

Everything was going smoothly for a shocking amount of time until a twig snapped in the near distance. Amaryllis couldn't tell which way the sound came from, but with Ezro's senses he whipped his head to the left, informing Amaryllis of where the thing was. She pulled the red reins back firmly stopping Ezro from his trot to stand still. Amaryllis sat hesitantly on his back unsure of whether or not she wanted to dismount him. Staying provided her with a feeling of safety, but getting down would make it easier for her to protect him. All within a single thought, she swung her leg around and dropped down. Her armour rattled like dishes dropping into a sink. She pulled her diamond encrusted sword out from her scabbard and raised it defensively holding it with two hands. Amaryllis had never held a sword before, nor did she know any fencing techniques. All she knew was that as soon as she saw the creature she would swing like a madwoman.

More rustling came from the left. The forest bloomed with thick, dark leaves, so when the creature emerged from the bushes and out into the small open space Amaryllis would only have a *second* to react.

She waited impatiently for the creature to present itself. Her anticipation caused her knees to wobble and her arms to twitch. The sword seemed to be vibrating in her hands.

The rustling grew louder until there was a thud on the other side of the bush. A low gurgling sound came from within the leaves, then a flash of dark green sprung right into Amaryllis' face. As soon as the green figure jumped through the leaves, Amaryllis swung aggressively with a loud grunt. When the sword made contact with the thing it made a sharp, clanging sound as if she were hitting metal. It flew a few feet then landed on all fours making the gurgling sound again. It was a goblin, and it was hideous. It had dark green, hard scales that acted as body armour. An arched back with pointed vertebrates poking through the skin, long bony fingers and toes with long, sharp nails, slits for a nose, a strange shaped skull, and yellow eyes with tiny pupils. As it gurgled, yellowish-white spit bubbled from the corners of its mouth.

Ezro whinnied and stood on his hind legs, then stomped his hooves into the ground over and over to try and scare the goblin off.

Amaryllis looked closely at the goblin's back, then scanned its entire body for a weak spot. It charged at her again in a flash of green, and once more she swung at it with her sword. This time, she followed it through the air and continued to swing. It was on the ground hissing as she swung and jabbed at it. She kept the goblin there for a few minutes, not gaining any advantages nor losing them, but she couldn't seem to really damage the darn thing. It was like trying to cut down a tree with a spoon.

She screamed in frustration as she swung frantically. Her tired shoulders burned and grew heavy so her attacks became weaker. After one final, frail swing, the goblin escaped from Amaryllis' fury, crawling away from her to circle Ezro. He brayed loudly as he stood on his hind legs. Ezro stomped at the ground to fend it off but it just kept of charging, nearly biting into his leg.

Amaryllis marched over to Ezro with her sword held high above her head ready to destroy the creature which scared her beloved horse. The fast-moving goblin was difficult to track as it zoomed around Ezro's legs, but with one lucky swing Amaryllis contacted it right on the head to stop it for a moment. While it was disoriented, she began to strike it again over and over. Her shoulder exhaustion presented itself earlier in her second was of attacks, but this time she fought through her tiredness to continue to swing for longer.

Her arms finally gave out from exhaustion and she couldn't even lift them past her sides. Amaryllis groaned impatiently and the goblin screeched viciously in return, taunting her. Suddenly, from behind Amaryllis, Ezro dashed over and stomped the goblin's head in with his powerful hooves. The goblins face was crushed and flattened into a spit covered pile of green skin and sharp teeth. Amaryllis sighed quietly and patted Ezro's nose before she climbed onto his back.

Chapter 24

Amaryllis and Ezro continued to ride the same way they had before encountering the goblin which was cautiously and consistently. The only difference was that both Amaryllis and Ezro were less afraid of the forest. After facing the goblin, they felt that they gained power providing them with courage.

The harsh sounds of the forest no longer phased them. Their ride was almost like a casual stroll back in Arlon. Amaryllis stroked Ezro's mane.

"I am so happy that Charles lent you to me," she exclaimed. "This journey is passing by much quicker than if I had walked, plus you saved us from the goblin… and you're wonderful company." Ezro nickered and flipped his ears back and forth. Amaryllis smiled and looked at the red sky through the thick trees. "We can fix this. Well, I can. You shouldn't even have to be coming with me. I destroyed everything," she chuckled nervously. The pressure hidden by Amaryllis' state of shock finally presented itself. She could finally comprehend every event that happened. It came on unbearably strong.

"I destroyed everything!" she cried loudly in a shaky voice. "Oh god…" she leaned on Ezro's head and let her stress consume her. All of the trauma entered her soul. Her body surged with fear under horrid pressure that forced her to scream in a low voice.

As strong as she was mentally, she was finally destroyed and the world had a momentary victory in the battle of her life. She needed someone to talk to because her self-hatred was eating her from the inside out.

"*I can do it... I can do it,*" she mocked herself in a whiny voice. "I destroyed something that had been keeping the world safe for two thousand years. I released the most dangerous being in existence and doomed the life on Earth, and I think that I can just walk up to it and... what? Hit it in the head? Give it a little punch? *Remove* the pigment from its skin!" she whined thinking of Akar's witty insults. "I have telekinetic powers now, so maybe I can just make it implode? Yes, I'll kill it with my little experience with magic before it slaughters me with its entire lifetime of evil in a matter of a second... PERFECT! Earth will be restored! I can *do* it!" she groaned again, watching the ground move quickly below her as she draped her upper body lazily over Ezro's back. She let go of the reins and wrapped her arms around his neck to find comfort from *something*. She wanted to cry but found that she had metaphorically cried her eyes dry too many times and simply had no tears left. She shouted as an alternative to her misery.

Ezro snorted at her screams, annoyed. If he could speak, he would tell her to stop her pointless blather and that she had the capability to defeat Immortuos, but Ezro's inhuman thoughts were trapped within his horse mind. He stopped trotting as his way of telling her to shut it. The ground stopped moving and Amaryllis sat up. She squeezed her legs together. "Come on, GO!" Ezro snorted and continued to stand motionless. He didn't even move his head to look around. He was completely still.

Amaryllis slumped, slid down his side and landed on the ground. She stormed around to stand in front of him.

"Charles said you were a loyal horse... this is NOT what loyalty looks like," she snapped. Ezro knew very well that Amaryllis was losing her mind and he was trying his best to make her come to her senses and remind her of who she was. He stood silent. "You're being a *pain*." He continued to stay still. "You're delaying the *saving* of the *world*... let's GO!" Amaryllis broke down and put her head against Ezro's side. She started to sob as she wrapped her arms around him. As she was submerged in sadness, she became more observant and openminded. She looked at each individual bluish-grey hair on Ezro's back, then at the mucky ground littered with puddles bubbling with stench.

Without saying another word, Amaryllis climbed onto Ezro's back. As soon as she was seated he began to trot.

Chapter 25

It became more frequent for Amaryllis and Ezro to face dangers that were more difficult to defeat. As they trotted closer and closer to Immortuos' lair, they came across more threatening creatures in higher quantities. They encountered deathly souls, shadow figures, giants, and more goblins. As dangerous and petrifying as they were, all of those creatures seemed pleasant compared to what Amaryllis and Ezro were inevitably bound to find.

Amaryllis and Ezro were exhausted after a long day of battling dozens of forest monsters. The sun was setting and no more light shone through the red clouds into the thick forest to light up their surroundings. It was nearly pitch black, making the blood red clouds appear dark red in the night. Neither the moon, nor the stars, could be seen.

As the sun fell further below the earth, for each minute that passed, Amaryllis could see less and less.

Ezro began to slow down since he could not see his own path. They now moved at a cautious walk which wasn't fast at all. It was more like a cautious crawl. Amaryllis might as well have climbed down and walked on her own, but she felt safe atop of the big, blue horse.

To make herself feel better, Amaryllis spoke aloud, but she did so quietly, so as to not awaken or attract any creatures.

"It's getting quite dark outside. We'll have to find a place to stay." Amaryllis looked at her hands, which she could hardly see. She could barely see the horse she was riding, and felt like she was floating through the woods.

It was twice as dangerous to be vulnerable in the night, as opposed to during the day, since the shadow creatures blended into the darkness. Amaryllis' confidence and sense of bravery faded as the blackness of the night invaded the forest. Her heart thudded and her mind raced as she realized that she was exposed to the creatures of the night—who would be able to find her easily if she was not quiet.

"I don't know where we'll be able to go, but we'll need to find something *fast*," she whispered fiercely, leaning forward to speak into Ezro's ear. There were no more sounds to be heard. The forest was dead silent and the only sound present was Ezro's hooves clopping. Amaryllis looked all around, squinting through the dark. She looked for large trees, ditches, or caves to sleep in. Everything looked similar; very grey and fuzzy, almost pixelated.

Then, out of nowhere, Amaryllis remembered Akar and his magic lesson.

I must utilize what I have learned.

Amaryllis looked deeply into the grey fuzziness and visualized the galaxy of white flashes of shooting stars and the blackness that surrounded everything. She pictured herself floating in space, able to breathe, and without the pressure crushing her body into mush.

Her eyes shined brightly, glowing turquoise.

Still holding onto the connection with the universe, Amaryllis brought her mind back to Earth and used her hands as flashlights. Beams of white light shot from her finger tips lighting up only the areas where they pointed. There wasn't enough light so she initiated more light by moving all of the energy into her palms. Both of her hands glowed yellow and the light was much brighter. She could see more clearly. She waved her hands all over looking for monsters but, more specifically, shadow creatures. Because of their dark hues, they blended in with their surroundings, they were absolutely invisible in the night. You wouldn't know you were being attacked until they already had you in their cold, sharp grasp, and spit their red gunk onto your face to devour you.

Amaryllis waved her hands like crazy looking for gigantic silhouettes. The bright lights did not bother Ezro, even with Amaryllis' arbitrary waving. She occasionally shined her light into his eyes and all over his back, enhancing his blue coloured coat. Ezro was not worried and had no reason to be. He had no idea of how dangerous the shadow creatures were at night so he continued to ride normally.

The suspense of waiting for a monster to jump out at Amaryllis was killing her. She began hyperventilating. Out in the open woods with no protection but armour and a horse was enough for her to break down in fear. Tears streamed down her cheeks as she scanned her surroundings.

Her inconsistent breathing drastically changed into a raspy scream from the top of her lungs when something jumped out in front of Ezro in a flash of brown. Ezro whinnied and stood on his hind legs. Amaryllis squeezed with her legs to hold on, held the reins in her left hand and used her right hand to illuminate the creature, which changed direction as soon as it landed in front of them. Ezro dropped to the ground and snorted. Amaryllis waved her hands all over, searching for the thing but to no avail. She broke the connection with the cosmos and allowed the magic to fade from her hands and back into space.

Ahead of her, the ground was illuminated in dim blue and white lights. The lights shone brighter as the deer walked across them.

As Amaryllis finally grew used to the gleam of the grove she was able to identify the creature as a deer. The deer stood innocently with its big, black eyes fixated on her. It blinked gracefully, fluttering its lashes and reminding Amaryllis of swaying leaves in a soft breeze. The deer's long, muscular legs held its body perfectly still which revealed the liveliness of the glow of the lights as the light flickered against its coat. The blue light danced energetically upon the deer's body which began to look greyish under the radiance as Amaryllis' eyes continued to adjust from pitch blackness to the glowing grove before her.

Amaryllis found herself so focused on the elegant animal that she had forgotten she was straddling Ezro. She brought her gaze away from the deer to look down at the horse. He was perfectly still, it was as if he had fallen asleep.

Something appeared in the corner of her eye. She looked up from Ezro's mane to see thick, blue gas rising from the grove.

The deer shuffled nervously as the blue mist climbed its body, completely surrounding it. The deer suddenly squealed as a sharp sizzling sound filled the air. The deer's legs began to decompose and melt away. Its legs bubbled and blistered, revealing bloody, red flesh which fell off its bones and to the ground in a heavy, gushing plop. The deer tried to move, to escape from the carnivorous mist, but couldn't as its muscles had tensed up, clenching unbearably tight. Its coat shrivelled up into dead follicles of hair revealing its red, boiling skin. The deer wailed loudly sounding nearly like a human. The deer's skeleton was now visible all over except for its skull which remained hidden behind muscle and tissue that was yet to melt away. All of the organs had slithered through the ribcage and landed in a steaming pile of tissue. Blood flowed from the skeleton and collected in a huge puddle where the deer had once stood. Its face finally began to sizzle, and as the skull started to show, its black eyes rolled out of their sockets. The bare, lifeless skeleton stood still for a moment then dropped as if a trap door opened from beneath it, out of sight. The final scream of the deer hung in the air for a moment longer before what was left of the creature had vanished. The blood swirled in circles, then absorbed into the dirt, taking the flesh with it. It was if the deer was never there.

Amaryllis froze in shock, her body as stiff as a board. With hot, sweaty hands she squeezed Ezro's mane until her knuckles turned white. A scream settled in her throat, ready to be released, but her throat closed and all she could do was utter a gasp. With a blank mind erased by fear, she dismounted Ezro—who was nervously whining and shuffling around awkwardly—keeping her gaze on the spot where the deer had died. She walked up to where the blue and white lights shone. As she stood before them she realized they were glowing blue mushrooms with white spots.

She studied the grove of mushrooms and glanced from left to right. They never seemed to end in either direction. She looked at the fungus in horror, taking a single step back from them. The mushrooms were densely packed together with no room for her to place her feet to avoid them. They had to get through somehow. Amaryllis spun around slowly, facing her petrified steed.

"I don't know how, but we have to," she whispered to him. Ezro snorted and slowly backed up a few steps. Amaryllis thought of using telekinesis to push the mushrooms aside to form a path, but then thought of how movement caused the gas to emit from them. She thought of levitating. It would take a lot of concentration and the mushrooms seemed to extend for a while, so that was suicidal. Then she thought of climbing and jumping from tree to tree, but what would she do with Ezro?

"I must try levitation," Amaryllis whispered to herself.

She leaned her head back, peering at the tops of trees. She held her arms out by her side and focused on nothing but how much she weighed, how strong the Earth's gravity was, and visualized her body being lifted from the ground. Nothing happened for a while, but her determination allowed her to try multiple times until she finally levitated… one inch from the ground.

She looked down at her boots then back up to the sky and closed her eyes, focusing harder on the lifting of her body.

Amaryllis rose another inch then dropped to the ground. She'd been trying for what felt like the longest time but didn't go anywhere. The sky grew even darker and time was passing by quickly. She'd have to think of something else. In her mind, the safest way was to send Ezro back to the castle. She didn't want to risk losing him because of her weak and flawed magic. She wouldn't be able to go on if she made the mistake of dropping the horse into the grove of toxic mushrooms. But how could she send him home safely, running for miles and miles without being attacked by something? Ezro was a nuisance at that time.

"Ezro, thank you for your assistance; however, you need to go home now," she said, pointing behind her. The horse stood still, staring at Amaryllis with his empty black eyes. Amaryllis' chest tightened in frustration, then she thought of making him invisible. He wouldn't be bothered by anything… *yes*.

Amaryllis connected with the universe and focused on making every inch of Ezro's skin, organ, and hair, transparent. As she did, she watched Ezro fade away until she could no longer see him. She grinned, feeling proud of herself, then threw a tiny stick at where she last saw him and watched it bounce off of nothing.

Her smile faded.

Ezro would have to be petrified and temporality traumatized to run a full gallop in one direction for a long period of time. The fact that Ezro was invisible, was the start of the trauma. He whimpered and snorted nervously, still standing in the same place. He had faced countless monsters in the forest but what he didn't encounter was his most trusted companion turning against him and playing tricks on him. Amaryllis did not want to, but she felt she had to run up to Ezro and scream at him, yell at him, and hit him until he ran away at full speed. It was all for his own good.

Amaryllis tried being gentle before resorting to betrayal. She walked a few steps with out-stretched arms, reaching for him. When she found his face, she stood still.

"Ezro, you need to go, now," she ordered. "Go home!"

Ezro couldn't comprehend. He seemed to think that he was to assist her until the very end. "Go and see Charles," she said softly, petting him. His loyalty to Amaryllis kept him grounded. "It's impossible for both of us to make it across," she stated, pointing to the mushrooms.

Nothing.

It was pointless to reason with a horse.

Trauma cycled around in Amaryllis' brain constantly. Setting Immortuos free was imprinted in her mind and it had just occurred to her that she would send Ezro home the same way the *little girl* told her she would be freeing her.

Her hands glowed as she collected her *own* magic. It felt and looked the same as Immortuos' pretend purity which painfully reminded her of how powerful the demon was.

A path of bright white light shot out from her palms and she ignited a path in the dirt, leading hundreds of miles straight back to the stables.

"Go, Ezro," she demanded. As she predicted, Ezro didn't move at all. She heard no sounds of hooves stomping into the dirt, not even snorting or any signs that he was even there. Her commands were pointless. He was disobeying correctly.

Her chest tightened once again in a strong frustration which affected her nearly as badly as her frustration during the Choosing Ceremony.

I'll have to provide him a continuous command in his brain to guide him home, she thought to herself, and that was exactly what she did. She wasn't sure how and did not dare to question how her vision was breaking the biological laws of her eyesight. Her sight acted as binoculars, or a telescope, moving closer and closer to where Ezro stood without moving her body. She emerged through the invisible barriers of Ezro's skull and could clearly see his *brain*. She felt like a parasite touring the inside of the horse. She admired his brain like it was a preserved artifact, so impressive and important. Although there was no way to be able to see anything within his head, her presence acted as a light source. She moved into the front of his brain and effortlessly flew *inside* of his frontal lobe where she thought to herself over and over, "Follow the trail, follow the trail."

    Amaryllis found herself in her own body within an instant. Her heart jumped and she gasped as she realized her sight had returned to her own eyes. Relief fell over her like a wave when the sound of hooves thundering against the ground filled the air. Ezro finally left with the command she provided him. As soon as he reached the meadow, his visibility would return and the command would evaporate from his mind.

    Amaryllis sighed a sad sigh then turned to a big tree on the boundary where the toxic mushrooms met the dusty soil.

Chapter 26

Amaryllis grabbed hold of a thick branch and hoisted herself up with the pull of her arms and the flex of her core, then sat nestled in between compact, twisted branches. Her armour dug into the bark of the tree and put pressure on her body. It was a pain, along with an extreme discomfort, to wear men's armour regardless of how light it was. It limited her movement, not allowing room for simple flexibility.

She gritted her teeth and grunted as she hoisted herself up higher in the tree. She stared at her feet, making sure to stand in a safe place, tapping each branch twice with her foot to ensure stability before placing all of her weight down.

The ground became more distant and the toxic mushrooms grew dimmer as she climbed higher and higher. The fungi mocked her with their stillness. So much power existed in such a small thing and there was no way to defeat them with dignity. Avoiding them was the unfortunate key to victory.

As Amaryllis finally found comfort in her placement, she looked at the nearest tree which had branches just inches away for her to jump to. She inched along the extending branch keeping her hands gently rested on the branch over her head for balance. Her eyes stared at the dim glow of blue, with the memory of the deer being decomposed at the back of her mind. She could only imagine the pain in which it felt and compared it to being burned alive. This thought gave her goosebumps. She felt warmth rush to her stomach and the rest of her body felt cold. Beads of sweat collected on her hairline and her face glistened. Her breathing became shaken and shallow as her heart rate increased. Her muscles tensed as she made her way near to the end of the branch on which she stood.

Jumping could have a number of outcomes and the conspicuous event that Amaryllis was desperate to avoid was slipping upon landing in the new tree, descending to her inevitable death.

Her anxiety consumed her to near completion. Her world was spinning yet her head felt as light as a feather, her body a rock. The blue light flickered between forced blinks, pushing incoming tears away.

Amaryllis filled her lungs with air then jumped, endeavouring to make a firm, impactive landing in the next tree. Her body was motionless through the air. Every muscle was flexed, and she looked awkwardly stiff until her feet found a thick branch with a clattered thud. Her knees bent slightly upon her landing. She gasped then quickly reached for a branch above her to eradicate her wobbling. Amaryllis was now completely surrounded by the mushrooms and had officially entered the territory of the grove.

She allowed herself to sit down to calm her troubled mind, breathing long and heavy breaths, glaring down at the poisonous ground. Her fingers pressed into the rough and scratchy bark of the new tree. It was all she felt in that moment aside from her pounding heart within her trembling body.

Amaryllis' vision was fading. Blackness invaded her sight as she gazed through a tiny pinhole. Her lungs struggled to take in air no matter how aggressively she inhaled and gasped for it. She blindly crawled to the centre of the tree where all of the branches met at the trunk and shut her eyes. As she did, fatigue filled her body and no matter how much she resisted, she couldn't fight the weight of her eyelids or the sensation of fear combined with sleepiness. Amaryllis drifted off for a moment then jolted awake.

Immediately, she sat up with a fresh mindset, reset by the minute's rest she attained. Her heart rate had slowed and her body no longer trembled. Amaryllis grabbed hold of the closest branch and stood up, following the same pattern of inching along the outstretching branch and jumping onto the next tree. This occurred for an extensive period of time and Amaryllis had become accustomed to the rhythm of the pattern which she had created. She proceeded with extreme caution; however, her process had been significantly sped up as fear no longer enclosed her. Every once in a while she would slip on her landings, falling below the branches to what she thought was her death before grabbing hold of a branch at the very last second. She would scream then climb back up, take a break, then jump to the next tree. It certainly would not seem irrational to think that she would never become accustomed to her process, but that is where Amaryllis' strange temperament defied such thoughts. Gradually, her fears died slightly, the blue light became slightly less frightening, and the fact that she was several feet above the ground no longer affected her to the point of vigorous trembling. It was as if she had forgotten where she was through repetition, but when she looked down, the mushrooms continued to taunt her. She chose to feed on her own fear to drive her out of the grove and closer to Immortuos.

To her relief, Amaryllis was two more trees away from reaching the end of the toxic grove. She sat perched on the third-last tree with a tired but stern face, alert eyes, and wild wavy hair. Her journey through the grove was nearly over. She thought of nothing other than how great it would feel to walk on the earth once again. For all she cared, she was finished with climbing for a long while.

A squirrel just outside the grove ran into the blue mushrooms, sending puffs of odourless, blue toxins out of the ground. Amaryllis closed her eyes—which stung like fire—to avoid watching the decomposition of the small creature. Upon opening her eyes the squirrel was gone as if it had never been there at all. She sighed then stood up, overwhelmed by the closeness of her victory. She inched along the branch, jumped, then landed in the next tree. She would have become excited by standing in the second-last tree if she hadn't been climbing and jumping for so long. Instead, she was emotionless, tired, and felt slightly despondent.

As she shuffled along the last branch—

She heard faint, crackling sounds—wood snapping and squeaking. They grew louder. Instinctively, she grabbed hold of the branch above her. It was scratchy with massive slivers of wood protruding all along the branch, penetrating the flesh of her hands as she squeezed with all her might. She winced in irritation, then gasped as the branch she stood on fell to the ground, sending up clouds of blue. The dead piece of wood crumbled, disappearing into the ground. The mushrooms weren't only ravenous for flesh.

She remained calm until she heard cracking again. She aimed for the trunk of the tree, firmly pressing her hands down onto massive slivers as she swung across. The pieces of wood penetrated deep into her skin and would have impaled her completely if not for their flimsiness. Her eyes watered while her arms moved swiftly with her legs kicking intensely, endeavouring to beat the branch before it snapped free. She screamed in pain with each reposition of her splintered hands.

Without warning or evidence of a fracture, the branch gave way and down she went.

Amaryllis descended in slow motion, watching the night sky become more and more distant. She tried to stop her body from falling with telekinesis but found her mind was too disturbed for her to concentrate. Her heart was too troubled and there was not enough time.

Before she knew it, she fell into the mushrooms with a thud. The impact snapped her mind awake and released adrenaline. She got up as fast as she could and sprinted for the end of the grove. Puffs of blue arose all around her with each step until she froze. Every single muscle in her body contracted, clenched and cramped all at once. She stood awkwardly in a hyperextended form. The pain was unbearable. She could not relieve her torture in any way. Instead, she was eaten by insanity, staring at the trees with wide eyes and a trembling body full of wretchedness. The dark surroundings of the forest were turning white in pixelated form as her bright green irises turned grey. If she still had regular vision, she would have seen her armour beginning to dissolve to expose her flesh to the fungus.

Chapter 27

A steaming hot, burning sensation was present all along Amaryllis' gashed arms, legs and hands. A powerful fire burned her flesh in a constant pain with each second worse than the last. A loud and persistent scream fled from her mouth as she opened her eyes, which were whitish green. She was baffled by her new surroundings which were dark and difficult to see. A fire burned in the corner, and through fuzzy vision she could see a silhouette, a side profile glaring into the fire mysteriously. Her screams did not seem to bother the person although her wailing pierced her own ears.

Amaryllis could not formulate words as the pain was far too vigorous for her to do anything other than cry and scream. Her throat stung badly. All sorts of pain attacked her figure in every internal and external area of her body.

All information was unattainable except for the fact that there was someone in the corner ignoring her, and she was laying down in something. All else was an enigma. Her brain only concentrated on her misery.

I want to die, I need to die, I need to die.

The fire danced, embers sprung into the air as the burning logs split and cracked. The silhouette shifted slightly, keeping their gaze on the orange flames. They knew not to speak as it would be pointless to try to communicate with the woman who was suffering. They knew her senses would gradually return, making the grotesque torture of her burned flesh hurt more by the minute: her hearing would allow her to listen to nothing but her own bellowing, and her sight would scare her half to death if she looked at her body. There was nothing the stranger could do other than place her in a tub of cold water to relieve the burning and let her cry.

Why aren't they helping me? she asked herself, realizing her capabilities of a wider range of thought.

"HELP ME!" she groaned between sharp screams, not realizing she had said anything until the figure shifted hesitantly. At that point, she couldn't tell what was in her head and what wasn't. "KILL ME!" she pleaded, her face scrunched into a disarray of despair. All of her memories vanished from her mind. She had forgotten about her quest, Prince James, her parents, her enemies, and even who she was or where she came from. The desire to perish consumed her soul absolutely.

She cried a final scream of despondence and misery, then fell unconscious due to shock and overpowering and unforgiving suffering.

Amaryllis was asleep for hours. When consciousness returned, she did not scream as vigorously but groaned instead. The several hours she was unconscious felt like one-second, perhaps even one blink of her foggy green eyes. The intensity of her pain dropped significantly within her short time of being asleep. She was unaware of her slumber of recovery until she could see faint daylight peering in through cracks in the walls.

She noticed that she was cold, covered in goosebumps where her skin was untouched by acidic burns. Her shoulders, chest, neck, stomach and face were the fortunate body parts to not be eaten away by the blue mushrooms. The rest of her body was *covered* in third degree burns. She looked, only moving her eyes, from left to right to see she was enclosed by a wooden tub. Then she looked down to see her naked body submerged in water. Her torso did not horrify her, but as her eyes lazily moved down from her torso to her burnt legs, then her arms, she cried loudly as if seeing the culprit of her torture caused the pain to intensify. The sight of the burn activated all other burnt areas to sting wretchedly. Amaryllis passed out again.

She was awakened by a male's gruff voice. Her eyes opened and they were finally bright green again. All cloudiness had faded.

Beside the tub was a man with shoulder-length, straight, grey hair. He possessed a scruffy unshaven face beholding mean, squinty, brown eyes that seemed to withhold anger. His jaw hung open just enough for Amaryllis to see that he had slightly crooked bottom teeth. He said something, leaning over the tub to speak.

"What did you say?" she whimpered under the pain of her stinging skin.

The man's expression suddenly appeared blank and emotionless. He repeated himself. "I said, *you're lucky I found you.*" His deep voice frightened her. "That armour you were wearing saved your life. If it weren't for it, I would have just left you to die… you were so damn close too… to makin' it out on your own. Maybe just a few more steps and you would have been free." He cleared his throat. "I saw you dangling from that dead tree and figured you were going to fall."

Amaryllis did not know how to handle the given information. She was unsure of what the appropriate response was. She felt uncomfortable being completely nude in front of this man. He subconsciously respected her comfort by looking away from her body, and if he did look it was at the only at the horrible burns.

"I… did not know what was happening. The last thing I remember was trying to run out of the grove, but… then I was unable to move no matter how hard I tried and I couldn't see. All I saw was white. The forest was blank—"

"Then I picked you up and brought you out before the fungus got you all the way. You'd be surprised how quickly they ate your armour and long johns…but they bought me an extra second.

Without them you'd be dead," he paused to study her reaction, which was wide-eyed and concerned. "…your eyes were pure white, no pupils, and you were bleeding all over the place." The man crossed his arms as he finished speaking.

Amaryllis appreciated all that he had done, but she couldn't bring herself to thank him. The sight of her blackened, sticky, bloody limbs frightened her. She felt an urge to cry at the thought of never having her own, smooth skin again. Instead, it would be leathery and abnormally bumpy and stretched. She looked at her acid-affected legs and felt discouraged.

"I'm telling you right now—" the man's voice seemed to raise in anger… or frustration… Amaryllis could not tell but it boomed and seemed to shake the room causing her to defensively shrug her shoulders and shut her eyes tightly. "—that armour is what saved you. If you had not been wearing it then I would have rescued a girl with no flesh, no muscles, absolutely nothing but skeleton showing in the arms and legs. It looks horrid I know, but be thankful you still *have* your limbs." When he finished talking, Amaryllis relaxed her shoulders, but her lower lip curled and her jaw began to quiver. The man glared at her impatiently. He seemed to understand what she was going through yet at the same time he wanted her to overcome it quickly. "Just cry. Let it out. Go on," he exhorted, waving a hand at her.

The image of Amaryllis' flesh being eaten away in the toxic grove was vivid in her mind. Although she was blinded by the psychedelic toxins she could imagine the scenario clearly. The man's invitation—her permission—to reveal her inner sorrows frustrated her. She did not want to cry or suffer in any way anymore. She wanted to stand up from the cold bathtub, throw some clothes on and continue her quest, and she would storm out furiously to physically inform the man that she didn't appreciate his condescending hospitality.

She glared up into his mean eyes then looked down at her legs again discouraged that she couldn't express her annoyance in the way she desired. The man had waited a minute, saying nothing, then spun around and walked away. He opened a door at the opposite side of the room letting in grey light for a moment.

"Stay in the tub," he ordered sternly, then walked out into the Dark Forest, gently shutting the door behind him.

Amaryllis utilized the man's absence to examine all her burns. She obeyed his instruction and never left the tub, mainly because it hurt too much to make any movements. She couldn't even stand up. She noticed that the burns were worse on her left side.

I must have fallen onto my left side after the paralysis.

The acid ate its way up her left leg laterally, up her side and the left half of her back. On the right side only her lower leg was affected. Both forearms were burned, but the upper arms and shoulders were untouched. Her chest and stomach were also free of burns. She was most thankful for her face. She would be afraid to look at herself if her radiant complexion was gashed in deep burns, pooling with rich blood.

Now that Amaryllis' mind was free of suicidal and confusing thoughts, she could finally think of her loved ones. She thought of their reactions if they were to see her which nearly brought herself to tears. Her mother would fall to her knees and scream, her father too would break down and sob, and Prince James… she was unsure of what he would do. He would most likely rush to her side, go to hold her hand and jerk it back after realizing that it was burned. As an alternative, he would gently grasp her upper arm with his touch as light as a feather and—

The man returned, jerking the door open and shutting it quickly. Amaryllis jolted in the bathtub, startled by his sudden entrance. The water in the tub swished around.

He held a small dagger coated in a purple substance which dripped from the tip of the blade and splatted heavily onto the floor. Before Amaryllis could ask anything at all, the man began to speak.

"As soon as you're healed, you are to leave," he stated calmly.

She ignored his statement and asked, "What's that?" she pointed to the blade. The man lifted the knife close to his face and examined the purple liquid.

Keeping his eyes on the tip of the blade he mumbled, "The blood of a nornx... and it is imperative that I maintain their population surrounding my shack. Before you ask what a nornx is, it's a massive, merciless being that feeds on absolutely anything at all. They'll eat boulders, trees, animals, monsters, and I even saw one gnawing on the side of a mountain a while back. So as you can imagine, these things are insanely gigantic and need to die before they start biting into my shack." He took a cloth from a chest and wiped the gooey blood off of the knife. Amaryllis stared at the mystery of a man, wondering what was going on within his mind.

"When do you think you'll be able to get out of the tub and start walking?" he asked.

Amaryllis shrugged her shoulders which hurt the left side of her back. "Because of my condition, perhaps..." she trailed off, looking away from the scruffy forest man. "...I have been taught a few things," she continued, remembering Akar. "They could significantly speed up my healing process," she stammered in realization. The man looked at her skeptically. Amaryllis herself was skeptical, wondering if she could heal herself with magic. It was worth the try.

"Are you going to tell me or leave me in suspense?" he asked impatiently. Amaryllis hardly knew this man. She knew absolutely nothing about him but from observing his behaviour, she figured he'd be the kind of person to scoff at magic.

Chapter 28

Amaryllis stared at her burnt, red and black skin that secreted fresh blood mixing and swirling with the water in the bathtub.

She focused first on her cells which she could see forming in her bone marrow, producing red and white blood cells abnormally fast with the assistance of her magic. She watched the cells multiply, both amazed and shocked with her abilities. Since Amaryllis was so concentrated on the internal aspects of her body, she could not see her burns beginning to heal.

However, the man stood mesmerized at the end of the tub trying to hide his astonishment and bewilderment with crossed arms and his lips pressed into a straight line. His mean glare never changed, it would be pointless to look for emotion within his eyes.

Even though Amaryllis' body was submerged in water, her burns had stopped bleeding and dried up into scabs. The scabs then flaked off and faded into non-existence, revealing pink skin which faded back to her regular colour of pigmentation. It all happened in a matter of seconds, and within that time Amaryllis was filled with euphoria as she felt the pain vacating her body.

Once her process was complete, she jolted when she could no longer view the production of her cells. Her mind jumped into her brain in an instant and her body was pushed back by the unseen force, feeling like someone shoved her against the tub. She gasped as air forced its way into her lungs. She was mentally exhausted and felt as if she lost quantities of energy which could only be refilled with rest. She smiled at her spotless skin and absence of pain.

The man stepped closer to Amaryllis. His body in her peripheral vision reminded her of his presence. She looked at him to see his mean eyes appearing to be in shock... angry... she simply could not tell. Her smile faded.

"What the hell was that?" he spluttered, looking at her legs then into her eyes, whipping his head which flipped his hair. "Are you a witch or something?" he asked grimly, trying to assert dominance. If she was a witch, he wanted to seem more frightening and powerful. He had dealt with a witch before, and he really had to put up a fight against her. He was strongly intimidated and slightly frightened by Amaryllis.

"I am not a witch. I have been taught pure magic which comes to me from the entire universe itself," she muttered, afraid of his loud voice. Amaryllis looked down at her naked body and felt anxiety in her stomach. A minute ago she was a girl in recovery having to be nude for the healing process. But she had turned into a regular, healthy girl taking a cold bath before a man she did not know. "Could I have some clothing please?" she asked nervously.

The man walked over to a drawer containing ragged, black pants and a ripped, white v-neck shirt and walked back hesitantly, placing them on the damp wooden floor beside the tub. He looked like he wanted to say something with his mouth half open and a lifted chest as he inhaled, trying to get the words to come out. He respectfully turned around to let Amaryllis get out of the tub and change into the clothes he gave her.

Amaryllis stepped into the black pants. The dew—from emerging from the tub without a towel—sitting on her legs pressed and absorbed into the fabric causing water droplets of all sizes to speckle the pants. The same thing occurred with the white v-neck shirt. The clothes were slightly large, but small enough for her comfort.

During her dressing, the man stared blankly at the floor with the image of Amaryllis' *witchcraft* burned in his mind. Meanwhile, Amaryllis watched the back of his head the entire time pondering what the stranger's intentions were.

"Who the hell are you?" he finally asked, breaking the silence. He turned around to see her fully clothed, looking at him curiously. His question surprised her and it showed in her face.

"I am Princess Amaryllis of Serilion," she stated. Her mother had taught her how imperative it was to formally introduce herself at a young age. Amaryllis remembered all of the times her mother would quiz her at random, approaching her suddenly and asking, "Who are you?" She would respond quietly with slouched shoulders and an uncertain gleam in her eyes. The queen had not learned where her daughter's shameful, shy behaviour descended from until just a few days ago, but since Amaryllis had risen above those who fed on her misery, she had finally come to realize who she was and her quest was furthering the development of her character.

The stranger took a step back and tilted his head with a frown on his face. "You mean to tell me that you are royalty?" he growled, speaking in a way that frightened Amaryllis about confirming the truth, but she did so anyway as she was instructed to do by the Queen of Serilion.

"Yes, have you not heard of Serilion? I can understand. It is terribly far away from Arl—"

"Get the hell out of here!" he roared in a deep voice... far deeper than usual... almost inaudible for Amaryllis to comprehend. He sounded evil and frankly, demonic.

Amaryllis' heart jumped into her throat. She shuddered upon hearing his angered, gruff voice. She did not move as she was frozen in fear. Her heartbeat was the only thing she could feel. All else was weightless.

"I don't know what to say—"

"Say *nothing*... just get out," he aggressively pointed to the door with a distorted look on his face. He appeared to Amaryllis as a tiger, ready to pounce. His body was still but appeared to be full of raging energy, as if he were waiting for the first syllable of the next word she was bound to say. He took a lunge followed by quick steps to grab her.

He moved fast. He seemed to move from his previous distance to an inch away from her face within the blink of an eye. She simply could not react quick enough. He gripped her throat and squeezed tightly. Amaryllis dug her fingernails into his hands, but he did not loosen his grip. Her throat burned unbearably. She looked into his wide brown eyes, full of rage. She kicked him in the shin as hard as she could but he did not move. He said nothing as he strangled her. Silence was, if not, more terrifying than anything he could have said. He had the most frightening eyes. Amaryllis' lungs begged for air, her whole chest stung. Her eyes watered, and within them was a plea for mercy.

With thorough concentration she converted her fear into anger and used it to summon magic. She watched the man's expression drastically change from angry to shocked in an instant as her eyes glowed bright turquoise. His sudden surprise caused his grip to involuntarily loosen, and from there she lifted the drawer full of clothes and slammed it into his body with her mind. Her throat was instantly free as his limp body flew across the room with the drawers close behind. He flew into the wall and the drawer chest came soaring with a loud bang as it crashed into his body.

Amaryllis gasped loudly, gently massaging her neck with soft hands. She dropped to her knees and sobbed with spastic breaths. After finally being able to breathe, she stood up and cautiously walked to the chest. She peered overtop of the chest to see the man with closed eyes.

What was that? she asked herself. *He had gone through so much trouble to rescue me from the grove, and all of his efforts became pointless as soon as he tried to kill me himself. I can't think of any logical explanation… although it was my introduction which drove him mad.*

The chest of drawers returned to its native place with Amaryllis' magic, levitating slowly and bouncing slightly across the room until it found itself against the wall. The man snapped awake and got up to charge at Amaryllis once again as if he had never been unconscious in the first place, but she kept him still, holding him in place with her mind. Her glowing eyes taunted him while he snarled in frustration.

"What is your problem?" she asked viciously.

The man growled through his teeth. "People like you… you're all malicious narcissists." He wiggled around trying to free himself from Amaryllis' unseen grasp.

"People such as I," she began with an angered voice, but as the man's insult absorbed into her thoughts, she found herself thinking of the Choosing Ceremony along with the eight preparation parties. She remembered the selfish princesses, the egotistical Prince Eric of Arlon, the scowling kings and queens, and worst of all, the most vivid memory of the Prince of Werling taking Laria's hand and walking her away from the line. For her, royalty was a game in which she did not know how to play. "You're right," she whimpered.

Her response startled him. No king, queen, prince, nor princess would have ever agreed with such a statement.

"I'm sorry?" he asked. His tense body relaxed, looking airy and flimsy compared to his previous rage-induced positioning. Amaryllis' connection with the universe had been disrupted, broken by her flashbacks. The man was released from her grasp but he did not move.

"I agree with you," she said solemnly. Amaryllis appeared to the man as an animal who despised her own species, or a treacherous shadow creature who desired to be kind and gentle.

"Why is that?" he asked, grabbing a stool from beside the chest of drawers and sitting down. Amaryllis quickly summarized her life story all within a minute. During that minute, although the man despised royals, he empathized with the princess feeling the pain of her sorrow-filled heart. She then told him about the demon she had accidentally set free and informed him of her quest and her endeavour to find a solution to contain the evil once again.

He looked only slightly troubled at the unfortunate news of Immortuos being set free. He had not known of its existence until Amaryllis had mentioned it and could not yet understand the dangers of the demon with its freedom or the Forest of Enchantment's broken barrier. But as Amaryllis droned on about Immortuos, the man knew more and more of how deadly the situation was. She had to deal with hell itself.

"I don't mean to sound sorry for myself, but I honestly believe I am the unluckiest human being on this Earth."

"There is no need for you to justify anything, Princess. I would have to agree with you. I must apologize for my actions… now knowing who you are, I feel terrible about it."

Amaryllis nodded her head and accepted his apology. "You understand why I don't especially admire the other royals—?"

"Don't you *defend* those royal swines. You worded that poorly. Those people caused excessive trauma to your *soul*. Yes, I understand why you especially *hate* those people. And yes I will now tell my story. All will be perfectly clear," he promised.

Amazement filled Amaryllis. He knew the words that were bound to exit her mouth. He picked up on her cues, giving her the illusion that he had read her mind.

Chapter 29

"My name is John Edwards and, like your life, mine was also extremely unlucky and miserable. Now, it is merely depressing. I have taken refuge in this horrid shack but, before I lived within the gates of Arlon, serving the king. I was his personal bounty hunter and hitman, running bloody errands for him every hour. Mind you, man-tracking was not my desired profession, and it was rare that I actually had to capture someone to bring them in. Decades ago, I owned a cattle farm alongside my wife and four sons. I was a busy and happy man until one day, I went to sell beef at the market. The king rarely came down to the village, but that day just *had* to be the day for his visit. You see, the King of Arlon is a coldhearted man, a malevolent monster. He truly does not care for the good of his people, providing us with no benefits of living in the village of Arlon. He claimed nearly all of our resources as his own, taking away our food and starving us.

"The commoners' hatred could not be concealed and several people had thrown rocks that soared through the air like cannonballs, straight for the king's stupid head. I acted blindly and goodheartedly by shielding him with an empty crate since no one else would. His knights, who had walked down with him had fallen to the ground, nailed by rocks which rattled their skulls within their helmets. I was then attacked by several villagers which I had easily eluded and defended myself against. I had shown a skill I did not know I possessed and it was enough to impress the king. He abducted me from my family, took me away right then, wanting me by his side all the time. I did not hear from them, nor was I allowed to visit them, let alone return to my life. I was constantly *killing* enemies of the king because of the size of Arlon itself with its massive population, but he also happened to be a cowardly, cruel man, so the number of casualties per day was *high*. If I had been the bounty hunter for a long while I'm afraid I would have taken the lives of everyone in the village. I don't know of anyone who's liked him to this day, but, back then he was absolutely despised, and it was because he was truly a horrible king. A good portion of the village was plotting to execute him, so I had no choice but to kill all of those people. It was months of killing with specific demands to *never* converse with my family, or else I was to face consequences that I was never informed of…the only thing I knew was that I would regret it for the rest of my life.

"On a cold and rainy day, I ventured down to the village to bring a mad blacksmith to the king for a reason I did not understand. I did not bother to question it. My journey had been interrupted by the sight of my wife. She was there, in the middle of the street, wearing a black, hooded cape to shield herself from the rain. She was breathtaking. Her soft brown eyes were sad, and her short, curly brown hair stuck out slightly from her cloak. She looked like a pretty little angel lighting up the muggy village with just her presence. Before running to hold her in my arms, I stood and stared, absolutely frozen. My absence surely destroyed her in all ways. I had suddenly left her to run the farm, take care of our sons, and left her without the love of a husband.

"I could not be away from her for another second. I ran as fast as I could, splashing in puddles on the street, sending water flying. She looked up at the sound of my footsteps and smiled. Tears flowed immediately after. I held her close, feeling her heart race and her chest spasm against me as she sobbed. I apologized a thousand times and told her that I loved her and the children.

We hugged for the longest time, neither of us wanting to let go. I explained my abduction and the king's rules. I told her about my new profession and her reaction broke my heart. She sobbed harder, holding me tighter. Her husband was a killer but it did not seem to matter as long as I was alive and well. She talked about the farm and how our boys matured quickly to cover my role in the chores. I had never been prouder and in that moment I wished they were there. My wife and I hugged and talked in the pouring rain before I remembered the king's rules, filling my gut with fear. As much as it pained me, I pushed her off me so I could find the unstable blacksmith and return to the castle so as to not have to face the consequences of visiting my wife. Her eyes streamed with tears as I pried her off. She looked hurt and confused, standing still with urges to run back into my embrace. I reminded her of the rules and I, myself began to cry. She said goodbye and told me she loved me very much, turning around to walk away. Without thinking I ran up behind her, grabbed her shoulders and spun her around. I told her I loved her more than anything, that I simply could not express to her in words just how much she meant to me, then I gave her a long kiss. It was a passionate and loving kiss that I wished never had to end. Walking away from her was the most difficult thing I had to do. Far more difficult than any kill I ever had to make.

"So, I found the crazed blacksmith and brought him back to the castle effortlessly. On the rest of my journey, I thought of my wife. Even as I handed the psychopath over to the king, the image of my wife's sorrowful, yet radiant face, burned in my mind. I had longed for her for months, and briefly seeing her was not enough. Seeing her only made me more lonesome for her. Night eventually fell and time seemed to pass so slowly.

"The king barged into my small bedroom which was right next to his, and called me down to the ballroom. I hurried along down the stairs, ran down the hall and through the ballroom doors. The room was empty all ex-except... for my wife, four sons, and the king," John stopped as a tear rolled down his cheek. He squinted, burying his face in his hands, then lifted his head and continued.

"The king told me he knew I had seen my wife that day and the consequences I was about to face were inevitable. Hundreds of knights emerged from the shadows making a wall separating me from the king and my beloved family who was tied up in ropes. I fell to my knees and wailed, crying tears of misery and despair. There are simply no words strong enough to describe the sadness that oppressed my soul.

"One by one the king stabbed my family with a large dagger, and I could not prevent it as the knights stood in my way. Their shrill screams echoed in the large room penetrating my ears... I will never forget the sound I heard. I could not save them. I ran away from the wall of knights and over to the large window with the drapes closed. I tore the rope which opened and closed the drapes, then ran back to my original place, throwing it over the chandelier and tugging to ensure it was stable. I took a running start, swung overtop of the knights and my feet met the king's face. He fell to the ground, unconscious. I pulled my wife and sons into my chest and cried but I was too late. I held onto them with trembling arms as I examined their stab wounds. They were each impaled in the gut, bleeding excessively, their blood pooling on the floor and staining my hands. The knights spun around with their armour rattling. It was then that I had an epiphany of hatred. The sound of the clanging metal irritated me so greatly and forever were to remind me of their duties of protecting and obeying the orders of *royals*. The sight of my dead family lying lifelessly in my lap destroyed and infuriated me.

"Just as the knights began to seize me, the king sat up holding his head. He frowned at me, followed by a low groan. He looked at me as if *my* actions were inconceivable and uncalled for... how dare *I* hit the king... yet he had the audacity to penalize my breaking of his inhumane rules by taking the lives of the only people in my life whom I cared for… the only people I desired to live for. The knights grabbed hold of me and kept me still as the king put his face an inch from mine. His vacuous eyes locked on mine, then he proceeded to tell me I was banished to the Dark Forest where I was to die.

"But I am still here… I have been living in these treacherous woods for twenty whole years. Normally, I would have continued to live in the mainlands and ignore the king, but everything there reminded me of my family. Therefore *I* decided to obey the banishment, *I* voluntarily marched into the Dark Forest without looking back. I found that the melancholic tunes best suited my perpetual misery. I survived the first few weeks by travelling to new locations daily, taking shelter in caves and trees, until I finally built this shack to protect myself. I am certain I have seen every type of dark creature to ever exist because there is not a shrill scream within these woods that I do not recognize, and every single day, I think of my wife. I picture my most bittersweet memory that we shared twenty years ago in the street on that rainy day. I think of the birth of each of my sons and how they were growing into beautiful, responsible young men who were bound to accomplish wondrous things… but then I cry at the thought of their death within that godforsaken castle. Princess Amaryllis of Serilion, I despise royals."

John Edwards finished his story, covering his face to sob silently in his hands. His head fell between his knees as he sat on his stool hunched over in a ball of sadness. Tears formed in Amaryllis' eyes, and she tried to blink them away but they could not be stopped. A single drop fell down her left cheek and onto the wooden floor. She understood his pain. He had described his story so passionately, she felt as if she were there with him when the tragedy happened. Her heart ached and she could not imagine how he felt. Amaryllis felt that his attack against her was completely justified and if she were him she would have lashed out as well.

Amaryllis opened her mouth to speak but she could not think of what to say. There were no words that could ever reassure him. The only appropriate thing she could say was based off of apology, acceptance and understanding.

"John," she began. "I am so incredibly sorry. What you went through and what you're still having to go through… those memories… again, I am so sorry." Amaryllis spoke softly, wiping her tears. John nodded between his legs, too consumed by misery to lift his head.

"I'm sorry to have made you relive that," she uttered.

"No, it's all right," he sobbed. His deep voice was lighter and shaken. "I am sorry for lashing out and trying to kill you, but now you understand that I have been living in wretchedness because of a royal, and your introduction… it unleashed my rage and I reacted unconsciously."

"I would have done the exact same thing," Amaryllis assured him. Although he had every reason to lean over and cry, sadness did not suit John Edwards. He looked to be too tough of a man to show any sort of deep emotion. It was strange yet completely acceptable at the same time.

Finally, after a few more moments he sat up revealing his face. His complexion was visibly red and blotchy beneath his grey stubble. His eyelashes were wet; all clumped together emphasizing the sorrow within his brown eyes. His world was slowly spinning, taunting him with the absence of his loved ones.

"Twenty years feels like an eternity when you're alone," he sighed. Amaryllis nodded her head grimly. "I am not one to believe in miracles, but, for your sake, it was a miracle that I was banished to these woods so I could save the life of the princess who was to save the world from elusive danger. This world has done nothing for me but take my joys away; however, I wish to assist you on your quest to prevent further losses of families. I imagine the creatures have spread out extremely far already and are currently terrorizing people. Please allow me to help you… I will be nothing but your escort through the forest and the protector of your body. No creature shall harm you ever again."

Amaryllis sighed. She frowned at the memory of her encounter with the demon and answered John gruffly as the demon brought out her inner guilt and rage.

"Yes, I accept your assistance. It would be much appreciated. I thank you in advance, and I thank you for saving me from the grove. I believe I forgot to thank you earlier. I was in too much pain to think clearly."

With hope in his eyes, John stood up towering over Amaryllis. He lightly touched her shoulder and assured her that they would make it to Immortuos' lair intact.

He had found a pair of socks and leather boots and gave them to her. They left John's shack in a hurry, jogging through the Dark Forest in the direction of the jagged, unsettling, evilly constructed mountain.

Chapter 30

Now that Amaryllis had no metal resting on her shoulders that weighed her down she felt as light as air. She ran like the wind through a patch of densely populated, young trees. She weaved through them with speed and grace. However, her graceful speed looked mediocre compared to John's precise and far more elegant movements. He was much faster and he should have been since he had been actively surviving in the unpredictable Dark Forest for two decades. His stamina was preeminent, he never seemed to tire. He breathed calmly and consistently, and his face was seldom visited by distress or exhaust. Amaryllis was always a good few paces behind him fighting her tired muscles, heart, and lungs with her mind. She felt weak and cowardly to ask for a rest, so she didn't say a word and pushed her body beyond its limits.

All was well until her muscles gave up. Her legs suddenly felt like they weighed one thousand pounds and she had to stop. Her legs wobbled as she stood still.

"John!" she yelled, so as to not let him continue to run away leaving her behind. He stopped suddenly and turned around to see Amaryllis leaning against a black oak tree, panting.

"Are you all right?" he called, then started jogging towards her.

"I am fine; however, I am quite fatigued. I cannot move my legs," she sighed.

John helped her sit down on the roots of the black oak tree. "We can rest briefly but not for long."

Amaryllis glanced at the gargantuan mountain, filled with hope. It appeared so close but its massive size was what gave it that illusion. It stretched to be extremely tall but the width seemed minuscule. The mountain twisted and turned in random patterns, moulded and shaped by the mind of an unforgiving presence who was raptured to conquer Earth with hell. The mountain's disturbing aura killed her feeling of hope and replaced it with fear.

"If you were to estimate the length of our journey from here, what would you say?" Amaryllis asked through deep breaths.

John stared intently at the mountain. "One day, but perhaps two if we keep stopping like this."

Amaryllis could not tell if he was joking or if he was frustrated that her stamina was inferior to his.

"We can slow down if you'd like," he offered. "We *have* been running for a long time." Amaryllis nodded. "How are you not the slightest bit tired?" she asked in astonishment. "It's been well over an hour of sheer sprinting."

John gripped his dagger tightly, relaxed his fingers, twirled it once releasing it into the air then caught it. Such a question seemed ridiculous to him. "Well, I've been surviving in here for twenty years. I've been running for my life for *quite* a long time," he chided. With his wife's bloody corpse involuntarily presented in his mind, he clenched his jaw then tossed the dagger again.

"I understand that, but your stamina seems to be endlessly stable."

John gripped the blade then threw the dagger into a tree twenty feet away. Walking away to retrieve it, he shouted over his shoulder, "Let me know when you're ready, and we'll go."

Amaryllis looked down and thought of how tired she was. She hadn't had a good night's rest in a while, and she looked forward to being able to sleep comfortably knowing this bounty hunter would be keeping watch for the dreaded creatures in the night. Amaryllis found that whenever she thought of the idea of a shadow creature, she would give herself unbearable anxiety. Those things grabbed at her, gashed her body, nearly dislocated all her limbs from her body as they tugged at her, and their screams permanently had a place in the back of her mind. Goosebumps rose from her flesh as she pictured her traumatic experience, her stomach jolting with anxiety. She stood up quickly pushing through the discomfort.

"Could we perhaps walk some of the way?" she asked in a voice disrupted by nervousness.

John yanked out the knife from the bark with an aggressive jerk then made his way back. "Yes, but you must tell me when you feel capable of running," he stated.

"Yes, of course, I shall," she agreed. "Although it will not be for a long while," she muttered under her breath.

They began walking and Amaryllis was thankful she could take a break, but John was full of energy and had to fight a strong urge to run. He had never really walked through the forest before. He was always in a situation where he had to flee. The monsters had spread, and the forest was quieter. John was constantly alert, no matter how deviously misleading the place of darkness was he never let his guard down.

The forest seemed to have a mind of its own. An intelligent and omnipotent life-form that acted as an unseen force. Each ecosystem functioned with odd perfection and patterning, and all of the creatures seemed to know exactly where other beings were at all times. They either chose to attack or not. The key to survival was always being ready for unexpected attacks. Wherever shelter was taken, even though one may have felt hidden and out of danger, the creatures were always aware of your location and no walls would stop them from trying to enter if they wanted to.

John had been restless for most of his nights living in the Dark Forest, listening to howling, loud banging on the sides of his shack, claws of creatures being scratched into the walls, and the continuous melancholic melodies which haunted him.

Luckily, he had kept his sanity in ways unknown. Perhaps, his fond memories of his family kept him going... but how long could have thoughts of someone he loved without reminding himself of their absence? He was truly a strong man, and mental strength was what Amaryllis and John Edwards shared.

They had walked for some time, then John asked her if she was feeling all right to run. Without responding, she tried to jog lightly but her muscles cramped. She grabbed her upper leg and massaged it.

"I cannot feel my legs, and when I run they seize," she groaned, wishing that Ezro could have crossed the grove of mushrooms with her to give her a rest. She wondered of his well-being and whether or not her magic had worked in getting him back to Charles.

"Why not use your magic to rid of the pain?" he suggested. As he spoke he sounded unsure of every word he said. He was a brand new believer in magic and still couldn't bring himself to completely accept that Amaryllis knew secrets that the world did not.

"I can't seem to concentrate at the moment. It takes focus and energy," she replied. "I, myself do not completely understand how it works. All I do is—" she stopped herself, picturing Akar. She did not imagine that he would be all right with her exposing the secrets of magic.

"What do you do?" John asked curiously, but Amaryllis could not hear him through her attempted communication with the cosmos.

I stand in the meadow beside the castle of Arlon. The dark green grass is long and it hides my lower body. As the wind blows, both my hair and the grass gently dance. The sky is completely black, speckled with stars, and there are no crimson clouds in sight. The world is free of evil. I can see the Forest of Enchantment. The boundary's golden rays glow and, within the peaceful forest, nature is beautiful and filled with innocent herbivores. Deer, rabbits, and squirrels live happily in the safe place within the Dark Forest. All has returned to normal. I bring myself back to the meadow then focus on the brightest star in the sky. I allow my soul to fly from my body and up into space—

"What do you do?" John repeated loudly, bewildered by her trance and moment of silence. His gruff voice startled her.

All within a split second, Amaryllis' soul fell from space and implanted itself within her body, which stood motionless in the meadow of her daydream until it was struck with life. Amaryllis jolted as she entered reality once again.

"I was nearly there. I almost found a connection. I just needed to—" she refrained from mentioning that she needed to receive magic from a star, "—it's all right, but, I refuse to tell you about the process," She uttered impatiently. She managed to enter space although she was extremely fatigued and found it exceedingly difficult to concentrate. Just a bit longer and she would have filled her body with magic from the universe. "I won't be healing my sore legs, and we'll have to continue walking."

John grew impatient himself, wanting to understand magic and wanting to run. He picked up Amaryllis and held her like an infant in his arms, then began sprinting.

Amaryllis' surroundings whooshed past her in a blur. Her body was strongly supported by John's muscular arms. He ran with her as if she were weightless.

"What are you doing?" she yelled over the rapid tapping of his feet against the dirt. He did not answer. Amaryllis looked at his scruffy face in the shadows of the darkness of the forest. It was light enough to read his determined facial expression. He was once handsome, but the oppression of misery and loneliness, along with old age had affected his once attractive appearance.

His eyes could not have always looked so mean, she thought to herself. *The sight of his wife would be the element that raises his furrowed brows and extracts the despair from his eyes.*

Her heart ached with sympathy for the poor man until she was disturbed in an instant.

"Now, I'm going to throw you," he stated with his eyes shifting in all directions.

Her stomach dropped. "What?" she yelled, panicked. She scanned the woods for danger, but John was running too fast for her to be able to focus on anything.

Charging from beside them were skinny, human-like creatures running on all fours like dogs. They were oddly silent as there was a dozen of them and their hands and feet made no sound as they contacted the ground. Their abnormal silence startled Amaryllis, and her feeling of fear grew stronger as the bounty hunter suddenly stopped and threw her as high as he could into the air. As soon as he released her the odd creatures seized him. They were biting at his arms and legs, sinking their teeth very near to the bone. He screamed in agony.

As Amaryllis reached the peak of her toss and held herself in place using magic. She levitated directly above John, staring at the emaciated beings. She used all of her concentration to snap several pointed branches off of trees and fire them into all twelve creatures. They fell instantly, but one died with its teeth buried within John's flesh.

Amaryllis slowly lowered herself. When she landed, her glowing eyes faded. John was breathing heavily, wincing. He grabbed the jaw of the creature and snapped it. He threw the carcass away in anger with a grunt.

"What are those things?"

John stared at his wounds, looking mildly concerned. "Akaskeez," he muttered pressing on his wounds to watch blood ooze out of them. Amaryllis stared at the akaskeez with the broken jaw. Its bottom teeth were short and stubby but sharp. The top teeth were long, pointed, and even sharper. Its skin was a faint red. It was translucent with purple veins clearly visible. Its kyphotic spine nearly poked through the skin and, as it lay dead, its big white eyes stared lifelessly at nothing in particular. If the thing were to stand up and its spine were to straighten, it would stand to be seven feet tall.

"Don't look into their eyes," John warned with a quickness in his voice, looking up from his gnawed legs.

Amaryllis looked away from the creature. Her heart dropped. She had been looking, mesmerized into the blank white eyes of the akaskeez. "Why?" she asked nervously, hugging herself for comfort.

"They're not completely deceased yet. Their souls are contained in their bodies for a while and their eyes are the windows to their vicious souls… they'll make spiritual connections with your soul and follow you forever, haunting you. I would know since I have one."

"What do you mean?"

"The spirit of an akaskeez constantly follows me. You cannot see it but I can," he explained.

"What does it do?"

"It's done nothing too troubling. It latched to me several years ago. All it does is stare at me with its glassy white eyes and sometimes it gets in my personal space. I feel nothing, but it's quite irritating sometimes. Most times I don't even notice it."

"How long did you look at it for it to latch to you?" she asked timidly.

"Oh, quite a while… not to worry," he responded gently. "I could see myself—my reflection—in the beast's eyes. I was caught staring at my appearance which I didn't like. I couldn't look away from the man in those white eyes."

Amaryllis dreaded the idea of being followed by a creature as horrifying as an akaskeez. The disturbing features would be enough to torment her for eternity, and if they actually attacked her in spirit form she would faint from fear. She dared not even glance at its body, she kept her eyes on John.

"Why did you throw me in the air?" she felt as if her question was rhetorical but she asked anyway.

"To protect you. I knew you would do your magical... thing," he scoffed.

"Magic exists and you don't need to feel shame by believing in it. You won't lose dignity or your *manliness* by believing." Amaryllis assured him. She could clearly read his scepticism. "And perhaps you might appreciate it if I healed your wounds. I seem to be able to focus on the power now."

Amaryllis focused on his bite marks and restored them to normal within a few seconds. John sighed as the pain dissipated. She looked at him with a smile on her face, hoping to have connected with him and make him feel comfortable with magic, but he just nodded, then instructed her to heal her own exhausted legs so they could continue moving. She did as she was told and then began sprinting ahead of him. Her legs were energized, moving back and forth with long, rapid strides. She felt quick, much quicker than before; however, John passed her. All felt the same as before with her trailing behind and John tirelessly bolting ahead.

Chapter 31

Amaryllis learned how to keep up with John. Her strategy consisted of healing her exhausted muscles as she ran, which took great amounts of concentration, and thinking of things to entertain herself.

She avoided memories like the Choosing Ceremony and the seven parties before the important eighth one. She fished out the pleasant memories which she stored in the depths of her mind. She thought of Prince James the most, thinking of how she was to become his wife—the Queen of Werling. Thinking of the word, *queen*, caused her to shudder. It was unbelievable to her.

I am Queen Amaryllis of Werling. The words were odd to say in her mind. She had been introducing herself as the *Princess of Serilion* for her entire life. She had never visited Werling before but she had heard wonderful things about it. Surely the castle was larger than her own and perhaps it was more beautiful. All was unknown until she was to see it for herself.

She wondered about James' well-being and what he could be doing in that moment. She wished to see him, for the journey to be over and to have him hold her.

Getting to the mountain was a separate journey. Amaryllis could predict the outcomes of the forest, but she could not predict the outcomes of fighting Immortuos and that frightened her.

Amaryllis and John had been running for quite some time with no conversation. Even though Amaryllis was a few paces back she could hear faint, heavy breathing finally coming from John. It was relieving to know that he was capable of tiring.

There was a sudden, strong wind blowing against their backs, pushing them forward and cooling them off in the warmth of their body heat. The leaves and branches of the trees shook vigorously which gave Amaryllis the feeling that something minacious was to happen. If she were alone and did not have the bounty hunter, she would have panicked. The trees seemed to signify sinister events that were bound to happen, and she ran through these ominous sirens with no escape from them.

John stopped abruptly causing Amaryllis to do the same.

"What is it?" she asked, mesmerized by the frantic shaking of the trees and the chilling sound they created. She felt claustrophobic, feeling more closed in by the darkness than before. The shadows attacked her good nature and purity, making her stomach feel empty. She was full of apprehensive energy and felt the desire to hide, or run to the exit of the Dark Forest (it's not like it would be any better on the outside anyway). She could only imagine the fear that people all over the world were experiencing. Surely the demonic creatures and monsters from the Dark Forest were spreading across the world.

"It's nothing. Only the winds coming from the lake," he answered solemnly, "but, we have to slow ourselves."

"What for?"

"We have to calm our heart rates. Soon, we will come across a lake. I'll explain everything in a moment but for now calm down. We're walking from here." John had to shout over the winds. His loud and deep voice, along with the suspense that he continued, frightened her even more. She held her stomach and leaned forward slightly to cope with the anxiety within her gut.

They slowed to a dawdling type of walk which increased the pulsating intensity of Amaryllis' nervousness. It seemed horribly wrong to walk so slowly during the violent tantrums of the gale through the forest, but they did and John seemed not at all phased by anything. The howling, furious winds nor the Dark Forest bothered him. He showed no concern for Amaryllis' fright.

Although she was hiding it quite well, internally she was screaming. On the outside, she trembled as she walked with wobbling knees. Her independence and mental strength had finally reached it's breaking point. Desperation was all that existed in her mindset. She wanted to run into someone's arms; whether it be Prince James', her mother's, or her father's, and allow their comforting embrace to settle her shaking. John did not project himself as the compassionate type, so Amaryllis refrained from expressing her repulsive need to wrap her arms around him and shudder. Instead, she tried to ignore his presence by staring at the dark, twisted trees ahead to take her mind from the situation. She tried to bring herself to a pleasant memory in her brain but darkness smothered her.

She was close to wishing she hadn't stood up to the Prince of Arlon, and that she hadn't fallen in love with Prince James so quickly. Marrying the Prince of Arlon was *heaven* compared to where she was, but she hadn't wished for it completely because, although love had never been kind to her, she had seen a glimpse of what real love was like. Her time with Prince James was a factor in keeping herself motivated. She hated herself immediately for thinking such opposing thoughts, but also felt she did not need to justify that those thoughts were acceptable in terms of her conditions.

Amaryllis was at war with herself. Half of her wanted to climb Immortuos' mountain to bring pain and, afterwards, death to the wretched creature. The other half of her wanted to cower at the base of a tree and wait for Prince James to rescue her. Her mind raced with arguing thoughts as she glumly walked beside the bounty hunter.

Talk to him, she thought. *Distract your mind. Say something.*

"Do you know your way through the whole forest?" The question exploded from her mouth.

He looked at her with a raised brow, then relaxed it. "Well, not all of it but most of it," he answered gruffly.

"Surely you must have seen all of it after living here for so long."

"Most of it," he said firmly, not in the mood to converse.

Amaryllis' stomach dropped. She was again alone with nothing but her thoughts and she did not like it. She was terrified of her own mind. "What will you do once I set things back to normal?" she asked quietly. There was a long pause between them. Each footstep in the dirt made the situation more awkward with an odd sort of silence.

"I haven't thought of it."

"You don't have to go back to that shack. You could come to Werling with James and I. We would make sure that you have your very own room in the castle," she offered sincerely.

"Don't look too far ahead."

"I mean it. You deserve it, John. You must miss the sweet songs of the Earth:birds chirping, water rushing, the gentle winds blowing. You must miss what the Dark Forest isn't."

"I don't want to go back if my wife isn't there. It's the exact same out there as it is in here if she's not living," he mumbled.

Amaryllis did not hear him. "Perhaps you'll meet someone rather exquisite and she'll help you to gain your happiness back," she encouraged him, hoping he'd agree and see the bright side of helping her save the Earth.

John reached his arm out in front of her and stopped her from walking. "Absolutely no one has been, or will ever be, more exquisite than Judith," he raged through gritted teeth. A few years ago, tears would have welled in his eyes, but he seemed to have permanently emptied his tear ducts. A chance of sadness was forever replaced by an undiluted rage.

He possessed a constant look that caused discomfort and fear, but when he was angry he defied the rules of fright. When Amaryllis thought John was as scary as could be his face would change growing even more terrifying.

Amaryllis' heart raced and she stood frozen. John's heart raced too. His pupils shrunk to the size of pinholes, and he fought the urge to strike her. Their eyes were locked for a while, predator glaring at its prey. Amaryllis was unable to move. All she could do was look and listen, hearing her heartbeat rage in her ears. She suffocated with the last breath of air she inhaled; her gasp becoming trapped in her chest.

John's anger suddenly passed and his eyes appeared slightly less menacing. "Don't you talk about my wife ever again, *Witch*," he warned, letting his arm fall limply to his side. Amaryllis stared wide eyed at him, then exhaled explosively. She stepped back and distanced herself. "Yeah, you're going to have to wait a while." He pointed at a set of trees in the distance.

"What are you talking about?" she snapped, annoyed with herself for letting an old man have control over her fear and nervousness. He was quite scary in general, as he was tall and had incredible muscular strength which showed in his stature. His presence was enough to make the bravest person shudder. Something about him was extremely mysterious and daunting. When angry, he unleashed a whole new level of intimidation. She had every reason to be scared but she did not like it.

"Our heart rates must be slowed," he scowled in a way that implied that *she* was the simpleton, then grabbed her and pulled her along. John knew the effect he had on her. He knew she felt uncomfortable. He could tell through her big, green, staring eyes and her tense shoulders, but he didn't attempt to make her feel comfortable. He didn't care.

She allowed him to lead her, pushing away the anger he ignited. Her cheeks were flushed in annoyance and frustration, hating herself for her sensitivity.

The bounty hunter pushed through many small bushes that irritated him with their presence. He hit them with a strong arm swing, and, if they snapped back and whipped him, he would pull out his dagger and cut them with slashes of frustration. He pushed a big bush aside to show Amaryllis a hidden lake.

"They can hear you," he whispered darkly.

Amaryllis shook her arm free from his grasp. "What are you talking about?" she barked.

He let go of the bush and it snapped back, once again hiding the lake. He held up a finger to hush her. "Quiet," he whispered. "They hear you."

She frowned at him. "What?" She would have sounded more afraid if she wasn't so fed up with John's inconsistent and confusing behaviour. He respected her enough to assist her and protect her on her journey, but he was so easily triggered. Amaryllis could not really blame him. He hadn't talked to or even seen another human being in two decades, plus *everything* had been taken from him.

"There are fish in the water that can detect the heart rates of other creatures. They try to scare their prey to increase their heart rates. It gets more blood flowing. When they feel they've scared you enough, they come up and attack. They take whole chunks outta you, and they gnaw right down to the bone," he warned sounding frightened himself. Seeing how afraid John was, Amaryllis too became afraid. Her heart only became more startled. It was all she could feel.

"There's no other way around the lake?" she asked with a shaky voice.

"Well, yeah, but that's an extra three days." He moved the bush out of the way again. "Look at how close we are to the mountain."

Amaryllis shuffled around to look beyond the lake. The mountain was close indeed. She assumed the sun was nearly setting. She could see the red clouded sky above the wavy lake, but the clouds were still too thick to be able to see the sun. After the lake, Amaryllis was determined to set up camp for the night.

"We have to swim?" she whimpered. John nodded. "How long will it take?"

"Not too long... it's longer than it is wide," he sighed.

"Is there any way we could fight them off if our heart rates get too high?"

John shook his head. "No, those things will tear you to shreds. Once they want you, they have you. That is it."

Amaryllis shivered and crossed her arms. "So, be brave or die?"

"No, the bravest person is as vulnerable as a coward. You need to distance your mind. These things use sharp movements and sudden loud noises to scare their prey. Any creature of any kind is bound to jolt and have their heart rates raised. It can be reactionary and inevitable. Be *strategic* or die. Relax."

"That is horrible. I find it difficult to relax, especially now. If anything, I am more frightened." Amaryllis looked at the choppy lake and imagined it swimming with big mouthed, sharp-toothed fish waiting to sink their teeth into her.

"I've done it once. I didn't know they were in there and that's the only reason they didn't get me. The thrashing did not phase me but as soon as they roared...yes that's right, the fish *roared*, and jumped out for me to see what they looked like, I got the hell out of there."

Amaryllis widened her eyes. "What do they look like?"

"I mustn't say," he cautioned. "I don't want to worry you anymore. Just... let's work on slowing our heart rates then we'll go," John suggested. He paused to think of a lie to tell Amaryllis to ease her anxiety, a lie that would only work to calm her down and not to mistakenly kill her faster. He brainstormed until he thought of something he wasn't completely sure of himself. "They don't attack until your heart picks up significantly, so even though they may be rubbing against you, or ramming into you, don't be alarmed. They don't feast until you are notably startled."

"I understand that. It's just that I think I will be easily startled and won't even last a minute. If only we had a raft…"

John widened his eyes and shook his head slowly. "Oh no-no, they can hear the pulsations through the boat. They'd tear it apart then you."

Amaryllis moaned and put her hands on top of her head. "At this point, it seems wiser to go the long way," she whined as she spoke, which was something she never did.

"It is beyond horrifying, I know. Some may even see it as sudden death, but I truly believe we can make it across here." He gazed at the wind-stirred water and spoke solemnly. He had begun his process of relaxation by accepting the circumstances. Amaryllis glared at him like he was insane. He laid down at the base of a bush separating them from the Dark Forest and the lake and closed his eyes. Keeping his eyes shut, he motioned for her to do the same. She did.

They laid squished between bushes with their eyes closed for a while. During their attempt of pure relaxation, John was gently talking to Amaryllis soothing her into a trance of weightlessness. She did not know how but his gruff voice dissipated into a gentle, kind voice that he must have possessed as a young man. His goal was to relax her to a point of near sleepiness. What he didn't know was that Amaryllis had come to terms with the task at hand, and she was mentally prepared to face the fish.

They stood up feeling lazy and lightheaded. Amaryllis was more at ease than John since he provided her with effortless relaxation—all she had to do was listen. She listened to the hollow, whooshing gales moving the water around. The lake which reflected the red sky crashed with high waves.

If Amaryllis were to analyze the lake a few minutes ago, she would have pictured the red lake as a bloody pool consisting of her own blood. In her hypothetical fantasy, John would have survived—swimming out of the lake with no emotional attachment to Amaryllis' death.

"Ready?" John whispered almost inaudibly.

"Yes," she answered softly remembering to distance her mind and think somnolent thoughts.

They stepped into the lake, water rushing into their boots and soaking their clothes the further in they went. The cold water gave them goosebumps, and the harsh winds made the shivering worse. As they moved slowly into the lake with clenched jaws to prevent the chattering of their teeth their feet could no longer touch the bottom. They swam in a breaststroke style as slow as possible.

Without thinking too much about it, Amaryllis looked blankly at her surroundings. She looked, only with her eyes, to the tree line. She missed the pure beauties of the Earth before they were shadowed by the red clouds. She looked to the mountain. It was her motivation to carefully swim through the monster infested waters. She was so much closer to Immortuos with each minute that passed.

A large wave was coming in her direction. She couldn't pick up her speed to swim up the wave, so she let it fall over her head submerging her in water briefly. She was excessively cold once her entire hair became wet, but she fought herself and ignored the excruciatingly awakening and flesh-raising waters.

The wind sounded louder after becoming completely wet. It seemed to penetrate and flow through her ears more aggressively, sounding heavy and more hollow.

The cold water burned Amaryllis' skin, worrying her greatly. It was so cold that it felt hot. When the body is exposed to cooler temperatures the heart is forced to pump faster, making it harder to warm the body. The lake itself was a trap. When animals with rapid heart rates from the cold water were petrified by the fish their heart rates would increase. The fish's scare tactics did not require much effort.

Amaryllis realized this after a few minutes and the thought itself startled her, but she refused to let it affect her. She couldn't even warn John about the water being too cold as she could risk increasing both of their heart rates.

From her left, a large ripple formed which showed through the choppy water.

Oh no... Already? she thought. Her relaxed mind delayed her reaction but she was slowly becoming more alert because of the temperature of the water. It was inevitable to resist the snapping awareness that the frigid water caused. In the bitter, empty feeling of the water, Amaryllis could only feel her heart beating. Although they did not show themselves, she knew she was surrounded by them. Amaryllis was almost glad that it was a windy day. If the water was still and transparent, she may not have dared to enter the lake at all to risk seeing the monstrous fish.

Another ripple was made...this time to her right. It was much closer than the first, splashing her face with skin-numbing droplets. She looked to John who did not seem bothered. He looked back at her and nodded as if saying, *you can do it.*

They continued swimming slowly, and as each second passed Amaryllis noticed how uncomfortable she was with the cotton fabric of her clothes sticking to her skin. It was only making her colder. It pressed against her hard goosebumps making her cringe.

Again, she looked away from the lake and up at the sky. From behind her, a big splash occurred, but she ignored it keeping her gaze on the strangely beautiful yet disturbing sky.

Another splash—it was bigger and louder, yet it was further away.

It was a horrible idea. They weren't even one quarter of the way across and already they were swarmed. If fear didn't increase their heart rate, then the cold would. Luckily, that wasn't enough for the fish because if it was Amaryllis and John would have been dead after five-seconds of being completely wet.

We should have taken the long way. This is idiotic. We're dead. Perhaps it is possible to turn back, thought Amaryllis.

We're all right, we're all right. As long as we remain calm and ignore the fish… we're all right, we're all right, thought John.

Amaryllis' main concern was the temperature; if they did swim across the lake successfully, as soon as they emerged they would suffer symptoms of hypothermia. She thought of keeping them both warm with magic but too much concentration was involved. If she was deep within her focus, and she was hit with a small irrelevant splash, she would jolt back into her body with a chaotic pulse. She could not levitate over the lake, bringing John with her… if she let go, they would plunge into the water consumed with a feeling of surprise. She could not control the minds of the fish… her pure magic was no match for the evilly programmed, thoughtless minds. Magic was almost immediate suicide.

Yes, walking would take an extra three days, but it would be better to arrive alive with the delay of restoring the good than to never make it at all and leave the world inevitable of destruction.

Amaryllis didn't want to waste her movement by looking back at the shore, but the thought of turning back inhabited her. She looked to the sides of the lake to make an inference of where she was. She guessed about, or slightly more than, a quarter of the way across, swimming with only harmless splashing and no contact.

Somehow, they managed to keep the insanely alert minds relaxed, which allowed them to dismiss everything happening around them. The fish tried to thrash around to startle them but to no avail.

Amaryllis looked to John to see his stern face filled with concentration. He felt her gaze, but refused to look at her. They continued to swim exceedingly slow—

Amaryllis felt something hit her leg. It slithered up against her chest, jumped out of the water in front of her face. She watched the long fish soar above the water with appreciation that she had not seen its face. It was large, metallic grey with sharp fins and a thin body. After reaching the peak of its jump, it dove back into the water a few feet in front of her. It was a fast swimmer, so there would be no way to escape the fish in a frenzied chase.

It was impossible to elude feelings of discomfort, and it was especially impossible to prevent a fearful heart from beating faster.

Calm, calm, stay calm. Don't worry... do not worry, they shall not get you. Not now, your time is not now.

Another fish rammed into her but into her side. She winced then turned her head to John. Water splashed as a group of fish circled him. He looked not the slightest bit concerned. He just shook his head then looked ahead to the shore as he swam.

They had a few minutes of swimming left, and all Amaryllis could think of was to not get too excited. They were nearly out of the hellish lake and it was difficult to keep that thought out of her head. It was so cold she could barely feel her limbs anymore. She wanted out so badly.

A fish jumped in front of her again revealing the side of its face. Amaryllis' stomach dropped upon seeing it so clearly. Its features were incomparable to anything she had ever seen. Knowing the appearance of the creature changed everything. Whenever she was touched or circled by one, she would picture its horrifying eyes staring at her frigid, slow-swimming body with a savage impulse to sink its teeth into her. All it waited for was a frightened heart, and as time passed while Amaryllis kept her heart rate calm the fish grew angrier and more aggressive.

Their bodies had become completely numb. The only way they knew they still had movement was by looking at their pale white limbs through the choppy waves, beneath the blurred surface of the water. With clenched jaws and tense muscles, they pulled the heavy water back, and with ice-like legs they kicked and kicked as strongly as they could. While putting in their best effort, they moved slower than before.

The shore was so close and the fish population had grown immensely with hundreds of fish that circled them at great speeds sending gargantuan splashes above the surface. It seemed that with every second more fish joined the vicious circle making the splashes bigger.

Amaryllis and John were too close to death to be phased. Their vision was blurred, they could hardly hear the splashing water being stirred, the only thing they could hear was their pulse.

Amaryllis' limbs could no longer move. Her head fell beneath the surface submerging herself completely. Her feet touched the bottom of the lake with about a foot of water above her head. Finally, the shallow end was near. She kept her eyes closed, afraid to look at the fish. She crossed her arms and held her stomach feeling neither her fingers nor the contact of her hands against her belly. She couldn't even feel her feet against the sandy floor of the lake. Amaryllis was frozen.

Her throat suddenly burned, she needed oxygen. She opened her eyes cautiously and held her eyelids still when they were half open. A blurry grey outline of a big fish floated near her face. She opened her eyes completely to see that it was opening its jaw revealing long, pointed, black teeth. It was disturbingly still. Amaryllis tried to push off the ground. It was incredibly difficult with her frozen legs but she managed to bring her head above the surface.

The cold wind penetrated her face, burning. Her ears were on fire. She was so cold that she felt hot. The fish too surfaced, like alligators, staring at her with a wide mouth. Amaryllis swam around the creature and floated to the shore.

John was laying on the ground next to a large tree. From her location, he looked as white as a ghost. He could have been dead.

Amaryllis was able to stand. The water reached her shoulders as she walked, and the further she moved the more the water moved down her body. It was up to her calves when she fell to her knees, which stung in an ice cold fire. She put her hands out and caught herself. She turned to the lake to see hundreds of grey fish heads staring at her. Keeping her eyes on them, she crawled out of the lake and onto the shore.

Chapter 32

The cold wind pressed against her body flowing right through her wet, cotton clothes to sting her frozen skin. Her hair hardened, frozen like ice. She laid curled up in a ball lying in the dusty soil, her wetness mixing with the chunky dirt, staining her clothes and exposed skin brown.

"John?" she croaked, spinning her head to look at the white figure, now leaning against the tree. Turning her head allowed her to realize how cold her ears were. She turned her right ear to the sky to be exposed to the wind while her left ear pressed against the ground. Although she could hardly feel it, her ear seemed as if it were to fall off, or was mushed into the ground as the weight of her head rested on it. It was awkward to talk as she could not feel her facial muscles, lips, or cheeks. Her breath was hot as it left her lips in a thin puff of air. She brought her hands, which were covered in dirt, to her purple lips and breathed hard into closed fists. It had little to no effect on her coldness. "John?" she repeated after a few breaths.

Coughing came from John's body but no words were spoken. Amaryllis tried to sit up, but her frigid body refused to move. "What do we do now?" she called.

No response…

She had to think on her own. Amaryllis thought of warm fires and the sun's rays. She coated her body with a faint, sparkling, yellow gas directly from the universe itself. As time passed, the gas became more vivid and strong, heating her body. As soon as she could feel her fingers and toes once again, she stood up and walked uncoordinatedly to John with wobbling legs and a heavy upper body.

Amaryllis did not realize, but her magical abilities were increasing in power. Stimulating her body to such harsh temperatures awoke something within her brain, within her soul. Her concentration had improved well, almost too well. She was aware of *everything*. She could hear and see so much at once. Her vision seemed to have a wider perspective. Even when she wasn't looking in a particular direction, she was still mindful of what was going on in that direction. Her senses seemed to have become enhanced after her hypothermic experience.

After eluding her fear for the entire duration of her swim, she was finally able to express herself on land. She thought of the fresh, horrifying experience and shivered, briefly covering her magically warmed skin in goosebumps.

She stood before John, appreciating her own warmth. Looking at him painfully reminded her of *her* condition a minute ago. Her muscles felt as if they were still frozen just by looking at him. His lips were white, skin pale, and his eyes were half closed; they fluttered as if struggling to support the weight of his eyelids. He looked at her, forcing his eyes open wide. No matter his condition his eyes always appeared mean even when he was near death.

"I can't—" he whispered, trembling. "—see you."

To John, Amaryllis was hardly notable. Her blurred figure blended in with the trees. He blinked several times, frustrated that his vision was not improving. He gently waved his arms about trying to reach her. Amaryllis had never seen him appear so frail even with his muscular build. If she were to touch his shoulder she felt it would shatter. He grabbed her leg above her boot. Through the thin, cotton fabric John's ice cold touch sent shivers up her leg giving her goosebumps again. She noticed that his hands squeezed tight, then loosened as he glared lifelessly at the crimson sky. Amaryllis gasped at his condition and momentarily felt guilt for hesitating to warm him. She couldn't help herself. Seeing him that way shocked her.

As magic had become easier she almost effortlessly summoned magic and healed his hypothermic symptoms. His skin brightened from pale to fair. His trembling ceased and overall, he felt the warmth of the gold coloured magic penetrating his skin, then pressing against his organs. Both Amaryllis and John were finally warm and dry.

They looked at each other solemnly, then Amaryllis revealed a smile which emerged from surprise. They had swum across the wavy, monster infested waters, which was ice cold and brutal with additional gales of fierceness, they had managed to stay calm in an alerting environment with ravenous fish attempting to kill them, and they did so thinking of hardly anything. Amaryllis chuckled in an exclaiming sigh, looking to the water with adrenaline flowing through her veins.

John glared at her blankly. He looked to the lake with a slight feeling of regret. He had entered the water with an absurd thought kept in the back of his mind, he wanted to die. Of course he wanted Amaryllis to succeed, but he was thinking of picking up speed as he swam to lure the fish to bite down on him and end his existence in seconds. By doing so, Amaryllis would have surely panicked, killing herself. John did not want that.

He looked at his hands which were no longer stiff and discoloured. He remembered considering sinking to the floor of the lake to drown. He was going to inhale litres of water to kill himself faster, then scream to finally release his twenty year build up of depression and misery; his hurt from the absence of his wife and children.

He looked at Amaryllis. She stood there with her soft grin slowly fading. He thought for sure she would be able to detect his suicidal thoughts with her… witchy, magical… abilities. He hated all of it, yet he appreciated it. Her magic saved him physically, but the prevention of his long desired death killed him mentally. He wanted to die in that moment more than ever and wished he had drowned, or was devoured. Most of all, he hated the feeling of being *read*.

Before allowing her to say something, he spoke, "Let's go. It's almost night," he grumbled. He did not thank her for warming him, he did not mention any feeling of victory for crossing the lake, nor did he show any pride in Amaryllis or himself.

Like anyone would have been she was uncertain of swimming across, but he assured her she could do it. Now that she had done it, he showed no care. Amaryllis had noticed his inconsistent behaviour when she first met him, and it was so easy to see it right then. She *hoped* for a sign of happiness showing he was glad they had survived, but she did not *expect* such happiness. So, instead of asking him what was wrong, she held all possible questions and followed him into the woods glancing once more at the mountain before it was to be hidden by the tall trees.

Through the darker hue of the sky, it was evident to be night. The red sky graduated to a dark maroon and within the forest, underneath the branches, it was nearly pitch black. Amaryllis and John climbed a ginormous oak tree with branches two feet in diameter. They climbed to the top to avoid the tall shadow creatures lurking on the grounds. Amaryllis' paranoia of encountering a shadow creature made her tremble. It was fairly noticeable, almost like a faint, continuous seizure, but John showed no concern. As long as they were above ground they would be fine, so he let her shake and shiver in fear. He was completely aware of his portrayed carelessness, but felt it was acceptable. He believed that by allowing her to suffer internally she would realize that she would be safe when no danger came.

The night passed slowly. John hadn't had a good night's sleep in twenty years and Amaryllis was too consumed by her paranoia to relax her body into a slumber. They did not converse; instead they laid uncomfortably between thick branches with their eyes closed. Their closed eyes should have been an automatic spawn for sleep after the exhausting day, but their minds kept them wide awake.

When morning came, and the maroon sky brightened to its original colour resembling fresh blood, John's eyes cracked open. He looked over to Amaryllis whose eyes were shut with fluttering eyelashes as she tried to sleep. Under the shade of the trees, Amaryllis' radiant features dominated the darkness, as her spell of warmth was still in effect.

John climbed down the tree with precise movements. He moved smoothly and effortlessly until he dropped to the ground allowing his bent knees to absorb the energy of the fall. Upon landing, a cloud of dust from the dead soil rose up to his thighs and the scent worked its way into his nostrils. The smell of dusty dirt had become so familiar to him that it smelled like nothing. He gazed up to the top of the tree where Amaryllis laid still. He could hardly see her. He only spotted her through memory of how high they had climbed. The hiding spot was strategically wise; however, his back was stiff. He arched his back, cracking it. Doing so only relieved the pressure slightly but it still helped.

John peered through the gaps in branches to find a portion of the mountain still standing as furiously as the day before. If anything, it disturbed him more and more with each glance. He was not prepared for what was to come. He believed there was no training process powerful enough to prepare even the most eligible warrior for this battle. Not even he, who had been exposed to evil for twenty years felt ready.

He looked at the top of the tree once more to see Amaryllis climbing down. She was not as fast as him, as her years of living the palace life did not expose her to physical labours, but she moved well with an unknown strength. She dropped to the ground, bending her knees instinctively like John to absorb the impact.

She looked tired with small bags under her eyes, but did not feel how she appeared. Her mind was too alert and much too anxious, to calm herself down. Her body was exhausted, in need of rest. She learned to resist her body's need to fall lifelessly to the ground, but the feeling of tiredness still consumed her. She could not rid of it completely. Upon awakening, her stomach had already inhabited butterflies. Immortuos was so close, and she was nearly there, afraid, yet excited, to finally face the demon once again. This time, she'd be prepared.

John started walking knowing all too well that Amaryllis would follow him.

She looked up to the sky as a mechanism to calm her nerves, but it did the opposite. Normally, looking up to the blue sky, imagining what the fluffy white clouds would feel like and taking a deep breath worked in Serilion, Arlon, and other kingdoms she would be visiting at the time. But in the Dark Forest, and everywhere in the world, the blue sky still remained as a defeated, bloody, crimson sky affected by Immortuos' wrath. The sky was not dead, but it was ill, and it made Amaryllis shudder. She missed the blue sky. Her favourite one of many remedies—getting lost in the seemingly endless blue sky—was unavailable to her, so she closed her eyes for a moment as she walked behind John and imagined all in that time: what her future would look like. All within a moment, she pictured colourful skies, fluffy clouds, rolling hills blooming with flowers — Werling — with Prince James standing before the castle gates. The butterflies in her stomach flew away, and she was at ease, until she opened her eyes to be greeted by the unnaturally twisted trees shadowed by red, and the continuous, sinister music she had nearly forgotten about. The music itself was fading as Amaryllis and John approached the opposite end of the Dark Forest. Amaryllis had never seen or even heard of what was on the other side. All of the kingdoms' palaces stood south of Arlon, scattered arbitrarily from east to west. Arlon was the most northerly palace in all of the chain of kingdoms, and north of Arlon was the Dark Forest. The undiscovered land, from what Amaryllis could no longer see was filled with mountains, and standing as the tallest was Immortuos' which could not have existed before. From what Amaryllis remembered, as she crawled out of the lake, her only sight, the very tip of the mountain, and if she could see the tip from *miles* and *miles* away, the mountain was truly gargantuan. She wanted to glance at the mountain again to search for her inner motivation to kill Immortuos, but the trees' leaves were thicker near the border of the Dark Forest, so instead she pictured the demon as the little girl it pretended to be. Its awkward behaviour that she desperately wished she should have noticed then, its strange exaggerated sentence formulation that was clearly forced. A part of Amaryllis wished the demon was right in front of her, but the more logical part of her did not. She remembered the disturbing transformation from a small child to a ten foot tall demon. The sudden gales of wind and the swirling red sky that enhanced the fear the demon was unconsciously provoking frightened Amaryllis even in her memory. Out of no where, John spoke.

"We're an hour away... possibly more," he grunted. Amaryllis hugged herself, feeling her goosebumps through her cotton shirt. The wind did not flow through the trees, but the morning temperature was frigid.

"I thought we were closer than that?" she asked.

"I'm not talking about distance, I am talking about time. The mountain is close. If we were to walk directly there we'd arrive in half an hour, but there is one last thing we must do."

"And what might that be?" she asked, surprised. Amaryllis was so eager to finally emerge from the Dark Forest; to escape the feeling, along with the sounds it excreted to terrify the ones who entered, the ones who did not belong. She wanted to get out so badly, but she would never tell him so.

"Tunnel," he replied bluntly. "Either we head straight to the mountain, which means we travel through the largest grove of toxic mushrooms, or we crawl through a tunnel beneath the grove to avoid the toxins. The only thing is, there will be things you will not want to see in this tunnel. It's quite long, cramped, damp, and inside are things that you literally do not want to see…that is their specialty."

"Well, you're making the grove of mushrooms sound better. I'd rather jump from tree to tree than squirm through a hole filled with things I don't want to see. What are they? The things?" Through her voice, no one would have ever known she was nervous, but the idea of the *things* bothered her greatly. They could be anything. Her imagination ran wild with visuals of rat-faced creatures with human bodies crawling all over her until finally sinking their teeth into her skin, taking out large chunks of flesh. She could not help but think of something horribly disturbing, especially when John strongly stood by the idea that she would *not want to see them*. It seemed like the less frightening way of saying, *these creatures will haunt you with only a glance.*

John twirled the fabric of the end of his cotton shirt and squeezed it, thinking of what he saw the last time he entered.

"These monsters I have not named, so we will call them Things, but trust me, take what I say literally…you do not want to see them. Think of something you do not want to see and that is what they are."

Amaryllis shuddered. The unknown appearance of these beings excited the dark parts of her mind, the part of her brain responsible for her anxiety and nightmares. Her heart raced in her chest. "Can you please explain them more?" she begged. She needed some type of information to calm her heart, anything to ease her fears whether it was an in depth description of the creatures, or a tale of a character from a fairytale, something. The silence made her imagination run wild, and she felt for some reason that John was trying to frighten her out of spite. It was odd, sometimes he showed a small degree of kindness, and other times utter cruelty. Amaryllis thought it was still him adjusting to the fact that he was assisting a royal after what royals had done to him... but he offered his help to her with integrity knowing Amaryllis was not like most royals. Perhaps at the time, John thought he could overcome his general hatred, but it was clearly still difficult for him.

"I cannot explain them anymore than I have. I do not know what these creatures actually look like, what their true form is. All I know is that they transform into the thing or person you either fear or hate most," John said lazily.

Amaryllis sighed with relief. "I am certain that I will be seeing Laria then...and Eric for sure."

"No, no, there will be more. There are always more. They flip the memory you have of these people. You will be seeing them with a twist."

"A twist?"

"Absolutely," John's mean eyes stared down into Amaryllis'. His eyes were dark and shadowed by the trees; the whites of his eyes eaten by darkness, his irises black, "They are distorted. You don't want to see them," he repeated gruffly.

Amaryllis did not know what to picture in her mind. *They are distorted* echoed through her. "And this *must* be the way we go?" she asked, trying to speak in a way that hid her nervousness.

John nodded, his expression stern. "Unless you'd rather risk your chances in the grove," he suggested with a harsh tone in his voice.

Amaryllis frowned. "I've been through a grove. I know what to expect—"

"You know what to ex—Amaryllis, don't you remember what happened?" John stammered, cringing at the memory of Amaryllis screaming like an animal in his bathtub, and picturing her flesh eaten down to the bone. He remembered how some pieces of skin floated to the surface of the water and how awful it smelled.

Just thinking of awakening in John's wooden shack to her own screaming made her flinch in pain, as if she could still feel the burns. "I know what happened," she snapped. "But you make the tunnel full of distorted Laria's and Eric's sound worse than toxic mushrooms."

John halted, holding his arm out to stop Amaryllis. She walked right into his extended arm, her body felt the resistance and he pushed her back. She looked at him impatiently. With the arm that stopped her, he pointed to the ground.

"What?" Amaryllis asked before finding a small hole in the ground covered by long, dead grass.

"That's the entrance," he breathed. He looked at her, trying to read her expression. Her face was stern, with dark green eyes darting from the hole in the ground to the trees. "Would you like me to go first?" he asked, studying her behaviour. She was suddenly difficult to read.

Amaryllis looked at the hole with curiosity and anger.

Faint laughter came from inside, both shrill and deep, mixed into one strange composition.

"No, I'll go," her voice was deep. John had never heard her speak so low before.

Chapter 33

She eyed the small hole as she moved the grass out of the way. The hole expanded greatly with each clump of grass she plucked. It was now three feet in diameter as opposed to one.

The hole was six feet deep vertically, until it angled downwards, gradually curving horizontally leaving her with a very small space to crawl through. She dropped down and the smell of damp soil entered her nose immediately. It was nearly pitch black down there. Light streamed in faintly from above allowing her to only barely see herself. She held her hands up to her face to prove to herself that it was nearly impossible to see anything. She could only see the outlines, no specific details. She put her hands on the walls surrounding her feeling dirt hardened by moisture.

The laughter grew slightly louder.

"Remember, they are only illusions!" John called from above. His voice was faint, he seemed so far away, and Amaryllis felt so alone. However, she did not regret going first. She needed to get to Immortuos faster even if it meant reaching the other side before John did.

If I must get through this, I must move quickly. I must disregard what I see.

Without thinking, she dove onto her hands and knees and began crawling through the hole at a fast pace. She did not overthink her entrance, for if she did, she would have frozen in fear unable to proceed. Her hands were no longer visible, nothing was, everything blended into the darkness, and she seemed to be crawling into nothing. The only thing she heard at that time was her own breathing. The sounds of her heavy panting bounced off of the dirt walls and penetrated her ears. Her knees, and the palms of her hands, were already scraped from the hard, flakey dirt she scampered through.

John called to her once more, but his voice was muffled almost inaudible. He stared into the hole, his mean brown eyes full of worry. The sounds of her shuffling underground faded into nothing, and as soon as they did John's stomach dropped. He worried something awful had happened to her already, then reminded himself that she was all right, she was simply progressing further into the hole.

He waited patiently for a few minutes. He feared if he was too close to Amaryllis the things would combine their memories into one, and he did not want to see the outcome.

The last time he entered the hole was about eight years ago when he was escaping a group of dragons. He had been burnt badly, bleeding from his wounds and nearly sobbing. They could not fit in the hole to chase him, so they waited on the outside, blowing flames inside which pushed him to crawl farther and farther into the tunnel. When the tunnel was illuminated with each blow of the dragons, skeletons, along with a bloodstained dirt floor were revealed.

The longer he waited, the more his sudden anxiety devoured his courage. He did not fear being alone in the open; however, he was not prepared to face a distorted version of the King of Arlon crawling at him full speed like a spider.

Amaryllis had been crawling for some time with no encounter with any creature. It was what they wanted: to build up the suspense, to create an anxiety-filled anticipation too unbearable to live with.

Her own gasping was all she could hear. There wasn't much oxygen available in the tunnel and her hyperventilating only made things worse. Blood pounded in her ears. Her heart thudded in her chest. Although it was too dark to see, she could feel her vision disfiguring. Breathing was difficult, overwhelmingly difficult.

In the darkness of the pitch black tunnel she knew her hands and knees were bleeding from excessively pressing the weight of her body into the crusty dirt. Dried blood stuck to the remaining insides of her cotton pants which were worn down, and warm, sticky, fresh blood poured from her scrapes. Her hand scrapes stung the worst even though the wounds were smaller than the wounds on her knees.

After a short period of time she learned to dismiss the pain. It was only easy to dismiss since breathing hurt more.

Suddenly, she dropped hard to the floor of the tunnel, collapsing from her crawling stance. She gasped and wheezed. She clasped her hands together in pain. Dirt and sharp stones from her right hand moved into her left, and left into right from her firm pressing. Leaving her hands with no weight on them, exposed to the air in the tunnel, seemed to make her hands sting more, and putting pressure on her palms hurt in a way that made her want to push harder.

Her chest ached with frazzled lungs as she gasped for air, the pain moved into her throat.

Without suffering for another second, Amaryllis summoned magic in the form of bubbles of oxygen. With her glowing turquoise eyes she could see them floating about in the darkness. They looked like the stars in space. She directed them to enter her nostrils and mouth instantly relieving her chest and throat pain. As they continued to fly into her nose and mouth, she took a huge inhale then exhaled slowly. With a wave of her hand, the bubbles vanished, and she left herself in the oxygen-lacking air of the tunnel. All she needed was to calm herself. She could last a while longer without it.

She sat up, putting her weight on her hands and knees once again, and began to crawl at a much slower pace than before. It was foolish to waste oxygen in a place like this.

Her dried scabs of blood broke open as the pressure on her knees became repetitive again.

She thought of lighting her way with magical rays of light, but if she, "Did not want to see the things," it would be wise not to do so. Her gentle breathing echoed in the tunnel, but it seemed to echo for longer.

Amaryllis lifted her arm above her head and reached for the ceiling of the tunnel. She felt nothing, swinging at air. She sat in a crouched position then hesitantly stood up being careful not to bash her head on the ceiling. Once she stood up completely straight, she reached her arm above her head, and on only her middle finger she could feel stone. She stood on the tips of her toes and placed her entire hand on the stone ceiling. She was in a cave.

Droplets of water falling into puddles could be heard, along with the echo of her footsteps as she took careful steps through the unseen cave.

From behind her, she heard shuffling. "You made it," a gruff voice said in a congratulatory manner.

Amaryllis spun around, losing her sense of direction. She no longer knew which way she was heading from before. "What?" she asked, confused, and frightened. She spoke in a high pitched, somewhat squeaky voice. The foreign voice briefly scoffed in a deep chuckle.

"It's John," the voice stated angrily.

"I never asked who you were," she shouted, her voice controlled by her fear. There was a long pause.

"The cave, it's easier for travel—no more crawling." The voice said in a whisper. Her stomach dropped. The sound was closer. She looked ahead of her squinting into the blackness of the cave. Her eyes felt closed although they were wide open. Frustration filled her, she could not see anything. "Isn't it nice to stand?" it asked from even closer to her, on her left side. Amaryllis disregarded everything John said.

"You're not John," she stammered. She was completely defenceless, unaware of her surroundings, too frightened to illuminate the cave with light.

"Amaryllis, come on," he barked. "It's me…John Edwards. Let's continue through the tunnel."

"I know you're not John!" Amaryllis blurted. The confrontation caused her chest to flutter with discomfort. Silence again.

"AMARYLLIS, THIS IS RIDICULOUS," the voice boomed. "BELIEVE ME!" The cave shook like an earthquake. Stones fell from the ceiling and broke into tiny pieces when they hit the ground. Each time Amaryllis disagreed with John, he grew exponentially angrier. She could no longer control herself. She screamed at the top of her lungs in a long, loud exhale. The cave reverberated in the sharp screech she made.

Silence.

"Amaryllis, please… it's me. I didn't mean to frighten you," he stressed. "I am sorry," he insisted, his voice now on the right side of her.

Tears welled up in her eyes. Her lower lip quivered. Her chest moved in and out slowly as she tried to calm herself. Her tears would not stop flowing.

It is not John. It simply cannot be him, she thought. She dared not say it aloud. She peered into the darkness.

"I'm sorry, John. I'm just frightened," she falsely explained, "and you've never been so angry with me before."

Silence.

"I apologize, Princess," he grumbled from directly behind her. If it truly was John he wouldn't care whether or not she believed it was him. He wouldn't be moving all over the place taking exceedingly long pauses to speak, and no matter how grumpy he got, he would usually make an effort to control his anger.

"It's fine," she assured between tearful hiccoughs.

"I'm glad to hear that," John said, his voice came from every direction. Amaryllis dropped into a squat and felt the ground for a piece of stone. She picked one up the size of an apple and readied her arm.

"Of course," she replied, squeezing the rock. The darkness of the cave swirled in spirals before her eyes. "I—"

"So, you do believe me?" he asked softly. Amaryllis could easily detect a sinister presence behind that voice. John would never have said any of the things "he" just said. There was undoubtedly a *Thing* with her. The darkness of the cave annoyed her even more with each second in which she could not see.

"Amaryllis?" he sighed. Her eyes widened as she felt hot breath in her ear. She swung blindly to her side and struck a muscular body. Hissing sounds filled the cave, followed by gargling and choking. Her heart jumped into her throat. She took a few steps back then illuminated the room with light streaming from her palms.

"John" stood taller than she remembered him. His mean eyes looked meaner; bloodshot and deep black, crazed and hair-raisingly frightening. He regurgitated chunky, purple blood and his abnormally long body spasmed with each choking sound. His shoulders quickly hunched forward then pulled back with each cough; some powerful enough to bring his head down between his legs, then the other way, arching his neck backwards behind his back. The blood splattered all over the walls of the small cave. His never-ending choking caused her to back to tense into an erect and uncomfortable position, to the point where she thought it would never arch again. Her muscles ached in a sharp pain, and a shiver ran down her spine as she watched "John" in horror. She met his eyes and let out a scream.

She did not know where she could have hit him to cause him to cough up blood—

John took two wobbly steps towards her, each leg spasmed as it briefly hung in the air before stepping down. Without warning, he coughed hard in her direction. Purple blood shot from his throat and onto her face. She shielded herself from the surging liquid with her hands, but the rest landed on her clothes and in her hair. It was hot and bubbled energetically against her scalp and on her clothes. The blood that landed on her palms momentarily caused a faded purple light to emit from her hands rather than gold. She screamed at the putridness then shook it off with the flick of her wrists. She shook her clothes and flipped her hair around to shake out the loose chunks.

The choking stopped abruptly. Amaryllis stood panting, taking slow steps back while keeping light on "John." She kept her eyes on his shoulders the whole time avoiding looking at his bloodstained mouth and fearsome eyes. The thing stood motionless, his dead eyes staring into nothing. The only movement Amaryllis could detect was his calm breathing. It faintly echoed in the cave.

With a snapping sound, which resembled breaking a stalk of celery in half, the thing bent sideways. Amaryllis felt her whole body jolt. She gasped. "John" took one slow step towards her, then charged full speed, his back still broken with his upper body hanging down beside his legs. Amaryllis tried to scream, but no sound came out. She tried to move but was frozen. The thing was a foot away from her when she finally spun around and sprinted as fast as she could to the far side of the cave. She shone her light to where she once stood. "John" was no where to be seen. She nervously waved her hands everywhere covering every square inch of the cave.

Nothing.

She sighed with relief. Leaning against the wall she sank down into a seated position with outstretched legs. Her body shook in need of an embrace. "I wish James were here," she whispered to herself. Of course, she meant it; however, she also didn't. She was glad to know he was safe in Arlon with the rest of the royal subjects. She just hoped he wasn't foolish enough to set out to find her. Amaryllis shook her head slowly.

Stop thinking about James, she ordered herself, *he'll only distract you. You're so close to Immortuos. Please stay focused. You won't be seeing James if you fail now.*

Amaryllis felt so relieved that, "John" had vanished, although she did not let her guard down completely. She could still sense a presence of some sort like he was invisible but still in the room. Her encounter with her first *Thing* went just as she'd imagined. She had hoped she'd be able to contain her fear but she couldn't blame herself.

Chapter 34

John placed his hands on the dirty walls of the hole. His heart pounded in his chest, and his breaths were shallow and quick. He eyed the small tunnel, his memory of his last encounter bringing pain to his chest.

Amaryllis surely reached the cave by now, he thought. He knew it was time to begin crawling through the tunnel, but he couldn't bring himself to do so. Each time he leaned forward to bend down he jerked upwards.

"I can't," he groaned between breaths. He held his breath for a moment. He thought he heard something.

He heard crying.

"Dad?" A tiny voice squeaked from within the black tunnel, "Daddy, is that you?" the boy whispered. It was supposedly his youngest son.

"Get away!" he yelled, his eyes glistened with moisture.

"Dad?" A slightly deeper voice called. John stared angrily into the tunnel expecting to see his four children emerge into the light.

"You're not them!" he hollered, "You're not... them." A tear streamed down his cheek followed by several more as he squinted.

"John?" a feminine voice asked softly. John shook his head, crying. He jumped up and hoisted himself out of the hole then rolled over onto his side and sobbed loudly.

"John, is that you?" she repeated, her voice still just as clear as if he were still in the hole.

"Go away," he cried harder after saying this. He knew it wasn't his wife, but it felt like it was, and the last thing he wanted to say to his wife was to go away. She may have died twenty years ago, but he was still affected by the deaths of his family as though they were murdered yesterday. Not being able to share his grief caused his pain to bottle up inside. He had never been able to let go of them.

His pupils constricted as he felt a tap on his shoulder. A shiver ran down his spine and his muscles clenched tightly. He sat up then whipped his head to face the hole. No one was there. He laughed nervously, more tears streamed down his cheeks, and sweat trickled down his forehead. He peered down the hole into the entrance of the tunnel. No one was there. He forced himself to drop down again. He stood in the same place as before listening for a sound.

Nothing.

He knew very well that he was being lured down, but he had no choice.

Without another thought, he slowly dropped to his knees and began crawling into the pitch black tunnel. He kept a steady pace knowing if he got too tired he would eventually find himself gasping for air. There was no sign of his family yet.

He occasionally felt something wet and cold beneath his hands and knees. Little did he know it was Amaryllis' blood.

John never thought he would ever have to return to the tunnel. His last entry was involuntarily. He had to go in. This time, it was by choice. A small part of him wished Amaryllis had persuaded him to take the long way through the grove of toxic mushrooms. Yes, it would have taken an extremely long time, but at least there were no monsters just inches from your face. It was frightening, and saddening, how your loved ones could have such an effect on you in the form of monsters.

"Dad?" a voice bellowed from behind him. He could not identify which son it was until it made the sound that his eldest son, Castor, made when his stomach hurt.

"Get away!" John warned with an unsteady voice. He jolted when he felt a hand grab his ankle hard. "Castor" was not strong enough to prevent John from moving, so he kept crawling hearing a dragging sound in the dirt.

"Dad, help me…" he whined. By the sound of his voice he was crying. "It hurts."

"You're not Castor," John snapped trying to keep himself from crying again. He shook his ankle free from "Castor's" grasp.

"What are you talking about?" Castor groaned followed by a yelp. "It really, really hurts, Dad."

John couldn't hold his tears back any longer. He didn't realize that he had started pretending his son was actually there. "Remember what I taught you?" John said softly.

"Take a deep breath and hold it for ten-seconds," he replied proudly.

"Yes, exactly…" John whispered, barely audible. John listened to the sound of a deep inhale then ten-seconds later he felt warm air against the back of his head.

"It worked I think," Castor chuckled.

"Very good, I am glad to hear." John's eyes could not stop leaking with tears. He felt the urge to turn around and hold his son in his arms.

"Dad, I love you."

John's eyes narrowed. He couldn't pretend anymore. It was too unreal.

"It's not real," he muttered, focusing on his consistent crawling speed. He looked down at where his hands would be visible if there was light.

"What, dad?"

"I said you're NOT real!" his voice boomed.

Silence.

John's comment drove "Castor" crazy, but it ignored its' anger and proceeded to tell John how he loved him so very much, his voice gradually getting deeper and deeper until its last word sounded like the voice of a demon. John shuddered. He raised his shoulders to his ears and shook as he felt goosebumps rise from his skin. The deep voice haunted him.

"Get the hell away from me!" John roared.

"Don't talk to him that way, John." His "wife" warned. "You don't want to traumatize him at such a young age."

"Shut up," he sobbed. "Judith" placed a gentle hand on his back, making him jump. He stopped crawling and stayed motionless on his hands and knees.

"What's wrong, John?" she asked contently, resting her hand on his shoulder. It was unfair how realistic the things were, how they could access memories and use them against people. He felt her rest her head on his back wrapping her arms around his waist. He shrugged his shoulders.

"Get off of me," he clamoured, cringing at her touch.

She didn't move. "I'm sorry?" she apologized, confused, "Just please, tell me what's the matter?" Her voice soothed and haunted him simultaneously.

"You're not here, but I need you to be," he stated, feeling sweat drip from his nose and tears tickling his cheeks.

"But, Johnny, I am here."

"No, you're not," he replied hopelessly.

"Hold me, John. Give me a hug. You'll feel better."

"No!" He shook his head and continued his crawl. Her head still rested on his back and her arms were still wrapped around his waist as he moved. Her legs dragged behind them.

"It's been a long twenty years," she taunted.

"Go to hell." He released himself from her grip with a forceful separation of her hands and a wiggle. She continued to taunt him as he crawled farther and farther away, her voice getting quieter and quieter.

Chapter 35

Amaryllis did not stay in the cave for long. Although she loved being able to walk around, she figured it was time to continue her crawl. She made sure she was not going out the same way she came in then used magic to heal her scrapes.

The tunnel beyond the cave was slightly larger than the last. The dirt was softer, which was relieving for her hands and knees, but the ground was more uneven. She entered the tunnel with less confidence, more fear. She had no idea who she was about to encounter next, and she was nervous to find out.

Amaryllis was frightened out of her mind, yet she was hopeful and believed she would make it out alive. Thinking clearly was a slight challenge, but she managed well. She found herself randomly thinking of the Choosing Ceremony.

"And Prince James takes the hand of Princess Laria!" she muttered, picturing the man who she loved take the hand of her nemesis. She subconsciously began crawling faster. Yes, James justified his involuntary choice, but the memory still hurt. As she crawled through the tunnel with determination in her heart, and fear on her mind, her imagination shifted from James to a bright blue sky scattered with fluffy white clouds. She missed the sky more than anyone in Arlon. As one who utilized nature as an escape, seeing the sky possessed by redness which casted perpetual shadows onto the land hurt her the most. Being in the tunnel amplified her lonesomeness for the sky. Her thoughts shifted again to her parents crying at the sight of her. She sighed, happy she was able to tell them what had been happening to her at that time. If something happened to her on her journey, she would go feeling satisfied with herself. She had expressed herself before leaving for her journey. She had finally stood up to Laria. She showed everyone what she was capable of. Amaryllis smiled, realizing her power.

Her smile faded when she heard breathing that was not her own. Of course, she was expecting another visit from a Thing. No matter how many encounters she had, she would never get used to them. The breathing was masculine and soft coming from right behind her. Her stomach dropped and her body filled with energy propelling her even faster through the tunnel.

"Amaryllis, where are you going?" It was "Prince James." Her heart pounded. Her hands smacked and her knees banged against the ground as she crawled rapidly. Normally, his voice would have soothed her, filling her with warmth and happiness but knowing it wasn't him haunted her. James was in Arlon. He was not here. Amaryllis opened her mouth to speak nearly confronting the thing that it was not the Prince of Werling but stopped herself when she remembered what happened with "John."

"I don't know," she replied truthfully, "I can't see, it's too dark."

"I can," he chuckled menacingly.

"Don't harm me," she pleaded.

"Now why would I do that?" he asked gently. It was a disturbing transition to witness; from listening to discomforting laughter to hearing the tender voice of her love. She shivered, feeling a wave of anxiety wash through her.

"*My* James never laughs like that," she stammered. It was extremely unfair. She missed James the most, and it triggered tears to hear his voice in such a distorted manner.

"Wait, Amaryllis," he pleaded, grabbing her lower leg and pulling hard to bring her down flat on her stomach. She winced then yelped as she hit the ground. Her fingernails dug into the dirt as he dragged her back. She grunted trying to free herself from his tight grip. He had both hands around her stomach squeezing so tightly it was hard to breathe.

"I love you," he mumbled softly into her ear, his lips brushing against her cheek. She gasped trying to suck in air. Her face felt steeping hot.

"I love you, too," she muttered through her teeth then felt something on her neck. It was sharp. She groaned feeling magic build up in each area of her body. Her body glowed yellow and her eyes turquoise. She looked down at distorted hands with long fingers digging into her gut, then she screamed as she pulled James' arms apart. She threw his body behind her—as though it was as weightless as a blanket—down the tunnel, hearing a faded, inhuman screech from far away. She screamed back at him out of madness then crawled as fast as she could. Her knees ached in inconceivable pain, so she reached above her head. She felt no ceiling, so she stood up and began sprinting. With one hand she illuminated the tunnel to see how long the ceiling would be high for.

Amaryllis gagged then screamed in disgust squeezing her eyes shut hard for a second. The tunnel's walls were stained with dried blood and other liquids she was afraid to identify. The floor was littered in decayed animal bodies and century-old human skeletons. Their eye sockets peered lifelessly at Amaryllis as she ran appearing as though they were following her. Amaryllis felt bile rise into her throat as she thought, *I was on my hands and knees crawling through that.*

She choked as she swallowed down the hot bile. There were so many skulls that she could not avoid stepping on them.

Someone was sprinting behind her. She quickly glanced back to see James charging at her with an exaggerated smile on his face which stretched all the way to the corners of his eyes. His greenish-blue eyes vanished revealing completely white eyes. Amaryllis screamed, gaining energy to sprint even faster. Her feet pounded against the skulls, breaking some of them and nearly getting a foot stuck inside. She looked back again to see James only about ten feet away from her. His smile bigger than before. His pale white eyes glistened as she shone her light in his face. His jaw dropped revealing a set of uneven teeth with a long black tongue dripping with drool.

"GET AWAY!" Amaryllis cried in anguish turning around to look ahead of her. James roared wetting Amaryllis' back with saliva. "Gross!" she exclaimed, contorting her face, cringing at the bubbly mucus. Her eyes narrowed, heat sparked inside of her, and fire ignited in her hands. Flames danced about in her palms. She abruptly stopped sprinting, spun around, and screamed at the top of her lungs as fire shot out from her hands like a flamethrower. James instantly caught fire and screeched in pain as its skin and organ tissue melted down to the bone. As soon as the screaming faded the flames retracted, settled, and danced playfully in her hands once again. Bones clattered to the skull-covered floor. Amaryllis breathed heavily through her mouth, her face illuminated in orange light. She looked down at the fire and shook it out, turning around to walk in the darkness once again.

Chapter 36

John reached the cave. He could tell because his shallow breathing began to echo all around him. His "wife" had faded away, and he was alone. All of his children had pestered him just before his arrival in the cave. He had pulled his dagger from its scabbard and blindly swung his arm about, hitting two of them and scaring all of them away.

He stood up, brushed dirt off of his pants and patted his scabbard to ensure his dagger was still there. He sighed, listening to water fall from the ceiling. It was a hypnotic sound that would have put him into a state of relaxation if he was not completely terrified. Like Amaryllis, the pitch blackness annoyed him, yet he was thankful for it. He surely would give in to the monsters if he looked into the eyes of his dead "family."

He enjoyed his freedom of movement for a short time. The things were not yet at rest.

John heard the sound of leather boots circling the cave slowly.

"Simple orders," a deep voice grumbled. "Very simple indeed…"

John clenched his hands into fists, his fingernails digging into his palms. He didn't realize he was grunting until he felt pressure in his head. "I hate you."

"You think that your hatred affects *me*?" The "King of Arlon" laughed, "You are nothing."

"I did *everything* for you—"

"You were my errand boy!" the king spat. "Only useful for your hide and seek skills...and your killings. You're a monster aren't you?" he chuckled.

John grunted so hard he thought a blood vessel popped. He knew better than to speak with the Thing, but he couldn't quite help himself. An illusion or not, the king was in a way here. John needed closure. He needed to express all of his anger then stab the "king" in the neck. "I was prohibited from seeing my wife and my children. I went down one day to fetch someone for *you*... my wife was there...what did you *expect* me to do?" John roared. "And you *killed* them as my punishment!" John silently withdrew his dagger squeezing it as hard as he could. He felt he had the strength to break it into pieces.

"It was what had to be done," the Thing giggled. John screamed as loud as he could feeling lightheaded afterwards.

"You deserve death! You deserve torture... *You deserve torture!* What if I tied up the Queen of Arlon and slit her throat?" John laughed like a madman, but the "king" showed no offence.

"You could do that! If you make it past my army of knights!" he replied cheerfully, taunting him. His voice came from directly in front of John. Not close enough. John had to be sure.

"As if killing my family wasn't enough for you, you thought it'd be a swell idea to send me to live wretchedly in the Dark Forest?" John hollered. The cave vibrated sending stones crashing to the floor. A large piece landed right on John's shoulder. He winced, falling to the ground. He had no idea where the "king" was now. His shoulder throbbed, and he could feel his pulse bounding where he was struck.

"I honestly think you deserved far worse," The Thing said simply. Its voice came from above, slowly lowering to the ground. John heard giggling to his right. It was extremely close sending puffs of air in his ear. John reacted quickly, jabbing his dagger to his right, hoping to strike something. He felt his blade penetrate through a thick object. An ear-piercing screech echoed in the cave followed by hot liquid trickling down John's hand. He pulled the dagger out then stabbed it back in, over and over in different locations, screaming the whole time. His hand was completely wet with blood by the time he was finished with his psychotic impulse. The thing fell to the ground.

Must have hit the chest, John thought to himself while standing up. He kicked the Thing's lifeless body, almost wishing he had a lantern to see the "king" with all of his stab wounds, but he feared seeing the thing's true form. Although it was an illusion, John felt the conversation was realistic enough to make him feel slightly better. It was the continuous stabbing more than the confrontation which really helped him.

John stepped around the Thing's body and stabbed it twice more. When he went to stab it a third time he gasped and nearly dropped the dagger when something grabbed his leg. The Thing was not dead. John felt a set of knife-like teeth sink into his chest. He squeezed his dagger tightly to help with the pain as he screamed at the top of his lungs. He stabbed the Thing, and it simply moved from his chest to his leg not reacting to the blade at all. Blood ran down his chest, his stomach and down to his leg. Tears welled in his eyes as he heard slurping and crunching sounds in his upper leg. He screamed as he stabbed the thing over and over. It still had no effect on it, if anything it chewed more aggressively tearing skin and chomping down on tendons. John's face flowed with tears of pain and frustration. He wailed like a child. Instead of stabbing, he reverted to slicing hoping to find an artery. He moved the blade back and fourth, up and down like a painter. He didn't stop even when he did end up striking an artery and blood exploded in his face. He sliced even when the Thing's jaw relaxed and dropped to the ground. His chest, lower leg, and upper leg stung in a radiating pain that seemed to attach to one another in one big stinging sensation. He was not finished yet. He kicked the Thing's body twenty times as hard as he could then stabbed it ten more times. He panted the entire time he did so.

John smiled to himself after his second psychotic episode. He had not smiled in decades. He shook his dagger for a good minute, getting most of the blood off of it before putting it back into his scabbard. His leg hurt the worst. He could still feel blood pouring from his wounds, he grunted angrily. He kicked the thing hard one last time before dropping to his knees and crawling into the next tunnel.

He frowned smelling smoke along with another putrid scent. From behind him he heard a growl. He crawled as fast as he could with his eyes watering the entire time, wincing at the pain in his wounds. It grew extremely painful when he moved quickly. The Thing had bit down all the way to the muscle. He crawled for a long time, crying the entire time, until standing up when he felt something brush against his side. He ran, hunched over slightly, daring not to waste a movement to feel for the ceiling.

Chapter 37

Amaryllis walked down the tunnel holding her arm above her head to feel the ceiling lower. She had been walking for what felt like an eternity.

She was beginning to feel claustrophobic. The walls of the tunnel felt as if they were shrinking, gradually getting smaller, waiting to squish her into nothing. She remembered how petrified she was of the Dark Forest in general. The unknown was horrifying, but now that she was exposed to what was inside, it only became more frightening from there. From flesh-eating groves to distorted memories suffocating its victims, along with each creature that lived there, the ecosystems were haunted, abnormal and full of monsters. It was a place of torment where humans did not belong.

The ceiling suddenly grew to be too tall to reach, which was relieving to Amaryllis' tired arm. She let it fall down to her hip, feeling pins and needles tickle her arm from shoulder to fingertips. Amaryllis had one less thing to worry about, but the Things hadn't made an appearance in a while and she was consumed with nervousness. She figured she must have scared them off with the flames she shot from her hands. It was a reactionary act driven by anger and fear. She was overjoyed with her power and she could thank Akar for that. She saw magic as the most effective defence against anything. It would win against the largest armies, the most powerful crossbows and swords if used proficiently. However, she did not yet understand her *full* potential.

The cracking sounds from stepping on skulls began to lessen as Amaryllis progressed further than anyone who ever entered—all except for John of course. She nearly had the confidence to light up the tunnel for the rest of her time inside. She was so annoyed with darkness that her body quivered with madness. Amaryllis frowned hard, shut her eyes tight and groaned quietly to relieve her frustration. Through her eyelids, a faint light seemed to peer inside. She opened her eyes to see she subconsciously formed golden light in her hands, chuckled to herself, then pointed her hands ahead of her to see down the tunnel. Amaryllis didn't bother putting the lights out as she needed to see as it was stressing her body that she was unable to see in a dangerous place. There were only a few bones lying on the ground with no blood in sight. Still no people to be seen.

I could be near the end, she thought. *Nothing's shown up in a while...I could pass time faster and get out sooner if I sprint right now. If I get tired, I'll take a break and load myself with bubbles of air.*

She made up her mind and started sprinting as fast as she could. Faster than when she ran from "James" and faster than when she was being chased at the Choosing Ceremony. Her hair flew behind her like a flag in the wind, her feet firmly tapped the ground, and she breathed as normally as if she were walking. She had become too familiar with running, she was quite good at it now. She wouldn't start panting for a few minutes. She fuelled her body to run even faster by pretending there were Things behind her. Not anyone in particular just a presence frightening enough to persuade her to run until she reached the other side of the tunnel.

As she ran, she wondered about John's well-being and if he was even alive. She was unsure of how he survived last time. He only had his blade, while she had everything. A source of light, air, fire... anything she wanted. She supposed if he could do it once he'd be able to do it again, but Amaryllis believed she'd never be able to return to the tunnel. One encounter was all she could take.

John is mentally stronger than I am I suppose. He's definitely still alive, but oh—how awful it must be to see his family.

Amaryllis suddenly halted, her boots slid in the dirt as she slowed. She shook the lights from her hands and waited for her eyes to adjust to the darkness. Red light peered into the tunnel off in the distance.

"The end," she gasped. She began running again, running even *faster* than before.

"Amaryllis!" She heard from behind her. It was a male voice, and sounded distressed.

"Get the hell away from me!" she yelled with a smile on her face and narrowed eyes that focused on the beautifully horrifying red light at the end of the tunnel.

"Amaryllis, wait!" he screamed. "Please, it's John-it's John!" Along with "John's" voice she heard gargling and screeching.

"No!" she panted, approaching the red light.

"Please, you must believe me! Please I am *begging* you! Amaryllis, stop running!"

"Not going to happen!" she laughed, drunk on the idea that she'd finally be leaving the tunnel.

"Amaryllis, I will die if you don't help me!" More growling followed after he spoke.

"Fine by me!"

"For god's sake, it's me—how can I prove it?" he screamed. "How are you supposed to make it to Immortuos without me?" She heard a yelp as "John" fell to the ground. Her heart sank and she whipped around, shining light down the tunnel.

John laid face first on the ground, screaming, dagger in hand while the "King of Arlon" bit into his shoulder. Amaryllis screamed, her eyes glowed turquoise. She pulled John all the way towards her with telekinesis leaving the King behind. Its big black eyes narrowed, focused on Amaryllis. She looked to John's shoulder which spewed blood then back at the Thing just a few feet away. Without another thought, she shot fire from her hands, melting the King of Arlon into a pile of organs and bones. It smelled terrible entering her nose and invading her throat which carried bile to her mouth. She swallowed it down then looked down at John who laid on the ground, his clothes drenched in blood. His mean brown eyes looked meaner than ever, but they didn't scare her anymore.

"What the hell!" he shouted, wincing as he stood up. "Just going to leave me behind to die?"

"You can't really blame me," she said firmly. "Considering where we are…and I'd already seen you. You were the first Thing I saw."

"What? You saw me?" He asked, sounding slightly offended.

Amaryllis shrugged her shoulders letting the light fade from her palms and leaving them in darkness. "Yes, it was horrifying," she whispered. "Who'd you see?" she asked trying to change the subject.

"Why the hell did you see me, Amaryllis?"

"I don't know! I saw you and Prince James!" she squeaked.

Silence.

"I'm out here risking my life for you, guiding you to where you need to be, and you see *me* in here?"

Amaryllis looked to the red light at the other end of the tunnel. Just a little more running was left. They had no time for this.

"I am not afraid of you, but I am intimidated by you," she admitted. John shook his head in disappointment, but he was aware how he appeared to her: a psychotic man—with a natural skill of surviving, killing and tracking things—lost in the absence of his family, letting it affect him, and nearly killing her for announcing who she was.

Amaryllis knew what he had been going through and what he was still having to go through. His behaviour was justified, but she knows deep down inside he was soft and kind-hearted.

"What did I say to you?" he muttered.

"We can talk about it later. We must leave now," she called over her shoulder illuminating the cave with her hands to see him. He stared at her the entire time she was healing his wounds. Once his skin had closed up, and he was overwhelmed with wonderful feelings, he began walking, careful not to show the magic's effect on him. He felt healthy and well-rested, almost happy.

She lit their way until they reached the exit: an asymmetrical hole covered in shrubbery and flowers with red light peering through the spaces between. John climbed out first making Amaryllis' heart flutter, and anxiety rise within her, as she did not want to be left alone in the tunnel filled with Things. She climbed up, pressing her body weight evenly into her arms and legs to hold her up in the tight hole but stopped halfway up when she heard a sound.

"Amaryllis," a dozen raspy voices whispered. "Amaryllis where are you going? Come back…come back!" They all spoke at the same time creating a powerful, yet quiet, noise to haunt her for the rest of the day. She shone her hands down the hole out of subconscious, idiotic curiosity and her breath was taken away as she tried to scream. Her muscles went limp, causing her to fall all the way back down the hole until she caught herself. Her eyes were locked on the true form of the Things. She couldn't move. They stared at her with sinister expressions spread across their faces, smiling teeth and big eyes wearing insanity. Her heart skipped a beat when John reached down the hole, grabbed her arm and pulled her out.

Chapter 38

Amaryllis laid on her side, just a few feet from the hole, crying. Fresh air never seemed so breathable. It was enjoyable to take slow, deep breaths. Her lungs seemed to sing happily with each breath. It was heavenly.

She used to think of the red world of evil as hideous and horrifying. She used to think the Dark Forest was the most evil and dark place, but that damned hole changed her entire perspective. The Dark Forest never seemed brighter, more lovely.

John too was thankful for fresh air, but he thought the forest was still as disgusting as when they entered the tunnel. The Dark Forest was not a place of relief, but he could see why Amaryllis thought it was. She had not lived there as long as he.

While she cried her eyes out, John tried his best to contain his uneasiness. His experience was just as frightening as the first one. He could never prepare himself for another. They seemed to be different each time, utilizing different memories from the brain to horrify in the same way.

Amaryllis sat up, revealing her red, blotchy, tearful face and glistening green eyes. She scooted away from the hole frantically making eye contact with John once she'd settled in a place far away enough from the sound of the Things. Looking at her, with tears still streaming, made it more difficult for John not to cry. He bit his tongue telling himself that his tongue hurt more than his emotional pain. He looked up and blinked a few times.

"I saw them," she whispered, sending a chill through his body. "I...saw *them*."

"I know you did," he mumbled, hiding the fear in his voice. He was only hoping that she would not begin to describe their appearance. He had his eyes closed when he pulled her from the hole to avoid seeing them.

"I cannot get them out of my head. I still see them so clearly," she whispered faintly. She sat far from John, and it was easy to see that she was shaking. Her quiet, shaken voice creeped him out making his brain run wild with preconceived ideas of what the things could look like. He wanted to tell her to drop it, to talk about something else, but remembered his second experience with the "King of Arlon." He needed closure, to scream at the king, and to stab out his build up of anger. If Amaryllis didn't talk it out now, it would haunt her forever.

"Nothing to worry about anymore," John said gruffly. "You're out of the tunnel now." He paced the forest floor, picked up a rock, chucked it into the grove of blue mushrooms behind them, and watched a puff of bright blue gas rise from the ground. In that moment, John wondered about the tunnel and if it was manmade or natural. It was quite smooth all the way with a consistency of elevation, and it was deep enough to not be too close to the roots of the toxic fungi. He chucked another rock putting all of his strength into the throw to cope with what he had to go through *again* with those Things.

"I suppose, but I find it difficult to breathe even though I'm away from them, even though I'm breathing fresh air."

"I'm not so sure about *fresh* air. There is nothing pure about the forest, and we're pretty damn close to the grove still," he said solemnly. Amaryllis didn't say anything. She tried to forget the things by remembering what the world looked like before she freed Immortuos, but she found the things running free in her mind, following her to her conscious thoughts. If she pictured the meadows in Arlon, soon enough the Things would barge into her pleasant memory and ruin it. She'd picture Prince James and see his face deform and contort into the face of the Things. She could not escape them.

"I think I just need to calm down somehow," she declared, looking at her surroundings. The grove behind them illuminated in a faint blue, lighting up the bases of the trees, crawling up the trunk as far as the weak blue light could go. The forest in front of them was filled tightly with tall, skinny trees. The thickness of the trees faded as the meadow drew nearer and as the forest soon ended.

"Of course, we can head to the mountain whenever you are ready." John said gently, his gruff voice sounded comforting. It felt like all of Amaryllis' organs twitched in fear and excitement. Her heart skipped a beat. She realized how close Immortuos was and forgot about the Things for a minute. She replayed the memory of Immortuos transforming from a young girl into its ten foot tall, blood-red skinned, evil self. She clenched her jaw, and her cheeks flushed red in anger. She squeezed the dead grass beside her, yanking it from the ground. The grass' roots weren't strong enough to give her any satisfaction, no mental release. The blades pulled too easily from the ground.

Immortuos used her kindness against her just like Laria and everyone else in her life. Amaryllis sighed remembering how recently soft she was, how self-conscious she had been, and how much she had grown during the past few days. She surely was not the same woman she was when she entered the forest. She had to grow up overnight to be able to survive. No soft-hearted person could ever survive in a place such as the Dark Forest. Amaryllis wondered whether or not she would end her journey with matching characteristics to John - serious and aware, wise and short-tempered.

She pictured herself standing atop Immortuos' dead body, with glowing turquoise eyes and blue flames spitting from her palms, and smiled from her cruel intention. It was amazing how the Dark Forest had changed her into a dauntless individual. She nearly forgot her past as the Princess of Serilion, and she wanted to forget it. She didn't like who she was then when she struggled in all areas of royalty, from confrontation to proper etiquette, but she loved who she turned out to be. No one could get in her way.

"How close is the mountain?" she asked, trying to hide the excitement on her face. John raised his arm pointing through the skinny trees.

"It's right through there," he stated. Amaryllis was completely filled with euphoria and adrenaline. The restoration of the world was soon to come. Her faults were about to be fixed. She smiled wide showing her beautiful, straight teeth, then her smile faded.

"Are you coming up the mountain with me?" she asked.

John didn't answer for a while. When Amaryllis opened her mouth to ask again he responded, "I don't see a point."

Amaryllis' heart sank. She looked up into his eyes which looked more innocent than mean. "Why not—?"

"Amaryllis, you're fighting Immortuos; the most powerful and most despicable killer the world has ever seen," he reminded her. "You have a…*magical* gift and I do not. Do you think that I will be a reliable use for your battle? No, I won't. You'd be trying to kill the demon while simultaneously trying to protect me, making sure I'm not dead. I will be a complete nuisance, only slowing you down. I can kill mortal beings, but… Immortuos…I'd be dead within seconds."

Amaryllis looked away from him, down at her hands folded in her lap. He was right. John was a capable man with mortal creatures. He was powerful in the regular world, but fighting powerful entities with magical abilities he was of no use. The telekinetic touch of an omnipotent demon was undoubtedly stronger than any force on Earth. John would be crushed instantly.

If Amaryllis had not met Akar, the sorcerer, her journey would have been pointless. She would have died in several different situations before even reaching the mountain.

"I understand, but does that mean…that we're parting ways?" she asked with surprise in her voice. Amaryllis had grown to like John Edwards. Yes, he was occasionally cold, he frightened her countless times and made her feel small when they first met, but he came all this way just to help her get to where she needed to be. He helped shape her into the strong woman she turned out to be while he gained nothing but a terrible encounter with someone he despised, lost people he longed for, and had brief hypothermia from swimming across the coldest lake. He saved her from death and attempted to heal her showing compassion when he had none left. John showed kindness to her that she would never forget. He tried to hide his liking for Amaryllis, to appear as a heartless man driven by anger, but he believed in her abilities and would never mention to anyone. Yet he was also intimidated by her. John thought he lost the ability to love, but he secretly loved Amaryllis like a daughter. However, he would never show it.

"I'm afraid so," was all he said.

Amaryllis got up from the ground and walked over to him with long, confident strides. She wrapped her arms around him. He looked down at her at first leaving his arms by his sides. "I want to thank you for everything you've done for me," she spoke into his chest.

He finally hugged her back. "Of course," he said emotionlessly, patting her upper back. Amaryllis was not prepared to say goodbye and neither was he. "I value your friendship."

"I value yours more than you know—but wait—where are you going if you're not coming with me? You cannot go back to that shack."

"Well, that's where I was planning on going," he said stubbornly. "Doing exactly what we had just done, but backwards."

"I don't want you living there anymore. You need a place in the kingdom."

John felt anger rise in his chest after hearing the word *kingdom*. He ignored it and asked, "Which kingdom?"

"Mine. Well, not Serilion. Hopefully it shall be Werling." She let herself go from John's embrace. "I want you living in my kingdom, preferably in the castle because it is what you deserve. It is the least I can do for you."

"I didn't really do too much to deserve a room in your palace—"

"But you did!"

"Not entirely, all I did was lead you places. Even then, you already knew where you were going."

"Well, I needed your guidance. You taught me how to survive in here."

"I think you always knew how to survive, Amaryllis. Your magical abilities can take you anywhere."

"Just admit that you helped me," she demanded. "So I can feel satisfied with myself. If you don't, then I shall feel like I used you without appreciation."

John Edwards smiled the tiniest smile. Amaryllis' lips parted slightly, her jaw nearly dropped at the sight of possible joy coming from John's facial expression.

"Amaryllis, I assisted you in the best way I could, but you really didn't need me."

"I disagree," she stated, mesmerized with his smile which seemed to be as rare as a blue moon.

"You're humble… are you sure you are royalty?" John joked in a monotonous voice.

Amaryllis smiled. She didn't recognize him anymore, she'd never seen his happy side. She wasn't sure as to why he was in such a good mood. "Why are you so happy?" she asked seriously.

John's minuscule smile vanished. "Because you're going to fix everything. It's just strange how we're parting now. I've been isolated for twenty years with only myself to talk to. I suppose I've grown used to your company. As much as I've enjoyed our journey, I am overjoyed to see you go. It's what you needed me for and now you're here. We survived."

Amaryllis grinned at the scruffy forest man who she'd grown to admire. He looked back at her with a straight face. Perhaps she'd see his smile in another while. One was all she'd get for now. "You're not really walking back to your shack, are you?"

"Where am I supposed to go?"

"Watch me from the tree line," she demanded. "I'll come for you when it's all done."

John nodded, gripping his scabbard. "I can do that."

Amaryllis' gaze shifted back to the hole of the tunnel. She had forgotten about the Things. Her heart jumped when they entered her mind again. A distorted Prince James played about in her thoughts. She sighed.

"It does feel odd to be carrying on without you." She admitted.

"You'll be all right. Now… go," he mumbled, putting his hands on his hips and gesturing to the mountain with a nod of his head. Amaryllis peered through the trees, shivering. Now that the moment had finally arrived, she felt she was not prepared to face Immortuos. During her time in the Dark Forest she was driven by anger. She had been fooled by a clever entity and wanted to kill it. She had forgotten about its strength. Immortuos was incredibly dangerous. It could kill humans with a mere flick of its fingers to the head, as powerful as hitting someone with a long, metal object. It had to be sentenced to an eternity in the Forest of Enchantment by a group of powerful sorcerers. Immortuos was too powerful to kill. They couldn't even baptize the Dark Forest. Immortuos seemed to be the ruler of the Dark Forest. Even though the demon was contained, there was no end to evil. And now that it was free, evil was running wild. The whole world was the Dark Forest now.

"All right," she said hesitantly, taking slow steps towards the exit of the forest.

It's time, she told herself. *You shall restore the Forest of Enchantment, you shall repaint the boundaries of the Dark Forest, you shall fix what you destroyed.* She shivered with both excitement and nervousness as she thought this.

She walked slowly out of the forest not looking back at John. She stepped out into a meadow, shielding her eyes from red light which was significantly brighter than what she was used to in the Dark Forest. Her pupils constricted focusing on the gargantuan mountain before her. It was magnificent. The base was fat gradually twisting and shrinking in diameter to the skinny tallest points — sharp and small enough to impale a fly's gut — which stretched high into the red clouds. The rocks were jagged and defined, far too steep for walking.

The meadow looked as if it were a lovely place before the mountain shot up from the ground. It was flat, populated with dried streams, dead grass and dead trees. Amaryllis noticed how warm the air felt, which was strange since she'd been migrating north the whole journey. Her question was answered when something she hadn't noticed caught her eye. The bottom of the mountain was hidden behind a rising whitish-grey gas; smoke. A moat of lava surrounded the base of the mountain.

Chapter 39

Her excitement vanished. Amaryllis walked across the meadow of dead grass with an anxiety that brought pain to her stomach. Each step closer to the moat of lava amplified the discomfort in her gut. Her eyes followed the mountain from its base — all the way to where the clouds hid the tip — and shivered. She glanced over her shoulder to take a final look at the Dark Forest. It appeared small and powerless like a regular forest. She had lived on the insides of the forest, which was, according to everyone she met, the most dangerous place on Earth. It was thought to be suicide upon entering, but the mountain, standing in the open meadow killed by heat and a lack of earthly qualities, overcast by flat red clouds, disturbed her more than any thought she ever had about the Dark Forest. She remembered how frightened she was when she first entered the forest to escape the kings, princes and knights. She felt she was not in control of her body's actions, letting it do what it wanted while her conscious self spectated her body's behaviour. She felt the exact same way while walking to the mountain. Her mind screamed at her body to turn around, to at least stand still for a moment, but her legs did not stop moving. Her eyes narrowed as she focused on the giant piece of rock and what was inside. Her green eyes were dark, filled with determination. She appeared prepared but did not feel that way. She knew what had to be done and had to resist her natural instincts to turn around and flee.

Her family played in her mind. The image of her mother tucking her in at night when Amaryllis was only young was vivid and made her smile. Her mother was young and beautiful without a wrinkle on her face. Her blue eyes sparkled in the shadows of Amaryllis' bedroom as she told her daughter she loved her. Another image of her father taking her on a walk through a rose garden continued her nostalgic smile. She did not remember where the rose garden was, all she remembered was her father holding her small hand in his. A recent memory flashed, so vivid she forgot where she was. She seemed to be living in the moment of her remembrance. James was fighting his opponent down the staircase, laughing and smiling as he dominated, then he stopped mid-battle and appeared before her, in front of her face. Being so close made her heart flutter. He whispered that he loved her. Then her memory jumped into another. She was holding James' hands before she was about to leave. He whispered that he loved her once more then Amaryllis was brought back to reality, the reality of the fiery, red world. Her heart was still racing, in love with her memories.

"My life must be flashing before my eyes," she pondered, finally in control of her body. She stopped walking, glaring at the mountain in anger. "This was my fault. This entire catastrophe was my doing." She thought of her loved ones. "I shall do it for myself, I shall do it for them." Amaryllis broke into a full sprint, her dirty clothes from John flapping in the breeze, her hair flying behind her. She panted, not because she was tired, but because she was angry. She was thirsty for a battle, she longed to inflict pain upon Immortuos, to send it away, back to the Forest of Enchantment.

The moat drew nearer. The smoke rising from the lava smelled stronger, and the air felt hotter against her skin and in her throat as she breathed it. She stopped at the edge of the trench-like moat eyeing the width. It looked to be twenty feet wide and possibly fifty feet deep. As she peered over the edge, the heat of the lava warmed her face in a blanket of heat. She stepped back quickly before giving the rising heat the chance to burn her face.

On the other side of the moat was the mountain with no land, nowhere to stand. Even the mountain was too steep to stand on. She looked up intimidated by the size of it. It was almost beautiful if it wasn't the result of Immortuos' awakening and its wrath against Earth for imprisoning it for two-thousand years. It was because of the story behind the mountain which gave it the power to release such a disturbing feeling upon those who looked at it. It truly represented what evil could do to something as pure as the Earth. It sprung from the ground, blanketed the blue sky in red, shading the entire world from the sun and destroyed the barrier of the Dark Forest. It was an absolute tribulation, killing hope in everyone around the world. All except for Amaryllis and those who believed in her of course, which were not many. Her parents believed she was dead just hours after she set out, and Laria, with the exception of the rest of the princesses, hoped she was gone for good. Akar knew Amaryllis had potential but magic was too new to her. He did not think she would be able to learn the secrets of magic on her own quick enough for her survival, but he was wrong. Prince James and John Edwards were the only ones who truly believed in her abilities. Prince James *had* to believe she would return home. After all, she was the love of his life, and he needed her to return. John Edwards witnessed the rising power of her magical abilities, he had no doubt she would become more powerful. He watched her anxiously from the tree line.

The moat smoked ominously taunting her at how she was to be burned alive if she did not cross successfully.

I'll jump across, she thought simply. *It's definitely possible with my abilities.*

Magic seemed so simple to her. It used to take so much concentration for her to perform the smallest things, but it seemed to flow through her now. Little did she know her bones became coated in transparent magic, along with her organs, her cells, everything.

She looked down at her legs flexing each muscle. Her quadriceps, hamstrings and calves unquestionably felt stronger. She was planning on enhancing her strength to be able to jump across the moat, but she really did not need the enhancements. If she had flexed any of her other muscles in different areas of her body, she would have felt the increase of strength in those areas. Her muscles were rock hard, her skin was tougher, nearly impossible to penetrate with any blade, let alone bruise. Her blood swam with a bright red hue of liquid magic.

Amaryllis had become immortal.

Having to constantly use magic that consisted of intense concentration, and being exposed to several near-death experiences each day, awakened something in her brain. She had been genetically reprogrammed and developed magic automatically just as—if not more—instinctive as the fight-or-flight response. It was always present, just waiting to evoke. Magic and science intertwined within her, and she did not know it. If one were to look at her they would notice how her eyes seemed to be filled with permanent enchantment.

To test her strength "by itself" and without her conscious thought of using magic she squatted down then accelerated into the air by pushing against the ground as hard as she could. She expected to jump two feet from the ground, but her stomach dropped as she seemed to fly into the air. The ground became so distant she could nearly see over top of the entire Dark Forest. She looked past her boots watching her surroundings get smaller in a vertical blur. The only objects that did not seem to shrink within her perception of depth was the mountain and it's surrounding moat. Her heart fluttered in surprise. Her eyes widened followed by a small grin spread across her face. After fifty feet, she reached the highest trajectory of her jump, feeling butterflies even more intensely than when she first pushed from the ground.

She fell.

The gravity that pulled her weight down felt much stronger, and there was a much more intensified gust of wind that seemed to surround her falling body than expected. Her hair flew upwards, but her arms and legs stayed straight in a soldier dive. She landed on the ground with a large thud sending rumbles of dirt away from where her feet impacted the ground. It did not hurt, not the slightest bit.

Amaryllis widened her eyes looking down at the fragment of Earth she disturbed.

"What the—?" she began, starting to comprehend what she had just done. She ran her fingers through her knotted, wavy hair and smiled wide nearly forgetting about where she was.

"I just—" she let her hair free allowing the wind to blow it behind her head. "—I just...flew. This is unbelievable," she laughed looking at the mountain.

Without wasting another second, she took a running start towards the moat and jumped. From beneath her, she felt the heat of the lava pressing against her clothes, through her skin but it did not hurt. Mid jump a large shadow briefly cast over her in a flash of black. She landed with her hands and feet against the mountain. She did not slide down since her powerful presence kept her stationary. It was as if gravity had turned sideways. She stood on the side of the mountain like she would stand on flat ground. She looked up to see nothing. It made no sense. The red, cloudy sky was clear. The shadow was humungous. There was no way something so large could vanish like that.

It was dead silent. All was still. Before, there was a light breeze blowing through the dead meadow, but it had faded into nothing. Amaryllis walked a few steps up the side of the steep mountain and stared above. She scanned the sky looking for any sort of movement. Her eyes darted back and forth between different places in the sky with a stern expression on her face. She walked a few more steps then all of her muscles tightened as something dove down from the clouds. It was bright red and matched the colour of the clouds exactly. It looked so small from so far away, but as it came closer to the ground it grew incredibly, inconceivably large. The red thing outstretched its wings just ten feet before plummeting to the ground, and it rose up sending a gust of wind through the meadow powerful enough to knock a house right over. It was far away, looking like a gigantic bird, larger than any creature she had ever seen. It was a dragon. Its features became more distinguishable as it flew closer and closer. The dragon had a narrow, slim face with a closed mouth pressed into a straight line with a few protruding teeth. Its eyes were bright yellow with black slits as its pupils. Its scales glistened, sparkling like polished diamonds. Its wing span was difficult to read as it flapped its wings in and out of its body rapidly, picking up inconceivable speed, charging towards her.

Amaryllis was trapped out in the open with no place close enough to hide behind. She stood her ground with her teeth and fists clenched in determination. The dragon was enormous, easily larger than the dragons she snuck by early into her journey through the Dark Forest. The jet-black dragons she saw before were about the size of the largest alligator, perhaps twenty-four feet in length, with a wingspan of thirty feet. But the red dragon—just a single flap of its gargantuan wings away—was incomparable to anything she had seen. Its *head* was twenty feet in length and ten feet in width. Its slim, muscular body was eighty feet long, its narrow tail was forty feet long and its powerful legs were twenty feet long. Its wingspan was nearly two hundred feet wide.

Amaryllis hugged the mountain as the beast soared over her with its yellow eye following her as it flew past. It left about a foot of space between her and its body. If she hadn't squished against the mountain as close as possible, she would have been hit knocking her body thousands of feet away from the mountain.

The beast was silent as it flew, a truly sneaky and unpredictable creature. Grey smoke snorted from its nostrils before it vanished behind the mountain sending a gust of wind to pin her against the rock. Her slightly lifted head banged against the mountain leaving a circular crack where her head smashed against the rock. The pressure held her there until the wind died down.

It looped around once more startling Amaryllis as the massive beast suddenly came into view. The wind from its wings pressed her against the mountain again. This time she smashed the side of her face into the rock. If she had not gained immortality, the pressure from the air of the dragon's wings would have compressed her body into mush, and the blows to her head surely would have crushed her skull into a thousand pieces. She was more irritated than frightened although the size of the dragon did not cease to impress her. She could never get used to it. It took her breath away each time it passed. It circled her five more times staring at her with its beady yellow eyes. Faint smoke continuously rose from its nostrils.

Rage built up within her chest in a fiery sensation. The dragon seemed to be teasing her—perhaps trying to frighten her. Being pushed down and having to watch the gigantic creature fly past her over and over angered her. She stood her ground as the beast flew by for the seventh time. The wind from its powerful wings did not press her down on its final lap, although it nearly did. The gusts of lifelike wind fought her, seeming as though they had a mind of their own; pushing her around aggressively. The wind howled in frustration as she wouldn't go down. As it circled around, she punched the dragon's stomach as hard as she could. The sharp scales absorbed her hand, and they would have cut it into shreds if she had not gained her power. They were sharper than the blade of the finest sword. Her punch did not affect the dragon at all, it felt like a simple touch, a tickle. The scales protected the dragon in an indestructible shell, and Amaryllis knew she would need to break through them to cause any sort of relevant damage. She waited for it to return, but it did not. She looked to the sky, knowing it was pointless. She wouldn't be able to see it, but she looked anyway.

She began to run up the mountain. To someone on the ground it would have looked like she was running up a wall. It was overwhelming to look ahead. The tip of the mountain was so far away. She ran towards the clouds, into the sky—she essentially had to run vertically. It was dreamlike, nearly unbelievable, yet beautiful. The red sky almost possessed beauty for a split second then returned to its menacing self.

Out of nowhere the dragon returned blowing orange flames from its mouth in a powerful upsurge. Amaryllis took the blow of fire and her body broke through the side of the mountain sinking further and further inside the rock. The mild warmth of the flames tickled her body. The mountain swallowed her with the help of the dragon's heat. Minerals of all sizes fell in her face highlighted in orange light. All she could hear were thunderous, deafeningly loud, lion-like roars with hints of screeching. The sound penetrated her ears rattling her brain. She gritted her teeth tensing each muscle. She screamed a raspy scream in anger that she could not even hear over the sound of the superior dragon scream. She pushed off of the rock behind her and flew forward towards the opening before getting thrown back by the weight of the flames.

Suddenly, fire stopped flowing from the dragon's mouth. The dragon's scream halted.

Amaryllis emerged from the hole with orange flames dancing on her cotton clothes and in her hair. Her face wore austerity with narrowed eyes and lips slightly parted as she breathed heavily out of her mouth in exasperation. The dragon had vanished again. At that moment, she wished she was a dragon so she could release her rage in a mouthful of protruding fire along with a scream, loud and tormenting.

She groaned as she jumped out from the hole and back onto the side of the mountain. She sprinted, grunting angrily with each stride. Veins bulged in her temple, neck, and in her arms underneath her flaming clothes. She ran so quickly the flames burnt out leaving her shirt and pants crusty and hard, covered in holes both large and small. Her skin was exposed nearly everywhere.

She thought of nothing as she ran. She was aware but did not think.

The dragon returned. It flew behind her about to commence another attack of orange fire until she sensed its presence. She turned around and shot her own flames from her palms back at it. The dragon gave into the heat for only a moment before firing back. Her surge pushed it back a couple feet, which took the beast by surprise. It made its pulse-pounding sound again shaking the Earth. The dragon's orange flames fought Amaryllis' blue flames. The span of their brawl of fire stretched to be one-hundred feet in length. Amaryllis screamed under the dragon's powerful roar, feeling her insides quiver with unease. The dragon's sound was truly horrifying, and the unbearable volume intensified the effect. She contorted her face as she screamed harder, feeling her throat beginning to sting. Her flames extended further into the dragon's pushing the dragon back slightly in the air.

While keeping her flames strong and vigorous, she looked around the dragon to see that *more* dragons flew down from the sky. There were about twenty of them nosediving from the clouds with aerodynamic positioning of their bodies, their wings pressed into themselves before opening last minute to lift them above the ground. They all headed for Amaryllis, roaring concurrently, causing the ground to shake in a powerful earthquake. She could feel small vibrations in the mountain. The lava in the moat bubbled, spitting into the air.

Her stomach dropped in an overwhelmed surprise, even though she already constantly possessed magic in her body as a gift from the universe. Her eyes glowed turquoise, but they only glowed when she used intense levels of power as opposed to her early practice of magic when they only glowed when she was spiritually in the universe. They had never glowed brighter than they did right then. Turquoise protruded from her eyes in a beam of light blinding three dragons in the way of the beam. They shrieked piercing screeches and collided into the side of the mountain sending rubble tumbling into the moat. The mountain rattled wildly. In the air, Amaryllis felt the vibrations course through her from her feet all the way to her head.

The dragon she was battling suddenly headed into the sky. Amaryllis followed it with her flames until it was out of sight, hidden in the clouds. Seventeen dragons suddenly hovered around her, spitting flames. She protected herself in a shield of fire instead of trying to fight back. Her flames were strong enough to withstand a concentrated blow but could not attack successfully against the quantity of monsters. She was not yet angry enough.

She kneeled down, watching orange flames filter through her blue shield of fire.

It was blazing hot, but she felt no pain. Only the lightest touch of warmth tickled her face. The weight of the dragons' combined fire rested on her soul. Her body was stable, but her soul began to shake in fatigue. She felt it in her chest.

"Come on!" she hollered. Her words echoed in her bubble of fire. Her chest ached tremendously.

Suddenly, her shield gave way, and the dragons' fire blasted her into the mountain. Like before, minerals fell before her as her body flew seamlessly into the rock. Orange light and dragons' roars filled the hole. She shut her eyes in exasperation still seeing orange light under her eyelids. She screamed silently then opened her eyes, her pupils constricted into tiny pinholes. Her green eyes looked red in the light of the flames. The dragons' roars faded into silence, and the heavy weight of the fire uplifted becoming weightless.

Amaryllis moved slowly, observing each detail of her situation: the bright, blazing fire; the melting rocks; and the darkness behind her.

Amaryllis crawled effortlessly out of the hole, emerging in even less clothing; only strings of fabric. She stood in the centre of the fire, so the dragons did not see her through the thickness of the flames. She stopped and stared at the soundless fire rushing past her, her red eyes wide and concentrated. Her clothes had completely burned away. She looked down from the rushing flames at her nude body illuminated in orange, watching herself become magically clothed. The magical dressing process began with perfectly fitting boots that stretched into snug leggings, which grew into a snug long sleeve shirt that extended into fingered gloves. The material was a fireproof, white armour that weighed almost nothing. Once the magical armour had finished building itself onto her body, she looked back into the flames. Perhaps it was a subconscious defensive tactic, which caused her to unwillingly create an armour for herself and what silenced the roars of the dragons, but nothing explained why she was suddenly able to walk effortlessly through the powerful surges of fire. Not a single thought ran through her mind as she stared into the flames with a solemn look on her face.

Chapter 40

Once she looked away from the mesmerizing orange flames, she jumped out of the line of fire flying high above the dragons' heads. They didn't even notice her as she moved so quickly in a flash of white. On her way into the sky, she noticed the dragons' black slits in their yellow eyes had turned red. She stopped accelerating, levitating motionlessly in the sky, still well below the clouds but far away from the top of the mountain. The sound of the dragons' roars returned, penetrating her ears once again, even from her great distance. She glared at them as they continued to spit fire into the mountain, but something was off. One dragon was missing, and it was the one which attacked her first, the one who taunted her.

She nervously looked into the clouds, and, like before, she couldn't see anything.

Where is it? Where is it? She thought.

A dragon's screech could be heard in front of her. It was loud, overpowering the roars from below. She spun all around but still could not see a thing. The dragons below her stopped spitting fire. They waited for a moment, waiting to see if Amaryllis would come crawling out of the cave. They were nearly satisfied until one of them looked up, spotting her. It narrowed its eyes roaring at her. It flapped its wings as it began to fly towards her. The other dragons followed, roaring the entire way.

Suddenly, a dragon swooped down from the sky, its body an inch away from her face. She jumped widening her eyes. It was the first dragon. Its roar overpowered the others sending a chill down her spine. It circled her waiting for the other dragons to arrive, which didn't take long. The others arrived in two more flaps of their humungous wings. They too began to circle her. Some flew high and some low. Some flew clockwise and some counterclockwise. Because the dragons were so big, there had to be a several hundred feet in between Amaryllis and the circling dragons. Their thunderous, raspy, lion-like roars transformed into screeches as they stopped circling her. They hovered sending gales of wind in her direction. She remained stationary not allowing the wind to push her around. The only part of her that the winds affected was her long, wavy, auburn hair; it flew every which way.

They all opened their mouths revealing fire that danced in the back of their throats ready to shoot. Instead of taking another surge of fire, Amaryllis allowed her body to drop. She fell quickly watching the dragon's blow their fire to where she once was. Twenty of them blew as powerfully as they could, but the smartest one dove down following Amaryllis as she fell. It dove insanely fast, its huge face just ten feet away from her with its yellow, red-slit eyes staring at her. Eight feet away…five…three…the dragon opened its mouth revealing a set of two foot long, bloodstained, razor sharp teeth and a long, forked, crimson tongue.

Amaryllis yelled in frustration, instead of falling slower than the dragon's dive to get eaten she flew, but it still followed her closely with a gaping mouth. She headed towards the mountain diving down to the moat of lava.

She hovered just an inch above the orange and yellow lava, looked behind her to see the dragon was still close, then she stuck her hand in the hot liquid and threw it back into the dragon's mouth. It rested on the dragon's tongue for a second then it swallowed the lava coughing out orange and yellow flames.

The dragon dove down into the moat then emerged completely coated in lava. Its wings flapped sending balls of lava into the meadow. Amaryllis looked behind her at the lava-coated dragon, its eyes wild, with the other dragons flying down from the sky. They copied the smartest dragon coating themselves in lava, some filling their mouths with it.

Five dragons soared closer to her spitting the lava on her. The weight of it brought her down thirty feet.

All of the dragons followed.

She spun in the air, shaking it off her body then shot up towards the clouds. She looked down at the many dragons pursuing her, overwhelmed. They didn't stop. It never ended.

She dropped suddenly heading for the mountain again. She found the most recent hole she was blown into and flew inside.

From outside, she heard screeches and saw several dragons bumping heads trying to see her in the hole. Soon enough blue flames entered, lighting it.

Amaryllis couldn't hear her heavy breathing over the dragons' roars. She sat down catching her breath.

How can I harm these dragons? They are immune to heat and heat is my only defensive resource. Their scales are their armour. I have punched one with extreme force… perhaps I can penetrate them with something.

Amaryllis was unsure how but she was able to resist the power of the surge of fire again. She walked out of the hole thinking of diamonds. Diamonds cannot be broken by anything but themselves.

Amaryllis held out her arm, and a single chunk of diamond appeared in her hand. She held it in two hands pulling both ends of the tiny rock into a five-foot long, skinny rod—two inches in diameter—with a pointed tip. She pricked her finger on the end of it watching blood squirt from her finger. The diamond rod made her immortal body bleed…it could certainly pierce the dragons' sturdy scales.

The dragons' fire faded into the air revealing their angered faces and Amaryllis' sly expression. She stood before them fiddling with the rod happily. It would be so easy.

One dragon lurched forward with an open mouth.

Amaryllis jumped onto its tongue holding the rod high above her head.

The dragon snapped its mouth closed. It let out an ear-piercing scream that shook Amaryllis' body. Its mouth opened and she jumped back onto the mountain. Blood spewed from the hole in its snout. The dragon roared in pain initiating a collected wave of roars from the other dragons.

The injured dragon tried to bite her again, but she protected herself with the rod, stabbing through its mouth once again. Another hole in its snout spewed with blood. It rained into the moat and trickled down Amaryllis' white armour. Her face was painted in blood.

The dragon cried and spun around to fly away, but Amaryllis was not finished.

She jumped onto its tail without the dragon knowing. The other twenty dragons followed. She sprinted up its tail, up its body, dodging its powerful, flapping wings, all the way up its neck, to its head. She leaned over to find its yellow eye darting all over the place until it spotted her. Its black slit constricted to be even thinner.

Amaryllis stuck the diamond rod right into its eye, pulling it out with yellow eye gunk on it. The dragon screeched a faint screech then began to head towards the ground with its gigantic, limp, lifeless body falling quickly. The dragons behind her roared in anguish for their fallen one, gaining an incorrigible rage that allowed them to fly faster towards her.

As a dragon flew above her, she jumped from the falling dead dragon and stabbed the overpassing dragon in the stomach. The rod wedged in its gut holding her up. She watched the dragon she had killed hit the ground sending a monstrous cloud of dust into the air and shaking the earth for a split second.

She used her rod as a pickaxe to climb the dragon. It screamed the whole time as she repeatedly stabbed its body and hoisted herself up higher onto its back.

The dragon flew faster, driven by pain, leaving the dragons far behind them. It spun in circles, trying to shake her off, but she held on watching the world in a hypnotic spiral. She could very faintly make out the castle of Arlon.

From Arlon, all of the royal subjects, all of the knights, dukes and commoners could see the battle. The dragons, from such a distance, looked like tiny birds. When they spit fire, it looked like an orange, feathery line. Amaryllis was too small to be visible, but Prince James knew she was there. He looked out of the tall, ballroom window with his eyes wide and watery. All of the royal families crowded the large window. It was twenty feet in length, but it didn't seem to be wide enough. He was nudged, pushed around as other people tried to see, but he didn't even notice them. Amaryllis' parents stood to the side of the window, crying. They were relieved to know she was alive, but how long would she be alive for? She was fighting dozens of dragons. The odds were unfair. If only they knew what had happened to her and how much power she had attained.

Laria watched the dragons in astonishment. Amaryllis was there fighting them. She had made it to the mountain. She couldn't help but smile. Something inside of her changed. Of course, she would always envy Amaryllis, and her envy increased knowing she was capable of surviving the Dark Forest, let alone fighting *dragons*, but she actually felt happy for Amaryllis, and happy for herself. If Amaryllis was successful, the red sky would disappear, and the world would return to normal.

While Amaryllis was gone, the castle doors and windows were banged on, and against, by charging creatures. Some monsters broke into the ballroom but were quickly killed by the princes. It was horrifying for everyone. Laria, like everyone else, wanted the world back and wanted the evil creatures to die away. Amaryllis was their saviour, she had to believe in her.

Amaryllis would have wondered if Arlon was watching her if she wasn't so focused. She made it to the dragon's head and stabbed it through its skull sending it falling to the ground. Immediately, she jumped onto another dragon and did the same thing. The dead dragons laid near one other in a massive cloud of dust with floating dead pieces of grass, dirt, and twigs falling to the ground.

The sky was full of hovering dragons that surrounded Amaryllis. Their huge wings sending powerful gales all throughout the meadow, shaking several trees in the Dark Forest. The winds made it all the way to Arlon, but by the time they reached the castle they had faded into a light breeze. The dragons didn't know when to quit: some spit fire, others tried to eat her, but nothing worked. Amaryllis outsmarted them each time.

She jumped from dragon to dragon stabbing them in the eyes and head with her diamond rod. Nearly all of the dragons laid in a pile in the dead meadow. There were three dragons left but only two were in sight. The smartest dragon flew into the clouds, hiding, possibly planning how it was going to execute her. The other two finally understood that they could not battle her, and they began to fly away joining the smartest dragon in the sky.

Amaryllis levitated three-hundred feet from the ground clenching her diamond rod in both hands. Her eyes were turquoise, her hair blew wildly behind her head, she looked magnificently majestic and, to the evil creatures that hid in the Dark Forest and the dragons in the clouds, she appeared dominant and terrifying.

She looked at the pile of dead dragons, their scales already began to fade into a muted red. She waited patiently for the final three dragons to present themselves. They did not make an appearance for what felt like an eternity.

Amaryllis had had enough and would not be satisfied unless she executed all of them, especially the dragon who attacked her first. She flew into the sky, and slowed herself down when her head poked through the clouds. She rose slowly, gripping the diamond rod firmly. The red clouds felt hot like fire.

She found herself in a pocket of air surrounded by the thick, red clouds.

"Show yourselves," she muttered, spinning all around, waiting for a dragon head to appear before her.

She waited patiently for a few minutes, but no dragon appeared. If it came to having to search the entire atmosphere she would. She built up energy within herself and flew forward until immediately halting when thunder boomed in the sky. Lighting flashed revealing three dragon silhouettes spread out around her. She silently moved forward with her diamond rod extended far in front of her. The clouds were so thick she wouldn't know she found one until she came an inch away from the thing. She ran into one, she felt it on the tip. She pressed as hard as she could impaling it in perhaps the shoulder. A screech filled the sky, and she was jerked out of the clouds, back down onto the suffering dragon. She had struck the tail.

The other dragons flew down thinking they could protect one another from her. As she sprinted up the forty-foot long tail, up its eighty-foot long body and the thirty-foot long neck, rain began to sprinkle from the sky. She dove onto its head stabbing through the brain. She leaped off the plummeting dragon and found herself jumping onto the mountain. She ran around it migrating slightly upwards until jumping for the next dragon. As she approached, the dragon spit its flames in her face, rushing past her in a powerful surge. It did not affect her. The fire was weightless. She did not land on the dragon, instead she jumped for its head and stabbed it in the eye. Immediately after, she swung over its head and shot herself forward chasing the final dragon. It was the one who taunted her on the mountain, the one who first pressed her into the rock, the culprit of her perseverance, her rage.

The dragon was demoralized. Amaryllis was too sharp-witted and strong; she could resist a blast of fire, she could fly just as fast, or slightly faster than it. The dragon's death was imminent and it knew it.

As Amaryllis charged the dragon with a disturbingly sinister look on her face, and the dragon actually responded with fear to her facial expression, her intimidation. Its eyes seemed to widen, and it flapped its wings as hard as it could, slowly losing her, until Amaryllis snapped. She wanted to fight Immortuos, not a group of dragons. She charged for the dragon, in an attempt to kill it and move on, reaching it in a millisecond. The dragon let out a shriek then broke for the clouds. Amaryllis watched its forty-foot tall tail rise into the clouds until it was gone. She grunted hard feeling her face heat up.

"You get back here!" she bellowed chasing it into the sky. One second she was below the clouds, the next she had located the dragon stabbing it somewhere on the body until they fell into the open air. She had pierced beneath its cheek then slid down all the way to its back, riding her diamond rod, cutting a thirty-foot long gash in its neck. She gritted her teeth the entire way down finally killing the last one. She stuck with it the whole way to the ground wanting to feel the satisfaction of physically taking it down.

They hit the ground—far from the pile of dragons—with a thud as loud as thunder. It was satisfying to ride the dragon on its way back to the Earth, falling with it to ensure it made it to the dragon graveyard. She was satisfied with her final killing. Amaryllis looked at its head to find its dead yellow eyes, but its eyelids were closed.

Dust, dirt, and dead grass rained from the sky as she stood atop the final beast peering through the cloud of dust at the pile of dragons, closer to the mountain. She ripped her diamond rod from its neck. It was coated in blood. Then she dismounted the creature landing in a pool of thick blood that reached her ankles.

She ignored it stopping to feel the sprinkling rain beginning to fall heavier.

When she emerged from the lake of blood, she walked slowly to the mountain. She watched the rain wash the blood away from her body, down the armour it trickled.

As she passed the pile of dead beasts power filled her. It took a long time, but she had killed them all. She had never been more sure of her abilities than right then watching the gargantuan pile of dead dragons become smaller as she headed for the mountain. Just walking past them took a long time and that reminded her of their hugeness and powerful strength.

Her armour and diamond rod were clean of blood and so was her face. Her hair was soaked, pressed flat to her head, but her body was dry with the snug protection of her armour. Rain began to pour, thunder boomed, and lightning struck the ground. It rained so hard, Amaryllis had to squint her eyes to see.

Chapter 41

Amaryllis jumped the moat again listening to sizzling sounds as the rain hit the lava. As she sprinted up the mountain, her eyes were almost shut trying to block out the pouring rain. Her eyelashes fluttered in her vision. The world grew darker as the storm rolled in, and Amaryllis couldn't help but think Immortuos caused it. Once she had run, she pushed off the mountain and flew all the way to where the mountain touched the clouds.

She crawled through the hot, red clouds to see that the mountain stretched for another fifty metres. She walked the rest of the way feeling fear rise in herself as she drew nearer to the top.

She lightly placed her hand on the tip feeling it was just as sharp as her diamond rod. There didn't seem to be an opening to the inside. She sat down, bringing her knees to her chest, letting the rain fall over her as she found herself deep in thought. She remembered what Akar said:

You'll have to restore the barrier by killing Immortuos… which will be terribly difficult since it is immortal… but every evil source or entity has a weakness. I don't know what it would be, but I pray that you will discover it.

"Every evil source or entity has a weakness," she repeated in her head remembering Akar's words. It was difficult to think of Immortuos having a weakness. A thing as malevolent as Immortuos wouldn't seem to possess any weaknesses…except for…purity. Purity is what contained it for two-thousand years, but is it what could potentially kill it for good? Amaryllis didn't know how to restore the barriers of the Dark Forest, nor did she know how to rebuild the Forest of Enchantment. She was going to have to kill it. It was the only way. The sorcerers couldn't do it two-thousand years ago but perhaps she could. She had to.

Amaryllis lost grip of her diamond rod. She snapped free from her thoughts to watch it fall a couple hundred feet, through the clouds, before flying down to fetch it. It bounced against a protruding rock nearly ricocheting upwards and stabbing her in the eye as she dove for it. She caught it hearing a faint cracking sound. Where the rod hit the mountain it left a big crack spanning four-feet wide that resembled a spiderweb.

Something sparked within her.

Her diamond rod was formed in her own hands. The mountain was formed by Immortuos' arrival. Amaryllis was a being of purity. Immortuos was a being of evil. The diamond rod constructed by purity impacted the mountain constructed by evil. Immortuos' weakness *was* purity. It had to be.

Amaryllis repeatedly hit the mountain with the dull end of her rod, watching the crack grow larger and larger, until a huge chunk of rock caved in and disappeared into darkness. Amaryllis walked inside of the hole finding she had plenty of room to walk around.

The inside of the mountain was almost utterly hollowed out in a large room with inconsistent patterns of narrowing passageways. From where she entered, torches of red flames danced on the far side of the inner wall of the mountain. Because the mountain was so wide, they looked like tiny matches from where she stood.

Rain water gushed in behind her pounding against her back in gigantic splashes. It was a nuisance. She attempted to patch the rocks back in their place, but she couldn't find the pieces anywhere. She couldn't see anything, so she used her hands to illuminate the inside of the mountain. The rocks were visible, so she replaced the rocks, as if she had never broken in, using telekinetic ability. It was seamless. As soon as she fixed the last piece, the thunderstorm, along with the downpour, could not be heard, exposing her to a deafening, penetrative silence.

As she explored the inside of Immortuos' lair, she noticed there was a hole in the centre about as deep as death. She wondered what it could be for. She shone light inside, but it didn't stretch all the way to the bottom. It was too long and too dark inside. There must have been something hidden at the bottom, and she was curious to find out, but she didn't let her wonderings consume her too much. She had to focus on Immortuos first.

Other than the monstrous hole, there seemed to be nothing inside. She flew over the trench to examine the torches. She took one down from the wall and studied the way the flame danced as if there was wind swirling about.

She was safe from the thunderstorm, the haunted land covered in dragon corpses, and the Dark Forest, which seemed, finally, so far away from her. However, inside the mountain, she was disturbed by the idea itself. The idea of where she was and who she was only a quick game of hide and seek from. Immortuos was, without a doubt, inside the mountain. It was in there somewhere.

Amaryllis stood up as straight as possible to show her anxiety that she was stronger than its presence. Normally, her fear would cause her to hunch over, hold her stomach, and breathe shallowly, but her posture was perfect, strong, and she breathed heavily. She was intimidating although she did not feel that way.

She eyed the inside of the mountain's walls. They were disgusting to the eye; red, white, goopy looking in some areas with random black spots. There was something about the variety of minerals and their shapes and colours that reminded her greatly of broken bones, both snapped, shattered and bloody. They reminded her of the deer she watched decompose in the first grove of blue mushrooms. The walls looked like a freeze-frame of the deer midway through its organs melting; splattered blood revealing sizzling tissue and white bones. Of course, the walls were dry, but it looked like something had been crushed against the walls then the residue had been lazily eaten leaving some areas lumpier than others.

The deafening silence in the mountain penetrated Amaryllis' body, flowing through her from the soundproof walls. It was a place that ignited uneasiness in her brave soul. If anyone else were to enter they surely would not be capable of containing their extreme discomfort, their fear. She wasn't panicking only because of her experience in the Dark Forest. Her anxiety tried to swirl and curl in her stomach, but she fought until it faded from pain into simply a feeling until her fear was gone.

She had grown accustomed to the mountain's disturbing features, feeling confident enough to begin to search for Immortuos.

Chapter 42

Amaryllis looked around the mountain for an opening, cracks, or any sort of entrance into another area. She completely disregarded the gaping hole in the centre fearing there was something down there that she did not want to see. Instead of going down, she decided to go up. After all, what was the point of forming such a large mountain with a tip that surpassed the clouds if it wasn't an important feature? Immortuos had to be up there.

She approached the wall furthest from where she had broken in, turning her back to the trench. It was inauspicious to face away from the hole, like something would crawl out and attack her from behind since she wasn't heeding the possibility of an attack. An apprehensive feeling settled in her stomach. Something had to be standing there. She looked back with a racing heart and a tense body, through the shadows, expecting to see *something*. Nothing was there. She sighed, turning back, then jumped to walk up the wall.

She walked for a while illuminating her way with her palms as the red torches grew dimmer in the distance. The disgusting red and white features from below gradually faded out showing regular rock and minerals that didn't remind her of death. She felt safer and safer as the giant hole became farther away. The area below projected a perturbing feeling so strong it tore her apart. She had just calmed herself with her heavy breathing. Her goosebumps finally settled, and her insides had stopped trembling as the red room couldn't be seen anymore, even with the light from her hands.

She walked one hundred feet up the wall, then another hundred, then another until she noticed the walls were angling sharply. She was near the tip of the mountain and the fear from below caught up with her once again. An unseen force picked away at her soul, her body shook in surrender, she could not resist the fear's effect. Proceeding further up felt wrong, going back down felt just as wrong, even staying where she currently was didn't feel safe. She felt the stares of angry eyes in the shadows of the mountain that made her skin crawl, but her light proved that no-one was there to be glaring at her with any sort of sinister gaze.

She made it as high as she could not able to walk any further. Above her was a small hole, a tunnel above her head. Gravity danced around her body lifting her to be able to crawl into the vertical tunnel. It tickled her softly, which would have made her grin if she wasn't so engaged, if Immortuos left her mind.

She shivered in remembrance of the tunnel of Things, breathing one hard exhale through her nose when she pictured their true form. Just imagining them haunted her into believing they had followed her there. She checked over her shoulders in trepidation then solace eased into her mind as she found no Thing in sight. To her misfortune, the mountain's tunnel was smaller than the one in the Dark Forest, nearly small enough to make Amaryllis feel claustrophobic. If she wasn't as lean as she was, she would have gotten stuck only to free herself with her inhuman strength of course, but as a mortal she would have been be trapped for life, to die shortly.

She wiggled efficiently through the jagged tunnel feeling sudden pokes and scratches against her thick skin as she seemed to fly upward. It took zero strength to climb. Her body subconsciously knew what to do, swimming like a fish in the sea. Some areas were more closed than others, but she succeeded in staying calm. A small area was the least of her worries.

    Amaryllis progressed through the tight spaces in a matter of a few minutes. During the last minute, she wondered how long she would be in such a small space for, involuntarily allowing rushing feelings of whelm to consume her. There was no way to tell time, so she didn't bother counting the minutes because it seemed to lengthen the process dreadfully.

    She finally emerged from the tunnel outstretching her arms to enjoy her space then let the unknown take effect on her. It was pitch black and oddly silent. Only the sounds of her breathing filled the area. She sparked white light in her palms before her fear of the unknown could enter her mind. To her relief, no creature accompanied her, nothing but the jagged, mountain walls stared back at her. She sat in silence for a minute holding her breath because listening to herself breathe in such a place made her hairs stand on end. She was puzzled and unsure of where to go next. The small room had no openings or even cracks of any kind that she could slip through. She seemed to advance as far as she could. If Immortuos was not there, then where else—

    A muted, jumble of cracking sounds prevailed the silent room circling her in a fearful ring of sounds. The sudden stridency narrowed her eyes into angry slits, revealing nothing but dark green irises with constricted pupils. Although the room was dark, and biologically her pupils should have dilated in the darkness of the room, her anger took over. They were nearly as small as a grain of sand. Her eyes darted back and forth trying to identify where the sound was loudest, but it was consistently blaring in each direction. With her diamond rod she repeatedly struck the wall to her right until a hole large enough to crawl through appeared. Rubble fell inside, and the cracking sounds grew louder. With gritted teeth, angry eyes, and glowing hands Amaryllis displayed unforgiving hostility. Beneath her armour were powerfully built, raging muscles thirsting to inflict pain. Her erect posture depicted her strength, her eyes told her story which she was still writing. She thwacked the mountain's walls once more to feed her damaging desires then jumped into the hole shaking the light from her hands.

Her armour sparked against the mountain walls as she fell down the hole. The space was devilishly tight; a claustrophobic nightmare. She turned her head to the side, in fear of scraping her nose clean off, looking up into the blackness of the crevice which amplified the knots in her stomach. An eerie, metallic, scraping sound vibrated in her ears. The armour was indestructible, but from the sounds it made it seemed to be falling apart.

She held her breath as she fell for what felt like an hour until her boots struck the ground in a hollow thump against rock. Her anger was still as strong as when she jumped, if not, stronger. The cracking sounds stopped as soon as she landed.

Chapter 43

Amaryllis grunted as she hit the wall in front of her. Her fingers were white, squeezed tightly around her diamond rod as she busted through the rock. Rubble rained into large piles after four powerful strikes then Amaryllis walked through the hole she had made. She listened for noises aside from her boots clacking against the smooth, stone floor. Again, all she heard was absolutely nothing. The sounds clearly originated from where she just entered, and they should have been intensively loud, but they had stopped abruptly. Again, the only noise being made came from Amaryllis as she breathed calmly.

A dark presence overwhelmed her, tugging at her soul, sending chills down her spine, and making her feel heavy. Surely, something was down there with her, waiting patiently with staring eyes, exuding its atrocity upon her. Feelings of exposure and defencelessness overcame her. She could see nothing, and she evidently possessed the ability to light the area, but knowing the unknown lurked before her kept her from moving at all. It was then that she realized that she was in a trench, which she feared just from glancing at. She was frozen, her heart being the only part of her she could feel aside from the trepidatious sensations. Her arms and legs stiffened like trees. She widened her eyes, annoyed to not gain a better vision of the room. As much as Amaryllis had endeavoured, as thick as her skin became, it was only natural to feel perturbed. Although the room was pitch black the sensation of the room enclosing her was present. Her chest throbbed in an aching discomfort, burning in a raging fire, nearly taking her breath away. It came randomly and suddenly; a constant feeling from then on.

Light it, light it, light it, she ordered herself but was too afraid. *Whatever is here will kill you in its element, the element of darkness. Light never reaches this pit, you will have the advantage…do it.*

"I can't," she mouthed barely moving her lips. Her heart pulsated manically, punching her ribs. She shivered in a cold sweat gaining movement in only her fingers. She clenched her hands into fists and clenched her jaw hard enough to surpass the jaw strength of a mortal. Her feet shuffled ever so slightly, her arms twitched.

Please light the pit. Please, please, please—

Amaryllis sighed loudly overwhelmed with stress. She immediately wished she had kept quiet. Her exhale reverberated up the pit moving farther and farther away until fading into nothing. Sweat trickled from her forehead down her neck and down her back. Her silence broke the refrain of balefulness. Before, her chest was exposed to the feeling of evil—the culprit of her pain—seeping through her body and squeezing her heart in a gradual press, but darkness seemed to suddenly crush, then eat away at her soul, as soon as she proved her presence to what ever being was emitting the evil.

Amaryllis gasped at the sudden pain then reacted. All in one moment, fire shot out from her hands sparking around the entire perimeter before growing into massive flames. The fire danced frantically crawling up the mountain walls. Black smoke swayed and swirled about, stretching upwards and entering her nose as she took shallow breaths. She stared into the centre of the room she was in, which was still shadowed, receiving little light from the fires. There was an outline of a figure just barely visible.

The cacophony of cracking returned suddenly rattling her eardrums. The rush of noise pushed her from her feet and onto her back. She landed with a thud feeling sound rush just above her face resembling powerful gales. She picked herself up fighting the sound as she stood up.

Light extruded from her hands revealing red and black, crusty, treelike structures standing in the middle of the hole. Her hands followed them up and up until her stomach dropped.

Before her, stood what she had been seeking, what destroyed the purity of the Earth: Immortuos.

Amaryllis' body trembled in a visceral rage. As she grew angrier, the fire surrounding the perimeter flailed faster, stretched higher.

The demon was thirty feet tall, standing perfectly still with its legs spread ten feet apart, and its arms hanging stiffly by its sides.

More than anything all she wanted was to pummel the demon, but as she pictured the juxtaposition of battling Immortuos, the positive outcome embedded itself in her mind. The only issue within the evident advantage of killing Immortuos was that she never might never receive the opportunity to express how it wronged the world, and more specifically, how it wronged her.

"What are you waiting for?" she spluttered squeezing her rod tightly in her hand hard enough for it to hurt. The demon remained stationary. The cracking sounds stayed at the same volume.

There were several questions she could have asked it, but there was no point in verbalizing her basic thoughts. She had instincts to ask if it truly knew what it had done, why it behaved so atrociously, and if it knew what she had to go through to reach it. All of these questions were rhetorical in regard to a being such as Immortuos. Immortuos knew very well what it had done, it possessed its intentions from the very beginning of its existence. Its wrath had been delayed two-thousand years, and it was more than prepared to carry out its intentions of destruction and death. All of its endeavours were absolutely meaningful with a sinister passion. Immortuos behaved atrociously because it was a being of darkness. There was no other answer. Amaryllis was a being of purity. She behaved the way she did from the environment she grew in, her heredity. Meaning, Immortuos descended from a dark world, a dimension of callousness and mercilessness. It possessed not the morals of an earthling. Destruction was normal, death was relished, mercy was frowned upon, love was unheard of, and of course Immortuos knew of Amaryllis' endeavours, it could sense her change in character. When it had used her for its escape, it sensed passivity, softness, and weakness, but now, it sensed awareness, aggression, and dominance.

Immortuos was intimidated, silenced by her advancing power that seemed to be progressing rapidly right in front of it. She didn't even notice her power was growing. She thought she reached the peak of her strength, but there was more to discover. Only Immortuos knew it.

"I risked everything to find you," she hissed, having to let go of her rod before crushing her joints. The memories of her journey played through her mind: informing the royal subjects of her departure to the Dark Forest in her dismantled, ceremonial gown; riding Ezro into the darkness; nearly dying in the mushroom grove; the lake; and the tunnel of Things. All through her memories she caught glimpses of different people she had not thought about for a while. John was one of them. She wondered what happened to him after her battle with the dragons. He was in the tree line spectating. He could be anywhere now. She hoped he was in good condition. Another person was her mother and her crying face watching her daughter walk away a second time. Amaryllis felt her mother's sadness. During that time, she pushed everyone away leaving without a loving explanation to assure her loved ones of her return.

She stood in Immortuos' lair now wishing she had been more kind and understanding, but after all, she did have to set out to fix her mistakes. She needed to spend each second with a purpose towards finding a solution to her prodigious conundrum of saving the Earth. She only hoped that her family would understand, especially Prince James, whom she was too distracted from to truly miss.

Immortuos appeared menacingly with Amaryllis' fire. No matter what she said, it stayed perfectly still, making the same constant cracking sounds. She knew not what they were, but she began to think it was the sound of the demon speaking. It was communicating through its own language of terrifying, shrilling, non-words.

"You'd better enjoy yourself while you can, in your little realm of darkness, because—"

The cracking sounds became louder, but Immortuos still stood motionless.

Amaryllis fought herself to control her impulses to just flat out charge at the demon. It was imperative that she expressed her sufferings first. "I won't even be sending you to a heavenly place to counteract your evil, your death will be permanent. Yes, you are currently undead, but I suppose what I'm trying to say is… you simply *won't* EXIST ANYM—!"

The demon roared shaking the entire mountain, which carried into the meadow. Immortuos broke from its state of stillness in a blink charging for Amaryllis on all fours. She had only a moment to react, which she used to summon strength into her diamond rod. Immortuos reached its arm out to grab her, and she drove the rod right through its skin until it poked out the other side. Immortuos shrieked then hit her with its opposite arm sending her flying into the mountain wall. She made impact with a groan then fell into the spitting fire. Immortuos plucked the sliver-like rod out of its arm and flicked it away. From where it was inserted, its red and black, burnt skin, bubbled in golden acid. Amaryllis crawled out of the fire, driven by infuriation then levitated into the air. Turquoise light radiated from her armour, along with her skin, and her eyes. She lit up the entire inside of the mountain temporarily blinding Immortuos and making the orange flames seem dim and dull. Extending her arms she released a concentrated beam of turquoise light directly at Immortuos' head. It shrieked over the rushing sound coming from her line of fire. Immortuos' pain strengthened the strike of light which made it wail louder and louder, caught in a cycle of torture. Amaryllis clenched her jaw and revealed her teeth as she used the power of the universe against the flagitious, undead creature. Before she could thoroughly enjoy her revenge, Immortuos grew twenty feet taller weakening the effect of the light. Amaryllis kept the light pointed at it anyway to make the monster suffer for as long as possible, until it grew another twenty feet. With each foot the demon grew the effect her universal summonings had lessened. She shook the light from her hands and lurched at the demon. Her fingered, armoured gloves dug into its flaky, bloody skin to hold herself up. She climbed its torso all the way to its face in a matter of seconds. Immortuos didn't even notice its own growth or her appearance of becoming smaller. She was merely a bug crawling on its body.

Amaryllis finally reached its face. Its eyes darted back and forth still shaken by her attack; the surge of the cosmos. It stopped suddenly, one of its eyes locating her on its cheek, and she watched the demon frown a distorted frown upon seeing her. Immortuos reached for her, its giant hand soaring through the air incredibly fast. The demon's growth was still progressing, growing an inch for each second that passed.

As Immortuos' tremendous, long-fingered hand chased Amaryllis all over its body, Amaryllis reacted summoning strength powerful enough to penetrate Immortuos' eye. Her body shot right through its cornea all the way to the retina. She was momentarily safe. A muffled, quaking shriek shook her body and rattled her ears. The demon opened its mouth wide, and allowed its body to react to the excruciating pain. Stringy, sticky, red blood dangled from the top to the bottom of its mouth. The screams blew the string-like blood forward, spastically shaking like flags in a windstorm. Immortuos covered its eye, and Amaryllis could see nothing. All she could feel was the goopy, squishiness of the demon's eye slurping against her armour. Amaryllis formed another diamond rod illuminating the inside of the eye briefly as her magical process proceeded. She gripped it tight then stabbed an arbitrary spot making the screams escalate several decibels higher. The demonic screams reminded her of a more horrifying version of the melodies of the Dark Forest until she could not think anymore. Her thoughts were suppressed by the thundering bellows which invaded her cranium. She stabbed it again, which made the screams worse. Two long figures suddenly wrapped around the sclera tugging the eyeball out of its socket. Amaryllis emerged from the eye flying into the open air, then landed on the ground. She turned around to see a distressed Immortuos with a hanging eyeball holding on by black muscles coated in blackish-red blood.

Finally, Immortuos spoke humanly using actual words. Its voice was thunderous and gravelly.

"You will rot in the depths of the darkest realm wishing for every excruciatingly slow second that passes that you never crossed paths with me." The demon barked, "You will never die, you will never see the light again. For every minute that passes, your hopes of escape will perish making each hour after the next feel like hell, which will make your days torturous. Unbearable suffering will crush your soul into dust as maggots burrow through your skin, as you cook in a perpetual fire, as the earthly soul is devoured by evil. You will forget who you are and where you came from. All you will know, all you will think about, is that you will never escape."

Amaryllis shivered as the demon's words vibrated through her skull. Its threats were menacing, yet they weren't enough to scare her away. As dominant, powerful, and intimidating the inhuman creature was, Amaryllis stood her ground staring at Immortuos' disfigured face with it's drooping eye. It was even taller now with its head nearly piercing the darkness into invisibility. She narrowed her eyes following the demon's eyes as it grew.

"The only place I shall ever visit is the Dark Forest to remind myself of the creature of hell I had awakened. The creature that both ruined and saved my life. The creature I had banished to the void of non-existence—!" Amaryllis began before being interrupted.

"You will suffer horribly without the essentials of humankind. I would rather kill you slowly, watching blood gush out of every orifice, and listening to your helpless voice plead for mercy as you choke, your throat brimful with blood. But the lack of human essentials would make you suffer that much more, that much longer. It will be eternal, and it will bring me great feelings of exhilarating pleasure. Without light you will shrivel into a hideous, emaciated damsel. Your beauty shall vanish. Without love you will loathe in neglect with a soul occupied with hatred. All of your kindness shall die. Being surrounded by evil will overpower your purity changing you forever into a being of horror, a spectre of distress." Immortuos smiled revealing long, thin, pointed black teeth. The demon tried to frighten Amaryllis' new, brave persona into the depths of her soul to retrieve her past self. When it encountered her she was in awful condition, petrified and cowardly. It was determined to make her cowardly, royal, dependent self resurface so it could break her indefinitely. Immortuos was intimidated by the new woman before him and distracting her from her powers was all it could do in defence.

Amaryllis ignored each grotesque word that slithered through Immortuos' bloody mouth staring intently at its long-fingered hands. It was the disguised hand of a *little girl* that caught her attention. The hand that commenced the alteration of the world.

"I will kill you," she promised. "You will suffer for each minute you've haunted the Earth for." She looked up at the demon standing one hundred feet over her, its face completely blank.

Immortuos could express one thousand ways to make Amaryllis suffer, one thousand different ways to break her soul until becoming a lifeless, ugly corpse, but no threat was enough to scare her. Immortuos understood the behaviour of the human race. It knew the way into the dark places of their hearts to traumatize them. It knew what scared them. Immortuos knew of its mentally scarring features that were difficult to gaze upon, and it remembered the fear in Amaryllis' eyes when she first saw its transformation, but she did not have it now. Her stern complexion wore determination, and she was not human either, not anymore. She was rather a superhuman.

Immortuos screeched furiously, reaching for her in a flash, giving her no time to react. Its gigantic fingers wrapped around her tiny body and squeezed. All that came from her was a faint gasp as her immortal body fought the unearthly strength of the vile creature. Immortuos' deadly grasp was strong enough to crush bedrock with a simple tap of its palm, but it could not crush Amaryllis.

She squirmed trying to wriggle free. As she tried, Immortuos grew angrier that it was not inflicting detrimental harm upon her, so it whipped her against the mountain wall. She busted through the thick rock all the way to the outside exposed to the pouring rain and continuous, crashing lightning.

As she seemed to fall in slow motion, she looked up to the angered clouds booming with thunder. Lightning flashed in the corners of her eyes. The rain drummed against her armour, and as she looked away from the clouds and back to the mountain she spotted where her body pummelled through the rock. Gravity flipped, and she fell upwards for a second before finding the strength to fly back into the mountain. She bolted through the rock feeling the universe fill her body without her command. She glowed in a sparkling, turquoise, gold, and purple light corkscrewing her body to build more force as she pierced right through Immortuos' chest. A sparkling ball of the cosmos hit the demon like a bullet.

As Amaryllis fired through the demon's body, a potent source of evil—originating from Immortuos itself—attempted to pick away at her soul, but the powerful, universal presence trounced it. Amaryllis could feel the two opposite sources fighting each other within her until she broke free through its back.

The demon roared louder than a red dragon. Amaryllis' small, yet effective, impalement felt like a gunshot wound. It burned in concentrated agony, her touch of purity stinging the demon like sizzling acid.

Chapter 44

Immortuos' growing process happened slowly yet consistently up until Amaryllis fired herself through the gargantuan beast. Stardust had fallen off her body and stuck to the tissue of Immortuos' as she pierced it completely. The demon was a victim to the unforgiving pain that light magic presented against dark magic. Both Immortuos' impenetrable body and its almighty presence that was simply impossible to demolish had just shown—like Amaryllis predicted—impotence to purity.

She was exhausted after summoning that much magic, but some of it had derived from the universe itself assisting her like a thinking, living creature. As Immortuos grew larger and larger, she would be required to summon greater amounts of magic which would inevitably drain her energy. The universe's infinite amount of energy simply could not fill her body fast enough to sustain her.

The magic in Immortuos' body seized, eating away at its body. The pain was unbearable, incomprehensibly torturous, presenting itself in sharp waves, stinging jolts, and a burning sensation. Amaryllis' attack hurried its growing process. Immortuos' body suddenly expanded growing too tall to fit inside the mountain. Amaryllis' body was the length of its smallest toe, its body large enough to make the red dragons look like birds. It moaned thunderously, and vibrantly, shaking the ground as it hunched over to grow through the mountain. The demon pushed through the rock almost effortlessly, like it was emerging from water sheeted in thin ice. Immortuos swung its arms out, busting rock, and sending massive boulders raining down towards Amaryllis. Just like that the mountain was broken by its own creator with a huge hole allowing the storm to blow in. She was exposed to the cold, oversized raindrops that seemed to pummel her one after the other with excessive force. Thrashing winds, summoned by the rainstorm, pushed the rain in all directions attacking her from each angle. While the boulders made their way to crush Amaryllis, she bolted upwards, squirming around them, even shoving them out of her path. She finally escaped the rocky rain levitating above the shattered mountain which appeared even more menacing, even more jagged with razor sharp points. The moat became filled with rocks. The lava rose from the moat blanketing the fallen boulders in a bumpy impression of burnt orange, sizzling hues. The pile of rocks lying around the mountain spanned over three hundred feet in diameter with the rocks nearest to the moat covered in the lava, spitting, fighting the rain.

Immortuos looked at the mountain with a look of pleasure spread over its face, ecstatic to realize the power it was gaining. It was strong enough to break the Earth, but the expression faded once it glanced over at the pile of dead dragons—the dragons Immortuos thought would defend the mountain. The ones that would kill anything that stepped foot near the moat.

Amaryllis watched the beast breathe heavily under the pouring rain and the growling sky. Its stock-stillness in the Earth's unforgiving weather brought goosebumps to her flesh. A wicked feeling radiated from the monstrous creature looking as if it were waiting for the first strike of lightning — a blinding flash — to turn around and snatch her when she was stunned by the sudden light. Something so gargantuan did not seem to be able to move any faster than a tortoise because of Earth's gravity, but Immortuos at any size could move as quickly as it pleased.

Immortuos looked away from the dead dragons and found Amaryllis floating in the sky, rain falling over her violently. The weather only phased her in the psychological sense that the world wanted to make her task much harder. The heavy rain was another obstacle, a distraction to limit her vision. The thunder swept the sky loudly, echoing outwards and ending in spine-chilling cracks to overpower the thoughts that she wouldn't be able to hear. The wind toyed with her, pushing her around, so that when Immortuos was not striking her something else was. The effects of the weather, wetness from the rain or the volume of the storm, did not bother her; it was the taunting inclemency. The annoying downpour, the deafening thunder, and the flashing pulses of lightning that mocked her and told her that the battle would only be getting harder from here.

Immortuos' gleaming, dead-black eyes narrowed in vexation reflecting Amaryllis' body. She first noticed how empty and lifeless they were then realized they were mirror-like. She could see herself quite clearly although she was about twenty feet away. Her white armour appeared dull, losing its brightness under the darkness of the thunderstorm. It then occurred to her that her reflection was what burned in the demon's mind. The image of her fuelled its rage like how the image of Immortuos fuelled her own. They both stood in each other's way preventing them from what they wanted.

Amaryllis looked like a butterfly next to Immortuos. She was puny, beautiful, and fragile but from within she conjured up her own vicious storm feeling more rage than she ever thought was possible to feel. The kind of rage that burned in your chest while your back broke into a cold, weightless sweat. The kind that built up for so long growing stronger and stronger as nothing was done to ease the anger, the frustration. It was the highest level of rage humanly possible to reach…only Amaryllis was no longer *human*, so her rage grew from there.

Rain drenched her hair and left big dew drops speckled on her cheeks and forehead. It pounded against the objects it hit making a sharp, echoey drumming sound spanning as far as the eye could see. As the rain trickled down her neck and wiggled into her armour she wondered why Immortuos stood so still, watching her. Perhaps it didn't feel the need to attack her, or the need to defend itself. Perhaps it was simply studying her or thinking of things far too evil for Amaryllis to picture. Whatever the reason was, the demon's silence and its motionlessness was horrifying beneath the flashing, crackling sky.

Suddenly, Immortuos held its arms out wide, tilting its head down to look at her with a narrower frown. Its arms moved from down by its side to its humungous wingspan in a blink making a reverberating cracking sound. Lightning flashed illuminating the tips of its pointed fingertips. Amaryllis' lips parted slightly for a small gasp to escape. The demon looked as if it were ready to reach for Amaryllis in another spontaneous movement. A sliver-sized diamond rod would do nothing to Immortuos now. Her best weapon was useless. The demon revealed a black-toothed smile stretching all the way to its eyes. It knew she felt defenceless, overwhelmed with its great size. Perhaps Immortuos would have it easy after all and its worrisome thoughts that Amaryllis was a threat could flee from its mind.

Amaryllis' eyes illuminated lighting her entire body blue. The universe swirled in her blood, danced in her mind, as it entered carrying millions of stars. As the cosmos poured themselves into her soul, her body glowed brighter and brighter. The demon's black eyes squinted fiercely to block the light. Amaryllis' vision was led away from the demon before her and transported into outer space. She watched the stars race towards the Earth in a picture of millions of shooting stars, emptying the universe into a temporary void. The entire universe rushed to her aid to assist her until it was over. Light painted the darkness in passing streaks until no more stars could be seen. It was pitch black. Her vision returned to Earth. The stars inhabited her body, illuminating the entire meadow, sending beams of light in all directions.

The kingdom of Arlon stared into the light, frightened, and confused.

She could barely see Immortuos in front of her, but it was shielding its face with two hands. The demon uttered a low pitched groan then swung blindly at Amaryllis narrowly missing her. Immortuos howled opening its eyes then striking her with the swat of its giant hand. Her body sailed a couple hundred feet back then stopped abruptly. Her body jolted into an erect posture, then she charged at Immortuos at lightning speed hitting it between the eyes. The beast fell slowly to the ground. Upon impact with the dead meadow the ground crumbled into a million pieces sending up an impenetrable, thick cloud of dust. Immortuos breathed heavy, unpleasantly horrifying breaths that dozens of different wounded animals would make if composed into one. Amaryllis made no sound. She breathed normally watching the beast with her icy eyes.

Immortuos sprung from the ground and grabbed her, immediately letting go after the stars coating her body burned the flesh of its palm down to the bone revealing black and red tendons. A shriek filled the air followed by a roar louder than the storm. Lightning struck the ground and Immortuos redirected it at Amaryllis. The forked lightning electrified her, brightening her radiating light for a split second. Her body stung in a raging pain from the electricity, her muscles clenched unbelievably tight, then she screamed. Her eyes darted across the landscape picking out the fallen boulders around the mountain. Using telekinesis, she lifted the rocks from the ground and chucked them at Immortuos hitting it in all places. Some rocks were covered in lava, some weren't. The lava coated rocks burned its body in sizzling holes, impaling it completely. Thousands of rocks pummelled the demon one after the other as it screamed in torture. Amaryllis watched Immortuos suffer her attack already thinking of what to do next.

The rubble had completely buried its feet, but all the demon had to do was lift its feet like it was stepping from a shallow pond to free itself. Immortuos bent down picking up hundreds of boulders then chucked them back in her direction. Each boulder sailed passed her with the closest ones only inches away from her body. She didn't even flinch as the stampede of flying rocks soared at her. She watched in complete awareness.

Immortuos went to snatch her again but caught itself drawing its arm back. The seizing of its palm seemed to shout, stinging harder as it reached for her. Surely one more touch would melt its hand clean off. Thunder crashed reminding Amaryllis of the rain she had forgotten about. She blinked water from her eyes for them only to fill with more water. She squinted hoping her eyelashes would catch the drops. They did not. Objects in her vision swam, blurry with never-ending water that she never noticed until then.

Immortuos screamed outstretching its arms towards her but not touching. Dark magic fled from its sharp fingers in a black fire. Amaryllis' chest became heavy and full, her soul under attack. Her turquoise beams fought the dark magic. It wasn't close to touching her, but its spiritual presence seemed to have no boundaries, creeping cautiously through the universe within her to pummel her soul. If she had no defence, the dark magic would eat her from the inside out leaving her as a skeleton inside of a decomposed, flimsy layer of skin flapped over her bones.

She barely had to fight back, the universe was doing most of the work for her. She joined the stars letting her anger and determination power her. The turquoise beams stretched farther pushing the dark magic back into Immortuos' fingertips. It shrieked as the acidic purity ever so lightly grazed the ends of its fingers. Angered beyond measure, Immortuos roared until the cackling thunder and rain could no longer be heard. She looked into its mouth, at the back of its throat, to see vigorous, black, bubbling bile. In an instant, the black goop shot powerfully from its mouth but was no match for Amaryllis' universally powered beams. The bile swerved around the light and continued to fly behind her.

Immortuos' big, black, lifeless eyes revealed panic. Nothing it did seemed to phase her in any sense.

She was nowhere near finished with the vile creature and it knew it. The beams of light swirled into a concentrated tornado of turquoise, twirling closer and closer to Immortuos to kill it. The demon roared defensively.

"*Mors ad te venit!*" Immortuos screeched. It backed away from the light but Amaryllis followed. "*MORIETUR!*"

"It is time for you to go!" Amaryllis shouted hysterically watching the demon inch away from her tornado of magic. Fear washed over Immortuos, opening its mouth wide to release a horrid screech, widening its eyes as death approached it in the form of a beautiful, artificial, earthly feature. Immortuos ran and ran. Amaryllis followed the demon wherever it went. After all, where could it possibly hide? It was the largest being on Earth. Of course, after a few minutes of running, Immortuos realized there was nothing it could do. It could not run, it could not fight the power of the universe nestled within a young woman who carried it with incredible, welcoming strength.

The battle lasted a long while with Amaryllis dominating completely to then having energy drained from her as Immortuos fired all kinds of things at her. From evil within itself, to natural objects like full grown trees, Immortuos threw everything it could see at Amaryllis. Anything to try and stop her from chasing it with what would end the being's existence eternally. All Immortuos had done was tire her, but she never lost enough energy to stand down, to give up. If anything, her loss of energy only made her angry enough to gain some energy back with only the power of her mind.

After running around the meadow for an endless amount of time, Immortuos dramatically and suddenly shrank in an attempt to hide from her and to be more stealthy. Amaryllis watched the gigantic demon's head fall closer and closer to the ground, shrinking smaller and smaller. She stayed in the air as it descended but not for long. As soon as it hit the ground, at its natural size of ten feet, Amaryllis dove down at lighting speed holding the tornado of purity—Immortuos' death medicine—in front of her body.

Immortuos headed for the Dark Forest hoping to find a hiding place to allow its thoughts to collect, to think of a plan to end Amaryllis forever. It ran with long, dirt pounding strides splashing in puddles with every step. The rainwater taunted the demon. It held pureness and was refreshing to all senses, reminding the creature of cleanliness, which it hated. Immortuos enjoyed decaying matter, the undead thriving in an eternal existence, all that reminded it of hell itself.

To Amaryllis, the rain was the Earth's way of beginning again, washing away the dirt. Once the storm ended, she was sure Immortuos would be long gone and the sun would shine again.

Amaryllis sprinted as quickly as she could, keeping her eye on Immortuos the entire time in a focused, determined stare. It ran frantically tripping a few times and fixing its clumsy mistake by running on all fours like a deranged dog.

Immortuos was moving too close to the tree line, so Amaryllis flung only a sliver of her turquoise tornado, as not to waste it for the power surge it would take to kill it, to the ground Immortuos was to step on. It shrieked changing direction. It now ran parallel to the Dark Forest then cut back towards the mountain. Immortuos summoned more energy out of nowhere, and bolted for the jagged, destroyed rock.

It ran through the rocks coated in lava, not reacting to the scorching heat in any way, while Amaryllis jumped over it all. Immortuos then began to dash up the mountain. Lightning crashed enhancing the sharpness of the jagged edges of the rocky mountain with it's blinding light. Amaryllis ran directly into the storm, vertically up the mountain, following the red and black, doglike demon.

She wanted to scream and yell at it to stop. It was doing the inevitable and continuing into the darkness, when in the end

Amaryllis was to kill it anyway. She wanted the sun. She wanted the blue sky. She wanted the demon to vanish at her hands.

Raindrops pummelled her eyes, pounded against her face and neck. The wind seemed to push her up the mountain helping her to move faster. It whistled sharply in her wet ears.

She followed Immortuos two hundred feet up the mountain until it jumped off floating down slowly in the thundering sky. Amaryllis let out a vigorous scream of frustration pushing off the mountain to chase Immortuos. Lightning crashed, thunder boomed, then Immortuos reached its arms towards the sky. Moments later, hundreds of red dragons swooped down from the crying clouds all roaring over the storm. Amaryllis had no time for this. She looked at the humungous winged creatures with flaming rage in her eyes. She did not dare waste any of the universe's magic to touch a single dragon. All was for Immortuos, to ensure it would disappear permanently. Using the entire universe's power would drain her to unconsciousness, so it had to be done right.

Amaryllis avoided the dragons by flying away from them and their hundreds of lines of orange fire from their mouths that the heavy rain nearly put out.

Immortuos was at the beginning of the line of creatures, followed by Amaryllis, followed by dragons which covered the entire sky.

"Fight me yourself, you *coward*!" she hollered, her voice overpowered by the thunder and the pouring rain. She looked over her shoulder to see angry dragon faces spitting weak flames then turned back to watch Immortuos land on the ground and zoom across the meadow.

Amaryllis used another sliver of the tornado leading Immortuos back to the mountain. It ran right where she wanted it; up the mountain again. Amaryllis' chest burned with irritation as she ran up the mountain once again. All of the dragons followed.

They ran and ran. Progressing up the mountain, Amaryllis shot another sliver, hitting Immortuos in the back. It screeched a piercing scream that made Amaryllis' eardrums ache. It ran faster into the storm and up through the clouds. Amaryllis broke through the clouds—above the storm—to see Immortuos' silhouette. She stared intently knowing better than to lose sight of it. Bringing Immortuos into the clouds was only to lose the dragons. They were no where to be seen.

Amaryllis used her own energy, not the universe's, to push herself harder. She became closer and closer to Immortuos until the demon stopped abruptly in the clouds. Amaryllis crept until she was uncomfortably close then she watched the demon look despondently around the thick clouds that *it* had put in the sky. She could sense its fear. It burned fiercely, tickling her soul with happiness knowing she had caused its terror.

A dragon's tail sailed by just an inch from Immortuos' face. It watched it fly past with slight hope that perhaps the dragons had killed Amaryllis, but the demon knew deep down that it wasn't true. It was impossible.

Amaryllis enjoyed the fear Immortuos was projecting. It was strong and lively reminding her of the dreaded fear she faced in the Dark Forest. Immortuos was suffering worse in those clouds in that very moment than when it spent two thousand years in the purest place in the world. Its torture was flourishing into a misery so dreadful, a human would instantly pass out from such overwhelming terror. The demon's muscular, manlike body trembled making deep bellowing noises of agony. Not knowing where Amaryllis was ate the demon alive and the fact that Amaryllis was staring at the back of the demon's head almost made her burst into maniacal laughter. Immortuos' torture brought her great joy but what was to come next would please her eternally.

Amaryllis reached her arms out before her allowing the turquoise tornado, swirling with the trillions of stars in the universe, to slowly leave her palms. It was cool to the touch, both the temperature of the universe and the murder of Immortuos giving her hard goosebumps.

The tip of the tornado struck Immortuos' head wrapping itself around its skull in a grip stronger than any force on Earth. Lightning struck, thunder cracked, and Immortuos let out a long-lasting holler of torture. The tornado moved down its neck, shoulders, torso, arms, and legs until the demon was completely submerged in the swirling stars. To a human its pain could be expressed as being burned alive in demented flames without the brain ever going into shock. It would feel the burning flames the entire time until it was eaten all the way down to the bone. Only when its heart stopped beating would the pain go away, but even in the afterlife, it would be haunted by its painful death for what felt like years in the place that didn't trace time. Remembering it for what seemed like an indefinite amount of time. Unsure of when the suffering would really end.

Immortuos burned in Amaryllis' universal windstorm, each star taking a small, vicious bite from the flesh of the undead. Slowly eating it down to non-existence, the stars chomped. The magic flowed from her hands tickling her palms as it left. Once the stars had taken a few bites each from the demon, they would return to outer space to float happily where they belonged.

Amaryllis screamed as the universe fled from her body. She screamed as her soul tried to hold on to her body without being pulled by the universe back into space with it. As her energy was drained, she finally attained revenge. She shut her eyes briefly and when she opened them Immortuos faced her. Its big black eyes—illuminated in turquoise light—begged for mercy as its flesh was eaten. She watched its body sizzle, melting down to the bone very slowly. The demon shouted something—perhaps pleading for forgiveness, for her to spare it's suffering; but Amaryllis couldn't hear over the sound of the swirling stars. Even if she could hear the demon's final requests, she would have ignored them and continued to release the stars but at an even faster rate.

The turquoise light filled the sky completely, painting over the red clouds and lighting the world brightly although it was night.

From the castle, the royal subjects watched the flashes of turquoise not knowing what to think. Prince James' heart pounded in his chest only hoping that Amaryllis was all right. He knew not what the lights meant. They were all oblivious, watching in horror, and in awe with the beautiful colour.

Immortuos decomposed by the minute. Amaryllis made eye contact the entire time watching the life drain from the wretched demon, but as Immortuos faded into nothing, *her* energy began to drain. She fought to keep her eyes open. She became lightheaded, losing her sense of hearing. She watched Immortuos die in a muted experience, which was acceptable according to her, but hearing the demon suffer was what she preferred. Either way, watching life drain from Immortuos was a burning image she would never forget. Although it brought her satisfaction, it also brought her fear.

The creature's body seized with jerky movements, twitching hysterically. Its eyes were wide, looking as though they would pop from their sockets, slowly creeping out of the demon's skull. Its mouth was open so wide to the point where it looked like its jaw would snap off completely.

The tornado became smaller and smaller, the turquoise light in the sky becoming dimmer by the second. The insides of Amaryllis' eyes were pink swirling with streaks of soft red lines and dim sparkling blue lights, and she could even hear the faintest sound of a soft breeze. She was delusional visiting a place in the depths of her brain…perhaps the place where her dreams lived. She forced her eyes open to barely see Immortuos through her fluttering eyelashes, her closing lids. Her eyes shut exposing her to her dreams again. Even in the pink world in her mind she could barely see. Her dream-self had heavy eyelids too. She opened her eyes to see Immortuos as a skinny pile of bones still with its horrific expression stuck on its black skull. Her eyelids slammed shut and she returned to the place in her mind where she could not see. She breathed long, heavy breaths that were difficult to take, nearly impossible. There was a heavy presence in her chest blocking her airways like a thick forest blocks the wind from entering. It was not painful but exhausting.

Her eyelids were stuck together, weighing one thousand pounds. The universe rushed out of her hands which fell slowly down to her sides. As her limp body relaxed more and more, the energy continued to drain vigorously. Immortuos was now only a black ooze, a liquified skeleton floating in the air. Although it took no structured form, Immortuos could still feel the painful burning. The black ooze acted as a blackhole, sucking in all of the red clouds, the evil creatures, and the overall evil presence the demon brought to Earth from the sky. The sky was filled with booming roars, shrieks, growls, and hollers of panic muting the thunderstorm.

The sounds travelled all the way to the castle, cracking the glass windows in every room. The royal subjects quickly stepped back from the giant ballroom window peering past the cracks at the red clouds being sucked into non-existence.

The final star shot from Amaryllis' right palm pummelling the black ooze several times before rushing back into space. The demon detonated, its particles filled the sky in a booming splash before morphing into raindrops which fell to the soil down below.

Immortuos was dead.

Chapter 45

Silence was all Amaryllis acknowledged. She had no idea where she was and she was not ready to open her eyes. All she remembered was the imaginary pink world with the red streaks and blue sparkles. Immortuos was a memory stored far away. She could vaguely see its trembling corpse melting into a black ooze, but she did not know what happened afterwards.

Her body felt weightless, it seemed to not be touching anything, just floating in an existence of nothingness. Suddenly her eyes popped open without her control. They burned, and they were stinging as light beamed directly into them. Defensively, she moved her hand above her head shielding the light. All she saw was the shadow that was cast beneath the back of her hand along with sheer whiteness that the shadow didn't take over. She was lying flat on her back with long grass growing up the sides of her body, dancing in a gentle breeze. As her eyes slowly grew used to the light, she sat up into a seated position. With her other hand, she gripped the long, healthy grass. It was not long until she discovered that the bright light came from the sun which finally made an appearance after being hidden for what seemed like so long.

Her vision was blurred. A vague serenity waved like a ripple before her with vibrant colours. She blinked her eyes dozens of times until she finally adjusted to the sunlight.

The orange meadow full of rocks, lava, and dead vegetation now bloomed with big, beautiful trees. Thick canopies of pink flowers tickled the long grass. Daisies, buttercups, and bluebells scattered the land and lively streams whispered into the breeze. Immortuos' jagged, deadly mountain rounded into a big family of soft, rolling hills speckled with saplings, shrubs and stones. Birds sang symphonies of contentment pleasing Amaryllis with their beautiful music.

The blurry serenity became crystal clear with a final hard blink. The sudden purity, and surroundings that she was dying to see took her breath away. Reality finally sunk in, and Amaryllis stood up with a burst of energy. Her body filled with a strong euphoria that spread from her heart to the rest of her body making her head feel light and her mind incredibly clear.

Immortuos was gone forever. All of the evil in the entire world had gone down with it. A pure sensation abundantly filled the air emitting perpetual joy.

The treacherous journey stripped her of her softness and her sensitivity (if she had stayed in the dark world for another journey's length her emotion would have vanished all together just like John's). No matter how much she had grown or how much wisdom she had gained a feeling of happiness would never fail to make her smile. Her emotion still held a place in her heart. Luckily, she had not lost it or else her reuniting with Prince James and her parents would have been sad and cold.

Amaryllis remembered Immortuos' death being exceedingly draining. The event rushed back into her memory by the second. She remembered how she couldn't keep her exhausted eyes open, how the demon ran frantically all over trying to drain her.

Her stomach dropped.

Immortuos' deteriorating face played in her mind repeatedly. Its face would be full and complete with a red and black burnt looking complexion then faded into a bare skeleton dripping with melted skin and gushing with blood. Over and over she saw the demon's dying face until the memory was hidden away by the hypnosis the meadow of purity was emitting. There was no use for evil thoughts in a place like this.

Amaryllis smiled softly overwhelmed with appreciation from the life-like presence of happiness for hiding Immortuos from her. She would reminisce later when she had an opportunity to share her story.

Surely if she thought of it now her mixed emotions of victory, fear, and relief would conflict dragging her into an abyss of trauma with no one to comfort her. So her mind devoured the joy of the meadow, hiding her horrid memories from her for her own sake. She had so much to think about. The fact that she *killed* the entity that several sorcerers could not, how she gained powers from the universe that made her truly potent among the human race, how she survived countless suicidal places and creatures. Her defence mechanism would only last her so long until the burden of the death of evil would eat her from the inside. She would need to pour her story out to continue on.

As if sending herself a reminder, John Edwards arbitrarily appeared in her thoughts.

John, she thought with a sinking heart. *What happened to John?*

Her worrisome thoughts conflicted with the positive, undetectable rays of the meadow as her mind raced with unanswered questions. She remembered telling him to watch her from the trees ine, so she scanned the… Dark Forest, which looked different. The gargantuan, sinister, twisted trees were replaced with colossal oak trees. As she approached the tree line, she noticed the forest didn't roar a horrifying clamour of moans, hums, and shrieks. It sang with flowing rivers and tweeting birds. The Dark Forest had become a Forest of Enchantment.

"John!" she called. Her voice didn't carry far—it died off as soon as the sound hit the gap between the two, big oak trees before her. She peered through the thick bases of the healthy trees looking for any movement at all. "John!" she called once more, even louder this time. The trees were so thick she couldn't see past twenty feet in front of her.

She stepped into the forest looking up at the massive trees stretching high into the sky. Golden rays from the sunlight shone down through the gaps between the leaves and branches brightening the dense forest. On a cloudy day it would be nearly pitch black.

"John, are you there?" she shouted. Her mind raced with hundreds of worries until the rushing thoughts vanished. She shut her eyes, and as she did she could see John. Beneath her closed eyes she saw him leaning against a tree, staring up the trunk. She opened her eyes knowing exactly where he was. She ran into the forest weaving around the big tree trunks for a while. As she ran, she spotted streams, wild flowers, and small creatures. The animals like rabbits, squirrels, and fawns appeared pleased that she was there visiting their home. They knew, like how the entire forest knew, that she was the creator of the Forest of Enchantment. They did not exist until she banished evil, and they expressed gratitude for the life she had provided them with a look of contentment. In a way, Amaryllis created new life, a rebirth. As she ran through the woods, the animals stopped what they were doing, whether it was eating or just scampering, and they would look at her wiggling their little tails. A full grown deer even ran beside her for a moment before running off.

Amaryllis weaved around one final tree, and there he was. John looked up from the green grass growing all around the roots of the tree he stood on. He grinned the smallest grin then his face relaxed to its intimidating resting expression. Amaryllis smiled, pleased with the environment she created.

"Well, you did it," John said merrily, pushing through his perpetual sadness to congratulate her.

Amaryllis nodded. "It was the most difficult thing I have ever done," she admitted, speaking as though the words were a burden to say. Reminding herself of the entire journey and the battle against Immortuos caused adrenaline to course through her veins. Her chest tightened with warmth. Thinking of the process exhausted her mind.

"What was?"

"Absolutely everything was. Starting from the very beginning until the very end."

"I can imagine, you have been through an excessive amount of stress…well, it's all over now—"

As John continued to speak, making positive remarks, Amaryllis zoned out of the conversation listening to the words, *it's all over now,* echo through her skull. What was she to do now that the war was over? She was a princess, a princess who had forgotten she was one. She was so occupied with her expedition that her royal background hardly struck her. She was a *princess* who completed non-princess tasks… even non-*prince* tasks. How could she go back to the easy life: being served at her command, being dressed and pampered, when she had just lived through hell? How could she return to dressing for fashion as opposed to dressing for the function of survival? As a princess, she was treated as an infant with no independence. Thinking back, she would absolutely hate it now.

"—Amaryllis?"

Amaryllis snapped from her trance. "Sorry, yes?"

"Did you hear what I said?" John asked impatiently.

"Honestly, no I did not," she replied placing her hands on her hips. Her white armour clanged as she shifted her weight to one side. John frowned at her, but instead of feeling frightened by his deadly stare she stared back at him without a single feeling of fear.

He sighed then said, "You must be happy to be returning home" through an exhale of exasperation.

Amaryllis found a window to enter her distant trance to think deeply, but she kept herself alert as to not annoy John anymore for her absence. "I don't know how to feel about that. I've been exposed to awful things for days on end so returning feels odd in a way."

"If I had a huge castle to return to, I would be there by now," John scoffed.

"No, you wouldn't." she sneered. "You wouldn't come to my castle if I offered it, would you? You'd just stay here and build a new shack in the enchanted forest."

John pressed his lips into a straight line nodding his head. "Probably," he admitted. "I'm not royal like you are, and I hate royals anyway. Would not want to be surrounded by stuck up people." He said his last words regretfully (as he spoke them), thinking he'd offend her for calling her people *stuck up*, but she didn't care, she agreed.

"That's why it feels strange to have to return to Arlon because I'm not stuck up anymore. I feel I belong here now, but in reality I know I belong in a kingdom." She laughed as she repeated the words *stuck up*. "And when I do return, I won't give in to their ways. I shall never be like that again, but on the other hand, I am eager to go back."

Prince James occupied her imagination, smiling, and waving at her. She smiled at the memory of their final embrace, then frowned as she remembered pushing him away.

"There are a few people I am excited to see," she admitted.

"Yes, that's definitely where you're supposed to be. You will make a fierce queen. Your people will fear you." John chuckled to himself at the thought of her own servants having to argue over who would tend to her, all frightened out of their minds.

"You think I'll be feared?" Amaryllis asked, half pleased at the idea of being feared and half worried. She would want her people to have faith in her regardless of her newly adopted assertive behaviour.

"Considering all you did…by *yourself*…yes they will fear you." John gestured to the entire forest with a waving motion of his hand. "And you did all of this?" he asked, his voice sounding lighter than usual succumbing to the euphoric nature around them.

"I suppose so," Amaryllis pondered. She only remembered killing Immortuos, not recreating the Earth. Perhaps the universe had helped or maybe killing Immortuos is what transformed everything into a magical place.

"You suppose so?" He scoffed. "Who else would have done this?"

"Killing Immortuos did this. I was too drained to have done this with much thought or even the slightest effort. Surely I could build something like this but replacing the whole forest and the meadow after losing nearly all of the life in me, impossible. It was the act of killing evil. The Earth healed itself."

John scratched the back of his head, moving his grey, shoulder-length hair aside to itch his neck. "Either way, *you* did this," he said firmly. "Don't give this godforsaken world any credit for anything." Deep down he wanted to hug her. He was proud and grateful for what she had done, and he had even missed her company when she was gone. He had lived alone for too long, and she had given him a glimpse of friendship that he needed. His friend returned in perfect health after her soul-crushing journey, saving him, and everyone else close enough to feel Immortuos' wrath.

"No, the world is beautiful. It is not *godforsaken*. If it wrongs you, it's for a reason that is beyond comprehendible to understand at first, but in the end it makes sense. You can perceive the Earth's lessons whichever way you choose, but no matter how bad it seems it's always for good. When I released Immortuos from its two millennium imprisonment, I blamed the world. I blamed myself. I was beyond shameful and angry, but it was neither my, nor the world's, fault. I did not free Immortuos intentionally, I did it thinking I was helping someone. I thought my life was over and my chance of seeking happiness was long gone. Until I decided to fight back. Through gashes and scars, toxic burns, and the cold touches of ravenous fish, claustrophobic spaces, and thunderstorms, I finally found what I was looking for. It was the most difficult thing I have ever done in my life, but I was determined to find happiness, to fix what I had done. If I had given up, blamed the world and went on with life as I left it, Immortuos would still be here. I would still be the timid coward I once was. Immortuos the most evil being known to all, and its release, was a *good* thing because I killed it away. It is gone forever. Evil is gone because of the fortunate mistake I made. All was meant to happen and I am glad it did. Like you said, it's all over now. I did what needed to be done, and now I must go back to Arlon."

John nodded his head pleased that she had so much figured out at her age. He was in his fifties, and he still hadn't moved on from his family's passing. He knew it was slowing him down, making his life more miserable than need be, but he couldn't get over it. He still held on to his grudge towards the King of Arlon.

"You know what, I will come back with you under one circumstance," he negotiated looking at her dead in the eyes with his head tilted forward slightly.

"What's that?" she asked, her suspicion making her voice deep.

"If I can access the King of Arlon, I will be satisfied...I will move on."

Amaryllis knew very well he wanted to brutally murder the king, not caring for the consequences. He'd sit happily in his jail cell for his remaining years with a grin on his face if he could only kill the one who killed his family.

"You know it is not going to happen."

"Then I'm not coming with you."

Amaryllis felt rage build up in her chest. "You're not spending the rest of your life moping around! Come back with me, get out of these woods, and move *on*," she snapped. "Don't you want to try to find happiness again? Hating and holding onto your anger does nothing. It is like drinking poison and expecting the person who wronged you to die. Come back, be strong, and move on. The king will get what is coming to him, and it will be worse than what he did to you...that's just the way the world seems to work. It's been twenty years, let it *go*." Amaryllis would have sympathized with him if he were a softer man, and if his family's death had happened more recently, but she was tired of his anger. He was a strong-willed person, and should know better than to rage on this way.

John was ready to scream. He felt light as blood rushed to his head. His memory of the murder was so vivid and clear, stored in the surface of his mind. Just like that, Amaryllis, whom he respected infuriated him. He wanted to strike her. He couldn't control himself. He sprang from the tree he rested against and charged for her.

All she had to do was hold her palm to his head to stop him. She knocked him down with a solemn expression on her face.

He didn't know how he went down so fast, but he began to get up until he hit the dirt again with a tap of her hand to his head. She knocked the rage right from his mind. He was more confused than angry.

"Come now," she said softly. "Don't make me do that again. Trust me, all right? Leaving the forest is what you need."

John turned his head slowly until his brown eyes met her sharp green ones. She stood powerfully, shadowed beneath the strong sunlight peering through the trees. He squinted as dirt fell from his forehead into his face. He was beyond foolish to think he could ever challenge Amaryllis. He stood hesitantly and slowly, worried she would strike him again by surprise. She waited until he was on his feet then took his wrist and guided him out of the forest into the meadow.

John instantly forgot about his bottling rage towards Amaryllis as soon as he stepped foot into the meadow. He would never admit it, but the meadow took his breath away—something that had not happened to him in ages. He wanted to shake his wrist free from Amaryllis' grasp, but he feared she would hurt him again. She sensed his discomfort and gently let go ignoring his stare as they continued to walk on. He looked at the rolling hills where the jagged mountain once was, the lively grass where it was once dead, and the flowers spanning as far as he could see. Although Amaryllis had already seen the meadow, it never failed to satisfy her a second time, taking her breath away once more.

After showing John the meadow to calm him down, Amaryllis was about to head back to the forest in the direction of Arlon, but a herd of wild horses came out of nowhere. John looked to Amaryllis with a look of relief on his face. He didn't want to journey to Arlon on foot. He had just about enough of full days of sprinting. Without speaking, they approached the herd. Amaryllis mounted a tall cream coloured horse, and John mounted a tall grey one. The horses complied acting with surprising obedience and tameness. Amaryllis imagined them trying to buck them off, but they were calm and seemed trained somehow. They did come from the euphoric meadow after all. Amaryllis and John led their horses into the forest in a slow walk swerving around giant trees until space began to open up and they could begin to trot then galloped through the forest.

Chapter 46

As soon as the red clouds had vanished, and the beautiful night's sky full of gleaming stars appeared, the royal subjects visiting Arlon cheered. Everyone hugged one another, celebrating the world's return and Immortuos' red world's disappearance. The sight of the sparkling stars was like a breath of fresh air, taking weight off everyones shoulders and relieving their fears. Amaryllis was victorious but was she alive? Yes, the world was back to normal, but did she save the world with the sacrifice of her life? No one knew. The question of her survival was debated in the room, ridiculous things being spat from tired mouths and hopeful things spewing from the mouths of the night owls who were unaffected by the late hour.

Prince James was exhausted from staying up all night watching the flashing colours in the sky—the battle from hundreds of miles away. He was filled with fear that his princess had been killed, yet filled with hope that she survived the battle. He took the side of the hopeful ones although he was tired and delirious. How could he believe she was dead? He had to believe she was returning to him just like she had promised. He longed for her to be in his arms and safe from danger. All he wanted was to hold her. The anticipation ate him alive. He needed rest to be able to think clearly, to be able to greet his returning princess at his best health.

As the royal subjects bickered about Amaryllis' survival, Prince James wandered out into the hallway. His tired body was guided by his tired mind down the hall. The loud echoing of his footsteps startled him as he walked lifelessly searching for a bedroom. He didn't even know where he was because his eyes kept falling to the floor, then closing. He barged into a random room which to his fortune happened to be a bedroom. All he saw was the outline of a bed and that was enough for him. He lazily pushed the door with intention of closing it but ended up leaving it slightly ajar. He didn't notice. He flopped himself onto the soft bed and drifted off after only a second of lying still.

Meanwhile, the King and Queen of Serilion were sleepless. They stared out of the ballroom window revealing the beautiful stars. They looked into the sky and hoped. Hoped for their daughter's return and hoped she would return in good condition. She left at a horrible time. She was only beginning to stand her ground and fight for herself. She was searching for joy and was near finding it until her whole world fell. Things only became harder for their poor daughter, and it hurt them, almost as much as it hurt her, to see Amaryllis in utter misery.

The king touched the queen's hand and she grasped his interlacing their fingers. The queen squeezed her husband's hand as sadness prevailed her. Her eyes resembled shiny glass, watering beyond her control.

"She's okay," trembled the king through a reassuring, forced smile. He wasn't sure, of course, but he wanted his wife to have faith. The queen's lower lip quivered, her hand squeezed tighter, then she nodded.

"She's okay," she repeated still nodding her head even after she spoke.

"She's on her way home now. You'll wake up in the morning, and she'll already be here," the king said after kissing the queen's hand. The more he spoke in a positive manner, the more he began to believe in his daughter's survival. Tears streamed down the queen's cheeks like waterfalls. Her skin became red and blotchy.

"I don't think I'll be going to sleep tonight," she muttered, wiping her eyes with one hand, only for her face to instantly become wet with tears again. "Not having her here, and with all of this uncertainty…I just can't take this, Laurence."

"I know, but trust me. We'll go to bed, and when we rise she will be here," he stated. Immediately after saying so, the king's heart sank. He shouldn't have made a guarantee as strong as that especially when it was in regard to his only daughter, but the queen seemed to have been affected by his optimism. She smiled, which looked discomforting to her swollen, blotchy face, but she smiled. She hadn't expressed even the slightest amount of happiness—no one had—the entire time Amaryllis was gone, so it was pleasing to see. The king's statement was positive enough to make his wife momentarily happy, but it would be his exact statement that would kill her if it were to be contradicted—if Amaryllis never returned. He shouldn't have spoken such powerful words.

Chapter 47

Amaryllis and John rode their wild steeds for hours through the Forest of Enchantment—which used to be the Dark Forest. It was astonishing how drastic the transformation was. The melody of horror reversed into a tune of natural sounds along with a perpetual, mystical purr. The most deadly creature within the forest was only a wolf as opposed to a shadow creature, which went down with Immortuos, and the vegetation was perfectly healthy, not dead and rotten. There were no dangerous obstacles to avoid; the blue mushroom groves transformed into ponds, the tunnel of Things became full of dirt—completely filled in to hide the caves; and the freezing cold lake inhabiting killer fish had turned into a pleasant lake full of ducks, frogs, and several species of fish. The Dark Forest had become a wonderful land of utter amazement possessing beautiful creatures of grace.

Amaryllis and John never had to guide their horses away from trees or even lead them in the right direction. There were spotless dirt paths without a single autumn leaf because of the forest's prematurity to other seasons besides summer—which seemed man-made. The paths were perfectly flat and all the same width of ten feet. The horses followed the paths, by instinct, in the correct direction. It was as if they could sense civilization. Amaryllis and John could close their eyes without worry and sleep the whole way back, but they were to consumed by the mesmerizing radiance of the forest to look away.

"This is absolutely unbelievable," John muttered under his breath.

Amaryllis heard him almost clearly but still asked for clarification to make sure he said what she thought he said. "It's what?"

"The forest; it looks nothing like it did before. Not even in the slightest way, other than it still being a *forest* I guess."

"Yes, it's beautiful here. It's beautiful everywhere," Amaryllis replied humbly. The forest was her creation, but she did not want to be one to sing her own praises. She wanted to thoroughly enjoy the world's rebirth, the world's *recreation*. For as long as Amaryllis had been alive, she'd never seen a forest as lovely as the one she galloped through on her steed. She really didn't *restore* the earth to its original form, she *improved* it.

"I feel like I almost don't belong in here," scoffed John. "It's too appealing."

Amaryllis let out a chuckle, but John was serious with a solemn expression on his face. He definitely enjoyed the stunning qualities the forest had to offer, but if he wasn't provided an obstacle each day in a deadly environment what was the point of his existence? The Dark Forest, in a way, distracted him from his losses. His home, his therapy, was gone.

"Well, it seems that a creature possessing rancid behaviour doesn't belong here... so, you really *don't* belong here I suppose," Amaryllis joked trying to make him smile, but she got more than what she tried for. John laughed a full bellied laugh forgetting about his misery for only a moment. Amaryllis' heart instantly warmed with love. John had a beautiful laugh that she was lucky enough to hear. It was contagious and soft, a childlike giggle coming from a full-grown man. Amaryllis smiled and giggled along with his laugh during his short period of giddiness. It was too good to be true, but after a few seconds he was grumpy and sad again.

"No, but really," he began. "It feels odd. I can't live here."

"Remember what I just nagged at you for? You're coming to Arlon, then Werling with me," she ordered. John wanted to resist, but he kept silent knowing that if he fought it then she would make the journey more difficult. He appreciated the thought, but he was not ready, nor did he ever think he was ready to move on from his family's death. He must stay to live the rest of his days lonely, missing his wife and children in the forest.

"Amaryllis, I don't wan—"

"John, you must come. It will be good for you. You must trust me, please," she said sincerely. John lowered his voice and looked down at the ground passing by quickly. He spoke loudly over the thumping hooves against the dirt,

"Amaryllis, with the most respect possible, you know nothing about loss. You don't know what its like to have your family torn away, killed before you while you could do absolutely nothing about it. You don't know what's good for me." The words came from him effortlessly, without a tear, without a stutter or pause. The memories did not bring tears to his eyes, but they stabbed at his heart. Amaryllis sighed sadly.

"I know that I know nothing about loss, nothing in my life compares to your despair—" she began, pushing away the thoughts of watching Prince James choose Princess Laria over her. Pushing away the potent feelings of neglect and betrayal and pushing away the thought of losing the potential love of her life, "—But it only takes common knowledge to know that spending the rest of your life alone would be torturous, whether you were suffering from a loss or not. I know that meeting new people would be difficult for you. You haven't seen anyone in twenty years, and you may not be ready to reenter the modern world, but you have to. No more living in the past, you must strive for happiness. Isn't joy important to you in any aspect?"

"Joy doesn't mean anything to me. I want my family. Their happiness is the only *aspect* of joy that I'm concerned for. But, they're dead. So, my own joy…never mattered to me in the first place. The only joy I ever had in life was waking up every single morning to my wife's beautiful face sleeping contently beside me, walking out of the room to wake my four angelic sons. But, they're gone. My joy is dead, unattainable, gone forever. Okay? It wouldn't matter where I live, my misery will consume me anywhere I go." John spoke with a sorrowful passion that Amaryllis hated. Her understanding of his past was clear, his family was exceedingly dear to him, but she hated how he gave up on himself.

"I'm not saying the memories won't be painful, but you have to escape the toll that these memories have on you. I know what I'm suggesting seems impossible and perhaps even inconsiderate in terms of your feelings but joy is possible. It is. I'm dreadfully sorry, but what you need is acceptance." Amaryllis truly cared for her friend, and she was determined to lead him to his happiness. She would never give up on him because no matter the wound's size healing is always possible, it's only natural. The only thing is that large wounds take longer to heal. They take patience, tears, and a little bit of misery. But in the end, after all of the rain from the never-ending thunderstorm, the sun is bound to shine. It can't rain forever.

Deep down, John knew what he needed. He knew that his excessive grieving was counterproductive, and the door leading to his journey of healing, his journey to joy, was reachable. It was right there, but he couldn't bring himself to walk through it. The door was locked, and the key was around his own neck.

He wouldn't even dream of trying to forget the most precious people he had ever had the pleasure of spending time with. He believed he owed them the respect of thinking of them even though it killed him each and every day.

He needed to be told that their death was not his fault, but he truly believed the fault was his.

He said nothing in response to Amaryllis' last remark silencing the two of them for the rest of the journey until they came upon John's shack hours later. It had adopted a pleasant appearance after the Dark Forest's transformation. The dark, dry, chipped wood aged backwards into a healthy, clean wood with flowery vines growing up and down the walls. Daisies and long grass crawled up the sides and even the windows and doors looked redone, new.

They slowed their horses down and dismounted them to explore the inside of John's newly, magically repaired house. John looked at the small structure in both disgust and in awe. The purity and friendliness of the house failed to meet his standards of poor living and sadness, and the fact that magic fixed up his shack surprised and slightly impressed him.

They stepped inside exposing their noses to the smell of warmth. A small flame danced happily in a little fireplace. A bed with light blue sheets was made up nicely, two chests of drawers stood on both sides of it, and the bathtub where Amaryllis sat in her decaying skin looked much cleaner than before. The room emitted coziness, which Amaryllis found lovely. She would have much preferred meeting John for the first time in this new room as opposed to the old one. This room made her feel protected and welcomed. The old shack was a nightmare to awaken in, but John preferred his nightmarish home over this heavenly one.

"It's—" he began then grunted and marched out the door. Amaryllis joined him shortly after admiring the home for a moment longer. When she closed the door behind her, she spun around to see John already mounted back on his grey steed. Amaryllis' cream-coloured steed stood majestically beside the grey one, its strong muscles showing through its coat.

"I don't think it would matter whether or not I demanded you return with me, you would never live in there. Would you?" Amaryllis asked seriously, gesturing to the cute shack behind her. John crossed his arms and shook his head.

"I'd fix it up," he replied gruffly.

"Fix it up? You mean destroy it?"

"Something like that. I would make it… more to my liking."

Amaryllis shook her head hiding a small grin on her face. She jumped up on her horse and as soon as she was seated both horses took off galloping. John twisted around to watch his shack grow more distant by the second. It was painful for him to leave it. He had built his home frantically to protect himself from the monsters of the Dark Forest. Just collecting wood was a difficult task to complete. He had to check over his shoulders constantly looking for dangers. Although he built the shack in a hurried manner, it stayed together sturdily for twenty years.

As the horses continued to gallop tirelessly, Amaryllis spotted a pond, which used to be the grove of mushrooms that nearly took her life, that separated her from Ezro. Without hesitation, the horses jumped into the water, which was shallow enough for them to trot through. John was soaked from his feet to his ankles and Amaryllis was as dry as a bone. Her armour protected her from every single element the world had.

"Ugh," John uttered annoyed with his wet feet. The water rushed right through the material of his boots.

The surroundings were different, but Amaryllis was beginning to know exactly where she was. Each area that reminded her of a troublesome, or near death experience, hinted at her location, her distance from the castle. Before she knew it, they reached the tree where she and Prince James had to hide from shadow creatures, where she was thrown.

The area forced not only memories upon her but dreadful feelings as well. She relived her emotional trauma once again from a new point of view. A single tear trickled down her face as she succumbed to her many emotions. She could feel Prince James' presence, she could hear him calling to her with worry in his voice. She relived her first encounter with shadow creatures and the stress from everyone pursuing her.

Her mind returned to the present, and she told herself to calm down.

It's not real anymore. It won't hurt you. They *won't hurt you. You aren't there anymore. You're here now.* She forced herself to recognize the new, friendly surroundings of the new forest. The Dark Forest was vivid in her memory. It was dead, but it still toyed with her.

Suddenly, a setting sun caught her attention. The horses entered the meadow, leaving the forest behind them, riding alongside the setting sky. John and Amaryllis slowed their steeds down and dismounted them. They trotted casually back towards the forest as Amaryllis and John watched them disappear into the trees.

Leaving the woods affected both Amaryllis and John. It felt wrong, like they were abandoning their home. Of course John's feelings of remembrance were stronger than Amaryllis', but her heart still raced looking at the forest from the castle side. She slowly turned away from the woods and towards the castle. It looked majestic in the setting sky, reflecting with colours of red, orange, and pink. She remembered how colossal Arlon's castle seemed, but after witnessing a demon stretch way past the height of the castle, and a mountain twisting beyond the clouds, Arlon was small, and Serilion seemed even *smaller*.

"Well, Are you going in there?" John asked softly.

Amaryllis turned around, her face shadowed away from the sunset. Her auburn hair behind her glowed, and her cheeks were just barely covered in golden sunlight. "Well, yes, but it just seems so…" her soft voice faded into silence.

John's hatred for royals momentarily vanished from his mind subconsciously to guide her back to where she needed to be. "They need you in there. Your family needs you, and I know it doesn't seem like it, but you really *do* belong in there…more than anybody else. Yeah, you'd easily outlive any one of those pricks outside of castle walls, but you're the only one who deserves a god damn castle." John spoke passionately delivering motivation that he truly believed in. "People like you need to be rulers...surviving the Dark Forest should be a requirement for each new king and queen," he chuckled. Amaryllis had the urge to laugh, but she ignored it and smiled a big smile.

"I'm feeling like I'm not ready," she admitted. John grinned, and she could see his giddy side on the verge of coming out. The side of him that laughed out loud shamelessly.

"Then it's the perfect time to go," he replied.

Amaryllis' heart skipped a beat. He was right. She looked at the tallest tower of the castle then looked back at him. "Go to the village and get comfortable. I'll come for you when things are resolved, when I'm on my way to Werling," she said thinking of the negative outcome of bringing John inside the castle. There would be a catastrophic conflict between him and the King of Arlon; a quarrel and a barbaric fight.

He knew why she was instructing him to go there. His hatred for royals came rushing back, so did his grumpiness. The King of Arlon laughed fiendishly in his imagination over his family's corpses. A wave of rage washed over him. His entire body emitted anger in an instant.

"Okay," he mumbled through a clenched jaw. "Good luck in there," he forced himself to say. He stormed past her without saying a formal goodbye. He walked across the meadow stiffly looking like he was refraining from breaking into a full blown sprint.

Amaryllis waited until he was no longer in sight before heading toward the castle. She did not want to risk the castle doors being opened for people inside to recognize him. She was in no rush to get inside. She walked moderately towards the castle doors enjoying each second of the gorgeous sunset painting her surroundings in warm hues.

Chapter 48

John approached the village. Faint music and cheers reverberated towards him, its happiness fuelling his anger. As he entered the village, the noise grew louder. As he looked around he saw no one he recognized, which he was happy about, but as a group of strangers danced around him, his slight pleasure vanished. He stood motionless staring at the dancing fools with hatred.

"What are you doing?" he snapped. They were not at all phased by his grumpy nature. They answered in soft, happy voices.

"We're celebrating!" they cheered.

"Well, get away from me!" he roared. The dancers stopped, looking at him with concern in their eyes.

"Do you not know?" a young girl asked.

"No, I don't care. Get away from me," John scowled then pushed two ladies aside to continue walking through the village, but the dancing ladies followed him stubbornly, not taking any hints from the grumpy old man.

"There is no way that *anybody* wouldn't care about this!" one of them called from behind him, jogging to catch up.

"My father is a grump like you, and even he was overjoyed to see it," said the youngest girl who had caught up with him. He stopped walking to stare at the three women following him.

"I do not care, now leave me the hell alone before I..." he breathed a deep breath to avoid threatening them. He truly didn't care about what was happening in the village. All he knew was that the village was punishing him, toying with him with its vigorous excitement when he was angered beyond words.

Without creating any more suspense for the not-so-secretive celebration, they told him why the village was so happy. They were celebrating hell's disappearance and the Princess of Serilion's success. Word had travelled quickly of her journey and all of Arlon waited anxiously for what felt like forever until Amaryllis brought the world back. The village fell in love with Serilion, especially in love with its brave princess. Now that John knew of the excitement, he began to notice banners hanging from houses reading, "Princess Amaryllis."

John could have told the girls that he knew Amaryllis but chose not to. He did not want to be peppered ridiculously with questions. He didn't even want to tell them that he knew about the saving of the world long before they did. Their happiness disgusted him.

"Yeah, yeah, I know," he grumbled.

"You know? But, you don't seem very happy about our freedom. I mean, the monster is gone—"

"Yeah, goodbye!" John snapped looking at them with fire in his eyes. He stormed off, but they did not follow him this time. As new cheering people crowded him while he advanced through the group all he needed to do was glare at them to warn them. No one dared to speak to him for the rest of his way. He took the smiles right off of their faces as he passed by then as soon as he was far away the people whose smiles he stole found their happiness again. No grump could rid them of their appreciation for their freedom for too long.

After a few minutes of squeezing through overly happy people, John finally reached his family's house where Judith, Castor, Harrison, Charlie, and Thomas once lived. The crowd died down by the time he reached his home, with only three stragglers who were just leaving the celebration to return home, but near the entrance to the village, the excitement still jived on. The three people entered their own homes, just further down from his own, then he was alone. Just him and his house.

No one had been living there for twenty years. It looked just like how he left it with the exception of some overgrown grass and several weeds crawling up the front of his house. The wood aged well, and the windows were intact. It possessed a welcoming, familial effect that tugged at John's heartstrings. A small part of him expected his family to be inside, getting ready for bed, but as he peered through the window to watch the setting sun reveal the dust and dirt that collected atop of tables and chairs, that small part of him died. He stepped away from the window in fear of the empty house then glared at the front door for a while. It wasn't until night fell upon him that he figured he must head inside. The stars shone brightly above him, twinkling peacefully. The village was silent all except for a gentle breeze that whistled in his ears. The world was serene attempting to calm John and guide him inside.

He was frozen, still staring at the door until a sudden gust of cold wind pressed against him giving him goosebumps. His gaze shifted from the door to a twenty-year-old pile of chopped wood just peeking out from around the corner. His body loosened, and he was able to move again. He collected a few pieces of wood, hauling it in his left arm, and summoned the courage to put his hand on the door handle. He scrunched his face and breathed through gritted teeth then aggressively pulled the door open stepping inside quickly. As soon as he let go of the door, it slammed behind him. He shut his eyes unprepared to look at his deserted home. He groaned from the overwhelming exposure to his family's absence. The house seemed to taunt him with its emptiness. His eyes cracked open, he gasped quietly, and his heart sank. He nearly dropped the wood in shock but tightened his grip to readjust it at the last second. Both the physical and emotional darkness of the house scared him. The gloominess screamed at him like a ravenous monster about to charge. The silhouette of each object in the house shaped into cursed items, releasing utter terror. He nearly expected to faint; his knees wobbled, his palms were sweaty, his heart pounded, and he was light headed, frozen again. The screams of silence penetrated his ears, the sight of the empty house tearing him apart.

Impulsively, he broke from his trance running to the fireplace. The wooden floors squeaked beneath him as he ran. As soon as he reached it, he tossed the wood inside, and after a while of attempting to spark a flame with stone and a piece of flint he had always kept at the foot of the fireplace a flame ignited. A lively fire grew bigger and bigger as the hungry flame ate at the wood. The fire cracked and spat, embers flying about. John moved away from the fire scooting back a few feet just to look into it. Its warmth sent his goosebumps away and lit up a portion of the room making it feel even more empty as light spread revealing its lack of care. Spiderwebs occupied each and every corner both on the ceiling and on the floor, mice poked out their heads from underneath some furniture, and dust flew about.

John did something he hadn't done for a long time, his eyes became wet with tears—he sobbed furiously. He brought his knees into his chest, brought his head to his knees and wept.

Chapter 49

The setting sky of warm colours faded into a bluish purple as the sun fell. Amaryllis stood hesitantly before the castle doors for only a few seconds before bringing her fist to knock. Her arm felt heavy, too heavy for her shoulder to withstand, but she knocked.

The doors instantly began to move creaking open slowly. Once they were fully open, Amaryllis slowly made her way inside. She met the two guards' eyes and watched their facial expressions change from stern, to shocked, then excited. The duke ran around the corner and his eyes nearly popped from their sockets. He had been asked by the King of Serilion to stand by the doors everyday from dawn until dusk to wait for his daughter's arrival.

"Princess Amaryllis!" the duke choked, too excited to speak normally. His words exploded from his mouth. He ran towards her grabbed her hand enclosed in armour and squeezed it tightly. "You've made it back! And—and—and—you did it! You killed Immortuos! This is too good to be true, my oh my."

Amaryllis smiled at him, happy to have brought out the happiest version of the duke she had ever seen. Although it felt odd to be called a princess, she embraced it. As the duke studied her, he noticed she appeared older. She was stronger, calmer, more confident. Her eyes were full of wisdom gained through an

IMMORTUOS

experience in which she had to mature quickly. Her armour was like nothing he had ever seen.

"Yes, I've solved the world's darkness and decay. Immortuos is dead," she replied then looked at the ceiling of the castle, then the polished floors. She hadn't been inside of a man-made structure as majestic as a castle since the very beginning of her journey, which felt like so long ago. Yes, it was smaller than the gargantuan mountain, but it still impressed her with its elegance. The interior of the castle used to overwhelm her seeming as though it would collapse on her at any minute with its dominating power, but now she dominated the castle. She used to feel small and insignificant, but she felt in control upon her return and for the rest of her existence as a changed person.

"We mustn't chat any longer!" he squeaked. "Everyone's been waiting anxiously for you!"

Amaryllis nodded feeling knots begin to form in her stomach. The excitement of greeting her family, Prince James, and everyone else was the only thing in that castle that had control over her. Her light-weighted boots clicked against the floor as the duke pulled her along the hall hurriedly. Amaryllis looked back at the doormen and held up a hand to wave. They waved back still wearing surprised expressions on their faces, in shock that she had returned. Of course, they had faith in her the entire time, but it was just strange to see her back, and she was so different.

They passed the ballroom, passed the dressing rooms, and approached a massive double door. The duke let go of her and let the two knights guarding the dining hall open the heavy doors. He jumped with excitement the entire time. She could see him bouncing from the corner of her eye.

The doors opened completely revealing a seemingly endless dining table lit with dozens upon dozens of candles. A huge window parallel to the table revealed a clear night's sky. The candles on the table illuminated the faces of familiar royals. Amaryllis entered the room, and everyone stood up from their seats, wood buzzing against tiles. She heard a feminine scream, that of her own mother's, followed by rapid footsteps. She spotted her mother wearing a sad face, running as fast as her legs could carry her. Her father too ran from his seat, but her mother was far quicker.

Tears welled in Amaryllis' eyes. She didn't expect to cry, but she did so quietly, without any spastic hiccoughs. She smiled outstretching her arms for her mother to run into her embrace. They wrapped their arms around each other saying nothing for a minute. Her father joined in, and he too said nothing. The others in the room watched the reunited family with racing hearts. They all smiled effortless smiles. Some cried, some didn't, but they all smiled for Amaryllis…even Laria smiled. Prince James refrained from sprinting at her. He held in his excitement as best as he could to not ruin her family moment.

The King and Queen of Serilion had no words for their daughter. They didn't know what to say. She was beyond powerful; she had just defeated the most evil being in history and no words strong enough could express how impressed they were with her bravery. No words could express how much they missed her. No words could express how proud they were of her, but they tried.

The king let go of his daughter to speak to her, but the queen wouldn't let go.

"Amaryllis, I do not know what to tell you…I do not even know where to begin," her father said gently. "I am so incredibly glad to have you back here, safe and in good health."

"Thank you, father," she replied, taking an arm away from around her mother to wipe a single tear then placing it back in the same place on her mother's back. The queen backed away to look at her daughter. The king put his arm around his wife, and they looked at their daughter with overwhelming love in their hearts.

"Thank you for coming back," her mother said through powerful hiccoughs. She had her mind set on her daughter returning in the late morning, and her nightly arrival put stress on her heart.

"Of course. I promised I would," Amaryllis said happily then looked over her mother's shoulder to see Prince James approaching. He stepped out from behind the Queen of Serilion and stood frozen in front of her. His watery eyes were revealed in the candlelight. He shook his head with a soft smile on his face. Amaryllis' heart skipped a beat upon seeing him. Another tear ran down her face followed by several more until they ran towards each other. Amaryllis jumped into her prince's arms both sensing euphoric sensations of love in their hearts. His body was warm and comforting, but she couldn't feel his warmth through her armour. Just his presence itself was comforting. She felt protected in his arms, and he felt protected in hers. Their faces were wet with tears, both not ready to let go of each other quite yet. The room buzzed, talking about how young love was just the most exquisite thing. Amaryllis' parents and James' father watched their children with happiness.

"You have *no* idea how much I've missed you," James whispered in her ear. His words amplified her happiness even more, and she was determined to amplify his in return.

"I am overjoyed to have made it back to you. I thought about you often on my journey wishing you were there countless times," she whispered back. The prince chuckled as if her affection could never surpass his.

"I thought about you every single minute of every day only hoping that you were okay. I constantly wished you were here," he replied. They let go of each other. Amaryllis faced the now seated royal subjects while James kept his eyes on her. Each person looked as if they were to explode with something to say. The King and Queen of Arlon read the room and the king spoke.

"Princess Amaryllis, if you don't mind, please take a seat at the head of the table. I'm sure we'd all like to hear you tell your tale," the king said proudly feeling the eyes of the royal subjects look at him in appreciation for attempting to get the princess to reveal details of her journey. Amaryllis looked at the King of Arlon with passionate disrespect, thinking of John Edwards. She saw the murder, the madness, still present in his eyes. He was too arrogant to sense her anger, but her mother and father, along with Prince James, noticed her drastic mood change. They said nothing about it, just watching her out of bewilderment. She walked around to the head of the table and the prince followed her. She sat on the left and James sat on the right. As soon as they took their seats, Amaryllis' parents found their own.

Dozens of eyes stared at her, the candle light brightening their faces and darkening their eyes. No matter the colour—whether brown, blue, or green—the eyes of the royals appeared black and without pupils. Each and every person was unrecognizable in the poor, dimly lit room. Even as she quickly glanced at James, who was right next to her, his features seemed different. Like everyone else's, his beautiful eyes were dulled by the candlelight, but she still loved to look into them. The candlelight played trickery on her. She would never be able to address anyone by their names as long as they were in that dining hall.

Suddenly, a set of teeth flashed from down the table followed by a low feminine voice that cried, "Well, we're all dying to know what happened!" she exploded, most likely a queen. Then, the room boomed with chatter; everyone shouted Amaryllis' name at the top of their lungs trying to overpower all other voices. The room chaotically escalated from yelling to screaming. Everyone stood up from their seats and began to walk to Amaryllis' end of the table. The King and Queen of Arlon, the King and Queen of Serilion, Laria, and Prince James were the only ones still respectfully seated.

Amaryllis looked at the hysterical crowd with readiness. Her facial expression wore seriousness with a slight frown, a more relaxed expression than her face when battling Immortuos, but it was similar. The wild behaviour before her reminded her of monsters, whom she could take down in a mere ten-seconds. She would easily dominate the room.

The burning question of how she killed Immortuos raced through everyone's mind driving them crazy enough to lose control of themselves. They needed to hear each and every detail to ease their curiosity. Amaryllis wanted to refrain from using her powers unsure of whether or not she wanted them to know of her immortality. If they knew, her treatment would be discriminatory and brutal. She would be treated as a witch and her journey of bravery would be ignored, but it was too late. Her eyes were glowing brightly, illuminating the table. It was a completely defensive reaction which she had no control over.

Well, it's too late now, she thought. The room filled with gasps and wide eyes. Prince James shifted in his seat beside her, leaning back and around in his chair to look at her glowing eyes. She smiled at him then stood up from her seat. She felt a gawking stare from him as she arose.

"Sit down," she said firmly to the crowd with the nod of her head. They hesitated for a moment, held still by their fear, then returned to their seats. Amaryllis' eyes returned to their regular green. The light faded from her eyes and only the candlelight lit the table once again. The King of Arlon looked at her skeptically wondering when and where she picked up her sudden leadership and dominance, completely ignoring the fact that her eyes glowed brighter than fire, almost as bright as the sun. He remembered her as a timid and sensitive child but that same girl did not return. Before him, at the opposite end of the table, was a warrior.

"I know you're eager to hear the gruesome details of my journey—"

"*Gruesome?*" a voice shrieked.

Amaryllis lowered her eyes for a moment and sighed. "Yes, the details are exceedingly gruesome and—"

"Your eyes, why were they glow—?"

"Enough interruptions!" Amaryllis boomed, her voice powerful and loud. If she was to tell her tale she would want to do so smoothly and efficiently, not wanting to spend too much time trapped within certain memories as to avoid post-trauma. She had only just returned and already she was forced to return to her journey through her vivid imagination; her immortal mind which acted as a time manipulator. Telling her story would be like reliving it all over again.

So, Amaryllis began her story. She started right from the beginning, her first encounter within the Dark Forest. She explained the horrid melodies, the haunted atmosphere, and the creatures in a perfectly accurate and terrifyingly descriptive manner. She told them how standing in such a place brought an overwhelmingly strong panic to her but over time she adapted to the horrors. Talking about her first experience with Immortuos filled the room with a tension of an awkward fear, which brought uneasiness to each and every person. They shifted in their seats squeezing the arms of their chairs as she described the unholy creature of darkness.

Amaryllis avoided mentioning John Edwards, completely cutting him out from the story. As she described her encounter with the toxic grove of blue mushrooms, she looked into the King of Arlon's eyes carefully avoiding any mention of her helping hand. He looked at her in anticipation almost *expecting* to hear of a shaggy old man: the one who's family he stole, but Amaryllis never mentioned him, which was strange and felt wrong. She was forced to take all of the credit for her own survival for her friend's protection. It was the right thing to do, but it certainly didn't seem to be. She continued her tale in the cold lake with fish that could detect a frightened heart, through more forest, and finally came the time to talk about the tunnel of *Things*—the most dreadful memory she had. She would forever keep her audience in suspense by not telling them who and what she saw down there. It would be an odd thing for her prince to hear, considering the Things took his form, and John Edwards was the other, so there was no point in trying to lie. She avoided describing their features all together, even their *true* features which made her pause from her monologue briefly when they hissed at her within her mind. She looked away from her surroundings before her completely zoning out and gaining full access into the memory. She was there again, frozen this time without John to pull her from the hole. She escaped her brain with a jolting feeling, her heart jumping when she returned to her surroundings. The royal subjects looked at her with sympathy, looking fearfully at Amaryllis in her state of remembrance. They were frightened just by her descriptions, glad she refrained from illustrating the faces of the things. Each individual felt they were present in a telling of a ghost story forgetting Amaryllis' glowing eyes, too focused on the intense details of her journey. Besides, she would explain her immortality in the end.

When she finally mentioned the mountain guarded by the gigantic dragons, a princess raised her hand.

"Yes?" Amaryllis asked. She wasn't annoyed, as her story was nearly finished and she hadn't been interrupted until now. She didn't mind answering questions, it was the cowardly shrieks and obnoxious shouting that exasperated her.

"I apologize, but may I leave? I can't bear to hear this anymore." Another princess, followed by another, chimed in saying the same things. They were scared and needed to leave. Her story was too petrifying. Amaryllis studied their frightened faces and nodded them out. As soon as she did, the three princesses shoved away from the table and jogged out.

"Stop!" the King of Arlon barked, "You are only permitted to enter the dressing room. As soon as we're done here someone will fetch you." The princesses nodded their heads spastically then bolted. They desperately needed to escape the room of fear. "Don't want them wandering around," he mumbled then looked at Amaryllis with intrigued eyes. "Please, continue."

Amaryllis felt a small wave of heat; of sheer anger. She didn't need *his* permission to speak, but she continued, describing her long battle with the fire breathing beasts. As she mentioned how she fought with blue flames, and a diamond rod crafted from her own hands, jaws dropped loosely. Many wanted to ask about her powers but were too afraid of her to verbalize their wonderings. They listened carefully to the details, absorbing the information, each word more important than the last.

And finally, after talking about the exploration of the mountain, she began the battle with Immortuos. More princesses, even a few queens, and one prince had to leave the room. The women went to the dressing room where the last three went, and the prince went alone into the men's dressing room as ordered by the King of Arlon. Only the brave and the fearful ones of being thought of as cowards remained. Laria was one of the fearful ones who stayed. In her mind, if she walked out, Amaryllis would win their little feud, but Amaryllis had forgotten all about Laria, she didn't care.

She finished talking about the battle by describing her loss of energy as power drained from within her, followed by her unconsciousness, and how she awoke in a serene land of happiness in the morning. Her story took an hour to tell. The candles were burned down nearly to the candelabrum, the flames dancing lazily as they died.

Everyone looked at her in complete awe and admiration. The King of Arlon smiled a small smile with the thought of Amaryllis marrying his son and how she would make a great queen to rule his kingdom along with Prince Eric. Then, his smile faded when he found himself looking at Prince James who looked at Amaryllis with love in his eyes.

Prince James was filled with an unbearable amount of pride impressed with her dauntless strength and her never-ending wisdom. He was completely in love with her.

The King and Queen of Serilion were filled with the same amount of pride, almost overwhelmed with their daughter's success. Her achievements could be rewarded endlessly…they should be rewarded endlessly.

The admiration never faded from anyone but the question finally arose. A prince she could not identify in the growing darkness that swallowed the room asked about her powers. He took the weight off everyones shoulders, but he also amplified their stress. The room feared her reaction to his question, but she wasn't hostile like they pictured in their worst preconceived scenarios. She was kind because she feared how they would treat her. Akar popped into her mind. He was knowledgable of magic, studied it, and used it well, but he was imprisoned. Amaryllis was knowledgable of magic through intense exposure and practice, she never studied it through books, she learned from experience. She was now the most powerful being on Earth, replacing Immortuos. Where would she be placed? *Nowhere…* there wasn't a single place or form of punishment that could contain her. If they didn't like her abilities that was a pity because no matter what they would attempt Amaryllis would always win with her immortality. She no longer feared their reaction. She was magically gifted and that's the way it was. She would never accept any form of hatred because of her "witchcraft."

"Well," she began. "I was taught basic magic from a sorcerer named Akar, which I used throughout my whole journey. Each task took incredible amounts of concentration and I struggled to perform at first, but as I constantly faced new dangers, I became faster and faster until I no longer needed to concentrate. Magic flows through me now, it is a part of me. I have been gifted with immortality due to extreme exposure to evil elements."

The room was silent. Looking at her in admiration, mixed with shock, wondering of the limits of her abilities. "What can you do?" the bold prince asked almost regretting his question when watching her face darken in the dimming candlelight. She smiled softly.

"I can do everything," she answered bluntly. Suddenly, each candle burned out, the flames shrinking into the metal candelabrum. The sudden darkness mildly startled the crowd of people. In the darkness, all in a matter of seconds, Amaryllis created new sticks of wax. Blue flames surged from her palms sailing over the table and lighting each new candle. Gasps filled the room, the bright blue light illuminating the shocked faces of the royal subjects. The candles danced with big, beautiful blue flames.

"That is the very least of it all," Amaryllis said solemnly. They did not hate her like she thought they would. Everyone had a blossoming respect for her that grew each time she impressed them. Her powers left the room speechless, which led her to believe they were afraid of her. "I know it's odd, but I would never harm—"

"Amaryllis, it's amazing," The King of Arlon chuckled. "Your powers can solve so many issues." He thought of an abundant source of resources, food forming in her own hands. He thought of gold raining down from a storm she generated to bring wealth to his palace. He thought of how easy it would be to eliminate criminals. Excitement filled everyone like children, absolutely in shock to be in the same room as an immortal sorcerer. Laria, including the rest of the princesses who tormented her, slumped in their seats, regretting every single harmless tease and especially regretting each time they physically harmed her. Amaryllis finally had what her past self longed for: love and respect. She looked at the happy faces before her, thinking of what she had achieved.

Chapter 50

The dining hall was filled with cheerful chatter lit by Amaryllis' blue flames. Amaryllis and James finally had time to speak. James asked her his own questions, asking her to go into more detail in some areas of her story so he could really understand what she went through. He asked what was on her mind in each situation, wanting to know everything as if he was there with her.

The King of Arlon stood up from the table, which no-one, except for his wife whom he politely and briefly left, noticed as they were deep in conversation. They all talked about parts of Amaryllis' story that either inspired or frightened them the most. He walked all the way to Amaryllis' end, and as he approached her Amaryllis felt anger boiling inside of her.

You destroyed John Edwards, you destroyed John Edwards, ringed in her ears. He leaned over bringing his face to hers.

"I'd like to speak with you in terms of the Choosing Ceremony. Things were left unresolved and unfair," he admitted quietly. James leaned in close to try to hear what the king was saying. Amaryllis looked at James, her heart warming immediately at the sight of him, then looked back at the king trying to push her hatred away.

"Are you offering a re-choosing?" she asked hopefully. James' eyes widened, nodding his head.

"Yes, the perplexing event of you running away made everything…difficult," he laughed anxiously. She narrowed her eyes. "Let's fix this," he said softly, truly caring for her happiness and not the ruined final annual party. She grabbed James' hand keeping her stare on the king.

"We would love nothing more," she said with a forced smile. Her imagination roamed wild picturing a cloud above the king's head which rained blood onto him. His eyes possessed wickedness.

I suppose I did not rid of all *of the evil,* she thought seeing right through the king's kindness and staring at his empty soul.

"Wonderful. We won't redo the entire ceremony, we'll only include you, Prince James, my son, and Princess Laria."

She didn't want to thank him but she did. After all, she was to experience the Choosing Ceremony once again but in the way she hoped it would occur. The king walked back to his seat and patted his wife's back gently. It was her suggestion of a re-choosing, not his.

"She wants it doesn't she?" the queen asked with a smile. The king nodded then called for the attention of everyone in the room. The queen's smile faded, she hoped for a "thank you for the idea," or some degree of credit, but she did not receive either.

"Because it is the only right thing to do, and because they deserve happiness, we will be organizing a re-choosing for Amaryllis, James, Eric, and Laria."

Everyone nodded in agreement remembering the disastrous ending of the Choosing Ceremony. The engaged royal subjects especially admired the idea. They wouldn't participate, there was no stress. They had already found their loves, and they would get to watch their acquaintances find their own deserved love. It was a perfect idea.

"It is eight o clock now. The ceremony will commence at quarter to nine," said the king. The royal subjects cheered and clapped. The king made eye contact with Amaryllis, James, Eric, and Laria. "You have forty-five minutes to prepare yourselves.

It will be the same as before. Get dressed, wait for the music. Once the music plays, make your way to the ballroom. It will end right this time." The king refrained from putting the guilt of the ceremony's failure all on Amaryllis although it was all her fault because he was slightly afraid of what she'd do. If he wasn't so arrogant, he would be completely afraid of her just like everyone else.

Everyone flooded the room, all except for Amaryllis and James. She hugged him tightly then kissed his cheek. She was careful of what to say as her fear of being neglected presented itself. She knew their love was strong, and he chose Laria by command of his father, but she was worried.

"I'll see you in forty-five minutes," she said softly, hiding the sadness in her voice, but the prince could detect it. He wrapped his arms around his beautiful bride to be feeling her smooth armour.

"I cannot wait to marry you," he laughed contentedly as if in disbelief that he was lucky enough to choose Amaryllis as his own with no outside afflictions. This time the ceremony would be absolutely wonderful. He would get to choose the woman he loved.

Amaryllis blushed, with the idea of being neglected pushed back slightly in her mind, becoming less of a worry. Then he pulled away from their hug and kissed her back on the cheek. She melted at the soft touch of his lips. Her worries vanished. They walked out of the dining room hand in hand. Amaryllis' armour annoyed the prince in the slightest sense that he wasn't actually touching *her,* but he was fortunate enough to have her back so he sighed and smiled.

The couple parted ways to prepare for the second Choosing Ceremony, saying a wholehearted goodbye before separating. They both swayed into the dressing rooms like autumn leaves falling from a tree with giddy smiles on their faces and redness in their cheeks.

Chapter 51

Amaryllis' armour pixelated into thin air, which would have exposed her nude body to Laria if she were't hidden in the closet searching for a new dress. Amaryllis sent a wave of white light starting from her toes and climbing up to her head to clean herself magically as opposed to bathing. Time was only long enough for her to put on a dress and makeup. She felt refreshed and beautiful as the light flew up her body. Her hair was knotless, her face was bright, and she smelled of roses.

She walked into the closet to see Laria's feet underneath the curtain of the changing area. She stepped into a faded blue, puffy dress.

"Beautiful dress," Amaryllis exclaimed, trying to create peace between them. She watched the material dance as Laria put it on, waiting for a response.

"Thanks," she muttered under her breath.

Amaryllis shrugged and turned away to gaze at the dresses on the hangers. No dress, no matter how beautiful, compared to her sparkly universe dress. Its remains went down with the forest it was destroyed in.

It was important that she chose a dress quickly, she needed time to calm herself. Her stomach twisted into knots of excitement that could only be untied by the loving and assuring embrace of her prince, her future king.

A deep, rich green dress caught her attention. It was long sleeved with a wide neck that would expose her shoulders, the skirt portion was long and smooth. It would hang loosely from her hips and flow to the floor, hiding her shoes. It would certainly match her emerald green eyes. It was good enough, absolutely beautiful.

She took it from its hanger and threw it on then picked out matching rich, green shoes and put them on quickly. She stepped in front of the long mirror and studied herself. She exuded a powerful energy, and her erect posture and muscular stature intensified her appearance of power, along with her resting stern expression gained through trauma.

After looking at herself in the mirror for a minute, she walked over to an arbitrary vanity and began applying makeup. She selected rouge that well suited her skin tone, brown eyeshadow, mascara, and dark red lipstick. She carefully yet quickly applied it all. It felt strange to put on makeup after being barefaced and natural for a while, but she enjoyed it. She loved how it enhanced her complexion, complimented her features.

Suddenly, Laria emerged from the closet in her faded blue dress. She may have actually looked beautiful if she didn't have such an ugly frown on her face. Amaryllis spun around on her stool to face her.

"Don't worry, you have time. It's only twenty after eight," Amaryllis declared. Laria nodded walking over to the vanity furthest away from Amaryllis'. A smile spread across her face, she looked at herself in the mirror shaking her head. "So rude," Amaryllis said under her breath. She couldn't believe someone so petty used to control her life. Relief filled her knowing that she did not have power over her anymore, but she was also filled with awkwardness. James had chosen Laria first, leading Laria to believe he wanted her as his queen. The dramatic change of knowing he wanted Amaryllis all along was difficult for Laria, since all any princess wanted was to be chosen by a handsome prince. Learning she was unwanted was devastating. Amaryllis almost felt sorry for her.

"Okay, listen… we need to talk about something before the ceremony begins."

Laria rolled her eyes and sighed. "Talk about what?"

"The whole situation with James and Eric…I'd like to know if you're all right with being chosen by Prince Eric," Amaryllis said, concerned.

Laria looked at her skeptically. "Yeah, why wouldn't I be?" she snapped.

"Well, you seemed upset over James, that's all. I'm sorry, but I really do love him and he loves me. There's no changing that." Amaryllis spoke with sincerity, and Laria responded with a crude attitude. As it turned out, Laria never cared for James specifically. She only cared about being chosen, and the fact that both Eric and James wanted Amaryllis infuriated her.

"I don't care about your stupid prince," Laria sneered, "I just want *a* prince. Now, leave me alone." Laria took out her anger with a brush and white powder sending cloudy puffs of white dust into the air. She furiously applied her makeup, hoping for her anger to ease, but it never seemed to reach its peak. It was never-ending.

Amaryllis sighed and put her hair into a beautiful up-do, which took almost no time at all. She spun around on her stool again. Laria bothered her now, but only in the aspect of Laria's sadness. She was definitely miserable to be acting like that. No confident person would ever dream of living the way Laria did, controlled by envy. Amaryllis wanted to help her. She instantly disregarded all of the cruel things Laria had done to her for one moment.

"Laria, you're beautiful, and I'm sure Prince Eric is beyond happy to have you as his queen. Several kings and queens believe you're one of the more eligible ones to rule. You'll be great."

Laria longed for a compliment as nice as Amaryllis'. It was kind enough to make her stop what she was doing completely. She sat still comprehending what she had just heard from the girl she had bullied since she was young. She was silent hoping for another compliment.

"Please turn around," Amaryllis ordered. Laria turned around slowly revealing a pale face with pink blush and red lips. Her brown eyes twinkled for a moment. "You look radiant," Amaryllis said gently with a smile, using her knowledge of cheering up a self-conscious person from experience with her mother's calm approach towards her when she was as timid as could be. Laria's heart fluttered happily. For a moment, she stopped comparing herself to Amaryllis and loved herself. But then, Amaryllis smiled beautifully, and Laria's heart sank. "I know it must be nerve-wracking to think of the future, but you have to believe you're destined for greatness. It's okay to be frightened."

Laria twisted her hair into an up-do similar to Amaryllis'. She let Amaryllis' kind words echo through her mind. She was in shock that she had even forgiven her at all after all of the rotten things she had done to her. She looked at Amaryllis with big brown eyes of sorrow.

Suddenly, a loud knock at the door startled the girls. Amaryllis looked at a clock on the wall. It was half past eight, not even close to the ceremony's start time yet.

"Who is it?" Amaryllis shouted.

A male voice shouted back, "Is Laria in there?"

"Yes," Laria croaked, standing up to head to the door.

"Come out here," he pleaded. Laria tried to smile at Amaryllis as she passed her on the way to the door but she was too upset to lift her lips. Amaryllis looked at her with empathy then looked to the door skeptically. Laria opened the door and stepped out. When she returned, she wore a content expression on her face with a small smile.

"Who was it?" Amaryllis asked.

"Prince Eric," she answered, trying to hide excitement in her voice. "He told me I looked beautiful, and he was overjoyed to choose me."

"Oh, that's wonderful!" Amaryllis said happily, clasping her hands together. The look on Laria's face was priceless, full of wonder and excitement. Eric's surprise visit was a great way to cheer Laria up for the ceremony. Amaryllis appreciated Eric's impulsive desire to say hello because now she didn't have to worry about her anymore.

"Look, Amaryllis," Laria began. "What you did for Arlon, for all of the world… I don't know what to say. It was simply heroic."

Amaryllis trembled with excitement. She and Laria were finally getting along after all of those wretched years. "Thank you, I appreciate that very much." They smiled at each other. "And now we get to move on in this new, wonderful world. Get married, move away, and become queen. You get to rule Arlon, that will be so exciting for you."

"Yes, and Werling is so beautiful, you'll love it there," Laria replied softly. Amaryllis felt warm inside, happy to be speaking so positively with Laria. They were ending on such good terms before saying goodbye to each other. They wouldn't see each other until the next generation of choosing ceremonies when their children would go through the tradition or until a kingdom threw a ball or another event that included all other kingdoms's presences. The timid girl deep within Amaryllis was finally at peace.

All it took was kindness and love to bring out the happiness in Laria. The love that she so desperately needed was finally provided by her future king and her new friend, which she took gratefully. Laria was difficult to love, she was difficult to spend time with because she was easily jealous and lashed out at those who were smarter or more beautiful than she was, and that's why she needed kindness more than anyone else. Laria was finally at peace with herself and Amaryllis was too. Their ugly past had been resolved, put to rest, and they both felt incredibly ecstatic about it.

The duke opened the door and music began to play. It sounded sweeter and created a stronger joy within Amaryllis than the last time she heard it. Goosebumps arose on her skin, and a smile spread across her face. Her heart raced in her chest and the knots in her stomach tightened.

She and Laria walked side by side behind the duke. He spun around and looked at them occasionally with a soft, wholehearted smile on his face. Happiness filled him to see them headed to their righteous destiny and to see them getting along. They were just as happy as he was about their new bond.

With each step closer to the ballroom, Amaryllis' knotted stomach became tighter and tighter.

After the longest walk to the ballroom, which was a part of the wonderfully wicked illusion that her anxiety played on her, they finally reached the doors. They creaked open sending music through the hallway like waves in the ocean. Her nearness to the instruments made the melody sweeter giving her another wave of goosebumps. The moon and the stars shone brightly through the windows lighting the room with natural starlight along with the chandelier lit in orange flames. Amaryllis looked up to the balcony to see the kings and queens, along with the couples as decided by the previous Choosing Ceremony. They all wore big smiles on their faces. Some shed tears and some clapped quietly as they princesses entered. They walked beneath the two spotlights, Amaryllis on the far right and Laria on the left. Before the music stopped, Amaryllis shot blue flames from her palms replacing the orange flames with blue ones which brightened the room even more. The balcony cheered for Amaryllis' act of magic, in awe with the blue fire. Amaryllis smiled up at the balcony then looked down at Prince James sitting in his double chair looking at her with love in his heart. She looked over at Laria who clapped silently for Amaryllis' trick with a look of surprise on her face.

The music stopped gradually, fading away seamlessly. Then the King of Arlon appeared with his booming voice.

"It brings great joy to me to witness love so strong within our children. I know the tradition hasn't been followed accordingly, but it almost seems better this way. This re-choosing is only fair because of course tradition is important, but our children's happiness is more important. After all, the purpose of the Choosing Ceremony is to bring happiness, to introduce love, not to force it in an arranged marriage." The king cleared his throat quietly. "Prince James of Werling, please make your selection."

Prince James arose from his seat slowly, trying to contain his excitement. Amaryllis looked at him with a dreamy look on her face that brought happiness to him. She looked so beautiful in her green gown that complimented her bright green eyes. He walked up to her and realized that within her eyes were the stars, twinkling peacefully in a galaxy of affection. He held out his hand, and she gently took it.

A sudden rush of excitement washed over her tightening the knots in her stomach as tightly as possible then released them in a wave of calm as the warmth and the touch of James' hand comforted her. The balcony cheered and applauded for them, Amaryllis' mother crying tears of joy for her daughter. She finally attained the happiness she deserved.

Amaryllis and James took their spots in their connected seats still holding hands. James leaned over the armrest and pressed his lips to hers in a tender kiss that took her breath away. They looked into each other's eyes with pure affection then looked over at Laria respectfully as it was her turn for happiness.

While watching Laria with Eric, Amaryllis couldn't stop thinking about how happy she was. Her joy consumed her completely feeling as though she'd be at an all time high for the rest of her life. No other feeling could compare to the true love she felt overpowering her body. Nothing she faced in the Dark Forest was as strong as this. She snapped from her lovestruck trance to clap for Laria and Eric who sat lovingly in their connected seats, holding hands. Her journey flashed before her eyes. It was all worth it. Each monster, each creature, each earthly wrath, and of course, ridding of Immortuos forever… it was all worth it.

Before she knew it, the Choosing Ceremony was over. She and James stood up from their seats and let the people from the balcony exit the ballroom first. The King of Werling approached his son and his fiancé with a shameful look on his face. Before expressing his deepest apology, he congratulated them first shaking his son's hand and kissing Amaryllis'.

"Again, I am so dreadfully sorry. There is nothing I can say or do that will ever make up for what I've done, but just know that it lives with me forever," he sighed. James looked at him with a satisfied look on his face. They were just the words he wanted to hear after his father delayed their engagement. But Amaryllis didn't like his apology, she appreciated it, but she didn't find it to be fair on *both* ends.

"Thank you very much, but please don't blame yourself. Don't take the fault. I am glad things worked out the way they did. In the end, I picked up queen-like traits from my journey, along with my immortality, and James and I *still* ended up together even after the world fell. Doesn't that tell you something?"

James looked at her in amazement, nodding his head. She was right and she thought of it all from a positive perspective, which he loved.

The King of Werling grinned. "Thank you, Amaryllis. And, yes, it definitely means something," he said with a wink then walked out the door. Amaryllis' parents approached them next with congratulatory hugs. The queen was in tears overwhelmed with happiness.

"You two will lead so well," she sobbed. The king looked down at his bawling wife and put his hands on her shoulders then smiled.

"She's extremely excited for you two," he chuckled. "As am I, I could not be happier." He put his arms out for another hug from Amaryllis. She squeezed him then squeezed her mother again.

"We don't have to say goodbye now...we can say goodbye in the morning," Amaryllis suggested, looking at her mother who trembled in dozens of emotions.

"That is a wonderful idea. Well, good night and sleep well. See you in the morning," The king said. He acted calm and in control but on the inside he was upset. He felt unprepared to give his daughter away, as was the queen, but she could not hide it like the king could.

"Good night!" said Amaryllis and James. Her parents left the room leaving them alone under the blue, candlelit chandelier. Amaryllis' feeling of euphoria vanished in an instant, her instincts taking over. She quickly glanced at the stars, then at the chandelier, then at every single detail in the ballroom. John's family was killed here.

"What is it?" James asked studying the serious look on her face.

"There's something I must do," she responded quickly, picturing John struggling to tell her the story of his family's death. "Come on." She took his hand and walked towards the door. Before they left, she turned around and waved her arm across her body sending a gust of wind to blow each and every candle in the chandelier out. They went out in a sharp, snapping sound behind them.

Each couple was provided with a large bedroom for the night before their departure for their kingdoms the next morning. Everyone had been staying in their designated rooms for several days as opposed to the one because of Amaryllis. No one even considered returning to their kingdoms until Amaryllis was either declared dead or until she returned. So, the King of Arlon provided hospitality for the visiting kingdoms until she returned. It was a stressful and suspenseful time for them all.

James led the way to their bedroom. The bedroom door had a big, royal blue coloured, "W" on it. He opened it to let her in then he closed it behind them.

"So, what is it? You never told me," he asked calmly. Amaryllis sat down on their bed letting the comforting mattress stuffed with feathers and straw break her down into a relaxed state. She wanted to tell James about John, but she feared someone may overhear. She feared the king was hidden in their room just waiting for her to reveal the missing component to her story. She knew not what he would do if he found out. Perhaps he'd force her to tell him where he was so he could kill him off himself since banishment to the Dark Forest wasn't enough. Or maybe he had forgotten about him, she would never know and she didn't want to.

She motioned for James to move closer. "We need to be as quiet as possible, all right?"

"Yes, of course," he whispered almost inaudibly, the perfect volume.

Amaryllis retold her story, but in a summarized version, this time including John Edwards and his sad tale. She explained where she had sent him to live, and she included how and why she invited him to Werling. James understood completely, even showing uneasiness from the new information about the King of Arlon.

"So, in the morning, you'd like to go and fetch him and sneak him into our carriage?" James asked, still barely making noise. The only reason Amaryllis could understand him was because she was reading his lips.

She nodded her head. "We'll have to sneak him past your father somehow. I assume the other kings know about the rivalry between John and the king?" Amaryllis asked.

James shrugged his shoulders. "I've never heard my father speak of it, but to be safe John could ride with the coachman while you, my father, and I are inside the carriage?"

Amaryllis' face lit up in the darkness of the room illuminated by the moonlight. "Yes, that could most definitely work, but we'll have to have John walk alongside the carriage until we're well away from the kingdom because if the King of Arlon *sees* him... it won't end well."

James shuddered thinking of the king impaling the Edwards family. "It's a plan then," James whispered with a faint nod. Amaryllis grinned slightly, pleased to know she would be taking her friend far away from his misery.

The kingdom of Werling was a three hour carriage ride from Arlon, which seemed far away enough to her.

Amaryllis and James changed out of their ceremonial clothes and found night clothes provided on their nightstand. They crawled into bed under the covers and discussed the plan once more before trying to sleep. James was more than happy to help his princess save the friend who saved her life. He would be forever grateful for John Edwards for helping her return to him. He wrapped his arms around her, and she snuggled into his chest listening to his heartbeat as she drifted off into the loveliest sleep she had ever had.

Chapter 52

Before dawn, Amaryllis jerked awake with John Edwards on her mind. She was still nestled in James' arms. She wiggled out carefully as not to wake him then grabbed a pair of slippers from underneath the bed. She slid them on then left the room closing the door silently behind her. The castle was dead silent, all was still and creepily motionless. She wanted to run for the door but her feet pattering against the floor would be too loud, so she walked carefully the entire way.

The door was unguarded with no doorman in sight. Amaryllis' eyes darted all over the dark castle looking for the King of Arlon in paranoia. In the depths of her mind, where her imagination was explicit, the King of Arlon chased her all over the castle bearing a sword in his hand. Also, in her mind, her immortality was not effective, it could not save her from the deranged lunatic.

She pulled the ropes enough to leave enough space for her to wiggle through, then she sprinted out the castle door. The crisp, night air pummelled her face, but she ignored the cold and sprinted for the village. The gate was unguarded and unlocked so she pushed it slowly to avoid the squeak of old hinges then continued her sprint.

She reached the village in a timely manner then slowed down to a cautious amble to walk stealthily through the sleeping settlement. She did not want to draw any attention to herself.

She peered through each window of each house until John's house screamed at her with its inner emptiness. His house looked well maintained although no one looked after it for twenty years, and that was the haunting part—it was the inside that was ugly with isolation. It emitted a wholesome feeling of hatred feeling upon her as she stood before it. John was definitely in there.

She let herself in. The furniture was stored with memories which turned to nightmares. They longed to be used collecting dust in thick layers. She looked to the left to see a dying fire, and a body lying in a ball on the floor.

"John!" she whispered. His body jerked a little, but he didn't answer. "John, get up!" she called a little louder. A groan came from the limp body. "John, let's go! It's me." She impulsively threw a blue ball of fire into the fire place, making a crackling hiss. John sat up from the dirty floor with a thundering heart. He stared at her with wild, wide eyes. She took a step back, startled. "John, are you okay?"

"No!" He hollered. "*No-no-no-no!*"

Amaryllis frowned, chucking a rock she found on the floor at his chest hoping for the pain to silence him, but he was still wild eyed about to scream again.

"John, *stop!*" she hissed through clenched teeth. She ran over to him covering his mouth. He screamed into her hand. "Shut up, *shut up!*" She kicked his side, slapped him in the face, then grabbed him by the shoulders and shook him. He wouldn't stop yelling and his panic-stricken face wouldn't fade. She grabbed him by the wrist and dragged him outside of the house. She whispered fiercely into his ear that he needed to be silent then hit him again in the face. The panic finally vanished, his eyes relaxed, and his body went limp in her arms. His brown eyes were soft and confused.

"What's going on?" he asked tiredly. His gaze met his house and his body stiffened, jerking away from Amaryllis who was standing just too close to the house.

"I've come to get you, so you can come to Werling with me," she whispered.

"Oh…"

"We've talked about this already," she reminded him.

"I know, but…"

"John you're acting very strange what happened to you in that house?" she asked, twisting the material of her nightgown anxiously.

"I never should have come here…their ghosts *haunt* me," he stammered taking another step back from the house. Amaryllis watched the man with pity. He had never acted this way in front of her before and his mentioning of ghosts disturbed her. She had gone into the ghost house, she been close to *them*. It was nearly impossible to take on a ghost. They had no physical bodies, no weaknesses. "Go on. Go and look at them." He waved his hand accidentally catching a glimpse of the kitchen window full of familiar faces smiling darkly at him. He gasped, turning away in fear. Amaryllis looked into the window and saw nothing, relieved they were only in his head, but worried for the poor, trembling man.

"John, it's okay. Calm down, everything is okay. They can't hurt you out here," she insisted, holding two hands up, showing her palms to him. He focused on the lines on her palms seeing the ghosts in his peripheral vision but refusing to look away from her hands.

"They are right there, can't you see them?" he sobbed.

Amaryllis studied the house, only seeing darkness inside, but no ghosts. "They aren't there John. Come on, let's go." She reached for his hand but he drew back.

"I can't leave them," he warned. Amaryllis reached for him again, but he smacked her hand away. "I can't leave them!" he repeated. She didn't recognize him anymore, he was suddenly mad from the thoughts trapped within his mind coming to life.

"Okay, okay..." Amaryllis began, checking the house once more for spectres to see none of them. "...so what do you want to do?"

He looked through the window and his wild eyes returned. He trembled in fear staring at the ghosts that stared back at him with evil smiles on their faces. Their eyes were red circles, their faces crusted in black.

"You can't see them?" he asked, raising a shaky, pointed finger to the empty window.

Amaryllis looked and saw nothing, but her heart raced. "John, you're scaring me," she admitted. "We should leave then the ghosts can't hurt you anymore," her voice trembled.

"No!" he screamed keeping his eyes on the ghosts. "I can't leave them."

"Why not?"

"They won't let me," he moaned in a deep voice.

"I assure you, if you walk away, they can't follow you."

"Yes, they can! They have been for twenty years!" he shouted still staring into the house. Amaryllis looked away from John and his haunted house for a moment to think. His family's death controlled him, owned him, possessed him, and the way to exorcise them from his mind was only to...have them back. Killing the king wouldn't ease his suffering although he would enjoy it, but since he wasn't willing to let them go, to finally say goodbye, Amaryllis would have to bring them to him.

She called upon the universe for help. Her eyes glowed bright turquoise, but John didn't notice as he was preoccupied with a stare down with his dead and distorted family members.

Amaryllis' body jolted aggressively losing a breath, then she felt weightless as her body fell back into empty space. Amaryllis travelled through dimensions, her body vanishing into thin air as she soared through a tunnel of bright swirling colours. She would have enjoyed her inter-dimensional travel if it weren't for the cries of her friend she was trying to ease. Instinctively, because of the stars within her, she knew where she was and where she needed to go. After another few seconds of soaring through the colourful dimensional walls, she halted, transporting herself to the afterlife. After a few minutes of flying around, she found the Edwards family. Her heart skipped a beat upon seeing them. She was so glad to have found them. They looked at her skeptically, unsure of who she was, but she didn't care.

"You all need to come with me!" Amaryllis said with urgency in her voice looking at the family of five which should be a family of six. She was far too determined, too focused on helping her friend to notice where she had travelled and what she had done.

"Go with you where? And who are you?" Judith asked. She and her sons had not aged a day past their death, so when they greeted John it would be right from where he left them. The only change he'd notice was their robes of white.

"I've come to take you to your husband, John Edwards."

John's children widened their little eyes, some exclaiming, "Dad!" or "Daddy!" excitedly, but their mother was skeptical.

"Please come with me. He's absolutely miserable without you. He's screaming, shouting, and he's claiming that he is haunted by your ghosts. Please come and help my friend, your husband."

Judith looked at her sons who began to cry for their dad, sobbing hysterically.

"How long has it been?" Judith asked with a trembling voice. She wiped a tear from her eye as her bottom lip curled.

"Twenty years," Amaryllis answered bluntly.

Judith gasped, bringing her hand to her mouth. *Twenty years* echoed in her mind, with each second that passed causing the echoes to become more distorted. She nodded. "Please bring us to him," Judith pleaded over the sounds of her crying children.

Without hesitation, Amaryllis transported back to Earth holding onto John's family through the tunnel of colour. She looked at their faces, watching for panic in their eyes, but she only saw bewilderment. Their mouths moved, but she couldn't hear them over the rushing sound of their speed through the dimensions.

A polychromatic, circular portal swirled around beside the house creating a humming noise. A shiver ran down John's spine as his back tensed up. He wanted to scream but his chest was full, locked, and he was frozen. The swirling thing seemed mystical and ghost related. He feared something evil would appear from it, but how would that be possible? It possessed wonderful colours, and its humming was beginning to sound peaceful. He sighed in relief as Amaryllis stepped out then he frowned. He studied the portal levitating a foot off of the ground, and the thousands of colours that swam through the swirling... liquid? Air? He had no idea what it was, but he suddenly hated it. He often hated her *witchy* acts.

"What is this?" he demanded crossly pointing at her portal with a jerk of his arm. He was finally free from his fearsome state and was no longer vulnerable to the ghosts in his mind, as he was too distracted by the magic before him. He was himself.

Amaryllis grinned gently and jumped down from the portal followed by five spirits. They were white and faceless until making contact with the Earth. Then their faces formed within their white misty bodies—which took the shape of their vessels from their past life.

John collapsed falling to his knees. He grasped the stone path for support but it wasn't enough. His head fell forward overwhelmed with emotion. His face washed over with a joyful sadness that made his eyes wet and his lips curl. His heart felt like it stopped completely, his chest was full. He sobbed frantically letting waterfalls drain from his eyes.

A cold touch to the shoulder caused him to rise slowly. Judith stood before him with a sorrowful expression on her face. He immediately got to his feet and went to hug her, but his arms went right through. Cold air hugged his legs. John looked down to see his four sons hugging him. Judith placed her arms around him and in that position the family stayed.

"I am so sorry," John cried, wishing he could feel the warmth of his family's embrace. Although, he felt their souls and that was enough.

"John, it's okay," Judith answered softly. She noticed his scruffy, older look and had to convince herself it was indeed her husband. She had seen him last with short, well-groomed hair, gentle brown eyes, and a clean-shaven face, but it was still her husband whom she loved, and his new appearance didn't bother her.

"No, it isn't. I knew I shouldn't have gone to see you, but I just couldn't help myself."

"And that is completely okay, it was a normal and natural thing to do. It wasn't your fault," she whispered.

"It was someone's…it has to be someone's…it was mine. The king warned me, but I refused to listen."

"Are you saying that if you hadn't seen me that rainy day then we would still be here? Because that simply isn't true. You would have found us another time, and another time after that. Eventually your loneliness and longing to see us would have driven you crazy. You would have broken the king's rule anyway…it would have been a little later. It wasn't your fault. The king simply had no sympathy, he had a cruel, greedy heart."

"It's his fault," John said darkly after a long pause, a long while of thinking. "The horrors he showed me, the image of you…"

"John!" Judith snapped. "I do not want you thinking like that anymore. You cannot live the rest of your life blaming that wretched man, or even worse, blaming yourself. It's been two decades, you mustn't stress your heart like that anymore. It is hurting me to see you this way, it's hurting *my* heart. It's okay to be angry, it's okay if it hurts. You may never get over it, but you must move past it. Please, for the sake of your own happiness and for the sake of my peace." She pulled away from him looking into his brown eyes with her white, ghostly ones. He didn't say anything for a while.

"I'll try," he uttered through his shaky voice. His wife shook her head and smiled softly.

"You will," she promised before leaning in to kiss him. All he felt was cold air, but he enjoyed the most loving feeling that the ghost could provide him. He closed his eyes, pursed his lips, and imagined the last time he kissed her in the pouring rain.

Amaryllis' heart raced with happiness, but it skipped a beat when John smiled at his wife and kids. They spoke for another few minutes all wrapped up in a ghostly embrace, but as soon as the sun peeked over the horizon, Amaryllis told them it was time to go. The royal subjects would soon awaken, and she'd have to beat them to the carriages before the goodbye speech from the King of Arlon. He would discuss the marital plans; where and when the weddings would take place. She needed to ensure that John would be returning with her.

John hugged everyone individually and said his own personal goodbyes accordingly. He said goodbye to his wife last, hugging her the longest.

"I love you," she said, whispering cold air into his ear.

He shivered. "I love you too."

Judith took her sons, leading them back through the portal. As they hovered around the entrance for a moment, their features faded away and became white, faceless figures again.

The portal shut with a sharp thrash, swirling away, smaller and smaller until it was gone.

John looked down at his feet then at the rising sun with a look of contentment. He felt whole again, complete. The distorted ghosts vanished from his house, from his mind. He was free of the guilt, free of the torturous pain. He looked at Amaryllis with a new set of eyes. They were no longer mean and hostile, they were friendly and gentle.

"Thank you," he cried, walking over to her. He wrapped his arms around the sorcerer whose magical abilities he now appreciated. He loved it for what it had granted him. The half-hour visit with his family set his soul free for eternity. Amaryllis hugged him tightly overjoyed to have helped him escape from the misery that had once controlled him. She helped kill the demons in his mind.

"Are you ready to go? We have to hurry," she urged noticing the village was significantly brighter from the sun which rose higher above the land. John looked at his house one final time saying goodbye to the pleasant memories he now had.

"Yes, let's go."

Amaryllis and John sprinted through the village just in time because when they arrived at the entrance the people awoke—stepping outside to breathe in the morning air and to take in the radiance of the morning sun. They ran through the gate and made it to the castle door.

"The doormen are probably there now," she groaned. A clacking sound of horse hooves on stone caught her attention. The carriages were being prepared in a line outside the castle gate on the path leading away from the kingdom. She spotted a white carriage at the end of the lineup with a big blue "W" on it and pictured James sleeping in bed. Hopefully he wasn't awake yet. Her absence may worry him. She never told him she would try to fetch John so early in the morning.

She thought quickly instructing John to get inside of the carriage representing Werling and he did as he was told. Amaryllis knocked on the castle door, telling them it was her, and they opened it.

"What are you doing now?" they asked her.

"Nothing, I just went out to see the sun," she answered calmly and convincingly.

"How did you get out? Did you open the door by yourself?"

Amaryllis nodded making up a story of how she wanted to see one final sunrise in the kingdom which provided her with lessons of love and forgiveness. The doormen were moved by her story and let her walk away without asking any more nosy questions.

She ran to her bedroom and found James sitting on the bed. He had just woken up. The sun shone in through the window highlighting his dark brown hair and enhancing the calm, sparkling ocean in his eyes.

Amaryllis shut the door behind her walked around the bed and sat next to him.

"I retrieved John," she whispered. He looked at her sunlit face, into her beautiful green eyes and grinned, then went serious.

"Where is he?" he asked.

"In the carriage, but it's all right because our carriage is at the end of the line. We'll stall your father to let him out then he'll walk beside us until we're out of sight."

"Yes, this will work… what time did you get up? I didn't even notice you left until I woke up without you in my arms," he laughed anxiously. "I was only slightly nervous that something had happened. Your timing was excellent," he spoke softly with his soothing voice, and it made Amaryllis feel safe and warm inside.

Amaryllis smiled at her hands folded in her lap.

"It was very early. I didn't want to wake you, and I wanted to return faster than I did, but the retrieval took longer than expected."

"Well, why? What happened?"

"John was being difficult, that's all." She didn't tell him about the ghosts or the inter-dimensional travel. She was too humble, too proud to flaunt her immortal powers around. James already found her to be extraordinary and her sudden magical abilities piled onto his admiration for her. He could not believe what she could do, it was so surprising and inconceivable. He had a desire to protect her and to make her feel safe, but he knew very well that she would be just fine on her own. Her powers let him worry less about her, but the only thing that concerned him was her biological clock. She was immortal. While he aged away, she would remain young and strong. So, he decided to love her each day like he was going to lose her; to enjoy her for eternity. He believed in the afterlife, but she wouldn't be joining him. That was all right, but it saddened him as he looked at her radiant complexion.

"Well, you're here now," he smiled. "We should get ready," he suggested, pointing to the closet across the room.

Amaryllis and James changed into corresponding outfits. She stepped into a white and blue dress with long sleeves and a v-neck. He changed into white leggings and a blue tunic. They were fixing their hair in front of a wide mirror when they received a knock on their door.

"Time to wake up!" It was the duke.

"We're already awake and ready to go," said Amaryllis with the same enthusiasm in her voice that the duke had in his. He opened the door then his face lit up.

"Aw, you two look marvellous together." Amaryllis and James looked at each other and smiled. "Breakfast begins in twenty minutes! Come down whenever you wish!"

They thanked him then he left to wake up the rest of the couples. They walked down to the dining hall and ate a great feast of eggs, oats, bacon, and fruit. After they ate, everyone headed out the castle door, admiring the castle's interior on their way out.

Chapter 53

The bright sun had the sky all to itself without a single cloud in sight; spreading its golden rays upon the land. It was warm with a light breeze tickling the royal subjects' ears as it sang to them. The young royals gathered before their carriages and their parents waited just behind them. The footman of each carriage stood beside the doors waiting to open them.

As Amaryllis promised, she said goodbye to her mother and father giving a wholehearted speech. She thanked them for all they had done for her, for raising her with unconditional love and providing her with all she could ever want. She appreciated them greatly and would never dare to dream about wishing for others as her guardians. Her pure heart was built by her parents' kindness showing her the beauties of the world as a young girl.

They responded with a speech about how proud they were to have her as their daughter. They simply couldn't compare their appreciation to anything else. What could they say to meet the greatness of her achievements and her powers? Their daughter was a magical being who defeated the demon who once terrorized the world, and who terrorized it once more, before going away forever. All they could tell her was how proud and amazed they were with her hoping their words were enough.

They said goodbye with long lasting hugs. No tears were shed, only happiness was present.

Then the King and Queen of Arlon spoke. "We'd like to express our happiness for another successful generation within the traditional Choosing Ceremony," everyone clapped politely thinking of how the ceremony was somewhat *unsuccessful*, but no one said a word and allowed the queen to continue speaking. "We were honoured to have hosted the annual parties as well, and we are overjoyed that our son, Eric, will be continuing the tradition with his queen, Laria of Galeston."

Laria blushed holding Eric's hand. They stood beside the King and Queen of Arlon, far from the carriages. The prince looked pleased with himself holding Laria triumphantly like he had won a prize.

"We'd also like to personally thank Princess Amaryllis of Serilion—who is to become Queen of Werling—for saving our lives and for saving Arlon. Amaryllis what you've done…there is simply no word to describe your bravery, and there is no word to describe your compassion, because you simply surpass each and everything you do with extreme greatness. We are honoured to have known you and to thank you…" the queen pointed in the direction of the village, "…there will be a statue of you in the centre of our village sculpted by the best sculptor in Arlon."

The crowd cheered and clapped for Amaryllis who smiled humbly looking away from the staring eyes. She gazed at the trees of the forest across the meadow. It was a magical place, but she would always first think of calling it the *Dark Forest* before the Forest of Enchantment. Her journey flashed through her mind again, and she looked at her memories defensively, ready to fight again. James put his hand on her back and looked to the crowd. He pinched her skin through her dress and patted her to pull her back to reality.

"Thank you very much," she said after wincing from James' pinch. The queen smiled wholeheartedly with a nod. The king took a turn speaking and, as he began, Amaryllis thanked James silently.

She tuned out the king wondering how John was doing in the carriage listening to his rival, then she tuned out her worrisome thoughts and listened to the birds chirping in the trees. She tuned back in when the king said his final goodbyes and the crowd began clapping. The footmen opened the carriage doors simultaneously, perfectly in sync. They practiced it the day before as ordered by the queen.

Amaryllis' stomach dropped, and her heart skipped a beat, as her footman whipped the door open to expose John Edwards to the king. She froze in panic studying the king's face as he admired the coloured, velvet interior of the carriages. She looked inside bewilderment consuming her completely. He was not there. She stood frozen in front of the carriage her mind racing. She broke out in a cold sweat. The happy, sunny day slowed down, spiralling hauntingly as she panicked.

"Amaryllis, won't you go in?" James asked. The footman offered his hand to assist her inside, but she wouldn't take it. The footmen weren't allowed to speak to the royal subjects unless spoken to as directed by the King of Arlon, but the footman couldn't help himself.

"Is something wrong?" he asked quietly hardly moving his lips as he spoke.

"Yes, I mean, no—everything is fine," she uttered through her anxiety sounding perfectly calm. She hopped into the carriage followed by James and the King of Werling.

The carriage was far larger than Serilion's with much more distance between the parallel seats. The seats were padded with royal blue velvet and they were much comfier to sit on, but she didn't make such observations with admiration. She noticed them at the back of her mind much later in the day. John's whereabouts worried her like a mother whose child didn't return home at the end of the day.

The carriages ahead of them began to leave. The horses hypnotic hooves clopping against the ground as they moved giving Amaryllis' frantic mind an idea.

"May I check something before we leave?" she exploded. James' father looked at her with wide eyes, but James understood her panic looking at her with sympathy. James suspected John, a peasant, had been discovered and taken to the king.

"What's the matter?" the king asked, leaning forward with a patient softness in his voice.

"The horses—I must make sure they're all right. I noticed them feeling distressed." Amaryllis opened the door and hopped down. The king looked at his son and James nodded his head.

"She's right. They may behave poorly on the way back. I don't think they've been fed for a while. Perhaps she's just picking some grass to feed them."

The king's face still wore bewilderment. "Yes, but she's awfully anxious. Isn't she a little too anxious over the...*horses*?" his father asked skeptically.

"Perhaps she's anxious, to be returning home with us and not to be returning to Serilion," James pondered although he already knew the answer.

"Oh..." the king sighed. His face relaxed. "...Poor girl. We must do our part to make her feel at home."

James sighed silently in relief.

Amaryllis felt the King of Arlon's stare as she searched around the carriage. She looked between the horses, but he wasn't there. She walked around to the other side of the carriage, but he wasn't there either. She checked underneath, but he certainly couldn't ride down there. There wasn't anything to hang on to.

She pulled her hair nervously holding back tears. James came around and hugged her. As he held her, his comforting embrace broke her and she sobbed onto his shoulder.

"He just left. He changed his mind, he didn't want to come," James insisted lying protectively to his fiancé. He truly had no idea what had happened, but he went with what Amaryllis was thinking. He would never tell her *that*.

"No, the king has him," she whimpered, sobbing harder. "He finally has him for good. He's going to kill him." James hugged her tightly, thinking of possible alternate whereabouts of her friend.

"Maybe he went into the wrong carriage. Maybe he's just hiding in the wrong one."

"No, I watched him come into this one," she insisted.

James pried Amaryllis off of him and stared into her shiny, wet, green eyes.

"I promise you everything is okay. John is too smart to let himself be killed like that." James knew he couldn't get away with giving an opinion on John since he never met him, but Amaryllis described him so well, and described his part in her journey so clearly, that he felt he *did* know him. He immediately regretted what he said until Amaryllis nodded.

"You're right, but… where did he go? I must check the village," she gasped stepping away to march down to John's house, but James grabbed her arm and pulled her towards him.

"You can't. The king is watching us right now. It's all too suspicious as it is. We must get in the carriage and head back to Werling. Trust that something had come up and he had to take off."

"John would never do this to me," she huffed crossing her arms. James wiped her wet face with his sleeve. She looked to the sky impatiently as he did so.

"Come now," James whispered pulling her arm. "Trust me."

Amaryllis frowned at the few pleasant memories she had of John. She pictured his contagious laugh, his smile, his soft brown eyes, and his happiness when reunited with his family. She imagined how devastated and angry she would be to learn of his death—his murder. As she daydreamed, James dragged her back into the carriage. The coachman clicked his tongue at the horses and with the snap of the reins they were off.

The King of Werling looked at the princess' sorrow-stricken face and said nothing. He met James' eyes, looking for a nod of his head to confirm she was all right, but James just looked away from his father and put his arm around Amaryllis to comfort her.

She looked out the window to see the subjects of Arlon waving at them. All except for the king. He stood with his arms by his side staring back at her through the window. She looked away, resting her head on James' shoulder, blinking her eyes to let a tear to wiggle out.

The pain stung viciously leaving her in a perpetual, never-fading sorrow. There was no way to lift her spirits. She looked out the window trying to admire the natural beauty of the land to cheer herself up, or at least to distract herself, but the pain was too immense.

After riding in the carriage for a few minutes, the castle was out of sight. She lifted her head from James' shoulder to watch it disappear behind the moving horizon. The tip of the tallest tower sank into the land then it was gone.

Suddenly, her heart jumped and her eyes nearly popped from their sockets. From behind a tree ran a man coming right towards her. He moved quickly with fast-moving arms and legs. She gasped loudly startling both James and his father.

"Stop the carriage!" the words exploded from her mouth. The coachman pulled on the reins exclaiming "Whoahh!" to the horses. They stopped their trot coming to a halt. The king looked at his son his face asking what the hell was going on.

"Don't worry about it," James said harshly, his greenish blue eyes appearing cold like ice. The king leaned back against the seat with a frown, but James didn't care for his father's concern at the moment, he was anxious for Amaryllis.

The coachman watched a scruffy older man stop before Amaryllis breathing heavily with a nervous smile. The look on her face startled John, so immediately, he explained himself.

"I overheard someone give the footmen orders to practice their *synchronized door opening*, so I bolted," he said defensively expecting her to argue with him or to hurt him by the enraged look she wore. "Don't...hit me," he breathed, holding his hands up to shield his face.

Amaryllis sighed, just relieved to see him. A nervous chuckle escaped from her mouth then she hugged him. John joined her in her nervous laughter until it escalated to joyous giggling.

"I was *destroyed*! That was so smart of you, but *ugh*—!" she punched his shoulder with half of her omnipotent strength. "—You scared me," she said monotonously. John winced, gripping his shoulder, but he forced a smile though his pain.

"Well, let's go to Werling," he said brightly, rubbing his stinging then aching pain in his shoulder. Amaryllis sighed in relief once more then turned to the coachman.

"This is my dear friend, John. He will be joining us on our journey back to Werling, but I don't want you to ever mention his presence here with us today, or ever. Do you understand me?" she yelled, her eyes glowing.

The coachman nodded. "Of course," he answered kindly despite being spoken to so poorly. Her glowing eyes met those of the footman.

"Yes, of course, your majesty," he said with a shaky voice.

"Don't call me that," she spat clenching her fists. Her eyes glowed brighter. She immediately recognized her poor actions realizing how cruel she was appearing to be, but it was her belief of John's death that put her in that place. She looked at John and her eyes faded back to green. The king hadn't captured John, he was alive and happy. She no longer had a reason to be angry.

"I apologize for my sudden outburst. It's just...imperative that John's name is never mentioned. Please." She spoke softly with true feeling of sorriness.

"That's all right. He won't be mentioned, not to worry," the coachman said with a reassuring smile. The footman agreed smiling too. They had been treated far worse by royal subjects. Amaryllis was certainly the kindest one to have yelled at them. The only difference between the effect of her outburst versus the rudest one was that she scared them more with her glowing eyes.

Amaryllis sighed as the heavy stress fell from her shoulders officially setting her free of all of her worries. Amaryllis and John stepped into the carriage, both sitting on James' side.

James shook John's hand. "It is great to finally meet you," he said. "I've heard many great things about you."

John grinned. "And you must be *the* Prince James?" John laughed quickly glancing at Amaryllis to see her smiling contently. James nodded then looked to Amaryllis with love in his eyes, flattered she had told John about him during her times of trouble.

The coachman snapped the reins and they were off again.

"Who is this?" The king asked skeptically, raising his voice. James looked to Amaryllis wondering whether or not she would trust his father in telling him.

"You can tell my father," James whispered into her ear. "He's trustworthy."

"*Who* is this?" he repeated.

Amaryllis explained that John was her close friend who had helped her on her journey. He had saved her and guided her through the Dark Forest. Then John proceeded to tell the king how she had brought his family to see him. He didn't mean to, and he knew this didn't relate to her story, but he couldn't get that good deed off his mind. He had to share his happiness with everyone.

The king shook John's hand with a smile. "Well, John Edwards, you are welcome to visit the palace whenever you so choose. You can choose any house in our village that you desire," he offered.

James spoke up. "Actually, Amaryllis wants him to have his own *room* in the palace, father."

"Is that so?"

Amaryllis nodded. John said nothing seeing what the outcome would be through reasoning between the royals. He didn't want to impose.

"Well, I suppose that'd be all right," the king laughed. "After all, in a month, I won't be king any longer anyway."

John's body filled with excitement. He was overjoyed to have his own bedroom in the palace to live the rest of his days in everyday pampering and care. No more survival or despair. He was headed for his well-deserved retirement from misery and danger.

"Thank you…so much," he uttered through uncontrollable excitement.

Amaryllis looked at her dear friend reminiscing all of the moments they had. From her first impression—which was that he was a horrifying hermit living deep in hell—to her last impression—in which his true character resurfaced. She was happy to have helped a poor man crawl out from his haunted hole of isolation, but she was even happier to see the outcome of her good deed of revealing his family to him. His stern, cruel resting expression changed into a peaceful one. He was happy both on the inside and the outside. He smiled often, showing his teeth to her more times in that one day than he ever did within the few days of knowing him.

Her future was finally handed to her through extreme hard work. All was meant to occur. She wasn't *supposed* to be chosen the first time for the reason of setting a demon free, which she terminated. Along the way she developed as a person losing her anxieties and gaining power. The world became brighter and she had everyone to thank. Everyones cruelty led up to the disappearance of evil. She thanked the princesses who abused her, James' father for threatening his son to choose the wrong princess, and although it was awful, she was glad to have met John during his time of grief. Each act of wickedness in the world is what helped rid of it forever.

Amaryllis' past was ugly and hellish. It was not too long ago that she was surrounded by evil perpetually consumed with fear but it felt like a different life she used to live. So much had changed in so little time. She was in love with who she had become—a superhuman who feared nothing, who didn't allow anyone to step all over her. She looked back at her past self and waved goodbye triumphantly looking at the carriage she was in and who she was with. She was heading to the beautiful kingdom of Werling with the man of her dreams. She had victoriously defeated the world after it scarred her mercilessly. All was finally working in her favour. After a long battle, she finally learned to fight. The world was hers.

CPSIA information can be obtained
at www.ICGtesting.com
Printed in the USA
LVHW040332190919
631534LV00001B/1